SOME ANGRY ANGEL

SOME
ANGRY
ANGEL

A MID-CENTURY FAERIE TALE

RICHARD
CONDON

McGraw-Hill Book Company, Inc.

NEW YORK

TORONTO

LONDON

SOME ANGRY ANGEL

for my mother and father

Space, from earthman's point of view, has three main divisions. The first and smallest is the solar system. The sun, with a diameter of 864,000 miles and its mighty force of gravitation, holds the nine known planets in their elliptical orbits. In addition, the solar system includes thirty-one satellites of the planets (not counting the earth's artificial satellites); thousands of asteroids, which are rather like tiny planets; comets and meteors. As astronomical distances go the size of the solar system is not astronomical: it is only about 7,350,000,000 miles across.

The next division of space is "our" galaxy: an aggregation of about 100 billion stars. Our sun is an average star in this "Milky Way." The nearest star to us after our sun is so distant that it takes light four and one-half years to travel to us. The galaxy itself is so vast that it takes light 100,000 years to travel from one edge of it to the other. Yet ours is a medium-sized galaxy.

Beyond our "Milky Way" is the third division of space—all the rest of the universe. In the unimaginable reaches of this really outer space are countless numbers of aggregations of suns. All these galaxies rotate and move in space. The most powerful telescopes can find no end to them.

The New York Times Magazine

Some angry angel,
Bleared by Bach and too inbred,
Climbed out of bed,
Pulled on a sock,
And, glancing downward,
Threw a rock
Which struck an earthbound peacock's head.
The peacock fell.
The peacock's yell,
Outraged by such treason,
Cried out to know why it,
Out of billions,
Should be hit,
And instantly invented a reason.

The Keener's Manual

ANY CLASH OF THE SYMBOLS
OF THE AUTHOR WITH THE
READER'S SYMBOLS, LIVING
OR DEAD, IS ENTIRELY COINCIDENTAL

In the summer of 1959, outside the hotel that would house the Tenth Anniversary Dinner for the Friends of Miss Friendship, in its halls and lobbies and arcades, on its wide staircase leading to the Grand Ballroom, in its elevators and bars, the human manifestations of holy eagerness made things seem more frenetic and crowded still, as though most of the population of the densely packed city had crowded into that area. The Pickpocket Squad was planted. Two epileptic seizures had occurred. Four lost children waited patiently to be found upon chairs in the Package Room. Massive blocks of people had converged on the hotel from as far west as Erwinna, Pennsylvania, as far north as Cold Springs, as far east as Quogue. Pilgrims from south of the city were represented by a pregnant woman from Courthouse, New Jersey, who carried a tall sign that said: SHE GAVE ME BACK MY LIFE GOD BLESS YOU MISS FRIENDSHIP. All of the people had been drawn in by the mounting shrillness in the day-to-day commentary published in *The Daily Press*.

The police estimate of the crowds within a two-block radius of the hotel, as reported in the *Press,* was 19,502 people. Police estimates tend to run 32 per cent higher than any actual estimate because that tends to suggest that the police work 32 per cent harder. Any *Press* estimate of attendance at one of its own special events was always 50 per cent higher than the police estimate because that tended to give the events a ring of success and excitement. Roughly, the true count was about 6,600 people, all gazing blankly at they knew not what in the drizzling rain.

Admission to the dinner was by presentation of one genuine letter from Miss Friendship and fifty cents. Hot dogs, potato salad, and rosé wine were to be served at running strips of tables in front of a dais mounted on a stage. On the dais were seated several of The First Ten Who Had Ever Written To Miss Friendship; they were the guests of honor. As Charles O'Neil, publisher of the *Press,* began his speech of welcome, the checkers had counted 1,743 guests into the Grand Ballroom.

Using special police and private limousines, considering the thickness of the crowds directly outside the hotel, the guests of honor were only about twenty minutes late. That huge, befuddled, mystified, enchanted, and hypnotized crowd was an enormous compliment to the art of modern communications. Almost seven thousand people waited in the rain for someone they had never seen, even in pictures, and would not, therefore, be able to recognize if they should then see. The *Press* had told them the dinner was to be a great, great occasion. That sufficed. It was simply another act in what had become the great twentieth-century vaudeville performance, conducted daily on a grind policy throughout the planet. The people had grown into a world in which entertainment was vital and must never end. The entertainments were clever and became exceedingly varied to embrace all aspects of life of the times. All the issues, great and small and including some that did not exist at all, were as floating islands that passed by the great grandstand where sat the savage, simple-minded people as they waited to be entertained on the river banks of time. The threats of death, then extinction; of mutilation, mutation, then annihilation were floated past, and someone in Washington or Moscow never stopped arranging for bigger, better, and more generous shows to come along. The system tended to confirm the widely held belief that there was no reality, hence reality could not threaten, could merely divert or entertain.

At the center of the dais on which sat the guests of honor, Charles O'Neil gripped the microphone of the public-address system in his left hand. "Ladies and gentlemen," he said, "and children, it is with considerable emotion that I welcome you tonight, when we will join hands and hearts in honoring a veritable saint of our time, Miss Friendship." There was a responsive sigh from the darkness in front of O'Neil. It hummed and swelled and O'Neil let it grow until it exploded into a rocket of cheers and applause. He let it fade almost away before he went on. "For many of you there will be an enormous surprise tonight—in fact, perhaps two surprises. But you can be sure that this sense of surprise will be a mutual one, exchanged between you and Miss Friendship. I have decided to tell you *your* surprise first, then to let Miss Friendship discover the other surprise without any outside help." The vast darkness below the stage and the dais burbled happily, with joyful anticipation. "Some of you have been to the *Press* and have met Miss Friendship. You folks, then, have had your surprise. To the others—to most of you here with the tribute of your love and gratitude—I have this to announce: Miss Friendship is a man." The darkness gasped with the sharpness of air rushing into a vacuum, then it became still as it chewed on that fact and decided whether such a condition could change anything in its feeling toward the savior. Most of the entities felt emptier and some felt cheated. O'Neil made everything better instantly and restored the balance of emotional power with his announcement of the second surprise. "It will sadden you to learn, and yet reveal the source of Miss Friendship's wisdom and compassion, that he has been unable to walk for many years, and that he has been confined to a wheel chair ever since he undertook this mission." The darkness sighed gratefully, reassured.

"However, as I have hinted, he will be surprised, too, because he believes he has been invited to a dinner for only these people with me on the dais—to meet the first ten people who ever wrote to him for advice and comfort—so you can imagine how flabbergasted he will be when he comes out upon this stage and sees almost two thousand of the faithful here tonight." The darkness giggled somewhere. It guffawed. It was highly pleased and as soon as all of it understood why it was pleased it rippled with laughter.

The television floor manager gave O'Neil the stand-by signal. O'Neil asked that the house lights be put on. The room was filled with light, revealing faces and bodies of every age, sex, color, and creed. They were faces and bodies that had known every shading of loss and pain. There was an insulated silence. The floor manager threw the opening cue to O'Neil, who faced into another microphone, angling his stance toward the lighted camera in the mezzanine box, above him and ahead of him, and said, "Ladies and gentlemen, faithful friends of Miss Friendship, it has become my privilege, as publisher of *The Daily Press,* to be spokesman for all of you tonight in expressing the love and admiration of all of us from the bottom of our hearts and in commemorating ten years of Miss Friendship's service. But you have not assembled here to have me address you, you have journeyed from near and far places to meet and hear a great, great man—Mr. Daniel Tiamat—our own Miss Friendship!"

A large man wearing black tie and looking magnificent with appalling haggardness, a huge torso, and a deeply seamed face under bright white hair, filled the shining aluminum wheel chair as it was pushed out of the wings from stage left by a tall, lovely, blond young woman.

The applause exploded. Like a fulmination deep within a mine, it burst into a ripping noise of great dimensions. They were on their feet applauding him. They pounded upon the tables. They clinked table silver against glassware and plates. A family of fourteen, from a great-grandfather downward, sang a jubilant, muscular hymn that could be heard exultantly, if faintly, over the enormous noise. The wheel chair was halted at the center of the dais, before the microphone. The huge man looked panoramically from his left to his right, all across that room. Then he closed his eyes. A silence waited for him to open them again. He motioned to the girl for something. She helped him to reach the crutches in the holster on the wheel chair. He pulled himself to his feet. The girl left him. The lights were dimmed to quarter-strength and a chalk-white spotlight appeared around his head and shoulders from the light booth high in the back of the room. The crowd waited while he sought emotional control of himself. They listened to hear his words, demanding his blessing.

"Those who have legs will stand," he said with a profoundly deep voice, amplified by the speakers placed all around the great room. There was a cacophonous scraping of chairs. "Those who have not been blinded will look about us, then above us." Heads went back, in token measure. "All of us, in one voice and with one mind and wish, if the brutality of our living and the shock of it have not snatched our voices and our sanity—all of us, with that one voice—let us curse God together."

II

Dan Tiamat's father was an eager young Irish immigrant who had begun his new life in New York as a swamper in a Third Avenue saloon with the biggest free lunch counter for blocks around. He had ended his days as a swamper in the same saloon, by then a speakeasy. He had been the oldest employee, the publican's granddaughter had told Dan, then grown to manhood, the day his father died.

Googlie Tiamat had indeed been an eager young man when he climbed out of the steerage hold at Castle Garden; eager not to work; eager to drink many liquors, light wines, and beers; eager, in the years that followed, to stay as far away as possible from the little family he failed to support on the small salary he earned, plus tips. Googlie had landed in 1897. He had found his darlin' bride, herself two days off the boat from Kilflyn, in 1908. Little Danny was born in 1909.

Googlie was not one of your desperate hard workers, burning to fling his mop about and spot the trousers of the customers. He worked slowly and unsteadily and made his friends. He had a tiny singing voice of the most delicate sensitivity, finish, and charm, in an extremely limited range of expression.

So limited, so delicate, so gentle, so, in effect, Irish, was his tenor voice that throughout its readiness to demonstrate to many of those who might have been sober at the time, it could sound disturbingly precious. To win a wager for a patron of his employer's public house one Saturday night, he had once sung the chorus of "My Wild Irish Rose" one hundred times.

Googlie Tiamat was a runty little foamer. His small, flabby nose hung off his face like a pulpy string under uncombed maroon hair of the kind and color once affected by Pat & Mike dialect acts. His eyeballs seemed to have been sprayed with a fine steam of ketchup and they always looked silly in his shallow, sallow face for, when he could not cadge a free drink from a customer, he would slug at the slops bottle, filled with the left-overs. He was a short-lipped man with a lot of mottled teeth. He weighed one hundred and sixteen pounds. It could have been an injustice to have called him a drunkard for he had been cruelly undercompensated physiologically so that when drinking with a patron who weighed two hundred and sixteen pounds, after the first four ounces of whisky Googlie would have, if tested, shown a concentration of 0.04 per cent alcohol in his blood while the heavier drinker would have shown only half that amount. If Googlie had known that his size and his weight were cheating him out of a doubled capacity for whisky he would have resented it deeply.

Dan's mother, Darlin' Agnes, weighed one hundred and seventy-one pounds. She was a jolly, steady talker with a cruel mouth and a laugh like a suit of armor filled with nails falling down a long flight of marble stairs. She could hit hard and effectively with her right hand, could throw objects with right or left, and her own singing voice was neither delicate nor precious.

As little Danny grew up, her chats with him were mostly about what a murderous, evil little man his father was. She yelled at Dan a lot of the time, but she never threw anything hard or sharp at him. She clouted him about the tiny tenement flat overlooking the exciting Third Avenue El which seemed to tell of the virtuous fun of big-city life by demonstrating that, if the poor could not get to see the world, then the city would ride the world past to see the poor, but the clouting was done out of a sense of duty "to improve a slowness of mind that come to you from the father." Darlin' Agnes never kissed Dan and never held him for any reason of affection. Neither the curses nor the advices and warnings about the father came from her to her son as often as she would have liked because she worked as a scrubwoman in the Municipal Building six nights a week and the boy was almost always asleep when she left and, as time went on, almost always out and away when she was home. Darlin' Agnes passed away in what the priest cited as "a horrible, horrible style or manner" when Dan was eleven years old. From the day of her funeral he supported himself, since his father had no comment nor contribution to make in the matter at all, in any way, shape, or form.

In the summer of 1923, Dan was a big boy and the big ones, even if they can drink more whisky later in life, get hungrier earlier. He worked in a ten-table pool hall, on the second floor over his father's employer's saloon, as a rack boy and an extra cue. He was a fine shooter. He had run a string as high as ninety-one consecutive balls, and his hustling brought in about three dollars a week. The neighborhood could not have yielded more than that to a known shark and it was not the kind of a pool hall a stranger would come from miles away to shoot a few games in.

After he was fourteen Dan was unable to straighten out his left forearm all the way because of the day a punch-drunk Armory fighter became weary of the way some of the lads liked to tease him by jumping high in the air in irregular rhythms, arms at their sides and stiffly erect; up and down, again and again, right in front of him, until the fighter began to sway. He tried to grab something to steady himself but his vision didn't coordinate very well any more and he would always topple over on his head, sprawled out comically on the floor, because that jumping up and down did something to the balance centers of his damaged brain. After they had made him fall down and get up more than thirty times, and they could continue no longer because of the wonderful laughter the whole game always produced, the fighter went berserk and threw every ivory ball, in seven colors of solids and stripes, from all the ten tables at whomever he could see. He broke all the windows in the place. A 3-ball, exactly the color of a ripe tomato, kept going through a window and killed a four-month old infant asleep in a carriage outside a saloon while its mother was having a beer.

The fighter smashed Dan Tiamat's elbow with a 9-ball and broke the pool hall's brand-new time clock. They put him away after that.

For the next fifteen months or so Dan was a Zeppelin pusher in the garment district, which made him stronger and bigger and hungrier. He pushed the wheeled racks of heavy coats through the predatory traffic of the side streets and main avenues of the West Side, against the traffic and across the traffic. He had to learn to move fast. It was an easy thing to get caught between a truck and a snarling taxi and then to take a faceful of carbon monoxide exhaust from a bus.

There was a strike. Dan scabbed fourteen months, until the union got back in and he was fired. Years afterward, with that exquisite lack of self-regard he clung to as he did to life, he often thought that if it hadn't been for that union he would still be there. It made him admire all organized labor.

Later on, Dan ran coffee, sandwiches, and cigarettes for a big weekend crap game run by two Italians named Gino and Four Eyes. It began every Friday night at eleven o'clock in the back of a taxi garage and wound up on Sunday morning. All his life after those long sessions, Dan could handle dice very well because he worked at it and Four Eyes, who was a distinguished dice mechanic (although he never played in his own game), took a liking to the kid and taught him the whole route. Dan cheated with dice right up to the time when he got a job on the day editorial side of *The Daily Press*.

He was callous about things like that. He had to get money somewhere and he knew that no one was going to give it to him voluntarily. There was never anything personal about cheating friends. Money changed hands, that was all and, after all, somebody had to lose. Later, when he had enough money to discontinue cheating and he had his new job and his new friends, he would say dice were not for him, whenever anyone tried to get a game going because, he would say, it was too easy to get cheated with dice. Pressed to prove this, he would reluctantly agree to demonstrate, in a manner that almost grew into an act, the principles of the blanket roll, the whip shot, the Courtlandt shot, or the Greek shot, and lecture briefly on such elements of die construction as flats, shapes, bricks, and tops. That proved he was through cheating. In fact, he did it that way to prove it to himself and for the reason that he could tell from the expressions on his friends' faces that they saw him as some kind of a modern-day Abe Lincoln and seemed to evince silently that if they could handle dice like that there would be no question of so exposing themselves. Later, he had to give up this cultural philanthropy altogether. One night, during a demonstration, a new man who had come in from a Newark newspaper suddenly placed Dan as the player who had won three hundred and ten bucks worth of cash intended for a life-insurance premium that had then been forced to lapse. Seeing Dan revealing these skills with dice, he naturally began a beef. Before he could really get going Dan anticipated what was in store and was able to cross to him quickly and hit him hard to avoid allowing the incident to embarrass his friends and co-workers. After he threw the man out of the building he explained that he had suddenly recognized the fellow as the man who had molested his little niece in Patterson, New Jersey, the previous spring.

Because Dan was a big boy and looked smart he got work much earlier than the other boys with the political club of the district during Registration Week and on Election Day. Dan was fifteen when he worked his first election. He and the other workers, all party stalwarts who could use the extra money, would assemble at the clubhouse at six o'clock on Election Day morning to have some coffee and crullers and to hear The Leader Himself, a wonderful man and a powerful dignitary downtown named James Fagin Ryan, talk inspiringly on the necessity, if not the duty, of getting the vote out.

After a few rounds of applause and more crullers and coffee they would meet separately with their individual block captains (Dan's was Mrs. Eliot Feeney) and receive the many envelopes holding one dollar each and the instructions to register, and later on vote, every bum they could find regardless of race, creed, or color. With the bulk of the envelopes went slips on which had been written names and addresses of the people, all loyal to the party, who had died during the previous year in the district. Dan would round up his bums in the bars and flophouses (always making sure to include his own father on the first trip) and have them driven to the polls, sign them in, then pay them off. Some six weeks later he would round up the same bums, sort them out as to correct "voting identities," then off they'd go to record their votes. These were standard practices observed by bums with some principles left; the ones who were grateful for what the democratic way and the right to vote had given them. All the other bums, the bulk of what The Leader called "our floating population," the typical let-George-do-it kind of slackers, would not permit themselves to be bothered at registration time. Either they had independent income on the day The Leader's drovers came around or they were just too proud. These would pass up the dollar for registering. They stepped forward only on Election Day, for the thrill of exercising their franchise and for the dollar, to vote the straight ticket against a name and address slip of the loyal dead who had been reregistered for recurrent voting by the block captains after the shock of the passing and the sorrow of the wake had gone by.

There was one militantly mutinous bum, seventy-six years old, who had been a hog farmer before his troubles found him.

His name was James Howells S. When he had the dime, he would announce his name that way to the desk men at flophouses saying, "I am James Howells S., sir, and I am too old for the Foreign Legion." He was a moral leader among the vagrants because of his unshakable principles on anything at all, one side or the other, firmly; and because he wasn't afraid of anyone, including the young skimble-skamblers just starting out as bums. He broke a large bottle of Instant Garlic on the bridge of the nose of a strong boy named German John Falcaro, a Sterno drinker half the old man's age, and James Howells S. talked to the lad while he kicked him until he winded himself, or so a bartender told Dan.

Nobody needed to know the old rummy's last name because if they knew it they would have had to call him mister in front of it, he said, and that was out of the question. Everybody called him Howls, the way some people are addressed as Gimpy or Slim. Most of them thought he was called Howls because of the manner in which he howled at every injustice he could ferret out of circumstance or memory. Howls didn't just mumble to himself or talk to himself the way a lot of other drunken bums did. Ruminating while he strolled the streets, he held a formal seminar with himself. When he was prepared, he declaimed to himself in a loud and incomprehensible voice. He was the elder statesman of his defeated community and was as much of a power in alleys and flophouses as The Leader Himself was in the district and the Board of Aldermen.

Howls always wore the same clothes, winter and summer. A gray felt hat with a cloth-cap lining came well down over his ears. He wore newspapers as underwear for insulation against heat or cold, a frayed rope around his emaciated middle, and shoes chosen somewhat carelessly from the bin at the Edward Jaffe Peace House. He didn't have much hair left and what remained looked like dirty rags. His face was broken and sad. His eyes were rheumy and red. He would drink anything up to kerosene and he was in ambulant alcoholic shock most of the time. He had a fine nose; a jutting, bony, and passionate nose. His teeth had gone long before so it was not possible to judge his attack-intent upon what was left of his life from his mouth line, but his chin, although fairly filthy from gutters and pavements, and often covered with the kind of bruise or scab that will happen every time if one slides across a pavement on one's face, was the chin of a man whose heart will snap off like a light switch before he would compromise.

There hadn't been a man in the Organization who had been able to get Howls to register *or* vote, and The Leader had had some of his best men try before Dan was sent in. A police sergeant, just to do James Fagin Ryan a favor, talked to Howls on a snowy day from a squad car and told him that he had better straighten himself out and get over there and vote like other people who were proud they were Americans and grateful they weren't starving Armenians. Howls stood up very straight beside the squad car in the driving wind. He was a little guy so he didn't have to look far down through the slit of the opened window to pierce the sergeant with his watery eyes. He spoke with a clear voice. "I am proud of my Armenian ancestry, Lieutenant," he said, "and I ain't et in two days."

The Leader had Angelo Guffanti offer Howls a nice dry cellar out of the wind in a corner of one of his ice, coal, and wood businesses but, under cross-examination by Howls, Mr. Guffanti was forced to admit that it would be necessary to lock the door after Howls had retired for the night, at 6 P.M. "I am a free man, sir," Howls told Mr. Guffanti and an assemblage of other bums who had gathered to hear the manifesto. "I will not be locked in at night like a dog, nor will I sell my vote like a cur."

Mr. Guffanti, whose English comprehension was somewhat limited, reported this statement to The Leader by saying that Howls would like a car instead of "like a cur."

"A car?" The Leader cried out. "Let him keep going on saying he won't vote and he won't be able to get a license to drive in this town!"

One morning, at about a quarter to eight, Howls and some

friends were having a few in one of the long speakeasy bars with the loud back-wall population of signs that offered gin, whisky, brandy, nevass, ouzo, mead, arrack, grappa, pulque, vodka, zubrowka, and other flavors of alcohol at ten cents a drink, when the bartender, a massive man with a battered face and the look of one who lacks empathy, came wiping and polishing the bar right in front of Howls.

"Listen, Howls," he said thickly, "whassa matta wit' chew? The Leader wants you should protect your own sacred right to vote. What? You can't use an extra dollar?"

Howls stared at him coldly, sipped at his short smoke, but did not answer.

"You like a drink now an' then, right? We got it here. Any kind you like, ten cents a shot an' no double bottoms, right?"

"Wrong."

"What's wrong?"

"About the double bottoms."

"So one buck is ten shots, right? So go an' vote like The Leader tells you, understand?"

Howls timed his response so that when he spoke everyone in the saloon was leaning forward to hear him. "When this joint elects to extend credit to me an' my friends," he said clearly and slowly, hiccupping lightly, "I will discuss my financial affairs with you." He set the triple-bottomed glass on the bar. "Fill it," he ordered.

The Leader tried every trick in the book because what had merely annoyed him at first had come to obsess him. The more pressure he put on Howls (and The Leader did tend to over-suggest because he was an extremely thorough man), the more Howls used that pressure as a stick with which to beat his own constituency.

Dan Tiamat was fifteen years old and well known in the neighborhood when the block captain nominated him for the annual post-Labor Day task of bringing in Howls' vote. As the unaccountable resistance continued, year after year, The Leader had passed from confusion to indignation. Gradually the word had seeped through to him that this year none of the bums were going to register or vote, that The Leader was essentially un-American to offer a dollar for what was, in the end as in the beginning, their birthright, and The Leader judged correctly that Howls was at the bottom of the rebellion. He wanted Howls brought into him but no one could find the bum. It was then that the block captain, Mrs. Eliot Feeney, said, "I have the lad who can find him, Jim. I don't say he can deliver him but he can find him and the dirty old mess will talk to him."

"Who?" asked The Leader.

"Young Danny Tiamat."

"Who?"

"Googlie Tiamat's boy. The father swamps for Big Johnny Finster."

"You know him, Jimmy," a red-faced man said with the voice of a wheeze passed through a wimple. "That big lump of a kid with the eyes that move too much."

"Ah," The Leader said. "Sure. Little Danny Tiamat. Not little-short or little-thin, I mean. Young, I mean. And a lump he is. He can talk to this filthy old wreck of a derelict, can he?"

"He can that," Mrs. Feeney said, "for the lad's father is like a brother in drink to the old man."

It was true that Howls saw Dan more as a boozy nephew than as a psychopomp. More, Dan had a good stomach in him and, for not too long a time in one sitting, he could put down shots of smoke, drink for drink, with the ancient bum.

"I won't sell my vote," Howls said at the outset of the *pourparler* that presently was held behind a billboard in a vacant lot. "They can't make me and since they'll never know my last name and I don't have any address, they can't go and vote me like a dead man either."

"Howls, listen," the youthful Dan said. "You are a thinking man. Everybody knows that. The Leader told me to ask you what you think would happen to a guy like you in Bolsheviki Russia where you wouldn't have any vote to save you at all?"

"I don't own nothing and I never will," Howls said. "I ain't owned nothing since I was fifty-two years old and that's one helluva long time ago."

"What's that got to do with not voting?"

"They can't touch you here or in Bolsheviki Russia if you don't own nothing, son. Always remember that. You're going to die like the rest of them, so die on your own terms, not theirs. Don't get no morals mixed up in it. Just set on your own terms —dirty and crooked, or fair and honest, or a mixture of both makes no difference. Just don't live on their terms and, by the God who loves you, don't die on their terms. They don't know nothing. If you do what I say you'll learn to know something."

Two nights after Registration Week, in the Edward Jaffe Peace House, over the Spaghetti Kitchen, Howls made his policy position known to eighteen of his bloc. It was an unnecessarily cold October night. They had come to the Peace House because the people there wanted to feed and warm them as much as to save them. Howls used the thematic spine within the word "Resist!" as his text.

There were interruptions as he spoke; some discourteous, some wearily cynical, some curious, but there is no need to record those comments here as he controlled his people at all times.

"You are as helpless a bunch of rumdumbs as there are in this world," he told them, "so I will talk about how much smoke one buck will buy for you. I say that one buck will buy exactly half as much rotgut as two bucks and maybe less. Some of you are looking at me as though like you could understand what I am saying. If you hear me, and what I say is clear, I will expect you to explain it all over again to the man beside you, and if there is nobody beside you, then reexplain it to yourself. In about ten days the hustlers are going to come to you. They are going to offer you one buck for your vote. Now, by this time—I mean some of you, not all of you—by this time some of you know that we have them scared that they will lose us. That makes us a very important group of men. They have sent the sergeant. They have sent an established businessman.

They have seen to it that the very people who sell us our booze have tried to change our course. Now, I say to you, don't hear those hustlers. I say, If we live in a democracy, I represent you and you represent me. If this world is a legacy of Jesus Christ, then I am you and you are me and each flock to its own fold." At the back of the room, without looking up from the pile of hopeless shoes he was sorting, Mr. Jaffe murmured, "Amen."

"We are here where we are, wherever we are," Howls proclaimed, "to be seen only with God's eyes and our own—may they be the same, may they mean the same—"

"Amen," whispered Mr. Jaffe.

"—and we are invisible to the Philistines who, having glued large coins over the keyholes through which they try to filter the sight of the soul, cannot see their own helplessness either. I say to you, *We are worth two bucks a vote!*"

On Election Eve, because he was nervous about that solid bloc of sure-thing votes, two hundred and sixty strong, which could be so decisive with indecisive issues, The Leader Himself ordered a nose-counting of bums, at a buck a vote. One hundred and eighteen of them babbled that they would most certainly be on hand at that price, but could they have two bits on account right then because they were hungry and hadn't had a shot for—hadn't had nothing to eat since Saturday? Every other drunken bum, an astonishing total of one hundred forty-two, held out for two bucks. In the end The Leader said he would pay the two bucks. Then he told Dan through clenched teeth to bring the old bastard to him after he'd voted him but before he paid him.

Dan Tiamat went off into the night. He couldn't find Howls until 8:20 A.M. on Election Day. Howls was asleep on a grating in the sidewalk over a basement steam laundry. He was drunk and he looked sick. He looked translucent, he was so old and so tired. It was a bitterly cold Tuesday. Dan propped him up against the wall of the building. He shook him.

· "Can you hear me, Howls?"

"I hear you, son." Howls stared at him, right in the eye, from behind the bloodshot pockets of rheum.

"I mean can you understand me what I'm sayin'?"

"I understand you, son."

"You won, Howls! The new price is two bucks a vote!"

"Yay!" It was a weak but spirited cheer.

"Come on. I'll help you up."

"Wha'?"

"Come on. I'll vote you. Then The Leader Himself wants to see you."

"You will vote me?"

"For double time. Come on. For two bucks."

In a most shocking way, the old man began to weep. The day had started poorly for him. "You didn't understand nothing I said, did you, Danny?" His face was even more destroyed by the grimaces of trying not to weep and his toothless mouth was working. "I will not sell my vote. I would no more sell my vote than I would tell my name."

Danny Tiamat, dazzled by the old man's fiscal victory, had indeed not understood.

Whenever Dan listened for his childhood, the music that had scored the libretto of poverty had been his mother's great shout of attack upon his father and the shatter and crash of bits of movables that were always there for the purpose, Darlin' Agnes liking the lively life. The fights were almost always joined over the same conflicting ideologies. Dan's father would inform anyone who wished to know that he followed the profession of waiter and Dan's mother would cry out, then and there, "He told me that to get me to marry him, the little cheater, but he was, an' is to this day, nothing but an ignorant swamper." Over the ensuing hubbub she would ask all present to demand that he produce written proof from the Waiters' Benevolent Association to substantiate his claims. This threat hovered over every social occasion attended by the young couple. Googlie could not turn away his pride when some devilish wag would stand before him and ask just what it was he done for a living, and Darlin' Agnes could not stifle her sense of outrage. She would whack him or a few of his friends for punctuation but the real action would not begin until they got back to the flat, where the sounds they made drowned out the rumble of the elevated trains.

The one stroke of luck Dan's father ever had was when he was chosen by a stranger, who had never patronized the saloon before and who was never to be seen again, to stand up and drink with him. The publican encouraged that kind of fraternization by the staff, since it kept money in the place that might have gone elsewhere. The stranger and Googlie were nearly two days at it before they tired out. Along the way of the friendship Googlie sang "Macushla" until the patron nearly hurt himself with the sobbing. When they were able to get the poor man soothed with aromatic spirits, and he was able to keep a whole drink down, Googlie got overtaken with the sadness that is now and then found in life and he slipped into his own crying jag. He wept and cried out the story that his own wife, in every other way a darlin' woman, would not believe he was a waiter but kept insisting that he was naught but a swamper and there was no way to prove otherwise as he did not carry a benevolent card because he did not believe in organized labor.

His friend asked a few penetrating questions and soon sized up the situation. At once he sent out for some sheets of white paper and, taking out a pen that was an ebony tube captured in an arbor of golden vines, he wrote out a long document with copperplate penmanship, formally establishing Googlie's membership of *la première classe* in the International Association of Footmen and Waiters. He sent for a notary to put his seal on it right then and there, and he signed it himself with a flourishing but indecipherable signature. That paper took the blisters out of the voice of Darlin' Agnes right up to the day of her death, God rest her soul.

She suffered death in an outrage of curiosity. At four o'clock in the morning of spring, out of patience with waiting for the elevator in the Municipal Building, she put her head into the shaft to ascertain its whereabouts, and there it was, virtually on top of her, descending without halt, with weight and power. Googlie got a nice sum out of it, the talk was.

Dan himself suffered in later life with the belief and the fear that all of the great men he walked among—the song-writers, the jockeys, the politicians, the hoodlums, the publi-cans, and the promoters—secretly looked down upon him for his ignorance and his origins. When he decided he could de-tect this revulsion, without a doubt or a question, he used the cutting power of his newspaper column to keep them on their knees before him. The column became his own daily certifica-tion into *la première classe* of the International Association of Footmen and Waiters.

Dan got his job in the Circulation Department of *The Daily Press* during a newspaper war. In order to assuage his con-stant hunger, which was a fear of hunger as well as a need for food, he sensed that this could be the permanent place he had thought he would never find, and he worked like a ferret trying to force entry under a brick granary. They made him a copy boy after two months of muscle work outside. Somebody de-cided that too many crackpots were walking in and out of the City Room, either to make threats or to attempt conversions, and someone large enough, who was not preoccupied with deadlines, was required to throw them down the stairs.

Dan had never gone further than the fifth grade in school, so he spent his evenings in the Main Reading Room of the Public Library. He read words, one at a time, with a dictionary at his elbow. Then he wrote the new words on a pad he had stolen from Woolworth's across the street, with its definition, ten times for each. There was nothing sporadic about this work. He kept at it every night, except Saturdays and Sundays, for three years, because nobody told him that there were night schools. The result was an intensive specialization in English vocabulary, grammar, and in that specialty of all writing in English, newspaperese. He taught himself to write for the *Press* by rewriting all the stories on pages one, two, and three, over

and over again. Other newspapers reflected the news slightly
differently, which meant that Dan made himself unemployable
by them: He had created himself to write for the *Press* and for
the *Press* alone. It was not that he had idealized the journalism
of the *Press*. He did not know how to get a job any place else.
At the end of three years he had gained such control of his
material that the words in his sentences seemed to sit, legs
hanging down, along the blade of the sharp knife of his most
specialized style.

Dan Tiamat ran scared all the time. When he rested, he slept
too much. He could sleep nearly all the way through his days
off because he allowed himself little else to do but to sleep and
to work. He worked like no one else on that paper had ever
worked; that was the truth, and Joe Downey said as much to
the publisher and to Benn Reyes, the city editor. Dan had no
interests beyond money and increased status.

He covered the *Morro Castle* disaster with his own money
on his own time. There are people like Marty Gabel, playing
the match game in the side-street bars today, who can still re-
peat his three leads verbatim from his stories that took readers
by the throat and dragged them into the holocaust through the
pages of the *Press*. Those stories got him a promotion. Lifted
right out of Circulation, he was made a district man and given
a raise.

At nights and on weekends, the way some cops will work
doggedly on a case even when they're not being paid for it, he
wrote a series on the city's psychiatric hospitals. The articles
frightened or fascinated so many people into buying the *Press*
that he was sent out to work on the state hospitals. At the end
of it he was stunned, standing there with a Pulitzer prize in the
one hand and a bound copy of his pieces in the other, and although the stories had done nothing to change hospital condi-
tions nor had anyone thought they would, they had brought
him nearer to the money and had moved him over the heads
of many others to a most prestigious rank.

He wrote Sports after that for a proper amount of time because the apotropaism of the newspaper business insists that

any really hot writer must come out of Sports, the illiterate area of journalism that calls for portraits of sweat merchants done in a suspension of knowledge of the rudiments of English grammar, vocabulary, and syntax. Theoretically, anyone who can learn to communicate successfully with the readers of Sports, can communicate with any other reader whomsoever. Dan had learned as much about newspaper divination rituals as any *pontifex maximus* in the business, so he sought auguries in the bowels of clichés and awaited his revealment.

He told himself that he knew his destiny. He had a deep faith that he would be named columnist someday. Then, lo!—the vision of the future became living history. As time went on, Dan became and remained one of the greatest columnists in that awesome and lonely profession, developing his "mighty leveler" style of attacking the great and pandering to the vicious and the petty, causing such readers to feel superiority over their betters and thus selling many, many newspapers throughout the land and enforcing fear of Daniel Tiamat himself. He became the hero of the dreams of the savage, simple-minded people of his time.

Googlie Tiamat, the ex-eager young Irish immigrant, died reading *The Irish Echo* on the morning of the first inauguration of Franklin D. Roosevelt. Dan, learning of his passing by post card from the publican's granddaughter, made the arrangements. (*"Surely you do not mean you would have us bury your beloved father in that, Mr. Tiamat?"*) When he had given the mortician his check, Dan did not accompany his father's body to Calvary, where his mother had invested in a plot years before. He hurried back to work, leaving behind the prison bars of poverty that always flashed back to threaten him whenever he saw bright sun working through the steel and wood trestles of the elevated railway that surrounded his memory.

"Considering life," the bartender said, "we should be thankful that we ain't dead. Or worse, to be sick our whole life in a bed. Ain't it the truth? Whatta you think, Ed?"

"Yeah, I know," the dishwasher replied, rubbing his

nose with one finger inside; the finger a groom, his nose a bride; his nostrils flaring, his hand astride.

The bartender leaned across the shelf, "If I was to tell you me myself was not just a bartender but a elf—how would you answer me—you, yourself?"

"Knock off, arreddy, wit' elfs an' fairies! You're awways talkin'. It never varies. Why try tuh fool contemporaries? I'm off at four. I'm goin' tuh Mary's."

The dishwasher riffled through his paper as a blonde came in on a shaky caper. The barman decided to make her taper. Her breath hung on her like blue vapor.

The barman returned, shaking his head. "Ed, she certainly ain't no thoroughbred. Using language like that, I say trouble's ahead. I wish she'd drink in Tim's place instead."

"What about elfs?" was the dishwasher's whine, bilious complexion more saturnine as he dripped off the stool with his huge behind, his cheeks bristling like a porcupine's.

"Well, just as sure as wet shoes squishes, and just as sure as God made fishes, after a life doing the dishes, what would you say if you got three wishes? Make a wish," said the barman, "go ahead."

"Stop talkin'," snarled Ed. "Set the ice instead. Or better yet, I wish you'd fall on your head." The bartender whirled and fell down dead.

So utter lack of thought for self; no thought for gain, no thought of self; had the gleam of bottle and the shine of shelf mark the passing of A Elf.

III

Dan Tiamat found an end to a long-lived romantic ache of his own when he was twenty-nine years old without ever learning precisely when it happened to him.

A seventeen-year-old female freshman was responsible for Dan's instituting his first and last mistress of formal status, Pilar Castaños. Had it not been for this freshman, whom Dan never met, Pilar would have had to return to live in Cuba immediately following her graduation from college, and that would have changed many things.

The freshman, on spring vacation from the University of Michigan, was physically assaulted aboard a cruise ship en route to Havana, at ten-twenty at night, by Pilar's father, who was on his way home following a business visit to New York. As Señor Castaños sought to embrace the young student most violently he was standing too close to the ship's rail and she, with the incomparable reflexes and considerable strength of her youth, repulsed him so forcibly as to push him over the ship's side, a surprise made possible by a defect in the rail's fastening or construction.

Señor Castaños died alone some thirty-five minutes later in a sea of green silver on a lovely spring night. The freshman was too shocked, too troubled, and too embarrassed to mention the incident to anyone.

The Castaños family refused to allow the disappearance to be recorded as a suicide for religious reasons, which necessitated some knotty legal maneuvers at the time of freshest grief inasmuch as the steamship line would not accept any recorded explanation that would merely state that the man had disappeared at sea while aboard their vessel, as that was tantamount to inviting a lawsuit. Somewhere between the memorial services at the church and the services before symbolic burial in the Castaños family plot, the problem was solved by the signing of a waiver of all claims by the widow and her one son, José, whereupon the death was formally announced as a "deep mystery" and given much attention in the Cuban press.

In all, it grew into a sadness impaled upon a greater sadness, but the young university student who had caused it all did not escape unscathed. The matter troubled her for many years until, much later than was entirely healthy for her, she spilled it out upon a psychoanalyst who gave her permission to forget it forever, which she did.

Pilar Castaños was graduated from Manhattanville College in New York just five weeks after her father's funeral. She was twenty-three years old. She had earned nearly three hundred dollars extra from her father's estate by charging the mourning weeds at a Fifth Avenue store, returning them for cash, then renting others from a theatrical costumer. After comforting her mother and spending as much time as possible with her twin brother, she had returned to her college in New York without intimating that she had no intention of returning home in June. Then, timing the letter to arrive at Botin on the very day of her graduation, she wrote to her mother to explain the fine opportunity she had been offered: a chance to stay and study with a woman professor of the Sorbonne who was on sabbatical leave in New York. (Pilar's mother had been strongly drawn to all things French all of her life.) The professor, the letter said, was an elderly, extremely well-educated Catholic lady, Madame Agnes Remotier, who, though a widow, had a married daughter exactly Pilar's age. With Madame Remotier, Pilar would be able to continue her studies of advanced French and Italian, and she requested permission that she be allowed to remain in New York.

Señora Castaños had never been a strong-minded woman and she had been forced, by customs of country and station, to remain unworldly for all of her life. As a direct result, she was somewhat inclined to underestimate that condition. For all the years of her marriage she had hoped silently that her only daughter would be allowed, in some manner, to see and to feel more than she had found. Her son, however, objected to Pilar's proposal with frantic vigor, but Señora Castaños held the money and the lost dreams so Pilar was permitted to stay in New York with Madame Remotier.

There was no Madame Remotier. It was in this name that Dan Tiamat had taken the small apartment on East Thirty-first street to formalize their status. From boyhood, from the day he had been able to read a tabloid newspaper, Dan had wished fervently to have a mistress. A mistress was a carnal caste mark to Dan. It signified powerful men and cigar smoke and preposterous intimacies accompanied by silken laughter. It meant

successful words, headline words such as "love nest." All of
this was to Pilar's favor, since Dan approached lust both wist-
fully and with awe.

Mistresses were an industry in ancient Greece, which was
a relatively long time ago. They are a reasonably normal result
of boys being patted on the head and given a cooky for brush-
ing their teeth a relatively short time before. Robert Graves's
somber tirades about the mistake made, for political reasons,
by substituting a Major Male Diety for the All-time, All-power-
ful Major Female Deity by King Sthenelus, the new Achean
overlord of the Peloponnese at "a township near Pisa in the
west of the Peloponnese, named Olympia after a nearby hill,
the lesser Mount Olympus," are cogent. Men are manufactured entirely by Woman. They are nurtured and taught by
Woman and, in consequence, tend to value beyond all else but
money, the approval and appreciation of Woman for themselves. All extensions of this innocence beyond puberty, of a
clandestine nature, are called infantilism by the sages. If a man
has lacked approval for all the early years of his life from
Woman he will never get enough of it no matter how old and
sage he becomes. For that reason, Dan Tiamat was in awe of
having a beautiful mistress to call his own. It was exceedingly
infantile, in its blanket-tossing of the reality principles by the
pleasure principles, but it was quite jolly and there seemed to
be no stigma attached to private sin, kept indoors. Dan actually
believed that it could be made to stay there. Installing his mistress in that apartment gave recognition to a formal mystery
that had ever existed for Dan as did the large amounts of money
he earned in the worst depression years; all fleshy flowers sprung
up out of erogenous rock.

Time is vital only to survival. It is no more than a monitor
of living. It causes events to stand in line to wait their turns
to happen in as orderly a fashion as their causes will permit.
It does not determine outcomes after the immediate results of
events have been deposited within the memories. When and
if Dan Tiamat awoke at the age of twenty-five or forty on a

morning still dusted by the memory of the softness of the soot riding a city breeze that had caressed his cheek in Central Park the first time he had ever remembered seeing green clumps of bushes giving mystery to a naked city hill, he did not know or care whether he had been four or eleven years old at the time. The memory is no kaleidoscope; it is more likely the same as a book or a pipe or a letter left somewhere in a large house where they may be enjoyed if they are found when they are needed. Time has little place in memory beyond its uses to focus greed and fear.

Whenever he remembered Pilar as he had seen her for the first time, Dan knew it had been winter because he could see snow in the background through the large window at the end of the hall away from the front door of Bernard Krigstein's apartment at 110th Street and the Drive. He couldn't remember whether it had been a Friday or a Sunday but he thought it had been in February. He had been a little buzzed, he could remember that, but not so buzzed that it could have been a Saturday.

Krigstein was a very good painter who had invited him to a party because he was a newspaperman and because he had sound, robust saloon manners. Krigstein and his friends were winding up to celebrate the painter's departure for Long Island where the Federal Government had commissioned him to paint a mural to be called "Communications" on the walls of a post office about to be completed in Jamaica.

Tiamat rang the door bell to the Krigstein apartment. Pilar answered.

Another girl guest who had been invited to the party by an unemployed sculptor—in that condition because he would only work with rose quartz—had brought five of her girl friends for protection against the sculptor's despair, which always set in after eleven o'clock and which had cost her a great number of hot and cold showers and jumping off the top of an upright piano after the last time. Pilar was a member of that guard.

Lights that seemed to be strung for eleven miles up the

Hudson River framed Pilar's head, far in the background, as she stood smiling at him. She was barefoot, which developed into a matter of tremendous excitement inasmuch as he had seen a South Sea Islands movie only the evening before. She wore Chinese red—dress, fingernails, and lips—against ivory skin, black eyes, and glistening black hair. She was a beautiful young woman who did not grow quite to the height of his shoulder and he was slouching from the cold and from the whisky. All of these things he remembered clearly from the winter of 1938, a very bad winter for sculptors. The events flew past the duckblind of his memory with colored feathers and rasping quacks the way they were supposed, usually, to swirl in whirlpool formation before the eyes of a drowning man.

As she looked all the way up at his eyes, as she stood in that doorway, she touched the top of the outside of her full upper lip with her glistening tongue then pulled it in slowly. It was as though he were an ant who had been caught in the lash of its stickiness. He began to tilt. He held the lintel of the doorway. An invisible woman laughed shrilly. Someone was playing the piano.

"Am I at the right place?" Dan asked.

"How can I answer that?" Her voice had the cadence and the rub of the Spanish language (in which she thought), but it was without true foreign accent. She pulled her shoulders back slowly. Her breasts lifted and came toward him. His glance caromed off his inhibitions. He stared at the center of the George Washington Bridge, high behind her head, where the moving lights of crossing cars made the window flicker like a motion picture screen. He stared beyond her for an instant, with widened eyes and a vague expression, looking like a *ayahuasquero* whose mind could see beautiful landscapes covered with monstrous beasts. He swallowed to widen his tightening throat. The floral smell of her, the smell of ferns sixty feet high, soaring from the moist, dark silence of a rain forest, began to smother his natural caution. His voice had roughened when he spoke again to ask whether this was the apart-

ment of Bernard Krigstein, the painter. She stood aside, smiling more personally, ordering him through the door with the
arc she made with her hips. She did not stand too far aside and
she did it so well that he knew with his body and his senses,
rather than with his mind, that she expected him to become
most fully aware of her body shortly, so why not then?—letting him brush against it barely perceptibly; an invitation to
frottage. "Promise, large promise, is the soul of an advertisement," wrote Dr. Samuel Johnson in 1759. Her mouth opened
and her lips moved delicately, if compulsively, as he passed
her, and she seemed to taste him. As though to guide him
across the threshold she touched his upper left arm, and many
years later, although he could not remember the day or the
month, and later, even the year on which this had happened,
he was still able to feel her touch, along with other memories.
"The unconscious system may be compared," Dr. Freud said
in a lecture at the University of Vienna in 1916, "to a large
anteroom, in which various mental excitations are crowding
upon one another, like individual beings." Time is merely a file
folder for the dull minutae of life. Emotions cannot be stored
in such a precise, economically dimensioned place; a year, or
months and a year, and then fifty or sixty of either with the
touch of a hand on an arm: thrilling sadly, unfiled.

She turned away from him to lead him toward the noises,
but he caught her arm and she turned to him.

"Let's go some place," he said.

"Where do you want to go?"

"Some place not so public. Like a restaurant or a bar." She
smiled at him, giving him one gasping look at bare lascivious-
ness, then she adjusted the same face to an expression which
enforced belief that the former look had never happened.
"Some place where there's a piano and a lot of strangers," he
blurted hurriedly.

"I know such a place," she told him.

"You'll need your coat."

"We won't be back?"

"No."

"I'll get my coat. Do you want to say hello to the host?"

"I'll call him next week. Please. Get your coat."

She held out her right hand with its long fingernails. "I am Pilar Castaños," she said to him. Just as formally, and with the dogged gravity of a man taking an oath for minor office, he took her hand, spoke his name, then did something that baffled him. He kissed her hand. She made a pigeon sound. Her eyes soared up to his eyes, as in a later time a jet interceptor might rise to hit an attacking missile. Her tongue reached for the top of her upper lip again, then she retracted it slowly. "Thirty seconds," she told him. "Maybe less." She was wearing a coat and a hat and they were ringing for the elevator in less time than that.

They didn't look for a place with a piano. Pilar had to be back at school by midnight so they went to a roller-skating rink near Van Cortlandt Park where Dan fell down as soon as he attempted to stand up on the skates, and cut his forehead badly enough over the left eye to require three stitches. After that they sat at a table in a frost-painted diner and ate, or pretended to eat.

"When will I see you again?" he kept asking her, and she kept turning the question by plucking handfuls of information out of his preoccupation. She had known who he was, she said, as soon as he had said his name. Krigstein was very pleased that he was coming to the party because when the mural was finished in a year or so at the post office in Jamaica, Dan had indicated he was going to get a picture of it in the paper. Could he do this? Could he get her picture to appear in *The Daily Press*? If her father ever saw her picture in a paper he would pull her back home to Cuba so fast that she would be able to answer this question Dan kept asking about when was he going to see her again. Her eyes brooded over his body. Yes, she lived in Cuba. Sugar. Sugar and government. Just one brother, a twin brother. Did Dan have a family? Ah, no. An orphan. That was sad. Really, she did not know when she could see him again, if she could see him again. She held his left hand, stretched across the table, in both of hers and rubbed her thumbs deeply into the fleshy pad of his palm. Examinations were going to come up very soon and— When would they start? It was only February? That was true. There was a *little* time. Would he like to see her again in one week? Saturday? For lunch? Yes, very good. Lunch and the theater and tea? Lunch, the theater, tea, dinner, dancing, and supper? Yes, very good. Oh. Oh, my! It was eleven forty-five. No, no. He must not. He could not. If he would put her into a cab that would take her to the top of the hill she felt that the good sisters would like that so much better that they would not stand in the way of her going down the same hill next Saturday. Her father was a very strict man who had given very strict orders. Her brother José was even worse. Kiss her good night? Absolutely out of the question. Her long tongue came out slowly again to touch the top of her lip. Then it retracted, a millimeter at a time.

It began feverishly, but although Dan saw her Friday, Saturday, and Sunday, and often as six times in three days, and was alone with her, in crowds, dancing, listening to the piano in the saloon they ultimately found, in taxis, and in horse-drawn carriages with very little windows, he did not kiss her (was not able to kiss her) until the third week in April, the day after she had learned her father had died. When Dan at last had kissed her (inasmuch as she had decided that the way was now clear to live with him, although she had not confided the decision to him), the great battering ram of their shared anxiety in opposition to their equal and always expanding senses of self-indulgence splintered and smashed all the high gates, crossed the swirling moats thick with crocodile, scaled the walls and the towers, and entered the castle to end the siege in an anagram of capitulation, triumph, and sensual avarice.

When she left for Cuba the following day, a Saturday, he traveled on the train with her to Miami, and not only did they never leave their drawing room; they seldom left one berth. Dan Tiamat had got himself a mistress.

For Dan and for Pilar, what followed was an endless summer of endless copulations. She would sit in the small apartment waiting for him to arrive, to spring upon him and bring him down upon the floor, the bed, a chair. When she stood, when she was alone in the apartment, day or night, her stomach and buttocks would roll slowly and ever so slightly in perpetual *danse du ventre*. As has been said in another connection, Pilar was very fond of what she liked.

Pilar passed time while she was away from Dan with tiny variations of the single theme. Although she went to a marvelous tea-leaf reader on West Seventy-second Street every Monday morning, and to a very good palmist-numerologist-graphologist at a restaurant on middle Lexington Avenue, for a short time on Saturday nights, she did not otherwise leave the little apartment in which they assaulted each other, except to shop. The seers concentrated on Dan's love for her (tea leaves) and her love for Dan (numerology graph) in exact terms of endearment's longevity, but these sciences, and the horoscope magazines she studied with fixed concentration were somewhat too coldly objective and impersonal. It was the newspapers that seemed to bring forces to bear directly upon her own sphere. To such contrasting types of invisible friends as Babette de Goren and Dr. Frances Moult, she wrote an endless series of anxious questions concerning the eternal pavan she sought to dance opposite Daniel Tiamat.

> Dear Babby: I am deeply in love with a professional man who is so rushed that he can only see me a few hours in the day, sometimes in the early evening, but mostly in the mid-afternoon. He loves me madly but does not mention marriage. Where do you think I am headed in this relationship?
>
> Latina

> Dear Latina: I think you are headed right out of your mind.
>
> Babette de G.

A favorite, gentling voice was Dr. Maria Van Slyke, a much less frivolous, much more delicately concerned Dutchwoman who had been knighted for the sympathy, freely given, to Australians with problems not dissimilar to those Americans who later wrote to her on the woman's page of New York's least conservative afternoon newspaper.

> Dear Dr. Van Slyke: I am wholly adored by a man who does not seem to be able to spend enough time with me and yet who, although he lives in the same city, seems to find it necessary to spend much more of his time away from me, at those most "crucial" hours when I need him most. I am a college graduate of good family. He is a professional man. We are young and "eager." Next year will be leap year. May I have your views on the precise etiquette for this folk occasion? Would it be proper for a young, pretty, loving woman to propose to a man?
>
> Señorita Bewildered

> My dear Señorita Bewildered: I am wholly surprised that an educated girl of good family could ask such a question. The answer? An unequivocal No. Try to consider man's role in this time of disheartening depression and restricted opportunity. He may be spending those hours away from you working until he nods at extra jobs while he tries to build a little nest egg for the dream house which you so impatiently crave. Trust your man, Señorita Bewildered. I have an intuitive feeling that your Mr. Right is getting everything ready to pop his question to you. Why not send 25¢ in cash or stamps for my enlightening booklet which poses this question: "Can Courtship Be Fun?"
>
> So very sincerely,
> Maria Van Slyke, Ph.D., D.D.S., K.B.E.

During the snowy winter months following Thanksgiving Day, Pilar took to buying newspapers at the out-of-town stand at Times Square to find other, newer oracles to whom she might write in her tireless search for The Right Thing. Of all available methods of divining the breadth, width, and height of Dan's love for her and hers for Dan, she preferred the experienced advisors of the daily papers to all others. They wrote directly to *her*. They were interested in her problems. She kept a careful mailing record so that she could write to a different lovelorn column every day and yet never duplicate her queries or their destinations.

Dan would beat his way to that cave whenever he could. He went through week after week thinking of nothing else but Pilar's body, her movements, the crazing sounds she made. When he would return to the recollection of all of these or one of them or six feral, blindingly, insensate lewdnesses she seemed to perform in her moaning, digging, rutting congress, his eyes would get wild in a subway or a bus and he would have to get off at the next stop to yell for a taxi to take him across town or downtown or uptown to feel her all around him. He was hopelessly addicted, hooked, and she was just as badly off. Love, in the normal sense of that cathedraled word with its flying buttresses and its vaulted ceiling that so gently touches the floor of heaven, did not seem to exist for Dan and Pilar. They never did the things with which lovers seek eternity. They had nothing much to say to one another. If they had interests in common they never discovered them because they were kept invisible. No walks in dark parks. No showers of flowers. No hours in little restaurants where the waiters would know too much about the humanities to think of talking to people like that about food. The apartment itself had had all the rubber wands and retorts of sexual ritual, but it had no books, no records, no television machine, no pictures. They had toppled forward into a concentrate of narcissism: the endless, wordless celebration of their own bodies.

Twenty years later, when the calendar had soothed him, he would remember her running, her face alight with anticipated sensation, across that living room as he opened the door, already

beginning to undress. She would be wearing a sheer negligee of
white lace and crepe de Chine and strumpet's mules with huge
immaculate powder-puff pom-poms and maddeningly high
heels at the end of her dark, perfect legs. That was what remained with him. She was running, always running toward him
on those teak legs and she wanted him with self-indulgent
desire that was close to craziness.

When that first summer was over, sometime in September,
a week or so after Labor Day, he had come up Fourth Avenue,
driving the man who was driving the cab, from covering a dock
fire on South Street, and he went bursting into the apartment
at high noon. Pilar, in that haunting negligee, in those brazen,
stilted mules, was standing in close embrace with a man whose
back was all Dan could see. He had the chilling feeling that
she was involved in the abandon of the embrace as much or
even more than the man, but as the door made its little sound
or a fraction of time afterward, she began to struggle to free
herself, to fight the man off. Then Dan was on them to pull
the man off and hit him heavily in the face, dropping him to
the floor. He lifted his foot, held in a heavy shoe, to kick the
man's face into the back of his head, but Pilar threw her full
weight into his shoulder, crashing him, off balance, into the
wall. She pinned him there and yelled, "No, Dan! No! He is
my brother." The man got to his feet, bleeding heavily from
the nose, and Dan watched him as he picked up a lamp and
crashed it down on Dan's head. Dan thought he heard the
noise of the lamp breaking, but not for long.

When he awoke he was lying on the floor. His head was in
Pilar's lap and her face was just above his, dropping tears all
over him as she rocked to and fro. His head hurt. It took time
before he remembered what happened and while it came back
to him they stared deeply into each other's eyes, not speaking.
Pilar spoke first. She spoke in sobs and the tears came in greater
torrent. "This is terrible, terrible, terrible." Dan remembered
everything then and tried to rise to defend himself, but she
pushed him down into her improvised cradle of flesh and lace

saying, "He's gone. He has been so sick, Dan. He does not know what he is doing. My mother wrote to me and I got it this morning. Oh, it is enough to break my heart, Dan." She pulled his hand under the negligee, high on the left side, and held it there with both of hers. "Pepé had a complete mental collapse. He was always a high-strung, nervous boy, and my father always treated him as an insect. He has been in a hospital, my mother said, ever since I wrote to say that I would stay in New York for a while. To see him like this. To see him so sick and confused. Oh, Dan, Dan, Dan. I am so unhappy."

"I'm pretty unhappy myself," Dan said. "I may have a fractured skull."

"No. You have only a lump. A very large lump."

"What the hell was he trying to do to you? Is that how a brother behaves with his sister?"

"He is desperate and despondent! I was comforting him. He needs me terribly."

"If that's how he needs you maybe they better lock him up quick and throw away the key."

"Why did you hit my brother? Why?" She rolled him unceremoniously off her lap and got to her feet, turning her back on him as she talked, and stripping the negligee off her lovely back. "Now that you have hurt him and perhaps driven him to do some wanton and violent thing because he is sick and frightened, you had better start to think of all of your friends in this city because we have to find him. He may do something terrible. They will hurt him. They may kill him." Dan pulled himself to his feet. As he rose slowly, groggily, he passed what appeared to be a line of small print under her left shoulder blade. He grabbed her shoulders to stare at it. She stiffened, unable to see him, staring straight ahead and beginning to breathe heavily, her perfect chest rising and falling as though a small boy were pumping her bellows from behind an arras. Dan read what he saw, printed in carmine upon creamy amber: *St. Joseph bless and keep Daniel Tiamat who is my life.*

"What the hell is this?"

"What the hell does it look like?"

He twirled her around. She was wearing those crazy mules and a thin gold necklace that held a minute crucifix. "When did you have that done?" he demanded hoarsely.

"I don't care. I don't care."

"When?" He shook her in a paraxysm of awed self-love.

"In Havana. After the funeral."

"You have carried my mark all this time and you never told me? You never showed me? You have loved me all this time and you never needed to tell me?"

"Don't talk, darling, darling, darling. Don't talk. My God, Dan!"

Pepé turned up in Bellevue the following morning. Within the week, Pilar was able to send him back to Cuba with a strong male psychiatric nurse.

Dan and his mistress continued in the same excluding manner, as though living on birds'-nest soup and proprietary breakfast foods on which had been sprinkled cantharides. They seldom went anywhere together. Dan did not truly know if she ever left the apartment. Pilar never said if she had. He brought her no presents beyond his body and his multiplying appetites. She gave him no comfort and no companionship beyond the unquenchable sexual holocaust. The tattooed sentence was explicit enough for both of them, it seemed, and any further experiments with sentiment were better left aside. It seemed that way, but during the early part of December, while they were at dinner, at Pilar's request, at a well-attended restaurant on Fifty-fifth Street, she asked him in a small, soft voice if he would come to her mother's house at Botin for Christmas and stay with them through the first of the year. He did not answer, but since she was not accustomed to his talking she saw nothing amiss in that. She explained that her brother was in a hospital in Switzerland. Her mother was lonely. Her mother

had implored her to leave Madame Remotier and come home
where she belonged at any time, but particularly at such a bad
and lonely time for her mother. She said that if she went home
she would have to stay home. She would have to remain with
her mother until her mother died, because that was her duty
and her mother's right. He did not speak then, but she went on.
The restaurant was not brightly lighted, perhaps not even well
lighted. There was not enough light to read a newspaper or to
see Dan's eyes. There was one exception, Pilar said. There was
one way whereby it would be possible to leave Botin and her
mother and yet take with her her mother's blessing. That way
was to marry. She could not remain at Botin without Dan. She
loved him more than anything in her life. If anything ever took
him from her she would not want to live, and if he ever left her
she would kill him or have him killed before she died herself.
Her voice was soft and loving and tenderly emphatic. This time
she did wait for him to speak.

"Honey, I—I don't know what to say. I mean—well, I mean,
you *know* that is absolutely impossible."

"Why is it impossible?"

"Why? You *know* why."

"What do I know? Why? Why?" Her voice was rising, and
as its height became shriller its width became harsher.

"Because I'm married. You know that. I'm married and I
have a child. You *knew* that. Don't look at me like that and
pretend you didn't know that."

"How did I know it? Did I have you followed to wherever it
is you live? Did I confront your wife? Did I make a scene in
front of your wife and your child?"

"Where did you think I went when I left you?"

"I didn't know where you went. I only waited for you to
come back."

"In eight months not once did I stay with you through one
night. Where did you think I went? Why did you think I had
to go?"

She waited until people three tables away, a party of six

who had gotten up ready to leave the restaurant, were almost abreast of their table. Then she threw the tiny tub of mashed potatoes covered with brown slime into his face. Then she pushed the plate with veal scallopine, spaghetti al pomodoro, and sticky film of marsala sauce and mushrooms into his face. She did not do these things with force to hurt his face, but she did them quickly and deftly so that all of the front of him that was in view was soiled, and before he was able to get to his feet, his reflexes being far less quick than hers, she had picked up the full plate of creamed spinach at his side of the table and placed it on top of his head, amid his boyish curls like a little china hat. As unrehearsed as it was, it got a tremendous laugh from the six people who had stopped beside the table when the action had started. Because they laughed so hard and so spontaneously the others in the room began to laugh.

Dan stood up, saw himself, the mess, and the shame, and struck out blindly at the person standing closest to him who was laughing the loudest. She happened to be somebody's crippled sister.

IV

Peggy Downey was nineteen years old when she met and married Dan Tiamat and, in following her own continuity from newspaperman's daughter to newspaperman's wife, it could have been that she knew as much about the business as both her teachers. She could talk animatedly about the good old days among the verb-mongers because she had heard all those lies. She knew which statesmen had brothers-in-law on the take. She knew which bishops who had been permitted to resign, and why; the approximate daily take of the slot-machine industry, which madams were operating; she knew the cursing patterns of the police commissioner, the mayor, the governor, and the President. She could discuss paper-pulp production and futures. She had conversed about newsprint tonnage costs, union beefs, alcoholism, legmen on opposition papers, circulation figures by zone, publisher expense accounts, police inspectors' home telephone numbers, the *Press* loan sharks' weekly handle, and all the other things that had interested and occupied her father, and then her husband. She had been breathing in the newspaper business with the vagrant city air since before she could talk.

Peggy's mother had died when Peggy was two. Her father had raised her. She was his great, close friend; his only remaining love in life; his pride; himself. Drunk or sober, when she had been little and he had had things calling to him from the darknesses of the city, he had always come home to dine with her, to listen to her, and later to pour out his difficulties and problems upon her, difficulties and problems that no one at the paper could conceive as existing for him because he was a sure man with a fine aim and quick decisions. Since he had died, much of him, when his wife had died, he and Peggy, in a way that was precious, grew up together and taught each other the strength they had and the direct and honest way they had.

Peggy's father was one of the final editions of prejournalism-school newspaper executives. He had been the deft-handed power at *The Press* for almost fifteen years, with half of those as regent for the O'Neil estate while the lawyers waited for the O'Neil son to finish school and learn the business. The year Peggy got married he was breaking Charley O'Neil into his first full year as publisher of the paper.

Raised as a repository of the functions and foibles of journalists (for her father had brought some two hundred of these home with him, from time to time, over all the years) Peggy had never been able to believe the statement in Pliny's *Natural History* that eating five almonds permits one to drink without experiencing intoxication, or that spirits drunk from an amethyst cup cannot cause drunkenness. Drinking and drunks had been as much a part of her life as hymnals, sick calls, and malevolent women are a part of the only daughter of a widowed country clergyman. That was the kind of a trade it was. Miners got silicosis. Matadors got gored. Press agents got ulcers. Fishermen got drowned. Newspapermen who worked for her father got drunk.

More and more frequently as her very strong, expandingly ecstatic marriage continued into time, her husband proved the extent of this condition of his profession. She did not blame herself, because she had never been blamed through her life, in a habitual or punishing sense, so she would not have known how to blame herself for something someone had done to himself, not to her. She felt no affront because her husband had chosen to drink, although she was in every perceptive and endearing manner a sensitive woman, and she did not see it all as a cruel conspiracy undertaken by him only for her humiliation.

Despite this objectivity she knew that that amount of drinking could not be good for him, but part of the complex known as maturity is measured by one's ability to understand that certain matters are another's individual responsibility, not to be haggled over, like a swarm of hornets to be driven away by the picnicker as soon as he is fully conscious that the hornets are there. She could not extract from his need his desire for alcohol and she was not at all sure that because he swallowed quantities of alcohol, this was the exact form of the pleasure he sought. So, she stood by him and did not rag at him, endowing them both with dignity in uneven, unsteady, but generous share. She always worried an odd notion that women existed to give to men, not to take away from them, and that men were there to give, in their own manner, as best they could, when they could, knowing surely how very much they needed to be able to give unquestioned.

Peggy did not brood about Dan's hidden unhappiness. She could not have comprehended hidden unhappiness. If that was a fault, it was one of her minor faults; one of her few faults. Everything she felt was out in the open because she did not need anything, nor had she been trained to fear the loss of anything of opaqued value. Because her husband was a patently happy, kind, fulfilled, and fulfilling man, she assumed, the few times she thought about it painstakingly and logically, that what he felt was out in the open as well, put there for her to see. This complementary essence did not make Dan more complicated than Peggy, as so many times the losers are explained away and the winners' feats diminished with the plea that losers are complicated and winners are not. A man bleeding from a bullet wound in his leg is no more complicated for it than a whole man drinking a mint julep in summer bliss in a hammock. Dan Tiamat had been wounded by poverty and that snarling lack of consideration which had resulted from his parents' wounds from the same beast causing them in their turn, to shoot their guns of anguished confusion at him. No responsible person could have called Googlie Tiamat a complicated man in any sense of that crutch-shaped word. If anything, Peggy was a far wiser and more sophisticated and more aware being than her husband, which was as it should have been. He could only sense what he needed, then move unseeing toward bandaged desire. She could sense and feel and think all at one time, on a level of feeling and intelligences that could be breathtaking as it met, married, and ratiocinated truths. She was unaware of any possibility of Dan's secret sorrow, because it was deeply hidden from his consciousness itself, buried in his shame of it. He was unaware that he had suffered a deep wound and that it was bleeding all the while he threatened the clocks.

Peggy was a sophisticated woman in the only emphatic or even acceptable sense of that battered term, which has been rubbed by the sensate into dowdiness such as might be seen in a sixty-eight-year old taxi dancer. Peggy was sophisticated because she had cultivated related knowledge over a broad spectrum of information and was able to evaluate what she observed against all of the more valuable and less valuable things she knew. By readers of movie fan magazines and comic books, Dan would have been considered the only really sophisticated member of that family, because he walked with crooks and heroes and knew the alleged heights and depths, but while he rode onward to examine and report upon these pieces of titillating juvenilia, to retail what he had learned to the infantile world of his readership, the very sound of the special siren installed in his special automobile drowned out the relative measure of the greater and smaller and limitless worlds beyond him.

Peggy was the wiser of the two because she had searched and watched and listened and sensed until she was sure her husband loved her, then she had accepted that as the greatest award likely to be received and had ceased seeking, ceased examining, ceased questioning. This concentric action was in no way a selfless thing. He compounded its bounty upon her. She lived by what Dan projected to her, and she lived for it.

Dan Tiamat was more limited than his wife in what he could appreciate. He was a man with man's superbly simple plumbing, so not knowing or even sensing the extent of his immortal blessedness because of her. When rutting, he continued to rut until his body was satisfied, his conceits assuaged, and the mercy for the stoppage of his gushing wounds was provided to him. Pilar Castaños was to remain his only formal mistress, but she was not to be his only extramarital bedmate.

Punch-drunk from the combination punches of poverty of every kind so long ago, it was very hard for him to give emotionally as well as materially. As the money flowed to him, and as the final rationale of an expense account permitted him to forgive himself for releasing some of it wastefully, he was finally able to gain a certain reputation as a check grabber, as a fairly sure touch for not more than twenty dollars, and as a totally fraudulent embodiment of the free-handed spender; but until he did, no matter how much he worked to retrain his consciousness so that he would look good, graceful, and powerful to the other totally fraudulent embodiments, his generosity was to be bracketed by the height of the fences of his expense account.

Dan Tiamat knew he knew, as secret and unspoken as such an ugly, dirty thought was to him, what would cause the next terrible depression that had to come because he feared it, de-

spite the woodenheaded reassurances he received from the same
people who had caused it the last time and who had not been
able to figure out what had made it happen the last time until
sixteen years after it had happened and who were now treating
what had caused the past depression with no possible way of
knowing the most human curses which would cause the next
one. Dan Tiamat knew he knew, and he hoarded against that
day as he grew more potent, as the blessing of his marriage grew
longer, as his daughter grew. One day, he knew, some legisla-
tion would be passed as a casual rider on some bill to benefit
the Bureau of Fisheries or another far-out agency, and the rider
would accumulate its own unexpected power, appealing to the
common greed, generating energy from seemingly nowhere but
finding life in the common greed, and it would suddenly be seen
as mandatory that expense accounts be eliminated, and with
all buying power abruptly withdrawn the national economy
would collapse right at the middle of the President's final quote
stating that no depression would ever be allowed to happen
again. As time went on, and on long after his marriage, long
after the Second World War, Dan Tiamat's world of the trend-
spenders rejected Fort Knox in favor of the Diners' Club.

He spent his feelings just as stingily. Giving is all of one
piece, whether with money or morality. Dan's emotional expense account showed the broads and his one formal mistress
on whom he spent his body and his childishness, while he generated contrition within the core of the love and eternal depend-
ence and enthralling devotion he held for his wife, so that in
his most Catholic of penances, in the name of his carnal guilt,
he needed to find absolution for what he had done in reckless
carnality by paying tenderness and incandescent attention, then
widening, deepening, and heightening love to his wife to assure
himself that he had not meant to do what he had done and to
ink out any memory that he had ever done it again and again.
He did not, in any passionate manner, deny Peggy what he
shared with others. Hunger is all of one piece, too, whether it
be the captive's scream for food or the free man's silent moan
for reassurance.

Peggy's own inability to escape from beauty by being unable to recognize ugliness made what Dan did and had to do
the object of self-judgment for him that it was. Other men have
expense accounts and little time to enjoy them. Other men are
crazed by fatigue from doing, then repeating through their years,
the valueless and futile moves required of them. Other men roll
in and out of beds and then go home to blame their wives,
hate their wives, beat their wives, or desert their wives, because
it follows that if a man is made to see himself in failure and
ugliness, his mirror must sink its teeth in his throat and threaten
his existence. But Dan Tiamat did not openly, consciously
blame his wife, and Peggy did not judge, question, or advise
her husband. To repay her, Dan loved her and only her, save
only his daughter.

It was not hard for Peggy to give. It would have agonized
her to have been deprived of giving and giving. She could give
so much that she could not give in even greater, more colossal
proportion than Dan's ability to take. Peggy was effulgently
grateful in the song she sang within herself to be able to love
so serenely and to be loved by her husband with such clear,
secure status, and she believed with all she had been given that
all people, but most particularly the people she loved, always
did the very best they could. This was more than enough for
her.

She did not accumulate steam, so there was no need to let
it off. She did not judge, criticize, or advise anyone but her
small daughter, because she had been given to see clearly, long
before, while raising her father and his friends, that such jaw-
flapping was a waste of time; that indeed men were built differently than women, and particularly around the ears.

Throughout their marriage Peggy was to be the flame and
Dan the moth; she the Holy Grail and he the seeker. Out of
all the women who might have come to him out of all the world
in his time, Dan had been given a woman who would love him
enough to treat him as an equal. She was an irreplaceable part
of his mind and his memory; the sensate, sweating, bleeding

skin that held his life together; the secret compartment of time that would hold the greatest joys and the most bitter burns of consuming grief.

When he was on his way in the newspaper business, sometimes drinking and sometimes disappearing, she was like the wives of whaling captains: the women who had walked around and around on the roofs of their houses when their men were out to sea for years, and if the record and the misty shapes of past people are true, none of them complained very loudly about the essential nature of the whale-catching business.

Dan was twenty-six when he met Peggy. They were crossing the Atlantic, east to west, on a Cunard liner. The ship was coursing away from the coast of France when he saw her for the first time and the conditioning within him, negative until then, became positive and the enzymes his body produced changed from neutral to militant. He was allowed by his instinct to decide that the time had come to wed and to reproduce himself.

He was testing the ship's stores, a glass at a time, in the walnut smoking room and facing a starboard window that looked upon the promenade deck while chatting about polycythemia among Peruvian Indians with the vessel's chief steward, when he saw Peggy pass. He grabbed the steward's forearm so suddenly and so crushingly that the man cried out "Aaaah!" in pain and shock.

"Who's that?"

"Hey! Dan! My arm! Leggo!" Dan let go and pointed. "Quick, quick! She's moving. Who is it?"

"Which one? Where?"

"That fabulous blonde. The one in lavender."

The bejowled steward, half erect, peered out the wide window. Dan was on his feet, eyes popping, jaw dropped, face pale. They both had the expressions of men staring at a massacre of defenseless settlers by savage Indians from the questionable safety of a low tree, when Peggy turned and looked directly at them. The steward waved, as though in explanation; a delicate wave, two fingers of his right hand moving slightly as though scratching the hovering back of an invisible butterfly. She waved. She turned slightly and called to someone off scene. Two other girls joined her. They waved. The steward and Dan waved back like castaways greeting an airplane. Since they were all merely four feet away from one another, the effect was overfriendly.

"Holy mackerel, I've got to get out there," Dan said hoarsely. "How do I get out there?" Scrambling around, he tripped over his own large feet and bumped into the tall, thin figure of a Prince of the Church, Denis Cardinal Grogan, Dan's prearranged cocktail date, and one of the few skinny prelates in modern church history.

"Sit down, Dan," the Cardinal said gently. "You seem all of a panic. Did you think I had forgotten our appointment? Did you know that your phrase *holy mackerel* is a euphemism for a particularly rude old French curse, my son?" Dan shook his head, dazed. "I thought not," the Cardinal said. "Sit down. Sit down." Dan looked behind him wildly, through the deck window. Peggy was smiling right into his eyes and he thought of his legs as turning to water. Cardinal Grogan looked out at her and waved with ecclesiastical swipes. She disappeared. Dan fell vertically into a chair. The Cardinal sat down slowly.

"You know," he said with his soft voice, "among the Wurramunga of Central Australia, silence is a form of mourning required for a year or two of all female relatives of a deceased male."

"Is that so, Your Eminence?" the steward asked with interest. Dan's mind turned over plot after plot as to how he could escape.

"Indeed yes," the Cardinal answered. "Consequently, the women have become remarkably proficient in a unique gesture language built upon elbow positions and motions of the arms and hands. Not that I had mistaken those young women for Wurramunga," he added smoothly.

"I, for one, knew you hadn't, Your Eminence," the steward said with the trace of a Scottish burr. "The rather pleasant-looking girl in violet has crossed wi' us before." He looked at Dan, who sat there dazed by the man's understatement. "She's a native New Yorker. Her name, if I'm not mistaken, would be Margaret Downey."

That evening, just before dinner, dressed in black tie, Dan dashed from public room to public room on three decks of the ship seeking Miss Downey. When he found her she was carrying a milk punch in her left hand and turning away from the bulletin board that held the rules for playing auction pool, which same had been fixed to the bulkhead of the smoking room. Dan was moving at about fifteen miles per hour, looking deranged by the suspicion that she had decided to get off the ship in mid-ocean after waving farewell to him. They collided. The milk punch dove out of its glass and covered Dan's trousers. They stared at each other in shocked silence. Dan, overcome with the inappropriateness of it all, dashed out of the smoking room like a burly Cinderelbert pressing midnight, sped below two decks on the handy companionway, burst into his state-room, and began to ring vigorously for the room steward while undressing in great haste until he realized he did not possess another pair of dining trousers, Savile Row not being famous for offering two pairs of pants with every suit.

By the time he went aloft again, after the room steward had performed his miracles, a heavy swell had set in, and Peggy was gone. He could not find her all the next day. He roamed the ship, above, around, about, and below. He covered both sittings at all mealtimes. At six o'clock, with the shattered nerves of a peyote chewer who has envisioned the combination to a rich aunt's private safe but cannot remember the last four numbers, he went to the chief steward's cabin and almost persuaded him to send out beaters everywhere on the ship but the stoke-hold. The steward telephoned his lady's aid on the deck which balanced Miss Downey. Intelligence was instantly available.

Miss Downey was quite indisposed by the sea, the room stewardess said.

All during the following day Miss Downey remained in her cabin, but at four o'clock the Atlantic became as a lake, which caused Dan's blood to pound and to emit hot and cold flashes. All at once it came upon him that although he had been seated at the captain's table in the dining salon, he had no idea where she had been seated, or at which sitting. He went directly to the chief steward's cabin.

"She's at Hungerford's table, second sitting."

"Who's he?"

"He's the chief purser. How else dew yew think a great boobie like thot could dine wi' all the beautiful women on the ship?"

"Well, the hell with him."

"I say that every trip, lad. Does not a whit of good."

"I mean, switch her to the captain's table."

"No, lad."

"Why not?"

"Well, for one thing, I'm not all that fond of the captain."

"Chief, listen to me. Would you like to be famous? Would you like to be the subject of a gorgeous article in full color in the Sunday magazine section of our paper?"

"You'd like to write aboot me? My colorful boyhood? My apprenticeship in the grand and glamorous hotels of Europe? Fascinatin' stuff like that?"

"You catch on."

"In that case, Dan. This is the very best I can dew," the chief steward said gravely. "A table for two. First *and* second sitting. How's that? You can linger a bit that way."

"How can you do that? I mean, there isn't enough room down there for the waiters to get through. A table for two? How?"

"That secret must die wi' me, lad." He broke into a broad grin, took Dan's hands, and clapped him steadily and vigorously on the back as though the nuptial ceremony had just been concluded. "And if you should run into the Prime Minister, perhaps yew'll be kind enough to recommend me for knighthood," he said.

Peggy brushed her ash-blond hair until it was a cap of lights. As she had not been in the dining salon at any time during the voyage, under the plan she and her dear friend the chief steward had evolved, the quarry, Daniel Tiamat, did not know that she was the sole owner of all rights on that voyage to a table for two, situated just far enough away from the music at both the first and the second sittings. She had not wasted the two days of self-enforced confinement in her stateroom. She had written many post cards that the chief steward would mail for her in England on his return voyage. She had worked on her wardrobe, and had reclaimed her hair and nails. She had rested and relaxed and now she was ready for her mission.

For a young woman of nineteen years who had spent almost all her life sorting out the polydaemons of the newspaper business, Daniel Tiamat at twenty-six, six feet two inches tall, with teeth like doll-house plates, and the prospect of a future that could recall Horace Greeley's, was a catch not to be left to the breezes of chance. Peggy had been stalking him actively, heart in throat, plan in hand, since the morning six weeks before when her father had mentioned at breakfast that in two weeks he would be sending young Tiamat to do an activities report on the depression fleshpots of Paris. Peggy had seen to it at once that her father conceived of the idea of giving her a graduation present of a trip to Europe that year, instead of the following year when she would finish her college education. Wardrobe soon became the greatest part of this gift, which the poor parent had had no way of anticipating.

When she sailed, she was prepared. She spent three contented, restful weeks touring England and Scotland, being far too intelligent to think she could interrupt effectively a healthy American male's first trip to Paris. She joined the ship Dan would be sailing aboard at Southampton. At once renewing her long-time acquaintanceship with the chief steward, she directed him as to where Dan was to be placed at 4:15 P.M. on the afternoon of the second day out, then anchored her target there by asking her father's old friend, Denis Cardinal Grogan, to invite the young man to interview him in the smoking room.

Although Peggy had seen Dan Tiamat only four times in her life, she had heard him discussed over and over again for some eight years. The first time she had liked what she had seen, Dan was emerging from her father's office. He hadn't seen her, he was that full of himself. The second time she had seen him had been at the Stork Club. He didn't see her that time either because he was faced in the other direction, and she had a half-hour, and more, to analyze his profile. The third time, having no idea who she was, he had tried to get a taxi away from her at Fifty-first and Madison by spotting it first, hailing it first, then trying to get into it first. An outraged glare from her had settled that ownership. It had been the only thing Peggy could have done, she decided. It would never have done, had she allowed a self-made Irish Catholic to pick her up on the streets of New York, as that kind had more cherished illusions about women than Spaniards, and, with her father in charge of the *Press,* she knew Dan couldn't get too far away from her. And, besides, she had still been tied up with the confinement of school at the time.

The fourth time she saw him she knew he would be right where she looked through the plate-glass window into the smoking room, courtesy of the Cunard Line, and she knew instantly from the manic thrashing about and milling and bumping he had done that *he* had seen *her,* at last.

Gazing mercilessly into her mirror, she applied some of M. Lanvin's aphrodisiac to her throat, forehead, shoulders, and either side of her nose. She was now ready to meet him at dinner and for the marriage that would surely follow.

She paused in the entrance to the dining salon, demonstrating what it could mean (as if anyone could ever forget what it meant) to have youth as a tribune. She wore a variation of lavender again, under her pale blondness, her melting pinkness, and her whiteness, reasoning that nothing succeeds like success and that the color had worked wonders on her objective previously. Her beauty was memorable because she had such regal carriage, but it was made even more acceptable by a truly witty face ready to radiate with mirth or to strew the largesse of compassion. She had fulfilling beauty, both close up and from a distance, which seemed more ready to listen than to talk, to endow rather than to absorb. Staring at her full, exciting figure, then at that face, then at those legs, then back at her figure, Dan Tiamat wore the expression of a fetched man. She saw him look at her in greed and awe from across the room, but he didn't see her see him because she hadn't seemed to look. Dan got pinker and pinker, then suddenly went pale. He started to get up even before she made a move in his direction, but apparently thought the better of it, just in time.

The chief steward approached her precisely on correct psychological schedule. "Ah, Miss Downey," he said mellifluously, "how good to see you feeling so much better." He indicated subtly that she was to follow him, and started forward with the gait of a movie butler. When they were within earshot of *the* table he said loudly enough for Dan to hear, "It became necessary to change your seating, Miss Downey. I hope it won't prove inconvenient. Old classmate of the purser's."

Dan arose hastily, stepped upon the hanging corner of the napkin in his hand, and was dragged face down upon the table just as Miss Downey arrived, but he was able to make it again to his feet unharmed.

"Miss Downey," the chief steward said with the unction of a cathedral organ, "may I present Mr. Daniel Tiamat, of New York?"

Dreams climb toward the stars upon brass steps rubbed clean. They do not need binoculars to better view the scene. Dreams have fists which beat upon your door, as old house dicks would rouse a lush sprawled drunk upon the floor. Dreams lack steel

*links to chain them to the truth, but cherish them before they
shrink; they are the minutes of your youth. Dreams cast
shadows forward. Bulk rises out of hope, with saffron sails
above the hulk that courses seas with decks aslope.*

V

When Pilar Castaños, in a gloating and malevolent mood of
triumph, left Joe Downey's office at the *Press,* leaving behind
her written, signed evidence against her lover in the form of
letters and the lease to Dan Tiamat's cherished "love nest," the
case against him was as complete as if it had been built by a
district attorney. Downey's world had come down upon him
and all around him. He was immobilized by dismay. For the
first time in his memory, he was unprepared to know how to
act. There was no thought of allowances for the accidents of
propinquity, youth, or the meaninglessness of lust. Downey
was where he was in the world because he had been born a
counter-puncher. As he sat alone in his office he thought only
in terms of naked retaliation for the sake of retaliation. He
had been slapped across the eyes with a frozen rope of what
he chose to see as scorn for him, and, after him and in that
order of importance, contempt for his daughter.

He and Tiamat were to have gone to the fights that night.
It was their weekly ritual. They had always met at Hungarian
Charley's, a horrendously noisy place across the street from the
paper, on fight nights. Pilar had paid Downey her visit at five-
thirty. She had departed at five minutes to six. Downey was
not conscious of how much time had passed after that. He sat
within the storm of his conflict, pulling himself gradually into
the shelter of his bitterness and resentment for what Tiamat
had done to him and to their own incomparable Peggy.

At seven-fifteen or so, when he was more than an hour overdue at Hungarian Charley's, Dan telephoned Downey's office

to find out what was causing his father-in-law's delay. Downey told him tersely that he'd better come back to the paper, then slammed the telephone down heavily into its cradle. Dan got there in five minutes. He found Downey in his swivel chair facing the nearly bare, polished work table that shot out at right angles from the huge Noah's Ark of his roll-top desk. There was one small desk light with a green glass shade on the work table. It brought out a patch of Turkey red in the old carpet. It etched Downey's grim mask of cold dislike and disapproving prejudgment.

"What's the matter, Joe?" Dan was smoking a big cigar. He hadn't bought it. The press agent for the world's biggest brassiere company had given it to him. Dan was wearing a flashy cream-colored flannel suit of Edwardian cut, with lapels piped in black, and a double-breasted vest with mother-of-pearl buttons. It took a certain kind of a man to wear a suit like that on a hot summer night.

Downey spat deliberately into the wastebasket at his side. Dan had never seen him do that before. "Sit down," Downey said. Dan pulled a captain's chair away from the wall and dragged it to the center of his side of the work table. Facing his father-in-law directly, he sat down.

"The Castaños woman left here a little while ago," Downey began bitterly. "Said her first name was Pilar. Seemed to think you were a great lay."

The expression that came over Dan's face, Downey thought, could have resembled that of a horse caught in a burning building, if anyone could have gotten a horse to wear a suit of clothes like that.

"You going to deny everything?" Downey demanded shrilly. "That's the drill, kid. Deny everything until you can think of something at least two per cent plausible."

Dan didn't answer.

"This is Peggy Downey's father talking to you." The words choked at the end of the sentence. Downey wheeled his chair around and stared out of the window toward Harlem and Canada. When he wheeled around again it was with manic vigor, and he said, roughly and rapidly, "Your doxy and I had a long talk. She brought documents with her. Everything but filthy pictures and phonograph records. A copy of the lease for the crib you keep her in. A bundle of obscene, disgusting letters telling about what you were going to do to her when you jumped her next." Dan shuddered. "And I read every one of them while she sat there, grinding her ass into the chair and tonguing those thick rubber lips. You've been married to Peggy for three years and this has been going on for one year and every minute of all that time you've been living as though you were my friend."

"Joe, now listen. Joe, I'm not going to say this is none of your business, because it isn't any of your business, but you *are* my friend, my greatest, closest friend and—"

"I'm no friend of yours, kid. Don't even talk about it. Forget it."

"Now, take it easy, Joe. Just a minute, now."

"I'll tell you how easy I'm going to take it," Downey said softly and with good control. He bit the end off a large cigar and jammed it into his face. He struck a wooden match and lighted the cigar carefully. "I'm even going to let you make a clean choice."

Dan dug the lighted end of his cigar into an ash tray and its acrid smell joined the other overpowering male smells in the room. "No choices!" he snarled in his street-fighter's voice. "And stop playing God or the heavy father or whatever the hell it is you're playing. She means nothing to me. She's something that drags me into bed and even though you saw her and watched her sit and squirm against a heavy seam in a very tight pair of pants she wears when she has to go out, I think maybe you're too old to understand what she can do to a man. Just lay off being the big judge. You think this is the first time something like this ever happened to anybody?"

"You'd be pushing a dress truck through the garment district if it wasn't for me."

"She's nothing to me. She's like a lot of curling smoke inside me."

"You might have been a swamper like Googlie if it wasn't for me. Finster's granddaughter would have put you on. They were people strong on tradition."

"She means nothing, Joe. Peggy is mine and don't go taking your biddy's disapproval there. You hear, Joe? I love Peggy. And we need each other, so don't go getting in deep over your head, Joe, because you can get hurt much worse than you think you're hurt now and I won't be the one who'll be hurting you."

The flat blue eyes looked at him with steady disgust. The skin became pinker all around the fringe of white hair. "Don't underestimate me, kid. I'm too goddam old, as you say, to go telling a man's wife about where he ruts and who he ruts with, because class alone will make a woman stick with a rotten man if it's put to her that way."

Dan began to think about Peggy with wild yearning with one part of his mind and about Pilar, with hatred and fury, with another. She had betrayed him in order to play a cheap theatrical scene with this old man whom no one could stop if he got started. He began to think of punching Pilar, of hitting her again and again and again. His eyes got red. He began to sweat under the light, creamy flannel suit with the piped lapels.

"We'll talk about the choices you can make," Downey said grimly. "I've thought it all the way through."

Dan's voice spilled out in a wild tantrum. "If you're not going to spill the whole thing to Peggy, then what the hell are you talking about? Choices? There's nothing else you can threaten me with, Joe, and think you can make it stick, so don't go playing with yourself and making deals like you were some god or something." He spewed out righteous indignation like a snowplow clearing a mountain road, and his eyes glittered as he spoke because he was beginning to feel the sure hunch that he was going to be able to work this out. It would be all right. He could feel that. Joe wasn't going to blab to Peggy, so it would be all right, because that was the only part that counted, and what the hell, he could bring Joe around as time went on and he would go to Pilar the instant this humiliation was over and he would beat her until she screamed, until his arms were too tired to hit her any more.

Downey spat into the wastebasket again. He looked at his son-in-law coldly and said, "Here are your choices, little man —you bold pig in the parlor of your betters, snouting about for a garbage-lined, lace-curtained parlor of your own. You can either quit this paper right now—and by cracky, as I know your grubby little character, as I know what has you greased and what makes you pant the prayers to self to turn you into a swell, I tell you the best thing you can do is to take that first choice and resign right now."

"Big deal." Tiamat sneered. "Why you simply scare hell outta me. What's the other choice? Do I pay a twenty-five-cent fine and you forget the whole thing?"

"The only other choice is that you accept a contract with the paper and become its big columnist."

Dan Tiamat was so confused that he seemed to try to swallow his Adam's apple. Here a man declared his enmity, then made an offer to turn him into a modern hero, with one incalculably ominous string attached. Downey hated gossip columns. He was known throughout the trade to have been voluble and emphatic on the subject, and he had said pointedly and publicly that he would not allow a gossip columnist on the *Press*. It was something neither the publisher nor anyone else ever brought up except conversationally, and when Downey occasionally talked about his attitude over a rye highball in Hungarian Charley's, or some place like that, he underlined everything he said with contempt for men and newspapers who lived by collecting and printing cheap, opportunistic, destructive rumors that turned people against one another and created a new, dazzling society of mediocrity.

"I don't think I understand what you mean, Joe," Dan said. "You mean like a gossip columnist?"

"The biggest," Downey said, "with all the tinsel fixings your larcenous, pimply conscience can make out of such a towering position."

"But, Joe, I don't get it. You don't want a columnist on this paper. Everybody knows that."

"You will call me Mr. Downey. Beginning at once."

"But what kind of a choice is that?"

"Mr. Downey. And by six o'clock tomorrow night you'll be the only employee of this newspaper who will call me Mr. Downey, because a staff bulletin will go out of this office tomorrow morning instructing every employee, and even the loan sharks and the bookies who cruise the building, to call me Joe—"

"I swear to Christ I think you've gone outta your mind!"

"—then we'll take to having staff meetings the day after that and you'll address your answers to me and you'll call me Mr. Downey. Is that clear, you cheap Irish trash?" His voice had mounted as he gave the orders and it quivered as he came to the end of it. He looked at Dan Tiamat as Carlos Juan Finlay probably once looked upon the marshy, fetid breeding grounds of the *Stegomyia fasciata*.

"Yes, sir," Dan said.

"Remember it. When we are with your family you will not address me at all. You will clear your throat and I will turn to you in an amenable manner."

Dan was a man with a supple, amenable manner. He had been suborned at the instant that Downey had known he would be. If he had not been suborned, he would have threatened to quit on the spot, for throughout the years he had agreed with Downey loudly over the infection and disgrace of gossip columns, and if he had not been suborned he would have tried to postpone judgment with bluster or blarney, but Dan had no conception of what he himself was. Downey, on the other hand, understood every shading of Dan's delicate yearnings, so he strummed those yearnings and the essence of Dan's self-delusion was captured within the shining fretwork of Downey's single silvered reference to a column. Dan was hooked. Downey was avenged. The ripples of that moment were to continue to spread outward and outward, repeating again and again into the dimensions of the future, and each ripple was to be wet with grief and to glisten liquidly over the mockery of despair.

"Will you please go over that once again?" Dan asked respectfully.

"I said, here is your second choice," Downey said harshly. "You can quit now, as I have advised you to do. You will survive that way. You fit exactly where you are and any paper can use you. You are young and you have relative good health, mental and otherwise. You have just enough power to suit your extreme limitations. All right. So much for that. If you refuse to quit you'll have to sign a contract with this newspaper. No tricks, and we'll triple your present salary and never pay you a cent more than that. You'll get rich from the other papers and you'll have your own outlet to complain about how much taxes the goddam country and the goddam state make you pay. I'll see to it that the syndicate pushes you hard until you're away up there past the biggest of them. You'll be your own man. You won't work for me because I wouldn't have you working for me, either way. You won't come near me unless I send for you and we won't speak unless your family is there, and that's the way it's going to be between you and me, kid."

Dan was beginning to realize, in a minimum way, the extent of the hurt and the loss he had caused his friend. It was coming to him softly and slowly because he had been paralyzed by the threat to himself and his fear of losing Peggy, but it was coming into his sensibilities now, as it would engulf him much later, that he would have to face his own hurt and loss because of it, but his sensitivity and his perceptions were already thickening with the taste of what was going to be his. "What the hell kind of a choice is that?" he said slowly and with great care. "You tell me I can make myself rich and famous and powerful overnight." Those qualifying words were magic medicine to Dan.

"Not exactly," Downey answered. "You don't make your-self anything. *I* make you rich and famous and powerful over-night. *I* do it to you. That's the whole point, kid."

"Yeah. Yeah, sure. But how could there be any question of choice? What kind of a way to get even with me is this? Okay. So, I'll take your second offer, the one with no tricks, and if you say no tricks I know that's the way it is. I'll sign the contract and the quicker the better, and I thank you for it from the bottom of my heart, but you have me pretty confused. I mean, I don't see how such a bonanza as this can get you even and I'm sorry from the bottom of my heart if I have caused you disappointment or if—if I have lost you as a friend."

"All right. I will answer those points categorically," Downey said with bleak hostility, "because this is the last time we will ever talk like this. You need that glory so bad that when you get it, it's got to hit you hard and bring you down. You haven't got the guts to make a lot of money, kid. You see the shine of it and your little pig eyes gleam with the pigeon-breasted prestige it can bring you among a lot of saloon keepers and hustlers. Money will be like whooping cough to you, kid, and you'll choke on it more than once, but you'll have to have more of it and more of it, like the rest of the gutless wonders who have sold out kith and kin every time for it, and the way you'll need it will be like a Hoosier fiend looking for a fix. That's all you are, kid. Just a frantic junkie clawing to get a fix. Then the fame! Fame forever comes to Googlie Tiamat's heir and son. You—up there—away up! A famous man to pimps and actors from coast to coast. A household word among all the idiots who read gossip columns, and celebrated as a name and a legend to press agents, politicians, hookers, and hoodlums. You'll be big and famous in a country of such fa-mous men, in this land of commercialized conceit where one peasant hires another peasant to do his bragging for him or to get his name spelled wrong in a column such as you will run. Big! And in this wonderland of hand-to-mouth celebrity that has all of the meaning of people who serve only self, you will be the biggest because you are the weaver of the rotting cheese-cloth cornucopia called a nationally syndicated column that they will pay the price of their dignity to get their names and their imaginary deeds into. Plus the power! Do not forget the power. A gossip column is a deadly weapon in the hands of a primitive conceit like yours. You'll wield the pistol and the whip like a lion tamer lording his absolute power over a mur-muration of fire-breathing mice. Money and your kind of fame and power have spoiled the best of them, kid, and you're not the best of them by far."

Joe Downey stopped and turned his chair around to look out the window to the north of the city. Then he continued, bitterly and with despair. "As for causing me disappointment, you have not. You have broken my heart. Until this afternoon I did not think those words were more than a romantic phrase." He ran his hand across his eyes. "I lost my son today, you might say, and I became a man's enemy. Right now, I could not tell you which of these is the more bitter to come upon." He turned his chair around. There were tears in his eyes. They stared at each other. Downey snarled. "And now that your wife thinks you're at the fights, why don't you go and find your doxy and give her the beating that must be titillating the little muscles in-side your legs right up to your groin?"

He leaned over again and spat his disgust into the waste-basket.

The little boys have yellow shoes covered o'er with tooth marks left by friends who'd barked for coins as a yellow dog, forsooth, barks. The little boys hold close their coins, their eyes a-spin, each ear a fuse, with heads as light as century bills, pawning dreams they cannot use. The little boys, though, cough the dust that rises from the folds of money. They never smile when they're alone. The weight of silence is not funny.

VI

Dan stopped a cab in front of the *Press* building and threw himself into it, giving Pilar's address. He was crazed with a passionate rage. He rode through the hot night in the light, creamy flannel suit, thinking of himself as an Edwardian dandy when he had bought it, but looking more like a movie cowboy with a penchant for dressing for dinner. He sat on the edge of the cab seat, mumbling to himself with rage, working himself into destructive fury, knowing that his turn had come and that she would be sorry she had ever decided to play games with a man such as himself. He did not permit himself to think of the astonishing good fortune this shameful, degrading action of hers had brought to him; he did not want to allow anything to seem to compensate for the vicious brutality of what she had done to him. When he was through with that little Cuban bitch tonight, he thought, it would be a long time before she could walk across a room to make trouble for anyone again, and when he left her with fewer teeth and a sore body, he would be rid of her forever. As he rode toward her he began to see her clearly in his imagination. He saw her heavy mouth and the black, feral eyes and the masses of black hair hanging down over her shoulders, and he became disgusted with himself to think that he had ever had anything to do with such an animal. He thought of Peggy's sweet, sweet smile and heard the music of her voice and saw the selflessness in her eyes as she looked at him and loved him, and he felt cheaper and more determined than ever before to even the score with the Cuban bitch and be done with her forever.

When the cab drew up in front of Pilar's building he threw a bill at the driver, leaped out, slammed the door, and half-ran into the building and into the self-service elevator.

He rang her door bell. He heard her stir inside. He heard her tremulous voice ask, "Who is it?" Through his clenched

61

teeth, with his fists knotted and ready to knock her across the room, with his legs tensed to spring at her, then to kick her body, he answered, "Western Union, lady." The door opened enough that she could peer out. He threw all of his weight against it, but it was chain-locked. He remembered no chain lock. There had never been a chain lock on that door before. As he puzzled this, staring right into her eyes, she began to scream at the top of her lungs. "No, no, Dan!" she shrieked at the full strength of her enormous voice, although she was out of his reach behind the chain-locked door. The sounds seemed to carom off the walls of the public corridor and hasten down the old open stairway to arouse all the living in the building. "Don't kill me! Don't murder me! Save me, save me! Rape! Raaaaape! For God's sake, Dan, don't murder me." He tried to pull the door closed but she had wedged a flatiron into the space between the door and the lintel. When he bent down to knock it away so he could close the door to stop those terrible sounds, she hit him from the top with a milk bottle, stunning him. As he pulled himself up slowly, her fist shot out and hit him with savage force in the left eye, and all the while she kept screaming strings of terrible accusations and horrible fears. As she leaned against the wall in his full view her negligee dropped open, and he gasped, as he always did, in spite of himself, at the beauty of her golden, pink-tipped to black-tipped breasts. She was a deep-chested woman and the volume of the racheted screaming noises she could produce was so enormous that it seemed to shake the walls. Her diction was so superb, even at full scream, that it seemed to slip all of the horrible words through the very bricks of the walls. He heard doors opening all around him. There were six apartments to a floor. Almost directly in his ear, as he turned to look into the shocked and frightened face of a fat lady, he heard her scream, in a nightmarish way, "No, no, my Gard, no!"

He turned and ran like a ballet dancer at feeding time, a streak of creamy white lightness that blended into one swath so smoothly that it could have been Donald Duck in full flight.

The instant he vanished, Pilar hurried to her telephone, dialed Operator, and pleaded with her to send a squad car at once because a man was about to break into her apartment to rape her.

Dan fled down those stairs like a culpable cutpurse, throwing his bulk from landing to landing on the stairs, feeling the lump on his head swelling, feeling his eye puffing and closing, while heads seemed to pop out of every door, hidden people seemed to be blowing police whistles out of windows at the front of the building, and one of the braver male tenants, seeing how fast the criminal was fleeing away from him, even yelled, "What the hell's going on here?"

As Dan reached the street floor and started in desperate panic to race across the lobby, he slipped on a bit of candy bar that some little shaver had left on the marble lobby floor and went high in the air like a cartoon figure to take a heavy, damaging comedy fall, coming down with his great weight on the base of his spine and seeming to splay out all over the lobby. A little old woman watched his every move from the doorway to her apartment. She smiled at him maternally. "You better get up, mister," she said. "The cops is coming gupp the stritt. If I was you, it shunt happen, I'd kip gung done to the cellar, mister. The main thing is—go!"

He could hear the siren on the police car. It seemed to sound just outside the building entrance. He got to his feet somehow, believing that he had broken his spine, but his panic soon helped him to forget the pain in his back or his head. As he started down the basement stairs he could hear the patter of big shoes coming in from the street, so he nearly jumped the full flight. He turned to start along a corridor to the service entrance of the building. Finding two men running toward him, he spun around and ran back. He knew he had some seconds' grace, since the police would first be directed upward to Pilar's apartment. There was a closet door just around the turning. He lost his stomach for a try at the lobby, pulled the closet door open, and slammed himself into the complete darkness inside.

The sudden insistence of his body upon all of the objects within —the brooms, pails, and lengths of pipe—so disturbed one large, open can of paint that it tipped upon its side on the shelf directly over his head, sending a torrent of sticky slime into his hair, across his face and down the front of his beautiful Edwardian suit.

In the lobby, from her doorway, the little old lady finally managed to convince the two policemen that the man they wanted had gone down into the basement. The two cops had a short meeting. One went up in the elevator to Pilar's apartment. The other started down the steps.

The smell of the paint in that airless closet was sharp and deeply disturbing. All the shocks of the past hour, from Downey to triumph to Pilar to ignominy, came upon him at one time and moved in his vitals like an electric mixer. He vomited violently and that part of the front of his creamy flannel suit with the elegant piping that had not been drenched by the paint was otherwise ruined forever. When he could vomit no more he still made awful retching sounds, and the combination of all of the terrible smells in that black and tiny space was punishing.

The sounds of his anguish betrayed his hiding place. He could hear a man's voice yelling, "He's here! The son of a bitch is here! Oh my Gard." The voice was directly outside the closet and Dan could hear something being slammed up against the door. Then another voice, a treble male almost orgiastically excited, began repeating "Whadee do? Whadee do?" The first voice shouted, "He raped a pregnant woman then he killed her the dirty son of a bitch an' I got him cornered like a goddam rat in this closet here don't just stand there fuh crissake go down that ally to the service door and bring that cop back here but I ain' splittin' no reward money with nobody yuh unnastan'?"

Dan heard the patter of big shoes. He sagged feebly against the wall of the closet. "Get back, get back. Away from that door, you. What the hell's a matter wit chew, you a suicide case or something?" It was a huge voice with hair all over it. My God, Dan thought, he is going to shoot through the door. It's a trigger-happy cop and he's after a goddam medal, and if he kills me making the arrest he'll be a hero. Was that crazy Pilar out of her goddam mind? Was she absolutely insane? He would never get out of this alive, he was sure, and he could remember her face while she had made those terrible, terrible screams. She had leaned against the wall, smiling at him as though she were a diva singing Carmen at full blast, enjoying every sound she made.

"You, inside! This is a police officer talking to you. You will open that door slow, you hear me? Slow, very slow, then out you come. All right, move out now, and come out slow or its some bullets in the tummy-tum-tum."

Tummy-tum-tum! That inanity upset Dan as much as anything else in the packed past hour. He began to sob steadily. He heard the sound of the object being kicked away from the door. Tears ran down his face, some of them from the fully closed, swollen, and purple left eye, and mingled with the paint. He grasped the doorknob in the sour-sharp blackness in front of him and pressed at the door with tiny strength, opening it infinitesimally. The policeman, standing at the side of the door, gun at ready, slammed the door out of Dan's hand and motioned him out wordlessly. The area had filled up magically with delighted, curious men and women of all ages. It was lighted by a single, brave twenty-five-watt bulb that seemed to give less light than a match.

"All right. All the way out. Turn. Thaaaat's it." The policeman frisked the prisoner efficiently. "Now up those stairs ahead of you. Up. Up." Dan moved forward, sniveling. In the poor light few of the crowd could see his closed eye for the mess that was his face. They moved in behind the police officer as he moved forward behind Dan, like sand pouring through an hourglass. Dan's progress was blocked on the stairs by the little old lady who had been so impartial about directing everyone to the basement. She had planted herself a quarter of the way up the stairs, directly in Dan's path, her stoutish daughter-in-law at her side.

"Hey, lady," the cop yelled. "Get the hell outta the way. Whatsa mattder wit chew? This here is a desperate man. Whatta you tryna do, get yourself killed?"

The old lady ignored the officer. She smiled shyly at the ruined and tainted Dan Tiamat and offered him the flatness of a brown paper bag and a stubby eyebrow pencil, saying, "Could you be so kindly to give me yaw rawtograph, mister, please?"

"Lady, fuh crissake," Dan moaned. "Have a heart."

"I said outta the way, lady," the cop bellowed, "an' that's an order. How long you think I can hole a man like this in check?"

"Don't get nervous, officer," Dan cried shrilly, feeling a gun barrel jabbing into his back. "I'll do whatever you say, but I can't move. Please understand that. This old creep is absolutely blocking the way."

"Watch your language there, buddy," the familiar treble voice yelled from the back of the crowd. "She just happens to be my mother." The mob moaned and rumbled its hatred.

"Give her the goddam autograph," the cop barked, jabbing Dan viciously with the gun. "Fuh gossake, lady, this guy may be a killer."

While Dan signed his name shakily, the old lady said, "Of caws he's a killer. What else? Gee, thanks, mister," she said sincerely to Dan. "Ah, that's okay," he mumbled.

The old lady and her daughter-in-law pressed themselves out of the path of justice and the cop moved Dan steadily up the stairs into the brightly lighted lobby. The area was even more densely crowded with people than the stairway behind the officer and his prisoner. It was filled, too, with the humming sound of "Whadee do? Whadee do?" but when the mass saw the prisoner in the full light it gathered itself into a gasp of horror, sending itself backward involuntarily. The frontal forefingers of the mass pointed at the prisoner. Some of its mouths said, "Oh my Gard" and "I'm gunna get sick" and one part of the beast uttered a sharp scream of shock. Dan's eyes followed the direction of the pointing fingers, looking down at himself and his beautifully cut Edwardian suit, unable to see the paint-stained right side of his own face. The policeman moved around to Dan's side, his gun even more at ready because he knew the taxpayers expected that, and looked to see what the mass was pointing at. The spilled paint was bright red and Dan appeared to be covered with viscous, gleaming, scarlet blood. His hands seemed red with gore, as though he had bashed and smashed at a troop of babies, and his face was covered with it, as though he had decided, in the final, frenzied, murdering moment, to pull his victims' hearts out with his teeth.

"What the hella you?" the shocked policeman cried in awe of this image of the wanton killer. "Some kinda fiend?" He crashed the butt of his pistol on the crown of Dan's head, subduing him effectively while the mass surrounding the two men sighed with great pleasure.

They dumped him into a cell at the station house, still unconscious. By that time it had been determined that the hideous gore was only paint. All the cops thought that was pretty hilarious and it put all of them into reasonably good spirits. Pilar took great care in getting dressed and made up so it was over an hour before she could be brought into a squad room to identify Dan as her assailant. She looked so incredibly beautiful that cops dropped things and stared at her. She wore a stunning white suit by Balmain and a frilly *café au lait* jabot. Her skin was golden, her teeth were perfect, her blue-black hair framed her face in a moving picture of the goal of lust. As she sat, her magnificent legs were crossed with the skirt just high enough to be dismaying, and she wore coffee-colored shoes with three-inch heels. They lit her cigarette and were charmed by her conversation, until at last one of the older men remembered to have the prisoner sent into the squad room for the confrontation.

Dan lurched into view, dazed and defeated, still groggy, and almost wholly unrecognizable because the left side of his face and the front of his hair were still covered with the glistening red paint.

"Is this the man, lady?" a stout detective, wearing a green silk polo shirt, asked Pilar.

"No, no," she said impatiently. "As I have told you, the man who tried to attack me was a stocky colored man with no teeth in the front." She pretended to peer more closely at Dan. What she saw made her want to cry, but she was careful not to get too close to his reach even with that many policemen in the room with her. Suddenly, as quickly as she had wanted to weep, she began to laugh. She roared with laughter and pointed her finger derisively. "It is my husband!" she cried out. "I didn't even recognize my own husband! He is a terrible mess, but oh, how funny!"

Her laughter was so hearty and so delightful that the cops began to laugh with her. Dan stood very still, balling his fists and clenching his teeth. At last, when Pilar could speak up, she said she would have to get her husband home and see that he was cleaned up.

The stout, green-shirted detective had not been a party to the laughing. He asked, "How do you figure your husband decided he had to hide in that little closet in the basement, lady?"

"Pardon?"

"I mean, you say this isn't the fella tryda assault you, but why was your husband tryna hide in a closet in the basement of his own apartment building?"

"But it is not his own apartment building. We are separated, although now, I think, this terrible experience has changed many things. Isn't that right, Dan, my darling?"

Dan did not answer, but he had gone under before her strength. Now he could not look at her even to glare at her. She was no longer concerned about standing close to him.

"But, lady," the detective said firmly, "you live onna seventh floor. Why should he hide inna closet inna basement? Is he a kook?"

"Officer, sir, please," Pilar said in a kindly but reproving tone. "My husband has a certain affliction. It came from the war."

"No!" Dan cried loudly, and it was so great a no that it added greatly to the believability of her story. He did not know what she was about to say but he could already sense the horror of the outrage with which she was about to smite him, merely one more weapon chosen with discrimination from the great arsenal of the woman scorned.

"He—you see, my husband—oh, it is so difficult to tell this while he stands there in front of us all, but he would never tell it on himself and that could mean he would have to stay here all night with that paint and mess all over him. So—you must forgive me for this, my darling Dan." She turned fiercely to the policemen. "He must always be near a bathroom. I know he thought that little closet was the nearest bathroom. You see, he wets his pants."

They beamed the glare of their pity on Dan. He sagged. He had lost.

He was released with a stern reprimand less than an hour later. She called a taxi. They got into it carefully. His back hurt from the fall in the lobby. His head was a mass of pain. She gave the driver her address and the cab moved along with them.

"How could you do it to me, baby?" Dan asked with a broken voice.

"Do what, sweetheart? Which part?" She held his hands in both of hers; in her smart *café au lait* kid gloves. She patted him lovingly. "Never mind that, dear," she said. "First we will go home. Then we will talk." She kissed him tenderly. She told the driver to stop for a minute at the drugstore at her corner. There she bought a large bottle of turpentine and some absorbent cotton. When they got to her apartment she took all his clothes off, oh, so very gently, then tenderly removed the paint from his face and neck and hair and hands.

"How could you do it to me, baby?" he kept moaning through all the ordeal. "I thought you loved me. How could you do such terrible things to me if you loved me?"

"I had to do it, my dearest," she crooned, "*because* I love you so much." She turned her attention to the Edwardian suit. "I had to discover, because you were married and could never marry me, whether you truly loved me. I went to Mr. Downey with all of your wonderful, passionate letters and the lease so that he would confront you and somehow force a reaction from you. I had to know if you loved me enough to want to rush back here and beat me after I had done such a naughty thing to you and to your wife's father. I knew it would make no real damage. You are men. Men forgive each other their women. But if you did not really love me, no matter how much you had said you loved me, you would never have come back here and I would have known that my life was finished here and I would have gone back to Cuba to my brother—and my mother." She kissed him lingeringly upon his slack mouth and she stared glassily into his feverish eyes. "But now I know that you love me. You have made me so happy today, my dearest Dan. My sweet, sweet, brave unselfish, dearest Dan. Oh, Dan. Ah. Aaah, sweetheart."

They made love frantically amid the heady fumes of the turpentine.

The little girls sip scarlet cups as sounds, full shrill with danger, shoot down through music, smoke, and hands that grope against each stranger. The little girls have eyes that glaze and satin breaths that bribe and beg for other calls and new sensations to edge toward shock along their legs. The little girls have lips for blood and scarlet cups to wound and fill. The little girls cry out for night to pluck out eyes, to maim, to kill.

Dan got home that night at one-twenty. He and Peggy and their daughter Carrie lived quite far uptown, on Riverside

Drive at 151st Street. The smell of turpentine, rather than the careful sounds he hardly made, woke Peggy. She gaped at his black eye, his markedly lumped head, and at the condition of his clothes and would have screamed with terror if he had not said, "It's just paint, hon," the instant she snapped the light on. He sat down unsteadily on the bed beside her and explained patiently how he had walked into a paint closet at Madison Square Garden by mistake, thinking it was the men's room, and thrashing around in there in the dark had knocked over this can of paint, then how, when he had got out of the closet a Garden special policeman had thought he was some kind of a killer or something and had hit him before the thing could be straightened out. He pointed out also that the Garden was insured and would replace his suit, but that the special policeman was just doing his duty, so since the paper and the Garden management were all good friends they had decided to forget the whole thing. He told her again not to worry about the suit: it would be replaced. "I should think so," Peggy said. Before she could say anything else, Dan suddenly began to gabble.

"Hey! Oh! That's not all, hon. I've been promoted. I've gotten a new job that is so fabulous I just can't believe it. Your father gave me my own column. A gossip column! On your father's orders."

"He did? I can't believe it."

"We'll be rich, honey. We'll be rich and famous. Have you ever had a surprise like that in your life?"

"Surprise? I'm flabbergasted," Peggy said. "Daddy never told me a thing about it."

VII

On the morning following his humiliation by Pilar, sickened by what she had done to him, Dan had his home telephone number changed. He didn't want to take the chance of having his Peggy bothered by a crazy maniac like that. He held Peggy in his arms and nearly crooned to her of the wonderful things they were going to do together and about the fame and the money they were going to have, because he was going to make that column the greatest thing of its kind the United States had ever seen.

"If ever a man deserved to be a columnist, I'm the man, honey," he said deep in his throat as he kissed the lobe of her ear.

"I'm perfectly willing to lie here and talk about business and your career, but I'd feel much better if you'd make up your own mind."

"Make up my own mind? Honey, I've been planning and working toward this since I was a kid, since I first read about O. O. McIntyre's suits."

"What has O. O. McIntyre got to do with a moment like this?" She moved slightly. She looked up at him. He swung his legs absent-mindedly over the edge of the bed. "I'm going to be very big, honey," he said. "I know just where I'm going. There are very, very few people walking around today who are as big as I'm going to be." Lying flat on her back, Peggy shrugged.

"I got to get downtown. I don't know where to start."

"I thought you said you were planning this for years."

He looked at her blankly. "I was. I have."

"Did you forget to plan how to start?"

He grinned at her. He began to laugh. He was so pleased with her that he leaned over to kiss her, and that ended that discussion of the column, the first of thousands of columns to come, for the present.

When he got to the paper he picked up a phone and called the Personnel department. He asked for Marc Rubin, one of the few men who had not smiled since the battleship *Maine* went down in the Havana harbor.

"What?" Rubin cooed like a nail moving across slate.

"This is Tiamat. You talk to Downey yet today?"

"No."

"Call him, then call me back."

"Whaaat?"

"You heard." Dan hung up. He waited for a few beats, then he asked for the chief operator. "Mabel, baby, if a woman, a slightly crazy fanatic name of Pilar Castaños, should try to get through to me, please leave her hanging. Okay?"

"Danny! You're a marrit man!"

"No, no, no. Nothing like that. This is a religious fanatic. Okay?"

"Any time, sweetheart."

As soon as Dan disconnected, the phone rang. It was Little Iodine Rubin. "So yah got yahself a nawfice anna secretary." It was a simple statement of status, but so vastly lofted above the tone of the exchange of forty seconds before that Tiamat felt a jolting thrill go through him. He rejoiced that he had called Rubin. How else? He was in! He was set! Rubin was actually being nice to him. Even warm to him!

"No dogs, Rubin. I work best if I have an intelligent, attractive girl I can show off for. You know?"

"I know. I know. Depend on Markie-Warkie. A column. Boy, I have said two hunnert times how much this paper needs a column and, boy oh boy, if you ain't exactly the speller to play that tune the very best." Dan could not believe his ears but he was convinced that he could actually hear Rubin grinning.

"Lissen, Dan," Rubin said. "You know what I think? I think you should move offa the editorial floor. A columnist is no working stiff, you know what I mean? Away. I gotta three-window office upstairs that I swear to God is as big as Charley O'Neil's. Which means bigger than Joe Downey's."

"I'll take it. When?"

"You'll move in tumorra morning an' you'll have a very intelligent an', believe me, very, very willing secretary waiting right there for you."

"Well, thanks—Marc."

"You take care a Marc Rubin. Marc Rubin takes care a
you. And good luck to you, believe me." They disconnected.

Dan waited tensely through ten days for Pilar to come storm-
ing into his office. Every night when he went home to Peggy
he dreaded opening the door, expecting to find her scratched
and crying in the middle of the room. When he walked along
the street his head moved nervously as though he wanted to
dart his eyes everywhere around him because he expected her
to fly at him out of a doorway or to run up after him on the
sidewalk with a rented car. But no such thing happened. Nothing happened.

He didn't do anything about her apartment for three weeks,
then he stopped sending the rent check. That changed nothing.
Either she had moved back to Cuba and had subleased or she
was paying the rent herself. After eleven weeks of anxiety over
what she could possibly be planning to do to him and where she
had gone to plan it, he had a friend in the Police Department
make an inquiry here and there. It turned out she was still living in the apartment. She had taken up painting and composing.
The cop started to tell him more but Dan cut him off.

After four months he felt that he had escaped from her. Or
that she had escaped from him. He wasn't sure which. It was
very confusing, but in many ways he was greatly relieved to
be rid of the obligation of racing to pounce on her from every
angle of the city; of hastening to that apartment at all hours of
the day.

When he felt absolutely sure he was free and clear of her, he
used the fact. It turned out to be the greatest thing in the world
that had ever happened to him, her barging in the way she
had, he told Downey. He had the chance to tell Downey this
because he had demanded a meeting in a loud voice right outside Downey's office, and for reasons of his own Downey had decided to be moved by that. As Dan wove his fantasy of what
he had done to get rid of Pilar, he believed every word of it.
He had let her have it, he said.

"How?" Downey wanted to know.

"Well, I grabbed a cab and I was out on the pavement in front of her building before it stopped. I banged on her door."

"With what?"

"With my fists! She was afraid to open up so I gave it the shoulder. She went backward into the room with it and I slammed the door. I grabbed her. I shook her, believe me. I yelled at her that we were through because we were never started. You know what I mean?"

"Whatta you mean?"

"I mean, because I happened to see this crazy kid once or twice here or there, she figures she can shake me down by putting the pressure on you and I told her she was lucky she didn't get herself arrested. I mean, that kind of blackmail is the lowest kind of blackmail."

"Yeah. Especially when she has the lease you signed in one hand and a pack of dirty letters from you in the other."

"You fell for that?"

"Come again?"

"That was the part! That was the low, criminal part of it that nobody could stand for! She went out and bought herself a printed lease form. That's all. She forged my name, then she typed those letters and she forged my name again. Listen, Joe, I don't happen to be able to control it if a crazy woman falls in love with me because I happen to look like her Uncle Max or something. This one is sick. You know what I mean?"

"I know what you think you mean," Downey said. He looked at Dan the way a man might peer at something unimportant through an empty coatsleeve.

"How is that, Joe?"

"You're a liar."

"Now, just a minute—"

"Get out." Downey swiveled in his chair and hit the intercom. "Send Rose Reiter in here with those budgets," he said. He ignored his gossip columnist. About five minutes after Rose

Reiter came in, and while she was explaining budget items to Downey, Dan left.

Ethnic groups living close to each other, and having the same or related languages, have strongly opposed views about adultery. The reindeer Koryaks are said to be puritans. Even the suspicion of adultery means death, and couples found in adultery must be disemboweled. The Maritime Koryaks, however, regard adultery as an honor and, should a child result, thank the father. Views about adultery in Western Christian communities are complicated by Christian mysticism, but in the West as elsewhere, although it is considered reprehensible by many cultures, adultery has always enjoyed a considerable popularity.

This is not to suggest that Dan had taken Pilar Castaños to bed to offend his father-in-law. However, Joe Downey, as Dan's discoverer, sponsor, and protector, had decided that the adultery had been designed to offend him. His daughter was involved only in a remote, doctrinaire manner. Downey overlooked the fact that the affair was much more a matter of concern between Dan and his wife than it was between Dan and himself. He remained Dan's enemy.

Pilar had given her erstwhile lover a lasting fright. He was, of course, quickly self-convinced that she was absolutely crazy. He remembered little things like that tattoo on her back and the time he had surprised her kissing her brother as if she wanted to swallow his whole head. She was absolutely unbalanced. He realized that he had forgotten that fact more often than he had remembered it. It had not only been an evaporation of memory; it had been a simple and common matter of leaving behind those things that are too heavy to be carried. If he had to have a mistress—if he *had had* to have a mistress —how could he have chosen a crazy woman who would not utter one word of complaint to him but who would march directly to the core of his existence to try to cost him his wife, his great benefactor, Joe Downey, and to get him fired? She was *crazy*. No bargaining about you give me this and I'll give you that. She had torn right in and said, in effect: "Daniel Tiamat is offensive to me. I want him destroyed." Thank God he had gotten rid of her in time. What would he have done if she had decided to go to Peggy, if she had really wanted to ruin him?

Dan seemed to mature overnight. He seemed to be able to recognize his blessings. He seemed to try to spend every hour he could with his wife, until she kidded him and joked about it in her way, which was exactly the right way, until he somehow tempered the guiltiness of his possessiveness.

"Honey," he would say, holding her cheeks between his hands and kissing her again and again, for he was an abundantly affectionate man in the manner that may have matched that of the late King Solomon, "whatever I do from now on, I do for you. I'm going to make this column the biggest thing they've ever seen, and I'm going to use it to do very big things, all for you and only for you."

"If it's for me, dear, please try to get a new source of jokes."

"Always remember this, baby, it's not what the joke says, but who said the joke. Get it?"

"No."

"If Groucho Marx says a joke, it is automatically very funny. If some unknown says some joke that you might consider funny, for me it has to be nothing. The readers like to know where their laughs are coming from. That's why America is famous for its sense of humor."

In time Peggy and Dan discovered that they felt much better if they discussed his work less and less, because as the column got better in Dan's view, it seemed to get worse in Peggy's. She decided to remember that, after all, she had been conditioned over years and years against Dan's kind of column by her father's unrelenting prejudice.

During the first year she went through all of it with him. His job required him to make the rounds of all the receptacles of glamour in the city. She made the rounds with him. She drank

ginger ale. He drank gin until he learned that he couldn't
handle that much liquor every day of his life and keep going.
He then worked out a method whereby he wouldn't have his
first drink until eleven-thirty, after the theater closings. For a
while Dan and Peggy stayed up until the last joint closed, but
even he came to understand how unnecessary that had to be.
The people who were very big went to only four or five joints,
and if he did miss a few hundred cafés, there were always a
couple of hundred press agents to fill him in on the action the
next day. Peggy helped him to understand that rest was important to his kind of work.

She sat at many tables with her husband and some of the
highest-seeded bores of their generation: film directors, danc-
ers, promoters, transvestites, gagmen, communications en-
gineers, hustlers, writers, bums, sportswriters, actors, athletes,
and agents—all the most exciting people of the day if one was
fortunate enough to remain out of earshot. They fostered unchanging conversation about one unchanging topic: self; but
because they all lived in the same air-conditioned *barrios,* eating the same food in daily public exhibitions matched by the
same bonifaces, extracting their dazzling wit from the same
columns printed in California the day before, and speaking
only to each other, it tended dangerously to seem like the same
conversation handed down to them by the hangers-on of Dia-
mond Jim Brady and Lily Langtry.

Peggy didn't care. She liked her husband. She loved to be
with him. She was thrilled to watch his confidence grow until
he seemed almost entirely at ease with a famous baseball manager, as though he were almost ready to acknowledge that he
was the man's social peer.

"I'm very lucky to be allowed to hang around with you,
Dan," she said one night.

"Lucky? Honey, don't you believe it. You're just as glamorous to me as all those people are to you."

"You're sweet. That isn't exactly what I was thinking of,
really. Tonight, I thought that if we went to one more club,

and heard one more compulsive screamer put his face to your ear and shout the story of what Groucho Marx said about Norman Krasna, I'd throw them through a bass drum."

"Honey, why didn't you tell me? But—I don't understand. I thought you just said you were lucky to be in a position to be around all the greats."

"Oh, I am! I did mean it. It just occurred to me that you could have been an editor of a morticians' trade paper or a Sand Hogs' journal and we would have had to hang around undertaking parlors or in tunnels under rivers listening to *them* talk shop, and I realized instantly that what we have to do is much, much better."

"We are living a legend, hon," he said solemnly.

As Carrie, Dan's and Peggy's daughter, grew older, Peggy gradually went into retirement from total night life and slowly a new schedule was worked out for Dan. He would work on his column at the new apartment on Fifth Avenue, beginning at about three in the afternoon. He would start his nightly rounds, alone, just before dinner. He made the theatrical openings and the big sports stuff after that, then a few night clubs and restaurants, and that was that. Dan could put away a lot of liquor between eleven-thirty and one o'clock, but he handled it as well as any of the other nightly drinkers who could also prove they weren't alcoholics. After a while, at no urging from Peggy, who would have been horrified at such a thing as urging anyone to do anything they hadn't chosen for themselves, he began to get home by one-thirty. She would wait for him, knitting or reading and listening for the baby, watching the greedy city crowd the night-blackened park, to listen with pleasure and praise to his nightly accounts concerning whom he had outtalked, outsmarted, and outstared during the preceding six hours.

In Dan's spoken narratives, as well as in his column, the word *very* was the ultimate qualifier of all power; an exclusive newspaper word property, just as a few years later it would be tacitly understood that the word *wonderful* would be the sole property of the television industry and the ultimate qualifier of all powers exhibited on that medium.

The nightly list of those conquered by Dan Tiamat represented the very biggest. There were the people who were very big in New York, L.A., Vegas, Miami, and so forth; another kind of people who were more exhausted but very, very big in London, Paris, Rome, and Jamaica; plus the really very big people who actually ran everything—the very quiet, very well tailored, very discreet, and very cultured men whose women sometimes chewed gum but seldom spoke, who could stare down a union leader or make a senator walk across a restaurant to say hello, or who could straighten out a judge here and there.

It was a thrilling life for Dan, from whose eyes fell enough star dust to bread a veal cutlet, so it was a wonderful life for Peggy as well. The very big people all loved him and he could prove that, but at the same time they had a good healthy fear of him, too. They all felt that he was a very funny fellow when he wanted to be, with sort of a dry wit, you know the kind, and yet, he would explain to Peggy, they all respected him and his column.

"Wouldn't they respect you and the column if they didn't think you were a very funny fellow?" Peggy asked him while they had a nightcap on the apartment terrace early one morning.

"You know how it is, honey. This town is full of merryandrews who haven't got to eat."

"You certainly have to eat. I'll bet you gained eleven pounds."

"Honest?" He was alarmed.

"Well, if you want me to be honest, I think you've gained about twenty-two pounds."

"It's that new sauce Béarnaise," he said bitterly.

"What's that?"

"It's a new sauce from Hollywood. It's made of sour cream and carrots and nuts and some mustard. It's probably loaded with calories."

"How was everything tonight?"

"Fine, fine. Listen, Peg, don't get me wrong. I don't care whether they think I'm a very funny fellow when I want to be, or not. They're mostly a bunch of creeps. But if they think I'm a helluva guy, why sit up nights to louse that up? Right?"

"Right? What happened tonight?"

"Al Parkay lent us his Mercedes."

"But, why?"

"It's really a marvelous deal. They have a very, very good trade-in, the Mercedes. Parkay got it from a certain party who had picked it up, you know, in a crap game or something, so Al took it on a tax write-off basis, but he has no use for it, so he says I'll actually be doing him a favor if I use it for, say, four or five years, then take it off his hands for, say, a thousand dollars. Actually, the Government will be paying for the whole thing."

"Is that good, dear?"

"Is what?"

"I mean, if the Government begins to give Mercedeses to every family in the country, that could irritate General Motors."

He looked at her queerly, then tried to smile. "It just so happens that we are not every family in the country, but I would like to meet anyone else in this country who would turn down a twelve-thousand-dollar car on a deal like this."

"But isn't the man who gave you the car—"

"Not gave, hon. He's lending me the car."

"I'm sorry. But isn't he a gangster?"

"A gangster?" Dan was horrified. "He's a gambler!"

"Daddy always speaks of Al Parkay as working for the Syndicate."

Dan shrugged slightly. "That could be. I mean, that's possible. But still, he's only a gambler."

"Well. That's a relief. But why should a gambler give you a twelve-thousand-dollar Mercedes?"

"I told you. He can't use it. He has a couple of cars and he doesn't like to move around much anyway."

"But why us, dear? Why not his mother? Daddy said he used to spend most of his time talking about his mother."

"His mother is an old Italian lady. She lives way downtown where the traffic is impossible. What would she want with a Mercedes? She'd think Al was nuts."

"I guess so. She'd probably rather have an Italian car, like a Ferrari."

"Are you kidding? She probably can't even drive!"

"But why us? I'm just asking, dear."

"He admires me, that's why! He likes the column and he happens to like a little publicity now and then so that various dolls will know his name if he meets them."

"Are you sure he's a gambler?"

"Sure I'm sure."

"I only asked because you never seem to say so in the column. I mean, you refer to him as Al Parkay, or Lover Boy, or Businessman Al Parkay."

"Well, after all, hon, the *Press* is a family paper. Why should we keep telling the readers about a lot of hoodlums and gangsters?"

By the time the column was three years old Dan Tiamat was a national figure whose daily pronouncements were read by sixty-five million Americans and an undisclosed number of aliens in almost two hundred newspapers. Dan was also on the air. He was the most colorful, if not the most factual, commentator on national radio by measure of both audience and income. He was consulted. Very, very big people consulted him before some very, very big moves were made, and in over 90 per cent of the cases they asked him to let the word leak into his column or into his microphone, or both. He was the great doge of the century of communications. He had developed the format and projected the contents of his column with enormous attention and greedy care. It leaned heavily upon names and upon Dan's opinion of the people behind the names. That he had never met, nor would ever meet, more than 0.12 per cent of any of the people he wrote about daily left Dan unmoved. The Column, as he himself had christened it, flashed behind-scenes canards, biased rumors, sinister fabrications, sick revenges, pimps' feuds, savage idiocies, moral wrongs, culpable treasons, hopeless confusions, bathroom jokes, incontinent falsehoods, crippling aspersions, shocking inferences, fawning idolatries, vicious assaults, unsuspected illiteracies, and relentless misinformation mixed with cloying sentiment and a profiteer's patriotism concerning motivations behind the movements of world leaders, ward heelers, starlets, and head waiters, and told of the certain consequences of these movements. Dan's syndicated omniscience was there to be shared. There was no one alive who would quibble if a tip-off in The Column happened to be wrong or even disastrously misleading; part of the mystery of it all was that they would forget they had read it in The Column in the first place.

The fact that Dan had not gone beyond the fifth grade in school was little known and by no one deplored. That was what had always been meant by "self-made man." It was not only part of the national tradition, but few of the great opinion molders of the time had needed to siphon their wisdom from a lot of books. Education was then, and would always be, for one's children.

Gossip (it was referred to as "personalities") was not all Dan dealt in. There were, of course, the jokes mailed to him by registered letter from the mighty, or clipped from *The Hollywood Reporter,* which presumably got them directly from the employed of that city. But also, from time to time there would be found Daniel Tiamat's emphatic belief in the Constitution of the United States, the Republic under a democracy, and the shadings of meaning behind the Fourth of July and Jefferson's birthday. And frequently Dan would dizzy his readers and infuriate the press agents with heart-warming stories about little people who had dared and won in love and life and who were, in a very unique fashion in the age of communications, truly wondrous religious little people; very, very little people.

This gift of the tiny touch was startling in that Dan's whole acquaintanceship was bounded by a jealous fence of rich jockeys,
executives whose cultures had been transformed by the creative
impact of the expense account, corpulent lesbians and thin
fairies, instigators of every nature, women who washed their
jewels in jet planes before landing as a simple gesture of friendship to press photographers, jolly hoodlums, execrable somme-
liers, wealthy thieves, sundry heiresses, and confidence men.
The only little men Dan ever saw to speak, in fact, were actors'
agents.

Dan would start to work at three in the afternoon, Sundays
excepted (it had been revealed in a three part biographical
study in Look), with a pair of scissors and three telephones,
which were in different colors as an asset when he was photo-
graphed in color. There was a typewriter close at hand: an
enormous eighty-pound Olivetti electric that could turn itself
off if anyone turned it on. He worked in his long, serenely
decorated living room, the size of a private fronton, overlooking Central Park. The room was done in shades of blue and
gray—sky blue against sea gray, aquamarine against slate gray
—with a sensible amount of navy trim to encompass all of it.
Peggy had been the decorator.

Mail directed to The Column was sorted by two expressionless young women whose names Dan never remembered but
who always exchanged Christmas presents with Peggy. Items
from the sorted mail were scissored out and pasted consecu-
tively upon sheets by Dan himself, while telephones rang and
he culled from the invisible voices whatever thin authority he
would require for the following day. This process was known
as "writing the column." It was said that no press agent would
dare call before three or after six on any afternoon between
Monday and Saturday. Several people who felt it more discreet
and less expensive not to employ press agents called him personally. Comedians making over twenty-five hundred dollars
a week would not permit a press agent to make the daily call for
them. There were three people who called him at seven o'clock

in the morning if they needed to, or got him out of sleep at night, and these were not government leaders or members of the clergy.

About 30 per cent of the mail still was directed to the *Press,* where Dan now seldom appeared and where reigned the young woman whom Marc Rubin had installed who did not exchange Christmas presents with Peggy. The mail sent to the paper was from the amateur character assassins, tipsters, and informers, and it was generally slim pickings. The harvest mail, which went directly to the apartment, was that which came from the professional informers. There were several grades of these informers. There were some sixty Broadway press agents of ducal rank (but a mere four were princes of the realm), about two hundred night-club and restaurant trudgers, perhaps thirty spokesmen for the living theater, five hundred heralds of the silver screen, seventy-nine hundred vocalists for American industry, and some forty-two thousand from the Federal payrolls under such droll classifications as information chiefs, press aides, P.R.O. section heads, advisory spokesmen, public education chairmen, and senators. All these Federal informers competed for attention with one another and with the White House rumor mill. They did not all communicate with The Column directly, but on every staff there was one man who could get through to Dan in exchange for a few top secrets in the areas of defense, finance, atomic energy, and witch hunts. This was not to be considered treasonable because the items they gave Dan were rarely, if ever, true anyway.

In addition, all the nations of the earth maintained visiting hustlers who lobbied from Washington or looked for edges from the open-eyed United Nations building in New York. They, too, had a choice selection of top rumors and fleshed-up used facts to be traded in return for sixty-five million readers.

All the newspapers of the country provided the daring-and-doing, I have-found-faith, what-use-is-money-in-the-end items that were the marijuana of Dan's special plea to be seen as all things to all men. The silver-lining copy placed within a high readership unit like The Column was essential to the newspaper industry so that it could, in a frantic sense, defend itself against itself. The big daily papers had `come to the point of reselling the same news in the form of a series of seemingly fresh editions that hit the street every two hours. This was a most difficult task. It brought about the give-them-what-they-want policy of the newspaper industry, which led to the arduous and expensive re-education of the entire public as to what it really wanted.

In order to sell all its uncountable editions, the newspaper industry had needed to foster moral anarchy and then to enforce its acceptance by the unending publication of frightening details in ceaseless and salaciously informative stories concerning obscure crime, adultery, betrayal, rape, degradation, indignity, race hatred, lust, graft, violence, prejudice, greed, fear, corruption, and suspicion until all America's children had learned that no adult authority was to be respected, until those children could become adults and prove that tenet.

While the daily papers sacked the morals of their communities to increase the readership of the multiple editions and to win higher and higher rates for advertising, their editorials and obediently regular news stories would deplore the effect of movies and radio and television and books upon the young, as though it were not the duty of the arts to deliver evil into a classical perspective and, in an ugly distortion carefully enunciated and then repeated, as though the newspaper industry had taken up the places and the privileges of the arts. The papers pressed on and on until, with the stubbornness of the slowness that it took the same industry to warn the people of the menace of world communism from 1920 onward until the people began to understand what it was their duty to believe, they finally succeeded in impressing murders of children by children into the normal way of life and at last made deceit, dishonesty, violence, and contempt for man the first of the great professions. While it dipped its pen in its readers' blood, the newspaper industry mumbled on about its sacred right, freedom of the press, and then gutted that right. Through his sops to dignity, through his slanders of his betters and his worship of all things successful, Daniel Tiamat handily became a significant figure of his hour of the industry.

It was a victory by default, made possible only because as readers shrank from memorizing all the specific in their papers, which taught them how to truss a teen-ager for raping, how to make a bomb, how to arm a street gang, how to rob a bank, or how to frame the mother of your children for a fast divorce, they chose Dan Tiamat's capsule versions of the same material. The very mindlessness of The Column held its millions of daily readers who were too frightened to scan more than the headlines that sledge-hammered home their directions for vice and violence; always teaching while always seeming to deplore. Square miles of forest fell each week to carry forward The Column and each year its readers were a little less sane than the year before.

However, if everything else in his limited life was distorted by his view through the bottom of a whisky glass or by his perpetual reconditioning by the contents of his column, Dan was able to retain his power to see Peggy the way she was: sane and lovely, saner than the flowers in May. He lived his schzioid existence as a columnist-husband for four years before Pilar telephoned him. The call came to him one night at Shor's at seven-twenty. He canceled dinner, the fights, and didn't show at any of the late joints. He got home at a quarter to two and went directly to bed, complaining to Peggy that he felt a bad cold coming on.

VIII

To emphasize the intensity with which Dan resumed his relationship with Pilar, let it be said that if he had studied the Slavic languages or the Mayan civilization within that same short period of time and with the same questing vigor he brought to the exploration of his mistress, he might conceivably have been asked to occupy a chair at the University of Kiev or invited to head the Department of Archaeology at the Carnegie Institution of Washington. The Cuban, on the other hand, seemed lethargic in the face of the swift reconciliation. After the first hour of Dan's studies, she even began to seem preoccupied.

When Dan snarled, "What the hell is the matter with you?" she looked up at him gratefully as though she had been waiting for some time for him to ask such a question.

"Oh, Dan! I am so worried. I am afraid I am going to be murdered."

"Whaaaat?"

"I have been carrying this fear with me for seven weeks, Dan. I have to share it with someone who will understand. It has become too much for me."

"Someone who will understand—baby, *I* will understand. Tell me. What's going on?"

She got out of bed and padded to the bureau, her behind jiggling as though that part of her, at least, was not worried at all. She took a letter out of the top drawer and brought it to Dan. Wherever she moved something always jiggled with unconcern. "It is dated March ninth," she said. "Seven weeks ago. It is from the senior psychiatrist at the sanitarium where we put my brother."

Dan frowned. "I thought he was locked up across the water. Switzerland or somewhere."

"He was, but then Mother and I moved him to this country."

With Pilar lying beside him in the bed, Dan read the letter.

> My dear Miss Castaños: With regret and with no little alarm, this letter is written to advise you and to warn you that your brother José has left this hospital without permission. His whereabouts are still undetermined. Police authorities have been notified and, I am told, a thirty-state alarm has been circulated.

Most importantly, we are concerned with your own safety and do most urgently request that you return to your home in Cuba at least until your brother has been overtaken and re-established under psychiatric care. I have taken the liberty of causing the Police Department to be notified in the City of New York and of furnishing a description of your brother, his delusions, and his homicidal tendencies.

You may be certain that, the instant that we are notified of José's detention by the authorities, we will notify you. I know you understand that you must not remain on any premises which José has knowledge of, unless these are your home in Cuba.

I send this letter with great apprehensions and, to emphasize the need for your departure, I must advise you, with regret, that your brother killed a nurse of this hospital during his escape from our protection. As sure as I have ever been in any prognosis, I find it urgent that I convey to you that José, having killed, will be driven to kill again. You are the target as long as you are away from your home in Cuba.

Dan reread the letter slowly, then looked at Pilar. "I'll handle this, honey. This takes our kind of organization."

"But what will you *do?*"

"We will find him. We will be very gentle. We will send him back to the hospital. I will solve everything."

"Oh, Dan."

"Do you feel better now? More relaxed?" He grinned at her lewdly and moved.

"Oh, Dan, you are wonderful. Aaaah, sweetheart! Oooooh, sweetheart."

Some time later, half sitting up in the bed, Pilar screamed. Dan gaped up at her. Her face was lined with fright and shock. She was attempting to point with one hand and to cover herself with the other. He twisted his body around to follow the point, hearing her say, "A man is *watching* us! Dan, Dan, it is a man watching us!"

Across the street, on the seventh floor of an office building, a man stood in a shallow niche on a narrow ledge between two windows. He was staring directly at them through a large pair of binoculars.

"Holy Jesus!" Dan yelled. He leaped out of bed in a great bound, naked and hairy, grabbing a clutch of underwear and trousers as he went, from a nearby chair. Standing behind the door to the bathroom, he hurried into these garments while he called the *Press*. "This is Tiamat," he said flatly into the telephone. "Gimme Reyes." He buttoned his trousers. "Benn? Tiamat. There's a nut on a building ledge about seven stories up on Thirty-first Street between Park and Lex. He's got binoculars but the way he's placed himself he may be deciding to jump any minute and I thought maybe we should get some photographers down here. Yeah. Thirty-first. You call the cops and I'll watch him here." He hung up.

"Dan! Oh, my God, Dan!"

Pilar was peering out the bedroom window. She had put a negligee on. "It's Pepé, my brother!" She closed the window curtains. "He saw us—what we were doing—with those binoculars! Get dressed. Get dressed. I have to go to him there. He will jump, he will jump. Oh, sweet Mother in Heaven, don't let him jump!" She stepped into a single-piece dress, slipped her bare feet into a pair of pumps. She wrapped a brightly colored kerchief around her head and started out the door.

"Wait!" Dan yelled.

"No, no! He will jump. I cannot look on his face after what he has seen us doing, but I must go to him or he will jump."

Dan was struggling into his socks. "Not like that, Pilar. Fuh crissake, there'll be photographers all over the place down there. Put some lipstick on."

"Do I look terrible?"

"You'll just look better when you get some lipstick on and comb that hair. Maybe it would be better if you lost that bandana and got into a black dress. This is a very big story, honey. I mean, you know, it could be."

She ran to the closet and snatched a dress from it. "And stockings!" Dan yelled. She found the stockings—they looked like handfuls of smoke—then disappeared into the bathroom. He had to wait, fully dressed and extremely impatient, almost six minutes before she was ready to leave. He peered out at Pepé from behind the curtains. Even seen from across the street, the young man's face was as white as worked Bellini marble. The binoculars dangled from a strap in his hand. His eyes, looking dead ahead, seemed sightless. His head, his face, and his body conveyed a sense of loss far greater than loss of life. It was the kind of loss that must have crept into the monodies of Lucifer, the escaped angel.

Dan and Pilar met the *Press*'s photographers as soon as they reached the street. Dan told them he had found the lunatic's sister. "I happened to get lucky and found her. She's all ours. Nobody else gets near her." And he had them line her up for three shots. He was in all of them.

"Now listen carefully," he told them. "I'm going up there with her. She'll talk to him. The cops'll be here any second. Ah, here they are."

A police car leading the truck of the Emergency Squad, both at full siren, rounded the Lexington Avenue corner. "You call Downey," Dan told the photographer named Joe Mansfield, whose Boston accent could burn like lava through the *A*'s of his sentences, "and tell him we've got it all taped out here. Tell him to send me two strong boys in case. This can get tricky. Hah? Go, Joe."

"Dan, Dan!" Pilar pleaded. Dragging him by the arm, she moved toward the building across the street. They began to run toward the building. A crowd was already beginning to assemble, everybody looking up like rubes on balloon day at the fair. Pilar, Dan, and a photographer named Bill Prass made the office-building entrance simultaneously with the police.

"Get the hell outta here," the sergeant advised them.

"I'm Tiamat from the *Press*." Dan's column now had an enormous amount of sales promotion. The sergeant made him instantly. "This is the sister of that guy up there. She'll be a big help to you. I found her so I'm helping you. As your helper I'm going up with you. Okay?"

They were standing on the sidewalk in front of the building. A heavy pair of binoculars came crashing down directly beside the columnist. If it had hit him on the head it would have gone right through to his belly. The sergeant dragged them into the entrance of the building. "Was that from *him?*" he demanded.

"Yes, yes." Pilar said. "He is sick. Oh, don't let him jump, sweet Lady of Mercy!"

The sergeant herded the three of them and two men from the Emergency Squad into an elevator. "Where to?" he snapped.

"Seventh floor," Dan answered. "I counted it." The operator closed the door.

"That's your brother on that ledge?" the sergeant asked Pilar.

"Yes, yes."

"What's he doing out there?"

"Queen of Angels, forgive me, forgive me!" Pilar wept, her face contorted with fear and remorse.

"Man has a psychiatric record, Sergeant. I just got the story from Miss Castaños. Been in two or three institutions. Very crazy."

"How do you like them onions?" the sergeant asked the men from the Emergency Squad. Their arms were filled with ropes, hoods, and nets. "Could it be any worse?" he said rhetorically.

"Not so bad, Sergeant," one of the men said cheerfully. He had a baby face. "With a real nut they jump the first time you try to call them in or else they hold out, and if he keeps holding out we'll eventually get him."

"How long to rig a set of nets?"

"Are you gonna call him in, Sarge?" Dan asked in amazement.

"To hell with that," the sergeant said. "With a columnist and a photographer here for openers, that's for nobody under the rank of captain. Or priest. Not me."

Pilar was praying in Spanish.

They walked rapidly along the seventh-floor corridor, trying every door. At length they found the office they wanted. A tall bald man in a black mohair office jacket and a young redheaded woman with a huge behind were leaning out of the window. The man was saying, "You will come in here at once. You get in off that ledge or I'll call the police."

"Get the hell outta there," the sergeant suggested from behind them, standing still. They turned. "Back," the sergeant said. "Slowly. Come on."

The bald man and the redhead moved away from the window. "He won't even answer," the man said.

"He's gorgeous," the redhead said, "absolutely gorgeous. What does he wanna do a thing like that for?"

The sergeant gestured to the four other people in the large room. "Everybody out! The Commissioner and the people of the City of New York gives yiz all the day off." The room was cleared. Patrolmen had now caught up with the sergeant's advance party. One was put on guard in front of each of the two doors leading into the office.

"No other press, hah, Sarge?" Dan said. "I helped you with the sister and I'll help you in the stories. Now you help me."

"That is a decision to be taken only by ranks of captain or better," the sergeant said. "You're inside, ain't you? Stop worryin'. Hey there, lady!"

Pilar was at the window, entreating softly and rapidly in Spanish. Bill Prass was shooting pictures from every angle possible, except that he hesitated to go all the way out on the ledge.

"Well, too late now," the sergeant said. "We shoulda watched her. If talking him in is gonna make him jump, he will now jump."

"Jeez, I hope Mansfield is working his camera downstairs," Prass said. Dan went to the window and stood close to the wall,

possibly back to back with the man on the ledge. He faced Pilar
as she looked out and pleaded with her brother. He reached for
her hand as she spoke. She looked at him strangely, disengaged
her hand, and went on speaking with her brother, who was out
of view.

"Come in, darling Pepé." It was in Spanish.

"I can never come in now," he said. "I saw you with him.
If my shame were less terrible I would have the strength to
jump from here."

"Pepé, *please* do not talk about that now. Please! Just come
in. Move very slowly and very carefully and come in."

"If I come in, Pilar, my love, my beloved sister, I will have
to kill you. I have a machete. I will do it quickly."

"Yes, yes. Kill me. Now. But come in. Step in through the
window and kill me."

"I want to look at you and talk to you. We will talk about
Botin, in Cuba."

"Come in and tell me. Come in. Please come in. Now."

For thirty-nine hours Pilar, police and Fire Department of-
ficials, the Emergency Squad, and a priest pleaded with Pepé
to come in from the ledge. A psychiatrist came from Bellevue
and studied the situation. The Emergency men could have
closed their nets, top and bottom, except that when Pepé saw
them preparing to release them, he produced a machete from
the left leg of his trousers and held it in both hands in front
of his throat, almost driving the eight thousand people in the
street into an ecstasy of hopeful fright. The psychiatrist immediately advised against closing the nets, as did a six-year-old
boy, speaking to his grandmother in the crowd. The nets went
back into place. The authorities hoped the nets would be wide
enough to engage Pepé if he leaped, while the throng in the
street hoped he would be agile enough to leap clear of the nets
when he went.

The sporting folk at Lindy's laid six to five that he would
not jump clear if he decided to go. The price on jumping, hit or
miss the street, was even money until he had not jumped during

the first six hours. After that the bettors really had to earn their money. When he was still on the ledge after six hours, a man had to bet a hundred to win seventy that he would jump, and bet a hundred to win twenty that he would not jump. The rules set down were that it would be a stand-off if the cops snatched him in or if he got talked off the ledge. Fringe bets were made on who would talk him in, if he got talked in, or who would be talking to him when he jumped, if he jumped.

Al Parkay was the only hustler with the head to look up the telephone of the office in which all the action was going on. He had no trouble getting Dan on the phone.

"Dan? Al Parkay. How do things look inside?"

"About even. He's crazy but he doesn't seem so restless. They talk to him but he doesn't answer unless it's the sister. Anyway, he has stopped threatening to jump."

"I certnee appreciate this."

"That's all right."

"Are you—uh—gonna stick there?"

"I stick here as long as the sister stays here. She's the control on the whole thing."

"Is it—uh—okay if I check you, say, every hour or so at this number?"

"Sure. Check me."

"I really appreciate. Just to prove, it's okay with you, I'm gonna roll a little action for you on this to make it more interesting."

"Very nice of you."

"If you were betting, how would you bet it?"

"No jump."

"Who's gonna talk him in?"

"The sister. He don't even hear the other people when they talk to him."

"How soon do you figure?"

"I would guess he'll come in when she collapses and she's very exhausted. Very. I would say about ten more hours."

"That long, hah? Well."

"We don't want it too quick. We got a paper to think about."

"You figure ten hours, hah?"

"Al, one thing. This is confidential information, you understand. If any of this got to any other paper we wouldn't like it at all."

"Listen!"

"Thanks very much, Al." They hung up, friends.

In all of the movements and emotional explosions that followed, Dan forgot about his arrangements with the hustler. He was agreeably surprised, then, two nights later, when he ran into Al Parkay and received an envelope holding twelve hundred and fifty dollars. "It was very good information, so it was a very good bet you made," Al said, grinning. He himself had come out a little over seventeen grand ahead. Bets had been laid off as far west as St. Louis. It had been a unique event among sportsmen. Parkay and Dan were fast friends, after that, for many years.

By the thirtieth hour, Dan had his fifth exclusive story on the tragedy and the public knew at last what Pepé's terms were. He had proposed that either he should be left with his sister in the office for approximately a half-hour so that he could kill her, or that his sister would agree to return by plane with him to their home in Cuba, in which case he would postpone killing her. "COME HOME OR I DIE" MAD BROTHER'S PLEA, was the headline in the *Press*. It sold a lot of papers.

Two airline promotion men tried to firm the thing up for their side by offering one-way tickets free of charge, including an all-expense tour of exciting, glamorous Havana. A very funny sketch involving a beautiful *señorita* with a broad Spanish accent and a funny guest-shot from a Broadway hit, with the comic trying to jump out the window every time the *señorita* packed her suitcase for a trip to Cuba, was heard on one of the big Sunday-night variety shows that radio could do so well in those days.

The whole event was a prodigious break for Daniel Tiamat and The Column. He scooped the country day after day. His picture was everywhere. He got the only interviews with the sister. He was the only newspaperman allowed inside the suicide office either by night, under the glare of the exciting police spotlights, or at the height of the day-time thrills. Other papers tried to get in, through their own connections, but the sister said that if they came in and anything happened to her concentration, and this resulted in harm to her brother, she would sue the papers and the city of New York. Even Joe Downey got enthusiastic about Dan's close connection with the story after that. He called Dan every two hours, keeping his tone impersonal, listened to a rundown on the action, and told him he was doing a great job.

The color story that every paper covered in the streets around the office building was enormous. Bars as far away as Thirty-fourth Street reported an 83 per cent increase in business. At one time or another practically everybody dropped down to Thirty-first Street, hoping they'd get lucky. During the two days of the event the streets were even more crowded than they were at night, because, besides the faithful regulars and the hustling concessionaires creating a fun controversy with their JUMP and DON'T JUMP buttons, there were a lot of children who had been allowed to skip school by their parents because there *was* a chance that the man might jump, and where could a kid have an experience like that twice in his life?

Pilar was so exhausted and upset after it was over that she did not get to see the stories Dan had written, and he never bothered to show them to her. A month after the event the *Press* gave its columnist a dinner at Toots Shor's, because he had written the paper's most triumphant story of the year, carried under a page-one head that said: PRESS COLUMNIST RESCUES MAD BROTHER.

What had happened was that Pilar was resting with the phony nurse the paper had provided (she was the sister-in-law of the head of Classified Advertising and had been unemployed for a long time from her profession in mortuary work), in a deck chair sent up by the Tri-It Comfit Chair outfit, when

Dan, who had continued to stay well back in the room for instinctive reasons, noticed a microphone being lowered into view in front of the window. Some smart guy at N.B.C. had figured a way to get himself a raise and was going to get a color story out of it even he couldn't get the brother to talk in English, if at all, by bumping the mike into the side of the building and doing a running narration of what was being attempted. They had cleared network time for him.

Dan ran like a wild man to the corridor outside the office and grabbed a big runner he had stationed there. "Get up on the roof and break the arm on the guy who is lowering that microphone from up there." He gave the goon a look at the dangling mike, then shoved him on his way. Then, forgetting his unspoken policy which had been formed when the binoculars had almost connected with his head, he rushed to the window, hoping to grab the mike and pull it in. As he reached out for it, Pepé saw him, and with a wild cry, rushed along the narrow ledged as though it were a trench instead of seven stories in the air over a hard street, machete held high, screaming in Spanish. He slipped just as he got to the window because his shoulder hit a decorative projection, and down he went. Reflexively, Dan grabbed at his wrist and held it. The crowd in the street went into mass hysteria. The noise sounded greater than that for Babe Ruth's sixty-first home run, but it stopped just as suddenly when it looked as though the man were going to be saved. The police sergeant, the same sergeant who had started out with them on the detail, held Dan around the waist and in a twinkling the specialists had moved in and had Pepé secured, lifting him to the ledge, then dragging him into the building. Pepé had fainted. Bill Prass's camera clicked. Pilar kissed her brother, then covered Dan's face with kisses (these shots were later destroyed by Downey), and the police and the doctors and the priest shook Dan's hand until he was afraid it would come off. He had not quite known how he had saved Pepé until it was over, and then he could not fathom how he had done it.

"In the most courageous, skillful, and distinguished single piece of journalism in this newspaper's history or, perhaps, that of any other in this city," Maxwell Miller, the oldest living newspaperman in the eastern United States, then a resident of Philadelphia, quavered into a microphone at the dinner of tribute the *Press* gave for Dan, "young Tiamat *owned* this great story until he was ready to make his move, then he *became* the story itself by an offering of heroism."

If Dan had been impatient on the threshold before, he was now in. He became and stayed very big with important people on that night. Subsequently he was awarded the Herman ("Addie") Addison Award of the National Newspaper Womens' Turnverein for his feat, and was successful in selling his treatment of the event to a major motion picture company for a handy sum in five figures.

IX

Three hours after Pepé had been taken downtown and Pilar had been satisfied that he would not be harmed, she and Dan had lunch in a dimly lit restaurant with banquettes, long tableclothes, and candelabra. She tasted daintily of this and that while he devoured her in his imagination. But she talked on and on upon the same subject—her brother. There seemed to be no way he could stop her, so he set his jaw, looked at the other women in the restaurant, and pretended not to listen to her.

Pilar talked about Pepé as he had been when a little boy and then a young man, as though by telling that story, relief hurtling from the past would rip through the words she spoke and her great burden of hopelessness would either be lifted from her or somehow shared. Because Dan had so enthusiastically returned to her, in her fatigue and weakness Pilar mistook his scrambling, infecting lust for love; because she lived for him and loved him, she suddenly saw his compulsive fondling of her body as tenderness, his talk, which poured from

him without punctuation, as a crying out of his love for her
and his need for her; and she believed all at once that if she
could confess to him she would be liberated from her sense of
doom.

"Dan, I have to tell you something. Dan!" His eyes had been
intent upon two pretty women who were talking fiercely across
the room.

"Yeah?"

"I must say something to you. I have to. Dan, darling Dan,
look at me."

"I'm here! I'm looking."

"I want to tell you why Pepé is so sick."

"Honey, let's talk about something else. Haven't we had
enough of your goddam brother?"

"Dan, this is important to me! It is something I have never,
never, never been able to tell anyone in my *life*. I can tell you
because I have to tell you! Because you love me and your love
lets me tell you to free myself because I am dying from it."

"Gee, Pilar. I'm sorry. Of course tell me, hon. I'm all ears.
Come on, now. Out with it."

She looked at him strangely, as though he had suddenly
been revealed as a Martian, as though he were some kind of
clot played by a skilled professional actor. An acid doubt tried
to reach the rim of her conscious mind to stop her, and it almost
did, but her need for his comfort and his belief was so strong
that she rushed the words from her. "Pepé has been so sick
because—because since we have been eighteen years old—"

"Yes?" He looked perplexed, the way a skillful animator
can draw a cartoon horse.

"—we have been lovers."

"You have been *what?*"

"We have made love to each other. Completely. We have
slept with each other. I got over it but he cannot and now it
has made him sick." Her sensibilities at last made her realize
what she was seeing in front of her. "Dan! Don't look like
that!"

He felt sick. He stared at her. His face was bloodless. He expected to vomit. She was a *degenerate!* She was a filthy, rotten, incestuous *degenerate!* She was sitting there calmly and bragging to him about having layed her brother, her own twin brother!

"I should think he would be sick," Dan said. He wanted to fling his wine into her face. He wanted to spit upon her, to shave her hair off, to jump upon her breasts in the running filth of the gutter, but he was a gutless wonder so he made a partial resolution of everything by calling for the check.

"What are you thinking?" she implored. "That was long ago. That was before I came here to college, before I met you. When I met you I couldn't go back. I, Dan, I—" She could see far into his eyes and she could see him fleeing, screaming his horror of her. She did not speak any more. She stood up and walked from the restaurant. He glanced at the check, threw a ten and a two on the table, and hurried after her.

They walked dispiritedly, bleakly down Fifth Avenue toward Washington Square. As they passed a supermarket on a side street, Pilar, who had begun to weep silently, said she needed some coffee for the apartment and rushed into the store. He shambled in after her, flogged by his disgust. Without thinking about it—a professional reaction—he walked toward the store's newsstand. He looked down at the headlines casually, then was transfixed by two lines of black letters: LEDGE MANIAC ELUDES COPS, VOWS VENGEANCE ON SISTER.

He wheeled in fright. Pilar seemed to be memorizing the labels on cans of sauerkraut one aisle away from him. He started to call out to her, then saw Pepé running crazily along the aisle toward her, shouting wildly and holding his long, razor-sharp machete high over his head. Pilar turned. As he came closer to her she moved without a flaw and swept a full shelf of canned goods to the floor in his path. Stepping on them as they rolled in every direction, he careened with his great forward momentum and a chilling scream into the bottles of ketchup and jars of peanut butter, mustard, and jam on the other side of the aisle. He swung the machete at her eccentrically as he fell and it opened her cheek laterally from the corner of her jaw to the corner of her mouth. It was a deep, wide wound. It separated the side of her beautiful face into two distinct and bloody flaps of skin. As Pepé lay on the floor for an instant among the oozing and still-rolling jars and bottles, Pilar struck him heavily with a large can of vegetable juice at the back of the head, at the base of his skull, out of mercy for him and not from fear.

Pepé subsided at her feet. The gushing blood from her ruined face spilled upon his face, then the shock crashed brutally into her anxiety to overtake again what she lived for, and she turned in a daze to look for Dan, her salvation from this and from herself, as two policemen came sprinting into the store.

"Dan, Dan darling!" she screamed, the words tattered and spent by the great tear in the side of her face. "Please! Dan!" One of the policemen dug his hands into the arterial pressure points at her neck and throat. Dan was gone. Dan had fled in mortal terror. The last handle of her will to remain conscious came away in her hand from the substance of her yearning. She fell forward, unconscious.

Dan Tiamat moved his family to Hollywood for the summer, the next afternoon. It was a pretty sudden decision, he agreed, but the big entertainment news wouldn't wait and the studios were bursting with activity. The three of them took the 20th Century Limited out of Grand Central Station at five in the afternoon. Downey came to see them off. Friends who had somehow picked up the news of the little holiday sent champagne and books, flowers and candy to the train. The Tiamats had a wonderful summer. They stayed on the Coast until October, almost six months, and Dan broke some great stuff from that city of the stars.

José Castaños was committed to a prison for the criminally insane. His sister, when she was strong enough, returned to assist her mother with the affairs of the big plantation at Botin, in Cuba.

X

Perhaps the highest point in Dan Tiamat's career of helping God to run the affairs of men came in the spring of 1949, when he was forty years old. Power had eroded him. The mirrors were pitted with the pox of his vanity. Booze had him by the sleeve and was tugging away for his complete attention. At his best he was as arrogant as a moving ostrich. He had proved that he could shake the world wherever actors, politicians, or publicans had tread.

His mission had become a crusade to give the nation his version of the news in two hundred and nineteen daily papers (no boilerplate) while he complained against ingratitude or clung tensely to soft, changing thighs under a restaurant table with his left hand and made cryptic notes with a silver, stubby pencil in his right. By 1949 he was very big with everybody. He also thrilled the nation with a weekly radio show for which people stopped eating, talking, or reading comic books. A musical play had been done from part of one of his columns. The boys had made movies from three of his other whole columns. Semiannually, in print, he commemorated the memory of free dinners he had had at the White House with two successive presidents. He was a Papal Knight although he and Cardinal Grogan were not speaking because the Cardinal had sold his memoirs to one national magazine after he had practically promised them to a very dear friend of Dan's who published another. He had tremors in the morning until the pills took hold. He had earned three hundred and twenty thousand dollars the previous year from all sources, and approximately six thousand people considered him a louse.

He was the complete New Yorker. He had been to Washington and back on night trains. He had been to Europe, once before his marriage, and again during the war. He had been to Cuba on his honeymoon with his only wife. Otherwise he had voyaged across water on two occasions: once to Staten Island when he had been a defenseless five years old (he had not been made to disembark) and again when he had voyaged from the foot of East Seventy-ninth Street to a prison on an island in the East River to wrap up a news story. He had not been seasick on either journey. He had been up North many times: to the Yankee Stadium, to Harlem, and to a funeral at Riverside Church, which faces Grant's Tomb. Dan Tiamat had hidden deep in the heart of the hive, but that had not kept him from yearning always to be some place, any place other than where he was at nearly every waking moment. He was a man discontented with self and with place and he never stopped wondering about things, such as what it would be like to be standing in the Angkor Wat at night; about bikinis of every color against tan skin threading through the traffic on the Boulevard des Anglais at Cannes; about the fervent, crowded fan-tan games which never ended in the basement of the Central Hotel in Portuguese China. He knew all about what there was to be learned concerning all of these places and others, from book after book, defying the first three hours of each morning's insomnia. He studied, with wrapt concentration, the sounds of the waters pleasuring the air at Iguassú, the summer sex of the Swedish people, *macumbas* in Brazil, the *penchak* of Bali, Bulgarian rose fields, the weekly printed guide to the whorehouses of Bangkok, the coast of Cornwall, and the honky-tonks of Calumet City, Illinois. He remained in perpetual awe of where he was not. The world he knew was a sore disappointment to him because the people in it seemed to be as weak as he felt he was.

While he put up with his surroundings, he lived as a man in his position should: eating patriotically his Red secobarbital sodium, his White barbitone, his Blue amobarbital. After he read his travel books in the earliest hours of each morning, he would sleep through six hours, drugged and dreamless, and when morning came he would climb to the top of his amphetamine-crested mountain to look at all the others with wild surmise, garrulous upon a peak near Darien. Daniel Tiamat was

a modern man. He controlled the spaces in which he presumed
he was living and wasted not one serene vision by tolerating a
jagged mood. If all the pills in all the pockets of modern men
were tossed out of the windows in all the threatening cities,
their streets would be more deeply covered than after the bliz-
zard of '88.

"Put a siren on Mr. Tiamat's car, sergeant.

"No check, Mr. Tiamat. Please! It's a honnuh anna
pivvelege!... Bet Gertrude's Cue onna nose, Dan. No
place. Onna nose.... I happen to have to insist that you
accept this pistol permit, Dan. A man like you can use a
little persuasion if you come up against the wrong ele-
ment, as we all do.... You aren't quite sure what a stock
option is, Mr. Tiamat? It's very simple. Let me explain
how it works.... Stay away from Little Marty, Dan. If
you see him, crossa street. Is coming big bang-bang to
Little Marty, you know what I mean?... Why shuddn't
you have a piece of this joint? You spend alla your time
here almost. Just to have you sitting is very good for
business.... Dan, do you have a minute? Dan, I hate to
bother you but could you take an hour or so and read this
script? I mean, if you like it, we'll do it, but I gotta get
a viewpoint with taste and imagination.... Honey, lis-
sename. Why can't I make it with you? Evvey guy in this
town wantsta make it with me, but I wanna make it on-
ney with you.... Hey, Mistuh Tiamat! Oh. Parm me fa
yelling. Lissen, Mistuh Tiamat, I got some beeyewdeeful
sample skins cerulean mink soft like a hanfulla condense
milk and I would considda it a pivvelege anna honnuh if
you let me run it up inta a coat fuh yaw wife.... I'll give
you a blank check, Dan. You fill in the name of your favorite charity yourself or better yet I'll put the cash in
your hand to save bookkeeping and you can hand it personally to your favorite charity."

Beyond his undeniable ability, Dan Tiamat had made it because he looked like Double Destiny. He was taller than anyone else in his field, or in very nearly any field this side of a
sideshow, for that matter. He had an uncorrected myopic condition that gave him an expression of burning intensity and

probing intelligence. He looked exceedingly Anglo-Saxon,
which is the sharpest edge in this country that boasts of being
a melting pot. He looked almost excessively Anglo-Saxon, in
the heavy weather-beaten Irish way that has made so many
political leaders. He had a jaw like an alligator's. The Choctaws
are not the only people who revere alligators and never kill
them. To compensate for this cruel cosmetic he had cultivated
a merry smile, wholly fraudulent, like a lovable priest in a
big box-office movie. A minor hearing deficiency caused him
to speak loudly; this suggested great self-confidence. In greeting
he gripped the extended hand with crushing clasp because the
publican his father had swamped for had been insistent on that
approach. His handwriting was large, not to say boyish. Middle European graphologists employed by industrial firms to
classify employees by this phase of their make-up have stated
that small handwriting indicates high intelligence. He had a
lot of hair, worn in the style of the late Wendell Willkie, and
because of an early nourishment deficiency it had begun to
gray prematurely, providing him with the top of a Texas senator
or of an admonitory advertising model in the white shift of the
medical professions. Tiamat looked like a winner so they made
him one, and after that he remained a winner for sure because
winners in every trade always get a lot of extra help.

"The homelike glow of the corner saloon is not ex-
ceeded except by the glow of a good cigar. Egad! What
a boon to hang here on the bar and puff out slow. A drink,
you say? I don't mind if I do and, in return, I have a little
tale for you—uh—tale, that is, a little story, as it were.
Ah, yes. Wherever there's a he you'll find a her.
"I knew a beauteous hustler once. Nellie, her name. I—
uh—hope you don't mind monologues. Every policeman
trusted Nellie because she was so very fond of dogs. I can
see her now. Egad! A sweet, old-fashioned two-dollar
girl. Nothing she wouldn't do for a friend. She'd pant
like broken bellows as she held you fast in love's sweet
glue. Just leave it on the bureau, dear, she'd say, trusting
you.
"Ah, those afternoons in the good old summertime.

Trolling on that shady dame, baby mine. Lolling above the sharp retorts of brewery horses while awaiting business news from all race courses. Mem-o-rees! Mem-o-rees! Why, yes, thank you, I will. Drink to forget, I always say, mem-o-rees to kill. What a thoughtful child that Nellie was. Please pardon me while I wipe away this stray tear from my eye.

"Looking back now, dear sir, I loved that girl for her crookedness and sweet corruptitude. She could roll a lush without losing a curl. She played the plectrum banjo in the nude. And if, in the course of steady defection, she'd find herself far from our midst, she'd drop me a card from the House of Correction, writ by kind prison matrons and signed with a kiss.

"I do not regret reversals which caused me, forty years ago, to sleep on straw, and I wish with all my heart that I had paused before I sold Nell to that joint in Panamaw. That was nineteen oh nine, but still I wait. (Not, sir, that I expect her to be true.) Perhaps, as we drink, she'll walk through that gate and in greeting make a bid to kiss you, too."

Life was coming on warm and strong for Dan Tiamat, that summer of 1949. It was as free as sunsets. There was plenty of whisky. There were cords of thick steaks with a black smell and centers like tea roses. The money felt as if it was printed on green cashmere. He was the doyen, the keeper of the fame; by omission he could kill and by commission, ruin. He did both, daily.

One night he was sitting in a joint in the West Fifties that had been built observing the tradition of a garbageman's Bushido. It had the correct pink air and dirty floors and expensive smells that indicated one might with luck finish a meal without being cuffed by the bluster of the fat bum who ran the place.

Dan was sitting at a large round table, unusual for him, dead center within the archway that separated the circular barroom from the mess hall, with four practitioners of palship, two of whom he had met for the first time about an hour previously. They were finishing dinner. On his right sat a gynandrous songwriter who wore twenty-dollar ties. A movie singer who had lost three wives to stinginess was at Dan's left. A dress manufacturer and Al Parkay, the gambler, faced him.

Al Parkay had a police record that featured four charges of murder but no convictions, and a sentence for indecent exposure in a five-and-ten-cent store in Newark, New Jersey. He looked so sensual that he gave the impression of having vicuña teeth. As suave as a movie butler, he was Dan's old friend, tried and true.

The dress manufacturer was a troubled man, convinced that his dead wife was watching him with his second wife. He had disliked his first wife and the possibility of her continuing psychic scrutiny terrified him. However, whenever he felt forced into doing anything in propitiation he consternated his second wife, whom he loved dearly. They had crossed on the *Ile de France* the summer before, on their honeymoon. He had had to throw all of her clothing, including her furs, overboard because he had been certain, more than at any other time, that his first wife was watching them and condemning them. Somehow, he had to show her that he could be as mean to his second wife as he had been to her.

While Dan chatted idly with a visitor to his table, the extremely well-dressed head of the National Schoolteachers Union, a man named Krolik, the four others at the table were engaged in relishing the forthcoming burial of Moe Girdle, a loser who was then waiting around upstate to be electrocuted. Mr. Girdle had walked into a restaurant on the West Side and, in full view of two hundred and sixty diners, shot a leading bookmaker through the head over a matter of thirty-two hundred dollars.

Although Dan had no use for Moe Girdle, when he heard Al Parkay remark that if anyone came out for a pardon for Moe Girdle, that guy would right away find himself outside in the snow with no shoes and no carfare, he took offense. *He* was the one who advised on the public pulse. *He* was the one who would decide things like pardons.

"I tell you what, Al," he said, turning away from Krolik in mid-sentence. "I'll make you a little bet." He turned slightly, caught the eye of the fat proprietor who was annoying three customers at another table, and winked broadly. "Al and me are going to make a little bet," he said loudly. The fat proprietor left his victims at once and lumbered to Dan's table.

"Bet me what?" Al Parkay demanded.

"What you were talking about," Dan replied.

The songwriter summed up in a high-pitched voice: "We were talking how Moe Girdle did not have the greatest disposition in the world. Then you said, Al, that anybody who pardoned Moe Girdle would likely be run out of town. Then Dan says he will make a bet with you on whether Moe Girdle will make pardon or make it with the electricity. At least, that is what I think was said. Am I right, Dan?"

"Not a pardon necessarily," Dan said. "Anything. A reprieve, even."

"Is that what you want to bet?" Al asked. "Because if that's what you want to bet, you got a bet. I'll give you odds arreddy."

"Odds?" Dan said with disapproval. "What kind of a ghoul are you? A man's life is at stake here."

"Some life," the songwriter piped.

"So what's the bet?" Al asked.

"I'll bet you against me."

"I know. But how much?"

Dan looked up at the fat proprietor and smirked. He turned to Al with his hard eyes. "If you win, I get out of the country and never come back. If I win you get out of the country and never come back." A second row of reverent spectators was now filling in around the table. The oafish proprietor stood behind Al.

"I don't get it," Al said.

"If you don't want to bet, don't bet."

"I dint say I din wanna bet. All I said was, I don't get it."

"Would you allow me to explain which is how I see this here bet?" the songwriter asked helpfully.

"Go ahead," Dan rumbled.

"Well, you make a bet, see? Then if Moe Girdle is dead in the Wednesday papers, Dan is got to get outta the country and never come back. This is a very, very dramatic type of bet. *Also* if Moe Girdle should stay alive in the Wednesday mawning papers, then Al needs to get outta the country and never come back. At lease, this is how I see the bet. Am I right, Dan?"

"Is this a bet or is this ever a bet?" the movie singer asked posterity.

"Shuddup, yuh crumbum," the oafish proprietor rasped.

"Very interesting," Al said. "I mean, it really is."

"I thought you might think so," Dan told him, "as you have always appreciated a real gamble." Everybody laughed at the sally.

"How do I know you'll pay off, Dan?" Al asked softly.

"Ordinarily, I wouldn't like a crack like that," Dan said, "but I'll figure that a bet like this just makes you unnaturally tense."

"Whatta you," the porcine proprietor asked Parkay, "outta yuh mind?"

"No offense, Dan. I mean it. But there is nothing whacky about a question like that."

"How could I welsh?" Dan asked, canting his head to indicate the loutish proprietor. "This loudmouth will have the story all over the country by tomorrow morning. If I welshed I'd be washed up every place. Just the same, you're entitled. I'll also write out a letter to my boss, Joe Downey, resigning all my jobs if I should lose and we can have a notary come in here and stamp it."

"You might even send copies of the letter to alla opposition papers," Al suggested.

"If you want."

"I want."

"Certainly. Why not?"

"If only to observe the letter of the lore," the songwriter said carefully, "what it is necessary to find out, perhaps, is how does Dan know that Al is gunna pay off?"

"Listen," Al said earnestly, "I am known to be pretty legitimate about a bet. You know what I mean? So I leave that part
up to Dan entirely. Any way he wants to insure the bet is absolutely okay with me."

There were now five new faces around them, brought over
by bellowed invitations from the lard-bound proprietor. Al
liked the feeling. Everybody was on his side. They all wanted
Tiamat to lose.

"First, do we have a bet?" Dan asked carefully. He could feel
everybody's admiration on him like sunshine. He was betting
on life and death and exile the way these creeps would lay
down a sawbuck in a crap game. He had not only become a
legend in this town, but lately he had been feeling it come over
him that he was a legend to himself.

"You got yesself a bet," Al said in a professional voice. He
leaned across the table with his right hand extended to seal
the bargain. Dan stared at the hand, manicured and scrubbed,
as though it were covered with running sores. "What are you
all of a sudden, Al?" he asked with a snort. "A sportsman?"
Everybody, including Al, got a good laugh out of that.

The dress manufacturer suddenly sat up as straight as a
nightstick. He had just had a vision of how this whole problem
of his marriages could be worked in reverse. If Sarah *was*
watching them, then every now and then she should suffer a
little. Gloria deserved a little break and Sarah deserved all the
heartbreak he could find for her. He stood up suddenly and
left the table.

"Where you goin', yuh crumbum?" the proprietor bawled,
deciding that the man was trying to sneak off to the telephone
to make calls about the bet and take the edge off it. When he
lumbered after the dress manufacturer he was astonished to find
him in front of the checkroom, waiting for his hat.

"Where yuh goin'?" he snarled. The dress manufacturer felt
a certain thrill that one of the greatest guys that the newspapers
kept saying God ever made should care where he went.

"Home," he said simply.

"Home?" The proprietor was incredulous. Two people came up to him to get his autograph and he brushed them away like a wrangler working young horses. "Whatta yuh mean, home? How can yuh go home, yuh crumbum? Don't you know what's happening in there? They're makin' history in there."

"I'm feeling sorry for my wife," the dress manufacturer said confusingly.

"Aaaah!" The proprietor turned away with contempt, but he was relieved—the bet was safe. As he waddled to the bar a woman tried to get his autograph for her son, who presumably was a child bartender with big dreams. "Get outta my way, yuh creep!" he said, and pushed past her. Telling her dentist about this actual personal encounter the next day, the woman observed that the proprietor was possibly the most colorful figure the twentieth century had produced. "He's just a great natural," she explained to the awed dentist. "He's a modern Falstaff or a Sir Joey Belch, like."

"Gimme alla change yuh got inna till," the suet-packed proprietor said to one of his haughty bartenders. With the silver in his hands he took off again, editing the story of the bet in his mind as he went, adding linchpins. He dumped the half-pound of money on the shelf under the pay telephone, then slammed the booth door shut. He reopened the door immediately. Why shouldn't everybody around the bar get the word to spread the word?

He yelled at a passing waiter, his smallest. "Get in there to Dan Tiamat's table and listen," he said. "Then get back here and fill me in." The small waiter nodded like a pigeon in a speeded-up movie and flew.

"Strictly speaking, Dan," the songwriter was squeaking, "I still don't see how are you gunna insure this type bet."

Dan told one of the waiters to bring him a phone. "What's your boss's number?" he asked Al pleasantly.

"My boss? What boss?"

"Come on."

There were now eighteen people standing around the table.

No one had taken the seat left vacant by the dress manufacturer because of the fear that the fat boniface might pour humiliation on them when he returned. Al looked up at the circle expressionlessly, then moved his eyes back to Dan's, chewing his lower lip with indecision. "I don't know the number," he said at last. "Very few people have that number to call this time of night." The waiter put a telephone instrument down in front of Dan. "What the hell, Dan," Al said, and there was the slightest suggestion of pleading in his voice. "Lou is a family man and he don't like it to try to do business at home."

"I know," Dan said. He dialed. It was a great effect and it paid off, distributing awe on the faces of his audience, who, in their own way, were very big themselves, some of them.

"Angelo?" Dan said into the phone. "This is Uncle Dan." His proud eyes swept the circle of faces. "Let me speak to your poppa." A North Carolinian literary agent watching Dan from across the table shivered at the thought of anybody, even his own kid, calling Big Lou Manganello poppa. A sports writer spoke out with the admiration and envy of all of them at that instant. "Oh, man!," he said, and Dan had the showmanship to wink at him while he waited with the phone at his ear. Al wiped his forehead with a purple and gold silk handkerchief that had his initials worked into it in red, from corner to corner, diagonally.

"Hello, Lou?" Dan said. "Dan Tiamat." A pause. "Oh, she's fine, Lou, thanks. How's Tessie?" A pause. "My little girl thanks you for her birthday card. Great. I'm glad." A pause. "Angelo sounds fine." A pause. "Is that so? Well, believe me, there seems to be a lot of those summer colds all over town." A pause. "Nothing urgent, Lou. I have a little contract, is all." He turned his hard eyes right on Al and smiled grimly. "Remember Al Parkay?" Al began to sweat in the middle of the best air conditioning money could buy. "Parkay. Yeah. That's the one. No, no, Lou! Nothing like that!" Al paled. "No beef, Lou, I can assure you." The literary agent stared agape at Dan Tiamat, trying to embalm forever this moment when he heard someone actually talking to the biggest hoodlum in the United States of America. His mind raced, wondering how he might later prove that he had been standing right there, one of the now thirty or so people who had been standing right there when all this had happened.

Finished telling Lou the details of the bet, Dan, simply, and with moving dignity, asked if Lou would personally okay Al's end of the transaction. Then he magnificently held the telephone up over the center of the table so that they all could say, for the rest of their lives, that they had actually heard Big Lou Manganello's voice. Every other table in the restaurant was stricken with silence. There was no chewing, gulping, or talking. Men and women at the bar, although they could see nothing but a knot of men, watched reverently, to be able to say they had been a part of it.

The voice was heard clearly by all. A loud, fantastically sincere falsetto, representing the great traditions of the Mafia in mid-practice of its public-relations policy, came out of the receiver as clearly as a macaw's. "Saytennly. I will gorrantee the bet one hunnert per cent. Please put Mr. Al Parkay onna wire, please."

Dan passed the telephone to Al, who covered the mouthpiece with his hand while he coughed delicately, as though he were about to run through one of Scarpia's arias from *Tosca,* then put the phone to his face.

"Uh—hello. Lou?" He swallowed. There was a long pause while he listened, his face getting redder, while Lou paid out his exact estimate of Parkay's judgment for allowing matters to reach such a point of embarrassment to The Organization. Al did not protest. When at last he spoke, he said, "Yes, Lou. Certainly, Lou. Of course. Listen, Dan is one thousand per cent with me, too." He looked across at the columnist as though he were trying to remember where he had put the poison. Thirty-six pairs of eyes, six pairs fitted with contact lenses, shone, and as many breaths were held. "Absolutely, Lou. Yes, sir. Certainly. Thank you very much, Lou." Al gently returned the telephone to its cradle. "Well, Dan, old pal," he said with a crumpled expression on his brutal face, "you better get some paper over to this here table and start writing out your previously mentioned letter to the newspapers."

The circle of faces broke outward like the edges of a design within a turning kaleidoscope, to be replaced by others. The rumor founders embarked upon their holy missions at bar, distant table, and telephone. The small waiter talked rapidly in a low voice into the poorly shaped ear of the cumbrous proprietor. Nodding steadily in the phone booth, the proprietor continued his conversation wth a number in Beverly Hills, California. "Frankie"—his voice seemed hidden deep within a spoiled cabbage—"this is the most fabulous bet ever made in my joint. I'm tellin' yuh. Life and death yet is the bet. Exile to outer space yet is the stakes. Big Lou Manganello gorrantees the pay-off. You following? Yeah. Sure. Certainly. I'll get a grand down for you on Dan."

At eleven-fifteen the same night Daniel Tiamat said hello to the cop on duty in front of the Governor's town house on Thirty-sixth Street. At eleven twenty-eight he found the Governor was relaxing with his model electric trains in the back basement, dictating memoranda to a male secretary while he switched and dispatched equipment over the vast system of tracks. The Governor had a Benedictine, Dan a rye and water. The Governor stared at Dan with raised white eyebrows.

"And what with the election only a year off," Dan continued agreeably, "I thought I'd stop by with this suggestion, as it were, no matter how late the hour." Dan could talk like a slob or a governess, as the occasion warranted. At the moment he was employing a construction known as open, or bluff, Irish charm.

"Very commendable, Dan," the Governor said.

"To get this grand plan to serve the voters moving forward, we'd need a commutation for a man named Moe Girdle."

The Governor sipped his Benedictine, looked at his secretary, and raised his eyebrows again.

"Morris Girdle has been sentenced to be executed tomorrow

night," the secretary said. He was a short man with thick ginger hair and high coloring. "You have turned down two routine requests for commutation from his wife."

"Who did he kill?"

"A bookie."

Dan cleared his throat. "He killed one of the leaders of organized crime in the State of New York," he said.

"Ah," the secretary replied, "he killed little Tommy Connery. We were in the Holy Name together. He was just another bookie."

"I was not speaking of a *pardon* here," Dan interjected carefully. "After all, I wouldn't ask the Governor to *pardon* a murder whose—uh—action was witnessed by over two hundred persons. I was suggesting a commutation—say to a prison for the criminally insane."

"Well, the man must have been nuts about something to blast Tommy in front of all those people," the secretary said equably.

"Exactly," Dan said briskly, "and as I see it, by commuting Moe Girdle, the Governor would be declaring war on organized crime."

"Would I now?" the Governor murmured.

"Suppose you signed a commutation to—say—three hundred years at Dannemora, or wherever. There couldn't be any grounds whatever for complaint—"

"Except from the prisoner himself, perhaps," the Governor replied with his famous grin. "But, go on, Dan."

"At the formal signing of the commutation you would issue a statement saying that if the Mafia has decided to exterminate itself, they will be punished for it, but not executed for it, while you remain Governor. The laborer is worthy of his hire, you say in effect. You then tell the people of New York City that if their authorities have become powerless to cope with organized crime, it becomes your duty to step in and stamp out this shocking condition."

"Hear! Hear!" the Governor murmured.

"Then you make news from coast to coast by giving Al Parkay, the leader of the U.S. Mafia exactly twenty-four hours to get out of the country."

"Who?"

The secretary shrugged. "A Syndicate gambler."

"Has he got a record?"

Dan nodded. "Four arrests for murder. No convictions. But he's no Mafia head, Governor. He's just a schlepper."

"The public doesn't know that," the Governor said.

"When my papers and my column and my network get through with him the public will know," Dan said earnestly, his alligator jaw jutting. "The whole thing will have national significance, if you know what I mean."

"But suppose he refuses to leave the country?" the Governor asked with polite interest.

"This is the perfect part of the whole suggestion," Dan said, extending open palms. "You have my personal guarantee that Parkay will go. And my column will back you all the way."

The Governor looked at his secretary and his eyebrows went up again. The secretary said, "It's not a bad figure, Governor. Parkay is nobody, so we can't offend anybody. As far as Girdle is concerned you would be sparing a human life, which is always good. You'll be striking a blow for public safety and good government by declaring war on organized crime, which could lead to an absolutely legitimate investigation on a national scale, and through all the action, of course, you'd be controlling a nice series of exciting, entertaining news stories that Dan can get the papers to carry forward for an indefinite period of time."

"Well, then," the Governor said, "let's do it."

"There is one thing, Governor," Dan said tentatively. "I mean my paper would appreciate it very much if you would—uh—consider doing something a little unusual. I mean, sign the commutation in our office."

The Governor looked across at the secretary, eyebrows up.

The secretary shrugged. "Why certainly, Dan," the Governor said. "After all, there has to be something in this for you."

"Consider sweet tales of hearts of gold. Ah, yes! How they warm a soul grown cold. A sweet waif, let's say, dear to behold—helped to better life by brigand bold.

"I have seen such, in this very bar, not long after the evening star had risen in the sky off there, afar. Twenty years ago—spectacular!

"A hoodlum yclept Young Salvatore came swaggering through that swinging door. Knocking codgers to the sawdust floor, he spat in the oyster stew and swore: 'Gimme a big, dirty glassa beer.' The barman, alas, just did not hear, so Young Sal slugged him forninst his ear, sending him flung on his union rear.

" 'So awright, arreddy! So work yer stick! So draw me a beer an' make it quick. You wanna get lumps? Yuh make me sick,' said suave Young Sal with his rhetoric. So the barman gallantly complied as a little girl, her blue eyes wide, came through the doors, very bona fide; shuffling on crutches, but dignified.

"She tugged demurely at Young Sal's sleeve. If eyes could grieve, her dear eyes did grieve. Her spell then must have started to weave for it caused Young Sal to try to leave. 'Oh, dear sir, it is my ambition to save heathen souls from perdition. Won't you give to establish a mission? Remember, I take no commission—directly.'

"He knocked her directly across the room, snapping a crutch, which costs, I presume. That lad could hit, and he lowered the boom, then he whacked her around with the joint's big boom. 'Listen, sister, leave me give advice.' Young Sal explained, words clipped and quite precise. 'Saloons ain't no place for liddul mice. Now get the hell out. It just ain't nice.'

"She what I mean? There are many gees, not alarmed by such delinquencies, who might have slipped her gratuities, but not Young Sal, and, thank God, not me.

"Youngsters today are a bit too bold. The delinquency problem is great, I'm told. But that lass was saved before sin could mold. Saved by a hoodlum with a heart of gold.' '

XI

The night Dan Tiamat visited the Governor and saved the life of a fellow human being, securing his place with his public and getting one hell of a story for the *Press,* was perhaps the peak moment of his life, hip-deep, as he was, in the affairs of men.

He let himself into his apartment shortly after midnight. Snapping on the light in the foyer, he yelled, "Where is everybody?" His dear wife's voice answered, from the study down the hall, which began its march through an arbor of framed photographs of Dan with the great, not the near-great. He strode merrily along the hall. The door to the living room was ajar.

Peggy was knitting something long and blue in the gray contour chair near the window. The glossy pink drapes behind her pale silver head and the blue-gray of her large eyes as they crinkled in her broad smile of greeting, set her in beauty and grace. "The king of the kids is home," he said. "Bigger, more potent, and more darlin' than ever." He squatted beside her and kissed her with the gusto of a big bite out of a shining red apple.

"And sober? I do declare, I think you're sober, Dan."

"You'd lose your bundle if you bet on it," he said, peeling off his jacket and pulling off his tie. "Ah, you should have seen their faces. You know what I did tonight? I ran Al Parkay out of town. Among other things, that is. In fact, I ran him out of the country."

"I thought he was a friend of yours." Peggy misinterpreted the expression on her husband's face. "He wasn't?"

"He's nothing." Dan walked across the long, high-ceilinged room to an elaborate bar, almost as elaborate as the one his father had lived in. "Drink, honey?"

"I do not drink honey. I'll take a gin and water."

"You do not drink honey. I'll remember that, honey."

"Thanks, honey."

Dan made two large drinks. "How's Carrie?" he asked as he worked.

"Much better."

"What did the doctor say about that rash?"

"Be gone tomorrow."

"Did you tell that goddam teacher to stop criticizing the child's politics?"

"We are handling it."

"But did you tell her?"

"Not yet. We need a little more evidence, then we'll bushwhack her."

"You know what I did tonight?" Dan handed Peggy her jar of gin, then kissed her again. He sat down on the cushioned window seat beside her. He held his drink in one hand and the gray telephone in the other and looked down at the zoo in Central Park, almost directly below him.

"Only partly."

"Listen to this. And you can bet that while I'm telling it to you people all over Vegas and L.A. and this town are doing exactly the same thing—talking about what I did. It's the most tremendous thing that's happened in ten years."

"Doesn't anybody like Al Parkay?"

"Parkay is only a tiny part of it!" He told her the complete story of the evening, not loading it too much because throughout the thing he looked pretty good anyway. "Hah?" he concluded. "How about that? Did you ever hear anything like that in your life?"

"It's sure a remarkable way to make a living," Peggy said. She grinned at him.

"Peg, you should have seen those *faces!*"

"I stopped going on those rounds with you because of those faces."

"Can you imagine what it'll mean for the paper—the Governor signing the goddam commutation right in the goddam City Room?"

Her face turned grave. "Yes. It will be very good for the paper."

"I gotta call Joe." He dialed rapidly, woke Joe Downey to instant alertness out of a sound sleep, and told him the whole story, sipping his big whisky between sentences, taking time to report exactly. He listened for a while, then he said good night and disconnected.

"Wasn't Papa asleep?"

"Not any more he isn't. I'll bet he has Benn Reyes on the phone right now. He'll have us on the street real early tomorrow and that hasn't happened for a long time." Dan hurried to the bar and made himself another drink, this time not bothering with water or ice.

"You're manic tonight."

"What? Oh, yeah. This thing has me all hopped up. Honey, you shoulda seen their faces when I dialed Big Lou Manganello."

"Well, after all, he is an American hero."

"Another drink?"

"No. I've hardly started this one."

Dan belted his drink down and poured another. He went back to the window seat. "This story is gonna sell a lotta papers, hon."

"Did you write your own piece yet?"

"The column?"

She didn't answer.

"Not yet."

"Did Papa remember to remind you to do it? I mean, for this early edition he wants?"

"Yeah. He mentioned it. I'll have it."

"So do it now."

The phone rang. He snatched it up. "Hi, Benn." He cupped his hand over the mouthpiece. To see Dan Tiamat talk on the phone made some people think of a kidnaper making his first ransom contact. Reyes, the *Press's* city editor, was dressing and telephoning at the same time from an air-conditioned bedroom in Brooklyn while his wife clattered up some coffee in the kitchen. "Not yet, but I will," Dan told him. "All right! Don't bug me on it." He looked over at Peggy and rolled his eyes to the ceiling. He listened to Reyes. He snarled into the phone. "All right, you jerk! Whatta you think? I'm new in this business or something? I'll write it when I'm good an' ready to write it." He slammed the instrument into its cradle.

"Oh, brother!" He slugged the whisky and went to the bar and poured another.

"The column, Pops."

He poured a short one.

"Benn Reyes is a good man," Peggy said matter-of-factly.

"He has a very funny attitude lately. I mean, actually, Peg—"

"That might be because you called him a jerk. He's a good man. That could rile him."

"I don't mean just tonight. I mean lately he has a very funny note in his voice. I can't explain it." Dan sat at the long ironing-board desk that came out at right angles from the windows. Facing Peggy, he pulled the electric Olivetti to himself on its wheeled table. He slid a carbon set into the machine and began to type steadily, with dead-pan sureness. He worked for nearly an hour. Peggy sat quietly, putting her knitting aside to make a fresh start on the Sunday crossword puzzle. The phone rang again.

"I'll get it," Peggy said automatically, reaching for the gray instrument on the window seat.

"I'm not here."

"I know." She pulled the phone toward her. "Hello?" She listened, then she spoke to Dan with her hand over the mouth-piece. "It's Beverly Hills and Bungalows."

He looked up blankly. Then it registered. "See? It's all over the country. I'm not here." He looked back at his work.

"Mr. Tiamat is not here, operator," Peggy said effortlessly. "No, I don't. Yes, I will." She looked serenely out the window at the Fifty-ninth Street skyline. "Operator Fifty-three. I have it. Who? *Who?* All right, operator. I'll tell him." She hung up.

Dan pulled the last page of copy out of the machine just as the door bell rang. It was an elderly Puerto Rican messenger from the *Press*. Dan gave him the copy in a flapped-under envelope and told him to ask his secretary for some passes to the Brooklyn Paramount. "Not me, mister," the old man said. "When I'm off I stick in bed."

When Dan returned to the living room he said, "Reyes sent a pickup anyway. How do you like a guy like that?"

Peggy shrugged. "Benn knows his business."

"Who called before?"

"Beverly Hills and Bungalows." The designation was a family joke that had originated from the legend on the note paper issued by the Beverly Hills Hotel.

"And who's there?"

"Steady now. Janice Rivers Pitt."

"What the hell could she want?"

"Darling, you know it would have been *lèse-majesté* for me to ask such a question."

"She must be back on the sauce." Dan walked to the sauce counter and built himself another large drink. His voice was thickening.

"Drink, honey? Oh, I know you don' drink, honey, but you wanna nother belt?"

"Don't tell me there's still some merchandise there."

"Cernlee. You wanna steinful?"

"Cernlee."

He made her a fat gin and water and brought it to her. He leaned over her unsteadily for his kiss. He walked to the window seat and fell on it upon his broad bottom just as the blue telephone rang. "I got it," he said, struggling up to his desk. "Hello? Oh, hello, Joc. Yeah. About five minutes ago. What? Am I sober? Whatta you mean, am I sober course I'm sober read the piece you don't think so. What? Yeah, I called him a jerk. What? Because he don't know what the hell he's doin' thaz why I callem a jerk. Whattur you, his father? What? Don' talk tummy like that, Joe. I'm not wunna ya workin' stiffs, I'm synnicate." He hung up and looked over at Peggy owlishly. "I swearta God they're all crazy tonight. I certainly pulled your poppa outta the wrong side a bed."

Peggy said evenly, "He probably thought you knew that people don't yell at hard-working newspapermen and call them jerks. As a matter of fact, I thought you knew, myself."

"I'm not people," he said. "I'm Dan Tiamat an' I goddam near pay all their salaries on that paper." He picked up the gray phone and dialed Long Distance. "Gotta fine out what Janice Pitt wants." He told the mouthpiece to get him Beverly Hills Operator Fifty-three. While he waited he looked down at the zoo lights.

Janice Rivers Pitt was a blood-royal movie queen in the second quarter-century of her reign. She was the widow of the late, great David Pitt, who may have been one of the greatest actors on the English-speaking stage and who had easily been the greatest drunk in any language.

"Dan! How the hell are you!"

"Janice! Baby!"

"Howza family?"

"Sensational. You back on the sauce?"

"In the way, yes. But not really. We were sitting around the new house having a little plain ether." Dan shuddered. "Dan, darling, I called to ask if you might know of someone going to London in the next few days."

"Not off hand, baby, but I could check around. Why?"

"Well, you see, darling, it's all rather embarrassing, but I'm moving from Bel Air to Brentwood and while the moving people were in packing things— You know how it's done, don't you, darling?"

"I'm fairly clear on it. Yes."

"Well, darling, if you don't think it's a small world— Please don't be stern with me about this, darling. You see we found this large jar in the back of one of the upstairs closets."

"Oh?" Dan shook his head violently.

"You can imagine my surprise, darling, but it was Davy. I mean Davy's ashes. I had goofed."

"But Davy's been dead for over—" Dan couldn't catch up with her.

"Fourteen months, darling." Janice Rivers Pitt tried to stifle a prodigiously sticky, ether-induced yawn.

"Davy's ashes?" He wheeled and stared at Peggy, not explaining a thing but his shocked incredulity.

"I tell you, Dan, I've been so embarrassed about this thing that I've turned an absolute plaid since the instant I realized what had happened. I mean, Davy's will was absolutely stern about insisting that he be buried in his family's plot in England. I mean, with his entire, populous family in Devon. I feel like an absolute ass, darling."

"This shakes me up," Dan said, and he looked shaken. Why did this woman have to inject doubt into the peace her souse of a husband had been promised after life? For years David Pitt had talked about very little else but how he would be going home to be buried. Somehow Dan felt that his own future had been threatened by this woman's shocking and callous indifference.

"It shakes *you* up?" Janice was booming, "What do you think it does to me."

"I thought a helluva lot of Davy, Janice. One helluva lot."

"And Davy loved you, too, darling. Do you think you could find me someone to carry his ashes to their final rest?"

"Find someone to—?"

"Yes, darling."

"Jan, hon, Jan, I'd hate myself if I let anybody else do that last duty for Davy." Dan was staring right into Peggy's eyes but he didn't seem to be seeing her. He was looking far past her, extremely upset at being told that there could be disappointment and struggle and emptiness in death. "I hope you'll understand, Janice, but I'll have to take those—that urn, I mean —take it to London myself." His eyes had gotten misty. Peggy

stood up suddenly. His eyes remained on the same level they
had held when she was seated.

"Understand? Dan, I have always said you were all heart,
but how can you? You are just about the busiest man in the
United States."

"It's the least I can do, Janice," he said dully, feeling despair
upon him like a too tight overcoat.

"You darling, wonderful man. Oh, Dan, you are a living
legend." He shivered. "You shall have this urn in your hands
by tomorrow night. Al Fisher, the publicity person who handles
me for Farber, that schtunk, and who is an utterly nice
and extremely sincere person, will be happy, I am sure, to fly
Davy to New York personally inasmuch as he has to be there
for—"

"No press agents," Dan said sharply. "Don't go turning a
thing like this into a circus stunt!"

"Fear nothing, darling. Al is the man that schtunk Farber
uses to keep things *out* of the paper. Oh, Dan, how happy you
have made Janice Rivers Pitt tonight and how truly have you
earned this story as your own exclusive."

He started to protest but she seemed to have hung up. Dan
replaced the phone slowly, then turned to stare across the park
toward California.

"That was Janice Pitt," he said.

"And did that sweet, sweet girl-child just call up for a chat
about her dead old Davy?" Peggy asked.

"Yeah," he answered absent-mindedly. "What a touching
thing. Christ, it tears me apart. We're going to London tomorrow night after the stunt with the Governor is over."

"You and Janice?"

"Janice? No. You and me?"

"But I can't go to London, Dan!"

"Honey! I pledged this! It is the final duty of my friendship
to the memory of David Pitt!"

"*What?*"

"While I was on that phone I suddenly saw Jan's gallantry. I suddenly saw what a tragic emptiness Davy's death must have meant to her."

"Oh, Dan. Come off it."

"Whatta you mean? He's been dead for fourteen goddam months and she hasn't been able to bring herself to let him go. Jesus, what an angle. It's like—like that Benét story, you know? That one where the old Southern broad keeps her husband's dead body in the bed beside her for years and years? Only this time it didn't come off the top of some writer's head. This time it happened to one of the biggest stars in the industry. What courage it must have taken!" Dan seemed to be talking himself sober. "She's been clinging to those ashes, then suddenly, out of nowhere, like that"—he hiccupped—"she must have decided that if she did it suddenly, quick, that she could make herself let him go. What a pang."

"Or ping, perhaps," Peggy said helpfully.

"It was Davy's dying wish that he go home to green Devon —to sleep forever in that mist, he said."

"Would you like me to play something solemn on the piano?"

"Anyway, we can stop by Dublin on the way back and you can pick up a couple of those tweed suits. Like in *Vogue*. You know?"

"Dearest Dan," Peggy said patiently, "I cannot go to London with you. For one thing, it's Carrie's tenth birthday two days from now, and we're all set for a carriage ride around the park, then into the Plaza for a lemonade."

"Honey, I'll get three great columns out of this!"

"I doubt it, love."

"You doubt it?"

"Davy Pitt, even when he was what you called alive fourteen months ago, hadn't been erect enough to work for eight years. You might as well try to get three news features out of Edwin Booth."

"They'll never forget Davy Pitt, hon."

"Well, you'd better not talk it over with Papa first. He'll think you're out of your mind for sure."

"Out of my mind?"

"Dan, come here." He approached her stiffly. "Hold me," she said. He grabbed her and pulled her to him, pressing her desperately close with one arm, running his other hand through her hair. "Ah, Peggy," was all he said then. The side of her head rested on his chest.

"Are you frightened of something, Dan," she asked.

He drew back an inch. "Me? Ho, ho!"

They stood closer together, not speaking until he said, "Why?"

"Only that you used the word *duty*, which is a word we all use when we make ourselves do something because we are afraid of what will happen if we don't do it."

"It's—it's because Davy told *everyone* that when he was dead he would be sent straight home to Devon, but all this time he's been in the closet of that Bel Air house with the flying bridge over the barbecue machines. He's been away from everyone, out of everybody's thoughts, because if there are those of us who did think of him after he was dead, we thought of him *that* way"—he gestured with a jerk of his head—"over in England. So the thoughts missed him and did him no good, and that's like standing straight up in worse than hell, to be all alone even after you're dead."

"Well, Dan, have it your way," Peggy said.

Al Fisher delivered Davy Pitt's ashes in an urn that was wrapped in white satin. With it came a letter instructing Dan to deliver the urn to Davy's sister in London. The sister was married to a member of Parliament, the letter explained, and she was terribly legitimate.

When the plane left New York for London, Dan had Davy packed into an old, battered doctor's satchel that he had bought in a pawnshop on Eighth Avenue. It was tucked snugly under his seat. He drank as the plane flew but he never lost consciousness of the great spirit within the ashes contained in the gift-wrapped urn in the doctor's bag. As the hours went along and the whisky was absorbed, Dan may have had the conviction that he was astride his own ashes, their guardian. If this was the case, Dan Tiamat protected his own ashes with more love and care and hope than he had ever demonstrated for his living flesh. He was drunk. He was drunk and ensnarled in the illusion that he was transporting his own ashes to some place where it would be clean and green in endless quiet with little white signs planted a hundred feet apart all over the perfect, rolled sod on which a neatly lettered sign would say NO SOUTENAGE. He lay back with his eyes closed and it came to him that he was about to be put to deep, deep rest to be reborn again in peace where he and Peggy and Carrie would be safe forever from fraud (self-fraud), cant (auto-cant), and sham (upon himself), away from the noise, far away from the noise of the racing men and women who careered through the streets of his mind, shrieking to gain a lead, then to try and hold it.

A passing stewardess, looking down at Dan's reposing face, thought for an instant his was a head which should have been printed on Irish money. Bone for bone, flesh for flesh, that was true. No leader of that starchy country throughout its history, excepting for a few invading Danes, French, and Spaniards had looked more Irish than Dan Tiamat. He had not the long-boned, horsy, aristocratic Irish look, but the vaudeville Irish look; the publican's kind, the ward politician's; the kind the fey and fevered attribute to the leprechaun. Dan looked nothing at all as Davy Pitt had looked.

David Pitt's presence had suggested the race memory of Richard III, yet now Dan's and Davy's marrow and their faces to God were indescribably intermingled within that urn as that urn existed within Dan's mind.

When a nation has produced the extraordinary quality of playwrights that England has produced over the centuries it finds itself demanding, through the eugenics of art and patriotism, that every thousandth woman do her duty and produce actors almost as prodigious. Taking into account the full span of British theatrical history, Davy Pitt had been one of the three greatest actors Britain had ever produced.

Other actors who had been more attentive to personal causes

than Davy had been to his, and many of them had been knighted for having displayed a fraction of his talent. Davy could not have been knighted ever, of course. He had been such a horrendous, crapulous, pot-paralyzed, vine-simple, gin-weary, brandy-popped, whisky-pooped, shirt-stained drunkard that the monarchs and first ministers who had gazed at Honors Lists across twenty-seven years of his art had allowed themselves to be dissuaded reluctantly. It undoubtedly had saddened them, for Davy had been a great, great Englishman; a great and valiant artist, gentleman, and friend.

At the London airport, a series of sheds accommodating the four winds, the polite customs officer read the death certificate and the burial consignment papers, slowly and carefully. Extrasensory perception reminded all travelers into this country that when English customs officers became extremely polite, instead of merely chillingly polite, they were approaching their most deadly effectiveness.

"Mr. Tiamat, how may we be sure, sir, that what is in that urn are the ashes of David Pitt?"

Dan shrugged, the inside of his head like a hive of quarreling pterodactyls, not knowing where to begin to answer such a question.

"Do you know for certain, sir, that this urn contains the ashes of the late David Pitt?" The customs man was wearing the relentless eyes that are issued by every nation's excise service except France's, and he had long amber teeth, like a comb.

"I didn't watch them cremate Mr. Pitt," Dan said slowly. "If that's what you mean."

"Um."

"I didn't see them sweep him up and funnel him into that jar and seal it, but those papers certainly look very official to me."

"Um."

"Why should anyone want to fool around with anything as silent as my ashes?" The officer's eyebrows went up. "I mean

Davy's ashes," Dan put in hurriedly, his bloodshot eyes beam-
ing resentment at the agent. "But I know Mr. Pitt is dead because I haven't seen him around the saloons since the time his
wife claims he died."

"The urn could also contain contraband, sir. Such as narcotics, jewelry, currency, et cetera. Our concern."

"It's a fine goddam thing when a great actor like Davy Pitt
has to come home for the last time in a melodrama," Dan said,
swaying, pushed by tenebrous melancholy. "Well, do what you
have to do. Go ahead. Take it into some back room and open
it." Then he cried out in an anguish of indignation, "But don't
you spill any of him on the floor of this shed!"

The customs officer leaned over and peered at the papers
more closely. "Excuse me, sir," he said with what sounded like
an entirely different voice, "but are you the Daniel Tiamat." He
seemed to peer more closely. "But of course you are, sir."

Dan nodded distantly, sobered as though from a sudden
flight to the misty, distant past. "That's me," he said.

"May I shake your hand, sir?" the officer reached over, took
Dan's limp hand as it hung by his side, and shook it vigorously. "It *is* good to face you like this, sir. You *cannot* know
how much your courage meant to me and my family. I *am* sorry
you were delayed by this business, sir. God bless you, sir."

The officer drew brachygraphic symbols rapidly upon the
urn with blue chalk. Then, with a reverential smile and the sort
of salute that ever will be reserved for the most gallant, he
pointed out how Dan was to leave the shed.

The London bureau chief for the *Press* was waiting. His
hearty greeting broke off Dan's interior linkage with the gone
days of the war. They drove into London and to the Savoy in
a robin's-egg-blue Rolls.

Davy's sister's married name was Mrs. Mori Krushen. Dan
telephoned her every morning at eleven o'clock for three consecutive mornings, and every afternoon at five. If he had been
sober he might have sent the urn to her by messenger and returned to New York, but he was obsessed with the personal

meaning of the need to hand it directly to Mrs. Krushen, to be assured of passport to his own eternal green peace. Besides, he loved London. It had been a great part of his life. He went forth to discover it again.

Someone has said that London is a grand city for walking. It is also a grand city for staggering, in that, under a rigid system of opening and closing the public houses throughout the day, all drinkers seem to fling their drinks back desperately, lest time be called before they can do away with six or so, and the supply is cut off. If Dan had not intended to drink in London, which most certainly was not the case, his intention would have been swept away by the joy of recognition on the faces of people at very nearly every turning; some at the sight of his face, others when they heard, or overheard, his name spoken. His hulking, great figure had not changed. He still seemed to be two and a half weeks late for an appointment at the barber's. His massive head, encompassing that lined and lumpy face, was like an old trade mark, instantly recognizable.

The fact was that Daniel Tiamat, as a war correspondent, had been one of the great heroes to the British people during the Battle of Britain. For what he had done beyond the call of duty, the British people had paid him their most extravagant tribute: eternal affection.

He was at first not entirely aware of the extent of this regard as he was stopped in pubs, on busses, at traffic crossings on this, his first return to London since the war. He had been so frightened all during those grim nights of bombing that he had been drunk one hundred per cent of the time and, more or less blacked out in the blackout, he had remembered little or nothing of what had happened to him. For this reason, seven years later he was continually surprised that people not only seemed to know him but that, occasionally, great tears appeared in their eyes as they shook his hand.

During the war Dan Tiamat had lived in a large two-room suite at the Savoy Hotel (then and later the best hotel in the world), and had been a famous figure in its bars and elevators with his webbed issue belt tight about his girth, holding a canteen filled with gin on one hip and a canteen filled with vermouth on the other. But he could not bear to stay in the place at night, once an air raid had started. He felt pinned by a vision of a huge bomb, always having a sharp point, falling laterally from the sky, entering his bedroom window, then landing to explode upon his person. Since bed was clearly not the safest place, all through raid nights Dan roamed the city, on foot or in the Studebaker lent him by an English friend, under a helmet and inside a two-hundred-and-thirty-dollar uniform, carrying a recording machine and interviewing the "little" people as though London were at the center of a widespread elves' convention.

It is possible that Dan may have been responsible for the widest popular use of that infuriating adjective "little," since he applied it to his audience and his interviewed subjects alike. "Little" described everyone within his sight as he broadcast night after night from roof tops, tube stations, bomb craters, hospitals, barracks, flying fields, and pubs—particularly the pubs, where the little man seemed to get littler and littler. After a time, a faithful listener could have gotten the impression that Tiamat had not seen a single Britisher who stood over two feet nine inches. No one who lived through the Battle of Britain would ever forget his resounding, fruity, throbbing, echoing, phony bass voice as it lurched out of wireless sets or off the sound tracks of reverent propaganda films. Dan Tiamat narrated three of the most popular films shown anywhere during World War II: *I Stood with Britain's Little Man, Little Men, Big Hearts,* and *Tiamat in Britain.*

"*I speak to you little men and women of Britain and to no one else upon this torn and suffering planet. I speak to you, my comrades, who are my pride of all the little men upon this planet. I speak to you, little people of England, Scotland, and Wales*" (it was the strangest thing the way nobody seemed to mind that adjective), "*about your golden courage and your triumph over the most infamous assault ever hammered home upon the dignity of all little men everywhere.*" It was the considered opinion of the O.W.I., the War Office, and the Association of American Correspondents in London that Dan Tiamat could not possibly have written this effective material; it was known that he was always too drunk to see his typewriter. They blamed an Australian nurse who had gone a bit crackers during one raid or another. She continually urged Dan to run for Prime Minister because he had such a wonderful voice. She had come to England before the war to study phonetics and speech. The trauma seemed to have been locked in on a night when she had been studying the sonorities, as treated in chapter four of Ridgeway's *Gutterals and Elidings*. The allegation about Dan's writing could have been true, but probably was not, inasmuch as he wrote his patriotic themes exactly the same way before and after the war. He had been writing that way long before he had shacked up with the girl. It is much more likely that she had plunged into her study of the sonorities after her exposure to Dan, rather than the other way round.

Only Dan Tiamat could have savored that adjective "little" the way he did. Early in life he had received the conviction that there were only three kinds of people: little people, big people, and very big people. A New York bookmaker who listened to one of Dan's wartime broadcasts from London asked Joe Downey why Dan kept describing everyone in the British Isles as little people. Downey may have provided another part of the reason, considering the hallucinations that must have accompanied much of his employee's constant drunkenness: "He's six feet four inches tall and he's working blind all the time over there. I expect that's how they strike him."

When a night raid on London began Tiamat would flee from the Savoy, across the courtyard and headlong upon the Strand, and keep running until forced to shelter or stopped by his own power by the first working party he came upon. He interviewed the same bomb-demolition crew three times in this way, without recognition at any time. Once in a shelter, he would assemble his portable equipment with gin-stiffened fingers, then tug at the sleeve of the person nearest him. "I am Daniel Tiamat of *The Daily Press*," he would rumble. "May I offer you a gin or a bit of vermouth?" Instantly one of his famous interviews would begin. They sounded enormously emotional mostly because the listener provided all that.

Dan's little people would be matter-of-fact, direct, and courteous. He would erupt with bass profundity and grunt a good deal, and these sounds would seem like just the sounds that should be made by a warrior for the truth who would pursue that truth even if he must die for freedom in that alien land. Had he made the identical broadcasts during peacetime all his listeners would have cried out, "Why, that bum is drunk!," but the fuzz around his voice, his stumblings and thicknesses, were beautifully at home in the sounds of explosions, the noises of bells and sirens, and various distant shouts and commands. The British people swore by him. He was a phenomenon of effective psychological transference. He was a walking materialization of gallantry for a people that took such a virtue for granted among themselves but, in Dan Tiamat, were able to project it and admire it in the theatrical courtliness of that great bear of a drunk who seemed to walk among them not seeing danger.

Dan told Peggy after the war that he would have lost his mind, had he had to be alone during one night raid. He said he had to run out where there were people ignoring the possibilities of their own deaths. He had to keep talking to people, he said, to be assured that he was still alive.

He was drunk for seventeen months. He was too drunk to remember to ask Downey to summon him home, and Downey wasn't doing him any favors.

Dan's finest hour in Britain was his coverage of the Merseult raid, in which five thousand Australians, two thousand Canadians, and one thousand Americans made one of the first two combined operations strikes of the war upon the French coast. Three thousand and twenty-four men were killed, wounded, or captured; most of them slaughtered in the frontal attack on the beach. The thirty-two tanks that were successfully landed were each hit and stranded. Every house along the innocent-seeming beach promenade had been heavily fortified. Enfilading fire from caves in the cliffs at either end of the long beach decimated the attacking force; even officers on the operations staff were casualties.

Daniel Tiamat was with them, the only correspondent to survive the action, therefore the first newspaperman to file an eye-witness account of a concerted assault upon Fortress Europa in World War II. He got a memorable book out of it, *Assault on Merseult,* which was the selection of a major book club, appeared serially in a leading weekly magazine, was immediately reprinted for the Armed Forces, and was translated into fourteen foreign languages. The film rights brought Dan eighty-five thousand dollars.

Dan had not known ahead that he would draw the Merseult assignment. Because it was to be an Australian and Canadian show, their press had been given the few news billets available. He had not, of course, had any inkling that the assault was ready to be launched. There had been the usual talk that it would have to happen one of these days, but until the assault was an accomplished fact, as Dan wrote later in his column, it was one of the best-guarded secrets of the war.

The day before had been a brutal one for Dan. For part of it he had been entertaining two Hollywood producers who were in London as O.W.I. consultants. His resistance was relatively low, in the manner of a water buffalo with chronic cataarh, and he had been fairly exhausted on leaving the film men. He had spent the rest of the afternoon knocking back a few gins with some Australian chums in their mess, some forty-five miles southeast of London, cheering the boys with some stirringly lascivious lies about movie stars he had known. Before Dan left, the Aussies filled his canteens with fresh gin. Being so far from London, Dan was wearing four.

He lost his balance while walking down a ramp on the way

to his jeep. No one saw him topple into a Services of Supply lorry that the loading chaps had been filling with army issue blankets. They had stopped the labor for a bit to have a smoke on the lorry's off side. Two of Dan's Australian chums, talking heatedly about various legends concerning the durability of Nellie Melba, had been a few lengths ahead of Dan before he had vanished. When they turned to speak to him as they reached his jeep, they were entirely puzzled. They peered about here and there through the gloaming, then decided that he had returned to the mess for just one more and carried on warm with their argument.

When Dan presently awoke, unharmed in his bed of blankets, he found he had a horrible, horrible head which was being made worse by the sounds of heavy boots moving on the stones all around him. It was more than he could bear. Blindly, he eased his body and head out of the lorry and tottered through the night into what seemed to be a tank garage. He could dimly make out the shapes of four huge tanks. He minced forward, whimpering softly, and bedded down slowly in the furthest corner of the garage. With stolid patience he drank off one of the replenished canteens and again fell asleep.

Thirty minutes later the tank carrier was towed out of the ways of the Portsmouth Navy Yard into the Channel, there to join the joint operations convoy headed for Merseult on a dead calm sea, under the cover of night. The force made its rendezvous two miles off the French coast, in total darkness, under radio silence. Transports, torpedo boats, supply ships, destroyers, invasion barges, long tank-landing craft, and two submarines made up the greatest invasion force of its kind ever assembled until that morning. An umbrella of three hundred fighter air craft would be engaged before the assault began, and two squadrons of Flying Fortresses, escorted by two hundred and fifty Spitfires, would plaster the enemy air installations at Abbéville.

At 5:12 A.M., the eleven destroyers began to shell the beaches. Two thousand shells were fired in ten minutes, each shell sent into each yard of the two thousand yards of facing beach.

The noise of the firing was horrendous, but it was as a mother's whisper to her sleeping child when compared, close up as Dan Tiamat was, to the racket made by the four great tanks as they made ready to move. Engines firing, smoke and fumes belching out everywhere around them, yet still confined within the closeness of the craft, the four tanks made concentrated noise so explosive, so inhumane in its ripping attrition, so horribly orchestrated into a roaring, pounding force of violence, that three of the craft's crew leaned overside and vomited. This action may not have been the result of the tearing noise alone, for the billows of thick, oily smoke was noxious. And yet to the soundly asleep correspondent, the smoke was a blanket, the uproar a lullaby.

A force of the Adelaide Light Infantry made ready to land, to be followed by the Calgary sappers. Then Dan's tank force would go in.

Shells from Caumartin began to bracket the tank barge that was Dan's cradle. Fighter aircraft appeared everywhere overhead. Some began their work of strafing gun emplacements on the beach and supply depots behind. The majority remained at levels of from three thousand to seven thousand feet to protect the invasion force from the enemy bombers that had appeared as if on rehearsed cue. The noise from the skies was added to the noise from the shore. Dan Tiamat muttered and turned his face to the bulkhead, for some reason disturbed in his sleep.

At 5:22 A.M. the operation began. The tank barge touched down. Slowly, cumbrously, as though aching to accumulate power, the four tanks rolled out. Two were immediately hit and stopped by mortars. The third ground on a ways and then swerved daintily, even politely, before it exploded. The fourth lumbered across the beach toward the promenade. It won fifteen yards before it was split open by a heavy shell. Machine-gun fire poured on the beach from both sides. Bodies lay motionless everywhere. Every crewman on the tank barge had been cut in half by the fire. Dan, at last awake, was alone.

He lay on the deck on his stomach, flush with the carnage of the beach, ears open to the screams of the dying and the expanding roar of the machine-gun fire. He studied the spectacle with the detachment of a man who has had many such bad dreams and has schooled himself to realize that dreams cannot hurt him. Closing his eyes, he willed the vision to pass away. It was the most realistic dream he had ever experienced. The sounds were vivid, the colors brilliant. Still concentrating to make the nightmare dissolve, he dropped again into a dreamless sleep.

The barge drifted away from the beach and was carried aimlessly out into the Channel. When a rescue party put its irons aboard, Dan was discovered alive, the only survivor. They handled him carefully, sure he had internal injuries, and put him aboard the headquarters ship, the British destroyer *Menlo*. Men took off their caps reverently as his cortege passed with solemn majesty to the improvised examination table in the wardroom.

"Will he be all right, sir?" one of the men pleaded softly with the surgeon.

"He will pull through, I am certain," the doctor answered. "Absolutely strawdinary!"

"No one like him, sir," the rating said. "I don't suppose we'll know men like 'im agyne."

"Amen," the surgeon muttered.

Dan returned to consciousness aboard the *Menlo* late that afternoon. He was too professional to be astonished to find himself at sea. With borrowed equipment and his three untouched canteens of gin he recorded thirty-six radio interviews with every type of survivor at the Portsmouth Naval Base that night, then went on the air "live" at 4 A.M., sounding as though he had gone through the very worst of it, to give his exclusive report to the great people of the United States, to be rebroadcast to all the world. His words, in the voice of a hero who had stared death down that men might be free, left that world inspired and shaken. It began, his quiet talk on that immortal broadcast, "The little man of the great and mighty British Commonwealth had his first chance at bat today. The monster that is Adolf Hitler cringes, trembling in his lair."

Now, seven years after his rendezvous with history, Daniel Tiamat was back in his beloved London.

Mrs. Krushen returned his calls on the morning of the fourth day. He had a cruel hang-over, and as she spoke he felt nailed through the head to the telephone, for her voice was as unexpectedly ugly as a woman's voice could be. Its pitch ranged from the hawking of a doomed mica miner who had smoked three packages of French cigarettes a day since childhood, to the peak appeal of a steam-blown lunch whistle. Her cadences struck as relentlessly as Cossack hooves on the fallen foreheads of beleagured Poles. In Dan's wracked state the sounds she made had him believing that a parrot trained by the English Speaking Union had answered the telephone. At first, he could not make any sense out of the words, so shocking were the sounds in which she dressed them.

"Mr. Tiamat? Mrs. Krushen here."

"Aaaaah!"

"I find myself scanning a sheaf of confusing messages which seem to treat with my late brother."

"Aaaaaah!"

"What was that? This *is* Mr. Tiamat?"

"Ugh, Yes." Her words were beginning to be separated from the noise they made.

"Did you leave these messages, Mr. Tiamat?"

He wanted to hang up and stretch out on the carpet. He stared blankly out of the eighth-floor window at the far bank of the Thames and Waterloo Bridge.

"Yes."

"Please explain. Mr. Tiamat." She took a deep breath as though to control herself. "You know Tiamat is a most extraordinary name."

"It is? It's just an Irish name. We come from Kilflyn, in the west."

"Not quite. Tiamat was the Mesopotamian mother of the gods who was destroyed by the king of the gods, and from whose body the heavens and the earth were created. Tiamat is the personification of chaos. But, no matter. We must not digress like this. Why do you keep ringing me?" Her voice shook through the last sentence.

"I've brought Davy home, Mrs. Krushen."

"I don't understand."

"You *are* the little sister of the late David Pitt, the very dead English actor?"

"I am." Her answer was below the level of a whisper.

"Well, I've brought Davy's ashes home to rest as he has always wished it to be."

"But, why? Why?" Her voice broke.

"Why?"

"You had no right to do that, Mr. Tiamat!" She began to weep harshly. "No right. No right at all."

He was dismayed. "No right? It was the one request in his will. Janice begged me to bring him here. I thought she had written to you about all this."

"Janice?"

"Davy's widow."

"Oh, Mr. Tiamat!" Mrs. Krushen sobbed. "I find I cannot talk any longer. You must forgive me. I simply cannot." The connection was suddenly broken. The silence took on velvet edges. Dan fell vertically into a chair, like a comedy ingénue, then forward on his knees to stretch out upon the mauve carpet like a tragic one.

Mrs. Krushen telephoned coolly the following day while Dan was trying to play the typewriter, attempting to do a piece on an unexpected delicatessen he had found the night before in Soho, and sipping whisky. She asked him straight out when they could meet and it was fixed for five o'clock that afternoon in the hall of the hotel.

When Mrs. Krushen arrived, she was thirty minutes late.
From a distance, Dan was able to recognize her instantly. Her
brother had had dank black hair that had fallen straight downward through the firewater fumes like a Piute Indian's, and it
had known the barber's shears as seldom as a Shakespearean
actor's should. Davy had had a nose like a cucumber, not as to
color, for its color had tended to be that of a squash, but as to
size and numbers of bumps. Davy had had enormous presence,
on stage and off, the carriage of Wellington, and the shoulders
of a Liverpool coal passer. Mrs. Krushen possessed these qual-
ities identically, including Davy's tendency toward port-wine
eyeballs and clothing that might have been passed on directly
from the off-duty wardrobe of Florence Nightingale during the
Crimean incident.

Dan, who was more than slightly drunk, had the fugitive
impression that this was the dead Davy walking toward him,
under one of the late Queen Mary's less chic hats. He stepped
forward reflectively, his right hand outstretched in greeting.
He was stopped in his tracks by her glare. "I *beg* your pardon,"
she said, as though he were a Panama City flesh booker making
his first move. As she spoke he became convinced again that she
was the right woman because her voice tones ranged from the
treble of a bosun's pipe to the boom of a sunset gun, and if her
breath could have been wrung out it would have spattered him
with gin.

"But—I'm Dan Tiamat!" he protested.

"Oh, Mr. Tiamat, what a terrible, terrible day!" she said,
reaching for his fallen hand and grasping it wholly. Vaguely,
he felt she was referring to the weather, but as she continued
to shake his hand like an aberrant lodge brother, he saw that
she was deeply moved.

"Shall we go into the bar?" he suggested tentatively.

"Do you have—that is, have you brought Davy with you?"
she asked.

"Not right with me. He's down there in the checkroom. Down
that little stairway." He pointed with his free hand. "If you want

him to be with us I can have him brought up here in no time at all."

"No, no, no!" Mrs. Krushen began to leak and bubble. "Oh, my dear, dear Mr. Tiamat!" She took him firmly by the upper arm and drag-pushed him past the writing desks, past a small, astonished page boy, past the far end of the grill, and up a short flight of steps to the American Bar, weeping and kawking and blowing her nose in short A-flat honks with her free hand.

In the bar, they were seated at a tiny table on the right side, in the furthest corner of the room. Somehow, Mrs. Krushen subdued herself, then came directly to the point. "Can you prove you are as you represent yourself, Mr. Tiamat?"

"I don't know what you mean."

"Please. You have said that his widow gave you Davy's ashes. Might I ask where she lives? The street address?"

"I don't know the street address."

"Ah."

"I never wrote to them and when I was in California they always had the studio's Publicity Department send a car for me or we met in restaurants."

"Don't you see how highly improbable this entire situation is, Mr. Tiamat? Davy has been dead for almost two years. A double gin, please," she told the waiter.

"Fourteen months. A double scotch, water on the side, please."

"I simply cannot fathom what you seem to seek to gain from this—this ghoulish representation. It all confuses me so."

"It was in his will. When he oversocialized he talked about nothing else! Your brother wanted to be buried with the rest of your family in Devon. There was a delay because his widow could not bear to let him go."

"Hah!"

"Surely all of this is a natural state of affairs, Mrs. Krushen."

"I am very much afraid it is not."

The waiter brought the drinks. Somehow, Mrs. Krushen got the double scotch by mistake, belted it, did not notice any difference, and nodded to the waiter for another before the double gin was placed in front of Dan. Dan belted it without noting the unexpected flavor, then nodded his wish for another.

"What if I were to tell you that my family has no burial plot and never has had a burial plot? And that we are from Ludlow, not Devon? Although it upsets me to have to say this to you, Mr. Tiamat, I am afraid this is another of Davy's cruel, cruel jokes."

"No, no, Mrs. Krushen. I have headstone receipts and photostats of the will and a consignment to the right plot in the right cemetery in Devon." He hiccupped.

"You must think me an unnatural sister," Mrs. Krushen said as her new double gin arrived and she belted it. She made a discreet sign to the waiter while Dan gulped his double scotch to stay abreast. "The same, please," he told the waiter.

"Do you drink a lot, Mr. Tiamat?" she asked.

"Well, I'm on sort of a vacation, you might say," Dan answered carefully. "I mean, I *am* relaxing."

"You should watch it. You really should you know. Alcohol is one of the *most* dangerous of all narcotics."

"Thank you just the same, Mrs. Krushen. Alcohol is no problem with me."

"Beverage alcohol is fecal matter, Mr. Tiamat. It is not made of grapes or grain or other attractive foods. It is these which are devoured by the ferment germ, and the germ then evacuates alcohol as its waste product."

"Please, Mrs. Krushen. I'm just trying to have a little fun on a little vacation."

"Is your idea of fun the thought of swallowing the excrement of a living organism?"

"I'd just like to make it clear that my coming to London was Davy's idea. I might even say it was his most precious wish— his coming to London—after he was dead, I mean."

"I loved my brother, Mr. Tiamat," she said. "You must believe that. But what can I tell my husband?"

Dan stared at her blankly. He was bewildered by her check-ered conversations.

"My husband hated Davy. This very moment, long after Davy's death, my husband still hates him bitterly. Oh, I can read your face! You think all of this is shallow and childish and that I seek only to shirk my duty." She began to weep again. Leaning forward on the small table, her expression agitated and torn by despair, and covered her face with her hands and wept steadily, trying to talk to him, or perhaps to herself. "I don't know what to do. I simply do not know what to do."

Dan, hiccupping in a rhythm which approximated that of a fat child learning how to skip, had become conscious of the embarrassment of the other relatively sober guests in the room. All were straining not to look at Mrs. Krushen with about only 3 per cent succeeding. He began to think about leaving when the waiter arrived with the next drinks. For the first time Dan reached his drink at the same time she reached hers. They knocked the drinks back. Dan rummaged in his pockets and found a disorderly clump of banknotes so large and so disar-rayed that it resembled a stage prop for a top banana in bur-lesque. He put a five-pound note at the center of the small table then arose, slowly and stuffily. He sidled behind Mrs. Krushen's chair and willed her to her feet.

She was almost as drunk as Davy used to get on a good day, but she did not stagger or weave. Davy had never staggered either, Dan remembered, until the fourth day of a bender, but by then, of course, Davy had even staggered sitting down.

He took Mrs. Krushen firmly by her arm and they retired from the bar, moving with the caution of extremely aged people down the short flight of steps. At the bottom Dan fell into a portside zig toward the wall but she righted him expertly, like the leader of a naval press gang. They did not speak again un-til they were seated on a divan in the hall near the revolving exits into the great courtyard. Dan held her hand, which was

large but surprisingly soft, and said, "Please don't cry any
more. I'll take Davy to Devon. Makes no diffrince akshully.
Same inna end. Happy t'do it. Helluva good frenna mine."

"I'll thank you to watch your language, Mr. Tiamat," she
answered in an overloud voice, as though the mixture of scotch
and gin had affected her hearing. "Furthermore, Davy is *my*
duty. Please have him fetched. I must go home."

Dan fetched the urn himself, returning from the distant
checkroom as quickly as he could. Mrs. Krushen got up unsteadily as he approached her again, extending the urn as he
came, as would a bearer of gifts. She raised her hands before
her with a quick, involuntary gesture, as though in reflexive
protection against physical assault, and released some of the
awful sounds at her command, falling backward two steps. She
began to weep more shockingly anew, repeating the words, "I
cannot do it. Please, Mr. Tiamat, do not make me do it." An
assistant manager and a displaced Texan started forward. Dan
took Mrs. Krushen by the elbow. Carrying the urn like a foot-
ball in the crook of his arm, he swept her across the lobby,
through the revolving doors, and into a taxi which was de-
positing passengers. He calmed the orthodox protests of the
doorman, breveted by the management to major general, with
a half-crown. Then he persuaded Mrs. Krushen to disclose their
destination. She lived in a mews beyond St. James.

She did not speak during the drive. As her key opened the
front door, a servant materialized. Mrs. Krushen said to Dan,
"I suspect you'll want a drink," and bolted.

The servant took Dan's coat. He tried to saunter in the direction taken by his hostess but soon settled for any forward
movement at all, carrying Davy under his arm. He entered
a large drawing room paneled with oversized oil paintings of
ladies and gentlemen who might have been limned while at-
tending costume balls or during employment as dress extras in
historical films. The place was strewn with ruddy Persian rugs
that were held to the floor by the heaviest kind of Jacobean
furniture. All of this was observed by a huge, inexorable

chandelier that could have been the eye of God. A tall, well-comported man with a port-wine complexion, who listed slightly to port and who had dead-white hair and an angry expression, stood some twenty-five feet across the room and greeted Dan with a voice which seemed to be intent upon not disturbing a throatful of melted fudge he had stored there to enjoy later. "I am Mori Krushen," he said. "And I know why you are here."

Dan did not offer to shake hands, not only because the man was standing so far away, but because he did not feel strong enough to shake hands. Not that he didn't sympathize with Mr. Krushen's point of view, because he did. He knew well that Davy had been a trial to his dear ones and everyone else. Dan sat down heavily, holding Davy in his lap.

Mr. Krushen's voice trembled as he said, "I want you to know that you are welcome here, Mr. Tiamat, but those ashes —that, that urn—must leave my house at once. If you wish, you may place the urn directly outside the front door, in the mews."

"But, it's raining out there, Mr. Krushen," Dan responded indistinctly.

"Nonetheless, I must insist. All of this is something I find I cannot discuss. I have been made unwell by it." He paled steadily as he spoke. He was breathing shallowly. "Please excuse me, Mr. Tiamat." He wheeled abruptly and left the room as Mrs. Krushen entered. They passed each other as blindly and as silently as two billard balls. Mrs. Krushen was carrying two tumblers and a bottle of gin. The tumblers were half-filled. "Cheers!" she cried out, with mock heartiness. "And I *do* hope you will come to dinner one evening soon, Mr. Tiamat." He had no answer ready.

"I am home now," Mrs. Krushen said emphatically, pouring two drinks, then handing a stiff one to Dan, "and I feel ever so much more sure. My son will be here shortly because his father has sent for him. You've been drinking a bit and you are not exactly a young man, nor are you entirely fit. This is not to threaten you. You have done your best to be kind, not having been told at any time that because of that urn and Davy's ashes my husband and son will make the coming year a rack of thorns for me. I couldn't bear it if my son were to hurt you, so you must give me Davy's ashes and leave. Please forgive me, Mr. Tiamat, but you must leave at once."

"Happy to. All mos' unuzhull. Take Davy." He proffered the urn.

"No!" She shoved her stiffened arms outward in a violent gesture to ward the urn off. "Please! Put him on the table, if you will."

"If you have a convulsion every time I hand you the goddam urn," Dan said harshly, because in the back of his fear and his despair she was rejecting him and the dignity of his death and his hope of a haven after death each time she did this, "how the hell are you going to get Davy to Devon?"

She looked at him coldly. "Davy's not going to Devon, Mr. Tiamat," she said grimly. "The top is coming off that urn and he's going into the dustbin and when he's there some peace may return to the men of this house."

Dan jerked the urn back to himself. He turned away from her and weaved across the room. He left the house and slammed the door heavily behind him. He tottered into the black night, clutching the urn close to him, stepping uncertainly on the wet cobblestones, indignation bracing his spine as the black ink of forgetfulness began to spill out across his memory from the far borders of his mind. He heard the door open behind him and he turned. A slab of yellow light, shaped like a golden coffin, fell upon the glistening stones. Mrs. Krushen put her head out. She peered into the darkness, unable to see him, a glass of warm gin in her hand. "Mr. Tiamat? Mr. Tiamat?" she called with her punishing voice. "You haven't said when we may expect you for dinner."

He stared stickily at her silhouette, framed in the bright light. "I'll hafta telephone you on that, Mrs. Krushen," he called back thickly from the center of the night. He turned and stumbled away, having in mind to hire a Rolls-Royce for the drive to Devon. He struck out in the darkness to find his hotel some-how. He got there several days later, but he lost Davy on the way.

Dan Tiamat's long fall began that night, in an actuarial sense. In a romantic sense, however, it was just part of the larger, longer fall. The London police found him in a gutter three nights after he had left Mrs. Krushen's. After a night in jail they reached the bureau chief of the *Press,* who made the arrangements for his release. The London man got him to bed at the hotel and called in the best doctor he knew. Dan was a shambles. From the hotel suite the London man telephoned Joe Downey in New York and made a terse, embarrassed re-port, making it clear that he would not have done so if the columnist had not been mentally and physically ill. There was such a long pause at Downey's end of the line that the London man said, at last, "Hello? Hello?"

"I'm here."

"Oh. Yes, sir."

"He's through," Downey said. "Put him on a plane when he can travel and cable me."

"Yes, sir."

"Dan Tiamat is through," Downey repeated slowly. "What do you think of that, son?"

The bureau chief stared through the open door at the slack-jawed body lying on the bed and tried to comprehend that Joe Downey was insisting that the great Dan Tiamat was finished.

"Who was the assassin of my youth?" the wild-eyed man cried to the bar mirror. He looked upon his silvered hair, in truth ashamed he could not see it clearer. "Did I spill it out, forsooth, or did I lose it as Snow White was taken by the hairy uncouth huntsman to be left in fright alone? Or was it wagered against some maudlin mockery like money? Where has it gone? Should I have sensed the indictment of the calendar? Odd, that I never knew the moment it departed. I should have liked to complain against the bestowment of silver in exchange for gold. Spiked I am; cold and old."

XII

The Tiamat residence in town, as opposed to the little place in the country, which was reminiscent of El Escorial, covered one floor of a large building in the Sixties on Fifth Avenue. Under its wide windows Central Park, an embarrassed plot of ground, counted its trees and waited. It was the same ground the glacier had ripped, that Peter Minuet had tested skeptically, and that at least one Union soldier had wanted to farm. Viewed from the Tiamat apartment on the twenty-fourth floor, it seemed to have been laid out like an ancient corpse of state, bound together with concrete embalming fluid, and set there to remind those who were left that they had come from some place sweet and green. Nature had sold her wares sweetly to stop the steel and bricks at the edge of the park, but the savage, simple-minded people of the city would yet erase this soothing place in time to come. They had begun. They were telling each other that it was the place of nighttime muggers and killers and that it was a great threat and danger. Nearly every park in every poorer city of the world was illuminated so that on summer nights babies could sleep and children could play, but such a move in New York would tend to save the park, and many savage, simple-minded people in the city were wrapped in dreams of ways of turning it into money.

The Tiamat dining room, large enough for the officers' mess of a cavalry regiment, was dominated by an old-fashioned Bowery-bought pool table. It was the kind of furniture that suited the wide, high-ceilinged room with its carved-angels moldings. The table looked so well where it stood that Dan had entirely forgotten that it represented one of his past careers. Three doweled wooden sections fitted across the top of it, to make it a dining table. These were removed instantly after meals because everyone in the Tiamat family liked to shoot pool. The tingling greenness of the table, bold in bright Kelly baize, was made more alluring by a heavy bronze captain's light, two feet nine inches in diameter, that could be raised or lowered at will and, as Dan told all his guests with awe, had cost eight hundred and fifteen dollars.

The morning Dan was due in from his trip to London with Davy Pitt's ashes, Peggy and Carrie were shooting a fast fifty points. Peggy had her hat on. She was waiting for her father to drive her to the airport. Carrie was ten years old. Peggy was thirty-three.

The stakes were reasonable. Every time one of them scratched, she had to put a nickel into a plastic piggy bank that waited on a sideboard. When a sufficient number of scratches were paid for and sufficient other fines collected, the loser intended to take the winner to lunch at Le Pavillon.

"Daddy's been away for ten days today," Peggy said casually, chalking her cue.

Carrie banked the 10-ball into a corner pocket. She chalked. "I know," she said. "Is he all right?"

"How do you mean?"

"Have you heard from him since yesterday when Grandpa called?"

"No."

"What did Grandpa say?"

"Well, Daddy is not one hundred per cent, not as fit as a fiddle."

"Is that why Grandpa's going to the airport with you?"

"In a way. He's also very helpful with the customs."

"Is Grandpa angry with Daddy?"

"I think so. Daddy hasn't filed for six days."

"Why?"

"Drinking, I think."

"But that's happened before and he's filed," Peggy, listening carefully, missed a long shot. "Hasn't he?" Carrie asked.

"That's why it's so important," her mother replied. "The machinery may be breaking down and if it is, I thought we ought to talk a little bit." They didn't look at each other but both became more and more intent upon the game as they conversed.

"Poor Daddy," Carrie said. She sank the 3-ball, chalked, sank the 1-ball, then moved to the other side of the table to study her position.

"I wouldn't say that," Peggy answered mildly. "Some people have ulcers and some have face tics and some have asthma. It's sort of an admission price to stay on in this world we live in. You've just had a touch of acne, as a matter of fact."

"Yeah, I know."

"I have fallen arches. Grandpa has soft teeth."

"Akshully, I meant poor Daddy because Grandpa is angry with him."

"After all, drinking a little too much is Daddy's only drawback."

"He never slams doors."

"Who slams doors?"

"Grandpa." Carrie was shooting smoothly and seemed to have settled down for a run. A dainty orange and blue, two-ball combination, dropped into a corner pocket.

"Carrie, why do you think Daddy drinks too much?"

Carrie straightened up and looked serenely at her mother, looking amazingly and beautifully like her mother. "I don't think I'd have a very good answer," she said.

"I'd love to hear it, just the same."

"Well, I think he gets restless. I think he worries and it makes him restless."

"That *is* a good answer."

"Is it?"

"Why, it's the whole key! Now, if for any reason like—well, like being hit by a big truck or just being away at a convention with Grandpa, I'm not here and Daddy seems to be nervous or restless or upset, from now on will you sort of talk to him and see if he'll tell you what's bothering him? And then maybe you can help him walk around the worry or pass right through it."

"Yes, Mother."

"And when I say, if I'm not here—it's just to be sure. As we have said many times, it is necessary to die, after all. And it isn't the dying that's the problem, it's the pile of unfinished business one leaves behind."

"But that's what people have children for."

"Yes, my darling girl. That must be why."

The blue heron, hurtling spear with wings, flew from the shout of morning. The light spread evenly, giving shadow. Honks of geese flew and a young wind spoke of Norway. Everywhere within the mind doors opened to yet another summer day. The world, itself ten thousand worlds apart from itself, awaited the bidding of the sun.

Dan sat alone in the double seat that was furthest front on the starboard side of the plane, into which he had been poured by all the King's (public relations) men. His sunken face had been punched concave by whisky and fatigue. It had been undefended by food and it looked as though some joker had applied lipstick to the rims of his eyelids. His overlong, graying hair was rumpled. Dirty stubble covered his lower face like a fungus. The left lapel of his dark jacket seemed to be covered with something someone else had tried to wipe off; a filmy, whitish, sour-smelling stain remained. It was just after dawn. The cabin was as quiet as an abandoned dovecote. There were fifty or sixty other passengers behind Dan somewhere in the darkness, but he wasn't aware of them. He was gummily conscious. He had been dropped into drugged sleep when he had boarded the plane, and he had boarded long before the other passengers in London. He did not want a drink. That was behind him. He had finished until the next time.

He felt sick, weak, oppressed by self-pity, and encased with transparent anxiety. When he had awakened, he could have been in a Cretan maze, in the stomach of a mammoth, or as dead as he had hoped to be while he was holding Davy's ashes to his bosom. For a frightening instant, he thought he'd been buried sitting up. Then he saw the sun bowling a path of light across the ocean below him. He fumbled with his blanket, then leaned on the alert bell until the stewardess arrived. She had

been briefed by a vice-president and three press agents that
Tiamat was a leader in the maharaja set, and she had been a
reader of his column for many years.

"Good morning, Mr. Tiamat," she chirped.

"Uh, morning. Ung. Whaz your home town, honey?"

"Portland, Oregon."

"Is at so? Well, well, well. My column runs in Porlin."

"Yes, sir."

"Porlin, Maine, too." He fumbled in his pockets until he
found a pencil and a ragged piece of paper, the name Jeannie
Jones scrawled across the back of it and the number Gerrard
7-5084. He turned the paper over. "Whaz your name, honey?
Gonna put your name inna paper in Porlin." His hands were
shaking. She leaned over and slid the pencil and paper from
his fingers. "I'd better write it for you, Mr. Tiamat. It's a fairly
exotic name." She leaned against the forward bulkhead and
printed her name. She put the paper in his hand and slid the
pencil into his breast pocket behind a dingy handkerchief. He
read it aloud. "Jeannie Jones. No, no, impossible. He stared
at her owlishly. "Is your name Jeannie Jones?"

"No, sir. My name is on the other side." She leaned over
and turned the paper over for him. He read aloud again. "Phylis
Lauritz, Porlin, Oregon. Stewardess. Pan American World
Airways." He put the paper into his inside pocket. "Make you
famous," he said. "Surprise your folks."

"Thank you very much, Mr. Tiamat. May I bring you some
orange juice?" She had almost said coffee instead of orange
juice, but those hands would never be able to hold a cup of hot
coffee.

"Where are we, honey?"

"We'll be in New York in two hours, Mr. Tiamat."

"Oh." He tried to sound casual, not to sound embarrassed.
"Where are we coming from?"

"This is Pan American Flight 103, westbound from London
to New York."

He could not remember leaving New York. The column?

How long since he had filed any copy for his column? The show. The image of a microphone came flying across his memory to shatter within his consciousness. The show was on Tuesday.

"What day is it? What day is today?"

"Today is Saturday, Mr. Tiamat."

"Thanks. Thanks very much," he said. "I'm gonna put your name inna paper." He closed his eyes. She tucked him in, then moved silently down the long aisle of the plane.

He was grateful to her for calling him by his name because at times like these he often believed he had been plucked out of his body and hidden within some stranger's form; inside some grossness shockingly different from his own clean covering. More and more and more he had become convinced in the past year that this was happening, although he could not fathom how it could have happened, and he had not dared to look into a mirror while he was thus a captive lest a spell be invoked or broken, causing him to remain forever a prisoner within this depraved form.

So it was Saturday. Then the show was safe. To hell with the show. His lifeline was that column. He tried to make his mind concentrate on Peggy. He tried to send out psychic waves that she would receive in New York and then go directly to the airport to meet him when he landed, but he could not impose any authority upon his concentration, so he changed his method. He lay back in the reclining seat and thought about Peggy's face, her sweet, sweet face. How did I get here? he asked the lovely vision. Why? He stared intently at his memory of Peggy, and then Janice Pitt's voice came to him and he began to remember Davy Pitt and Moe Girdle and the news photographers at the airport seeing Al Parkay off to France. That poor slob. He hadn't known where to go, and he couldn't go to Italy, which was *à la mode* in his set, because three deportees there didn't care for him much, thanks to several transactions he had undertaken after they had been deported. Al was a hoodlum with a problem because he was a native-born

American, and the Governor had not taken this into consideration when he had issued his ultimatum to organized crime. Al
had complained about the point to Lou Manganello, but Lou
had insisted that Al pay off the goddam bet, goddamit, to hell
with the ultimatum, because Big Lou Manganello had goron-
teed the goddam bet, and since Al had been such a schlemiel
to make such a bet he should get quick into the first plane an'
get outta the country. You hear? Lou had called Dan later.
Listen, would Dan care anything if Al Parkay happened to turn
right around at the airport in Paris and fly to Cleveland or
St. Louis where the boys would have some work for him? Lou
would gorontee it wunt possibly embarrass either Dan or the
Governor. Dan had said it would be perfectly okay with him
and then, half-conscious on that plane, his mind began to find
Davy Pitt and he remembered Davy the last time he had seen
him alive, trying to stand erect at the end of the bar at the
Absinthe House, his black hair falling straight down over his
eyes. How long since he had filed a column? He had been
writing something in London. Had he filed? Before he left New
York he had been four columns ahead, and he knew that was
right because he had called Joe Downey from the airport (although Peggy had told him it would have been better not to
do it) and Joe had said, among other loud things, that he was
only four columns ahead. Only. He'd never been four columns ahead in his life before that. Maybe everything was going to be okay. It began to look as though everything was going to be all right. He had left New York on a Thursday. It was
now Saturday morning. One column gone in Friday's paper.
No column in the Saturday or Sunday paper. So he was still
three ahead. He was clear until Wednesday. That must be why
he took such an awful chance of going to London. There was
nothing to worry about. He could relax and stop torturing
himself. All he needed was a little sleep, just a little, steady
sleep in his own bed. Just a little rest with his own family and
by Sunday afternoon he would be able to settle down and knock
out more copy, and then he could give a little time to his radio
show.

He still felt sick and he still felt weak, but he felt safer. He leaned his head against the coolness of the plane window and peered cautiously into the bleakness of his mind. He knew he was stumbling in the rat race. He was fighting not to be eaten, fighting to live by eating anyone else who stopped to rest. If only Peggy would throw something at him, the way his mother had. If only she would hang with all her dead weight from the lapels of his two-hundred-and-ninety-dollar suit in the middle of Toots Shor's and shriek out to everybody that he was a drunken bum and no good and a fraud who was breaking her hope and her heart.

The tears of self-pity were hot and large. They splashed down his cheeks to dampen his ruined shirt and his twisted, dirty necktie. Dan had had a knack all of his life for being right at the wrong time and wrong at the right time, and for the wrong reasons. He was off on his count of Saturdays by one week of columns owed. He had missed one scheduled coast-to-coast radio show. He did not yet know it but he had stopped running in the rat race.

Joe Downey loved his daughter more than he loved his work. That was a huge measure. When his wife had died of typhoid (it still dazed him to think that in a city as enormous as New York, with five boroughs and thirty thousand miles of maze, that his small household could have employed that one woman, Typhoid Mary, as a cook), Peggy had been two years old. He had immolated himself upon his work but after the first few months of pain, Peggy and her laughter had kept him from giving everything to the newspaper, then getting back little else but money. He began to bring his work home with him, and the men with whom he did the work. He talked over his problems with her and when she was little it was as though he were talking to himself, or as he would have talked to his wife. He took Peggy to the Palace once a week for the vaudeville and to the Polo Grounds to shout for the greater glory of the Giants in the sunshine. They saw the circus together every season—both the opening and closing performance.

Peggy was born a wise child and grew into a sweet child. She knew what made her father laugh and what could make him weep. She learned how to lead him out of rages and how to push him into unpleasant tasks. As she grew older she ran the house and she provided extra dimensions for the things he did away from his work and at his work, even if she had to stay awake part of many a night to figure out ways and means to do it. She was the indispensable child-woman.

When he learned, while standing under the large block letter D at the pier to meet her when she returned from her celebration of the graduation present, whom she had decided to marry, he very nearly collapsed with gratitude. For a considerable number of years after that day, Downey had tottered about under the vague impression that she had married Dan to suit her father, and it was a long, long time before he was forced to shake that happy thought. His darling, darling daughter had married the young man whom he admired most in all the world; a young man who would ever welcome him into their house at any hour of the day or night, and be delighted to drink with him, talk shop with him, and, conceivably, to name their first, second, and third sons after him. Downey had inhaled all this satisfaction like perfume.

Three years later a Cuban woman had come into his office with documentary proof that Tiamat was nothing, had always been nothing, would always be trash.

Fourteen years after that morning of euphoria on the pier, as he rode beside Peggy in the publisher's limousine along the East River Drive toward the airport, he was close to despair over Dan, so Peggy had his despair to cope with as well as whatever anxiety and sorrow she concealed within herself. The morning marked the first time since her marriage that her father had acknowledged to her that her husband drank at all. It was her father's professional indifference to the caricatures produced by alcohol that had allowed her to associate whisky with newspapermen in the manner that others might associate a sense of induced gallantry with Errol Flynn. As he spoke about her husband's drinking, her father spoke carefully and monotonously as though he did not entirely believe what he was saying and wanted to insure that she would question it in the same degree.

The relationship between Dan and Downey, while never again friendly in even the most fleeting fashion, had progressed far beyond the original bitterness. For one thing, Dan had gone on to make a large amount of money for the paper and for the syndicate it owned, so that Downey had soon swallowed his prejudice against gossip columns and maintained an unspoken respect for Dan.

Downey let his small hand drop on top of Peggy's long slender hand as it rested on the seat between them. He patted it. He removed his hand self-consciously then and placed it in his lap, but she reached over and took the hand back to the place on the seat and held it warmly to help him say what he had to say. He cleared his throat with the sound of bark being ripped off a redwood tree. "The time has come for us to face it for once and for all, lovey. Your husband is now a bum or on the near side of being a bum."

"Don't go all out now, Papa. You'll only make yourself feel bad later."

"I have to say it. Dan Tiamat is a bum."

"Think of Vincent van Gogh, Papa."

"Why?"

"You wouldn't call Vincent van Gogh a bum, yet God knows he was a drunk."

"Van Gogh was an artist!"

"Was Jesus an artist?"

"Now, just a minute here, Peggy—"

"He certainly suffered, God knows. And I do mean God knows."

"He didn't have the whisky habit."

"If my idea of St. Paul is true, you can bet there's a lot they didn't tell us."

"Peggy!"

"You're doing the talking. I merely answer in the hope of defending my husband."

"I'm not attacking him. He's attacked himself by being found drunk *again* in a gutter—*again,* lovey—and the only difference this time is that he picked a different country. But even that far away he managed to get into the newspapers of the world by making a pitiable scene in court about that drunk actor's ashes."

"So I heard," Peggy said. She patted his hand and her air of diffidence purely maddened him. He jerked his hand away and stared sullenly out the car window as they went up the gentle approach to the Triborough Bridge. He snapped off the end of a cigar that looked huge in his small face and spat the tiny wad of tobacco anywhere. He accepted the light his daughter gave him, puffed, and then huffed: "I have to tell you that he's thrown away his future in this business and—"

"I know, Papa. Believe me, I know how they will not tolerate drunks in your business. Who ever heard of a newspaperman who took a drink?"

"The union contract did away with the whisky. Let 'em get drunk and we can fire 'em."

"Then tell Dan's union. Why tell me?"

"I tell you, lovey, because he's through. I mean that literally. Through and through. The hundred and ninety-six papers who pay him have complained for the ninth and last time that he has hung them up for copy. How do you think it happened that that disgraceful story was printed all over the country in his own newspapers? They did it to have an out from their contracts and they want out not only because his copy is missing, time and time again, but because he can't write any more and God knows I never thought I'd be saying a thing like that in my life. And that's not all, lovey. The radio show is gone. And were they ever tickled to be handed such an out! He's missed four shows out of the last thirteen. He isn't selling the product because the public doesn't believe the news he hands out any more than they'd believe any other drunk."

"He's safe then."

"Whatta you mean?"

"You are going to fire him, aren't you?"

"I didn't say that."

"You were about to."

"I was not."

"Let's not think about anything now. Let's just get him home."

"What did you mean about Dan being safe now?"

"I suppose I'm thinking about why the women outlive the men in the United States of America. They live under feather pressure while the men take a few hundred tons per square inch every day."

"Never mind generalities."

"Then, specifically. Ever since Dan got what he thought he wanted in this business he's been drowning in that sea of celebrity. He's rich and he secretly thinks he's unworthy of it, and you know it. He's scared silly that something is going to take away his celebrity, his ten thousand intimate friends, his so-called power, and his so-called riches. He's scared silly, Papa, so he drinks. He's like a normal, average-size man who has to shave in front of those elongating mirrors that make him seem monstrously tall when he thinks of himself as a midget."

"He is a midget. And he always has been a midget."

"Is that so? That isn't the way you used to tell it to me."

"Then put it down to the fact that he was all right to drink with but I don't like him as a son-in-law."

"You were delirious with joy when I told you I was going to marry him."

"Well, the honeymoon is over."

"How long has it been over?"

"I don't count by days or year. He's a cheap man and a small man."

"You know, Pa, as far back as I can remember you told me that you would never allow a column like Dan's in the *Press*. Why did you change your mind?"

"I had a low opinion of that kind of a column, and my opinion is lower now than it ever was, but I vowed I would change my mind if I ever found a man who was lower than my opinion of that kind of a column."

"I think we'll just stop talking now. Or perhaps there is something else you can do. You can get out at the next light and find yourself a cab and go back where you came from."

"I didn't ask him to be a drunken bum."

"I said stop it, Papa."

"You've been too good to him," Downey said bitterly, staring away from her. "It might have all been different if you'd thrown a tight rein on him. That's what a man needs a woman for."

"Just shut up, Papa. Even if it means nothing to you, I love Dan. He's mine, and I like him just the way he is or anyway he wants to be, and I never thought you'd grow old enough to be insensitive to such a thing as that between my husband who loves me and me."

"Now, just a moment, Peggy—"

"Just shut up. You don't know what you're talking about, because if you did, maybe you would have been the big moral paragon who would have demanded that Dan live his life your way, studding the scene with exemplary laws of conduct and imposing your will on him, because I suspect that's what men are for, too." She tapped her chest pugnaciously with a stiff finger. "I run my life and up to a certain point, my daughter's. I do the best I can to be the best I can. And I'm not going to push my husband off any emotional cliff just because your wife believed in reading the riot act to you."

"Peggy!"

"Believe it or not, Dan does the best he can to be the best he can. In spite of those thousands of friends. In spite of those alleged riches. In spite of that useless, ludicrous, juvenile consequence which has no other name to be called by except that silly word *celebrity*." Peggy glared at her father. "And try to understand this. I *want* him fired! How's that for running somebody else's life? I want him thrown out of the newspaper business on his marshmallow head."

The limousine was bowling along Grand Central Parkway.

"Now just a minute, lovey. You don't mean that."

"Will you fire him?"

"He has a contract and there is no legal way we can fire him without the risk of a lawsuit."

"Do you really think we are making this journey to bring Dan home, sober him up, then send him out to grope for destruction again?"

"Now, Peggy. It's not as bad as that."

"You said he was a bum, Papa. Actually, he's a poor boy who is perpetually alarmed to find himself living on Fifth Avenue. He's a coffee runner for a floating crap game who has suddenly been made one of the dearest friends of some of the most vicious hoodlums, actors, gamblers, and businessmen of the times. Did you know that a Christmas card from a silly movie star is enough to send him right to the bar for reassurance that everything he has, he deserves?"

"But just the same—"

"Can you remember that last classically horrible drunk he was on?"

"Naturally. Of course."

"When was it?"

"Why can't you stay on the subject?"

"It was in March. This is July. And he was in the Polyclinic for six days after that. He started to drink because he signed a check to pay an income tax that came to more money than all the men of his dreary, Irish peasant family had ever earned, going back to Adam, he told me. The tax he paid was enough money to have kept the three of us for thirty-one years, based on what he was earning when he got his first real reporting job on the paper. He sat in that lawyers' office—it takes two lawyers to handle his problems—surrounded by three certified public accountants, the senior partners of their firm—and he signed that check and then he stared at his hands without a poor man's callous on them and he started to cry. Within two hours the story was out, all over town, then all over the country, that he

was so cheap and stingy that it broke his heart to have to
pay taxes to his Government, when all the time he was awe-
struck and frightened that all the invisible apparatus which had
brought in all the fame—which had made all the money causing all of those taxes—would collapse and he would be discovered to be just an average man—which is exactly and
preciously what that wonderful man is. So he began to drink
to hold the fear down. He was six days in the Polyclinic after
we found him and he missed two radio shows and sixteen days
of columns."

The big black limousine rolled into the restricted area next
to the apron at the airport.

*If compassion is a mirror, what are tears? Do they glint and
shine as beacons to the strangers? What are fears? What are the
hopes of man? Do our selves see us clearer through the glass
of others' plan? Can pity scourge scorn? By loving, can the
hungry hate we owe to witty self be starved? What can befall
us if we give? What remains but faith and strength if we should
weaken our disdain? Should we taste the salt of kindness, flavor
of living? Can it enhance the love of self, this gift of giving?*

XIII

When a man as selfish as Dan Tiamat shares lives with a
woman as selfless as his wife, they observe all the laws of op-
posites that have been the concrete for so many religions,
including the act of love. In terms of ornithomancy, Peggy
was like a flock of swallows, assured by numbers, flying south
at the scent of snow to preserve the youngest and weakest.
Dan was like a sparrow living in winter, flying close to the
ground, foraging for seeds in the droppings of horses, sensitive
only to the moment at hand and what it could bring to him.
Peggy was so feeling that she defended Dan's callousness. When
she got him back from London she was elated; she could see
sunlight ahead of them after a terrifying journey through a long
tunnel.

Five days after he had returned Dan had recovered suf-
ficiently that he was able to tie his shoe laces without falling on
his head. Another day passed before he had the strength to
make it to the office.

When he entered the anteroom of his private rooms at the
paper, on the quiet side of the building, through a door marked
PRIVATE NO VISITORS THIS MEANS YOU, his secretary wasn't
there. Her bare desk was just beyond a railing; his office was
beyond her desk, behind a closed door with a buzzer lock on
it, and his office was the same size as the publisher's and bigger
than Downey's by one-half. He strolled in with his customary
air, patterned after that of the man who invented dollar cigars,
but he was stopped by the puzzle of the desk being as bare as
a bardot. He walked around it as one might examine a space
ship. He tried pulling at a drawer. It opened! She was not at
her desk and the desk was unlocked. As far as his policy was
concerned, this sort of thing would be far better happening
in security offices in the Pentagon. The drawer was empty. He
looked in the other drawers. They were all empty.

He unlocked the door to his office and strode to his desk,
neither closing the door behind him nor removing his flat straw
hat. He dialed the Personnel Department. A nasal voice which
gave the unaccountable impression that the speaker was trying
to climb up a wall backward, told him that his secretary was
no longer with the *Press*.

"Put Rubin on."

"I'm sorry," the voice said. "Mr. Rubin is in a meeting. You
can call him back after four or in the morning."

"Call him back? Are you new here? Do you know who
you're talking to?" Dan's voice became strident. "Put Rubin on
this phone."

There was a pause. The pause got longer and longer. The
weeks of alcohol had left him flabby. His anger tired him
quickly. He had to sit down. He began to yell "Hello! Hello!"
into the telephone.

"What?" The sound stabbed into his head suddenly. It was
Marc Rubin's lovable nails-across-the-blackboard voice.

"What are you, Rubin, a suicide?"

"Yeah, yeah. I'm scared silly. Whatta you want?" Dan could not believe what he was hearing.

"There may be some sort of a misunderstanding here," he said evenly, "and if so don't get panicky when you find out. It can happen. To one mistake you're entitled. Do you know who you are talking to?"

"Come on, come on! I'm talking to Tiamat. Dan Tiamat, the ex-big man and ex-columnist of *The New York Daily Press.* Speak up. Don't waste my time."

Dan held onto the chair with his free hand. Through clenched teeth he said, "First, I want that girl fired."

"She offended you?"

"Yes."

"She gets a raise." Dan suddenly began to sweat profusely. "You wanna know where your secretary is?" Rubin asked. "She's on terminal leave. If she didn't leave you any letter of explanation you can figure out for yourself what she thinks of you, and my records show she's been with you for eight years."

"Are you drunk, Rubin?"

"You are the drunk, Mr. Ex-Big Man, not me. I've been waiting a long, long time for this day to happen. Right now you have no secretary. Tomorrow you'll have no office. If I had my way you wouldn't even have a typewriter. So stop wasting my time and go in and pick yourself up off the floor of Downey's office." The phone went dead.

Dan began to tremble, breathing like a stud walrus. Then it came to him clearly that the way to straighten out this misunderstanding was to go upstairs and break Rubin's nose and then have him fired, in that order, but he could not find the strength to get started. He dialed the publisher, the man who had made the greatest amount of money from him.

"Hello?"

"Charley O'Neil?"

"Yes."

"This is Dan Tiamat, Charley, and I want to know what the hell—"

"Save it, Dan. Don't include me in. This is Downey's business." He hung up.

Dan stood up slowly. He wiped his face with a handkerchief. His anger had burned up his short supply of energy. When he looked up, Gilda Muller, Downey's secretary, was standing in the doorway. She wore her hair like an Iroquois brave, her sweaters like covers on a moth-balled dreadnought, and on her, at her age, it didn't look good. Her eyes held the expression of matched steel ball bearings. "Mr. Downey will see you now, Mr. Tiamat," she said.

"You walked here to tell me that?"

"Mr. Downey had the starter report you as soon as you came in the building. He wants to make sure you get in to see him."

"Later. I gotta see Rubin." He tried to move past her but she filled the doorway. She stared at him as though she were about to spit in his eye.

"And how are all the other little things going, sport?"

"You, too, Muller?"

"In fat, black spades with pointy, pointy tops. This way, big man."

She turned and walked away from him. He followed her automatically. They moved along a corridor in tandem, she balancing on stilt heels, her buttocks moving like factory bobbins. As he crossed the City Room he noticed the faces of the boys, and they were not wearing nice expressions. He began to get the old, displaced feeling that he had come alive inside some stranger's body. He had known most of these men all of his adult life and they were looking at him with dislike and contempt, with pleased and untimid malice. He was possessed with the thought that somehow something had changed his outside shell. He had to find a mirror. He saw Charley Wells's face and he could not believe what he saw. He had paid Charley Wells's insurance premium two years ago. He stared at Al Gosse and Al had the grace to drop his eyes. Al's son had attacked a neighbor's little girl and Al had come blubbering to Dan to pull the cops off the kid, and he had arranged for a suspended sentence for the little pervert. Then it came to him that he had a different face for all of them, and, worst of all, still a different face for himself. He had seen his true face once. He had been walking across Madison Square Park in the springtime and he had passed a man on a bench who was staring at a basket of jonquils at his feet, his face filled with wonder and his hatband stained. Nothing had changed but his life.

Gilda Muller swung open the door to Downey's office. "Mr. Tiamat is here, Mr. Downey," she said musically, her eyes bright with pleasure. Downey was bent over the roll-top desk. It had as many pigeonholes as the key rack of a side-street hotel. All the desk's innards were exposed as though it had been disemboweled by a designer of modern offices. On view in the pigeonholes were a red yo-yo, a huge bunch of rusting keys, a flashlight, a copy of *Bride's Magazine* seven years old, two or three hundred memoranda of different colors, a stack of birthday cards held together by a sleeve garter, four rolls of Scotch tape, a large container of Selenex, a dandruff remover, and a rolled scroll that attested to Downey's efforts either for or against National Brotherhood Week in 1947. The Turkey red carpet, in prissy pattern, seemed perpetually embarrassed by two emperor-sized brass spittoons and clearly seemed to be trying to squirm out from under them. The office smelled of equal parts of barbershop and locker room. For many years Downey had worn a beret while he worked because of the force with which the cold, conditioned air fell upon his baldness. He wore a brown beret because he felt a blue beret would look too French. In the winter he wore the same headpiece because the building was old and the heat always leaked out of the pipes before it could be raced to his side of the building. Because he was short-waisted, he looked small as he sat beside that towering desk, flanked by the long, wide, polished work table.

Dan remained standing near the work table, fighting weakness, his hands balled into fists of bravado, although he couldn't find the stamina to sustain the snarling play he wished he could somehow bring off, or to execute some of the meanness he had always made to work for him before. A cold sweat covered him.

"Siddown, Dan."

Dan held onto the back of a wooden captain's chair. "What the hell is happening, Joe?"

"You made the full circle for me. I knew this would happen but even I didn't think you'd rot away in only ten years, kid." He bit off the end of a big cigar. "I said, siddown!"

"Whatta you mean, Joe?" Tiamat sat down carefully. It seemed incredible that his voice was almost a whine.

"Remember the Castaños woman, kid?"

"Well, yes. Of course."

"You remember how you sat here ten years ago and I told you you had broken my heart?"

"Yes, Joe."

"Well, we're even now. You've paid off. The horrible days are over, kid. You have ten days before the new assignment starts. Go get some sun and rest."

"What new assignment?"

Downey slid an advertising proof across the desk. "This ad has been running for a week," he said. Dan leaned forward to read the half-page advertisement facing him.

SEND
YOUR HEARTBREAKS
YOUR WORRIES
YOUR PROBLEMS AND YOUR FEARS
TO
MISS FRIENDSHIP
NEW YORK'S MOST COMPASSIONATE
NEIGHBOR
WHOSE DAILY COLUMN STARTS
IN THE NEW YORK PRESS
MONDAY, AUGUST 1st
IF YOU NEED A FRIEND WRITE NOW FOR ADVICE
AND COMFORT

Dan's large pale hands started to shake. "Joe. No. You can't.
I don't have to take this. Go murder somebody else. I'm not
gonna stay here and get killed like this."

"Get killed?" Downey snorted. "You're dead."

"Listen, Joe—"

"You remember that contract you were so eager to sign
when you had the Cuban bitch, when you couldn't wait to be a
big columnist with the money, the fame, and the power?" He
touched the advertisement. "The contract is still in force. This
is our new lonelyhearts department and you're going to run it
for us. You don't seem to understand just how through you are.
You lost all your papers and your radio show. Charley O'Neil
thought he could hold the basic twelve papers for you, but
they're gone. And I want you to understand that there wasn't
one of them who wasn't happy to get out from under the wreck
of you. Did you know that thirty-nine papers haven't carried
your copy for over four months, that's how bad it was?"
Downey swiveled away and began to shuffle the papers on his
desk. "That's all, pal. On your way."

Dan stood up shakily. He paid out an engraved obscenity
upon his father-in-law's dignity.

"All right, big man," Downey said. "I'll now have the office
boy's little sister throw you out of here."

He reached for the phone but Dan grabbed first. "Get me
Mort Nathanson at the *Graphic,*" he said thickly to the operator. He stared into Downey's blue eyes, breathing with difficulty. "Get all your lawyers and all the little lawyers in the
law schools and get them started on that contract, Baldy," he
said. "You have just lost yourself two hundred thousand readers, but your loss will be the *Graphic's* gain." He spoke into the
telephone. "Hey, Mort! Hozza kid? Hoz Sylvia? Judy? Lucy?
Oh, you heard? That's right. No show. No papers. No nothink.
You still wanna make a deal?" He stared at Downey and twisted
a horrible smile out of the crevices of his teeth while he listened
to Nathanson. "Okay. Good. Great. Two weeks to build up the
second coming, then I start to work on the *Graphic.* You did
a good day's work, keed. See you." He hung up with an effort.

He braced himself on the work table, then leaned over Downey's wastebasket and spat elaborately. His strength was waning. "Your move, tinhorn." He tried to snarl, but he could just about get the words out. He left Downey's office but this time he didn't walk across the center of the City Room. He walked around its edges like a dying squire pacing his acres for the last time. He concentrated on making it to the elevator bank, but when he made it that far he knew he would need to get into his office and lie down for a little while.

He opened the door to his outer office. Howard Pearl, the advertising manager, and Bob Schwartz, the purchasing manager, were there making expansive redecorating gestures that signified enormous good taste.

"Get out!" Dan said as he walked past them to the inner office door. "Out!"

"Now, just a minute, here," Pearl said roughly.

Dan turned on them with his old-time, snarling vehemence. "Get out! This is my office this week. If it's your office next week then come back next week. Out! Out!" He unlocked the inner office door, went in, slammed the door behind him, then forgot about the two men because he could not support any thought. He threw his straw hat on the floor and sank upon the leather couch, managing to stretch himself out, sweating, his heart pounding. He rested, eyes open, stretched out upon his back, for a long time. At last he felt strong enough to sit up. He looked at his watch. It was ten minutes to one. He dialed the telephone on the end table.

"Honey. Dan."

"Are you all right?"

"A little weak, maybe."

"Why don't I get the car and pick you up?"

"I just quit."

"You quit—the *Press?*" It was an incomprehensible condition to Peggy.

"Think you could get downtown for lunch?"

"But—"

"He wanted to make me the lovelorn editor. Your father. He

told me he had me all tied up in a contract and that I would
just take over his goddam lovelorn department and goddam
well like it. I quit. I mean, what the hell else could I do?"

"Where will we meet for lunch?"

"Hungarian Charley's?"

"Dan, it's so noisy!"

"Yeah, yeah. Okay. Jesus, I can never think of a restaurant
when I have to think of a restaurant."

"I'll meet you in the garden at the Italian Pavilion in twenty
minutes."

"Good. Right. Okay."

"I'll call for a table. Don't rush. Don't get all tired out, darling." She hung up and stared at the whiteness of her knuckles
as she gripped the telephone.

They sat under the beautiful green, red, and white awning.
Peggy read his fortune, with her soft, sweet voice, in the *bus-
secca,* again in the *bardele coi Morai,* so expressive were they
of the future, being wide noodles made with flour and borage
leaves, and finally in the great balloon of cognac. In all these
divinations she saw that he would be elected President of the
United States in 1952 (which did not come true), that they
would both live forever in expanding happiness (which did not
come true either), and that they would love each other always
(which did). Considering everything, she hit a good forecast-
ing average as fortunetelling goes.

When Peggy had him soothed with food, wine, cognac, and
blarney, she permitted him to let the ebbed torrent of his words
cover the rock of his resentment.

"Can you imagine me—me, Dan Tiamat—as pen pal to a
lot of slobs?"

"It's very hard to say. I mean, from the point of view of re-
ducing pressure on you and letting you enjoy life, it just might
be great."

"Great?"

"In a way it would be a privilege."

"I don't get you."

"Nobody asks for troubles, Dan. They drift in out of nowhere. They lurch out of a fog. Anybody in trouble needs help. That's how we survive, after all."

"Whatta you mean, that's how we survive? After all, what?"

"Don't you remember *Moby Dick?* It was your favorite once. You liked to read it out loud one summer, a long time ago."

"Honey, I wish you would stay on the point. One thing just keeps leading us to another here. We're not getting anywhere."

" '—the monkey rope was fast at both ends; fast to Qeequeg's broad canvas belt and fast to my narrow leather one . . . my own individuality was merged in a joint stock company . . . I saw that this situation was the precise situation of every mortal . . . he has this Siamese connexion with a plurality of other mortals.' "

The waiter brought hot coffee. His assistant shined the spoons. The captain served them another heart's ease of cognac while the maître d'hôtel hovered with an invisible rapier in hand, as though to run through any *cameriere* who faulted the service. Dan poured his cognac slowly into the black, smoking aromatic coffee in front of Peggy and a blending of three perfumes rose around them.

"You don't expect me to walk out on Mort Nathanson and go back and eat crow for your father and beg him to give me this lovelorn column, do you, Peg?"

"No. No, I don't."

"Then why are you talking about it in this mysterious way?"

"Dan, can you remember any five of the columns you wrote in the past month?" She watched her coffee, stirring it slowly. He stared at her blankly. "Even better, can you recall twenty columns—no, ten columns—you've written out of the thousand-odd during the past five years?" Dan held his head still, chin high, eyes rolling slightly, as though he were trying to peer into the past, but he could not or would not answer her.

"Don't let it get you down," she said soothingly. "Flapdoodle is flapdoodle."

"Flapdoodle? My columns are flapdoodle?"

"I don't think I meant it in exactly that way," she said. "I meant to indicate that perhaps your work wasn't as important as you thought it was."

"Was?"

"Well, for the time being. If we have two weeks off before you open at the *Graphic*, let's go to Havana. Do you know we haven't been to Havana since our honeymoon?"

"How can you say flapdoodle! Look at the money they paid me!"

"Oh, Dan! Look at the money they paid Louis B. Mayer!"

"I have dined at the White House with three Presidents of the United States."

"Yes. Sure. And we both remember who some of the other guests were, too."

"Listen, Peg," he said hotly, "if you're going to argue like this maybe you can tell me who else can remember any part of yesterday's newspaper for that matter."

"Oh, I agree. But if people can't remember the inhumanities and the triumphs, the disasters and betrayals, and the other hunks of history on which they were floated through yesterday, how can they possibly remember your flapdoodle?" She touched his hand tenderly. "Dan, I wish you could see how run down you look. And that's an understatement. I wish I could get you to understand what an empty horn this whole column career has been for you."

"All right. I agree, then. Let's say I understand. Then what?"

"I don't have any program. I'm not trying to sell you anything, I just thought that if you had a job—and after all, we are not pushed for money—if you had a job where you had to take the troubles, the personal troubles of five people seriously every day—"

"Aaah!" He was incredulously impatient.

"—just five letters a day, five days a week, and heaven knows that isn't much, those five people would remember what you had written to them for the rest of their lives."

"Is that what you want for me? Is that what you want? A slob's job writing a lonelyhearts column?"

"You know what I want, darling," she said quietly. "I want you to have what you want. I just want you to be proud of yourself."

"You're a goddam marvel, Peg."

"Are we going to Havana?"

He grinned at her broadly. "Maybe tonight. If we can't get a plane tonight we'll go the first thing in the morning."

XIV

Hawk clouds scudded toward stone nests under the west, pulling darkness in. Day sky filled with night and crests of wet threw their shining discipline upon the streets. Vats of light were flung, flashing a sudden grin upon the neon face of night. Spent day had fled into the sun, which lurched at the edge of the brimming world. It fell, just then, under the gun of thunder. A rushing wind was hurled and a warm, wet rain paid into the ground an ecstasy.

Havana was completing its first full day of unseasonal flash flood and, in the area of the city within a block of the harbor wall, the water was two feet deep along the building walls. After dinner the Tiamats rode away from the harbor, slithering through the velvet Cuban night, which was streaked obliquely by falling rain, the thoughts of each for the other as shining bubbles from two caressing glasses of champagne. They were rested again and ready, eager to find some new ingenuity in the night.

At Partura's they watched the bartender put a pineapple into a press and get the equivalent of a midget's opera hat full of juice, to add three fingers of Bacardi, tap in some powdered sugar, then shake the whole thing into a froth of great health with the sugar providing instant energy, the pineapple juice vitamin C, and the rum contributing the only reliable antibiotic available to all men. They had two of these, taking their time, crowded by the sounds of the trumpet and maracas behind them, smelling the wet, luxuriant tropical night, laughing over their secrets. They contained each other so intimately that they sat within a magic ring invisible to the strangers for well over an hour.

Heneghan came in at about ten to one. Heneghan was an anthropologist whose family's development of the plastic tea bag had left him an annual tax-free income of between twenty-five and twenty-seven thousand dollars for as long as he continued his field researches outside the metropolitan area of New York, where his family enjoyed living, so he had never needed Dan's column to increase his worth, and, had he known of it, he would have considered Dan's transmogrification into Miss Friendship to be an advancement. Heneghan had nearly perfect vision but he wore contact lenses so that he could change the color of his eyes at will or as his costume dictated. Although the true color of his eyes was muddy gray, that night they were Nile green flicked with chic gold. He was dressed in a stark white linen suit, like a Central Casting planter, with highly shined black shoes and a black string tie. He wore a guardsman's mustache over each eyebrow, which gave the effect of expensive fur awnings. His hair was oatmeal-colored, no one knew his age, and his skin was a dull ivory when he was drinking, which was during waking hours, and these skin tones gradually backed down during the night to reach, at last, the color of spring water mixed with absinthe. His face was round above generally plump body lines, and he was a most cheerful looking man who spoke as though surrounded by a rich atmosphere of nitrous oxide, and altogether he resembled a clean-shaven Santa Claus following riotous, post-Christmas debauchery.

Heneghan sat down at the Tiamat's table. He talked at all times as continuously and as effortlessly as a prerecorded tape, and he proceeded to tell them how he had come in from a harbor cruise aboard a sloop, some hours before, which had also carried a large vacuum bottle of gimlets (he still had this with him), two guitarists, a girl named Carmelita. He explained with regret that he had lost Carmelita and the two guitarists in a taxi when he had left it for an instant in traffic to purchase three cigars and a clean white suit. She had been swept out of his life by the insistence of the cars behind. Any search would be hopeless, he assured them. She was lost forever. He could not remember her last name and she had never known his.

"I missed her last name," he continued rapidly, with no hint of tiring, "because I—"

"Jim," Peggy interrupted at last, "you have been speaking in Spanish and we don't understand Spanish."

"It probably isn't even Spanish," Dan said. "He makes it sound like some lost language."

Heneghan's eyes lighted up like an expensive pin-ball machine. "My dear Tiamat," he said with delight, this time in English, "what an ear you have! I have been trying out a bakers' dialect of Pinar del Rio province, which is Carmelita's home state."

"Is Carmelita a baker?" Peggy asked.

"I think not." Heneghan leered. "But the reason I missed getting her last name is that Carmelita is the diminutive for Carmen, and it occurred to me instantly that perhaps she did not know that the ancient Italian goddess of prophecy was called Carmenta, who sang of the future and the past like a notice for an overdue insurance premium." He lifted the large vacuum bottle to his lap and unscrewed its top. He uncorked it. A paper cup appeared from his jacket pocket. He filled it with the cold, green gimlet juice. He recorked and fastened the top carefully again, put the jug on the floor, and sipped as he talked. "It is particularly interesting to me," he said, "because Carmenta was the mother of Evander, a demigod giver of certain mild laws, and, as a boy, I attended the Evander-Childs High School in New York."

"It's a small world," Peggy observed.

They rested. Possessing the illusion that they were far away from threats, they achieved instant repose against the tropical temperature of the café, which was open on two sides. The café's electric lights burned reflections into the wet streets. The sighing wind threw the rain downward in the sound pattern of burning opium.

After a while Heneghan got to talking about the night he had made eleven straight passes in a joint across the river from Cincinnati, and eventually that memoir led them to call for a check and a cab and to set out for Sans Merci and its oracular stick men who sometimes seemed to know exactly what would happen with cards, dice, or that little while ball, even before it happened, an odd thing but hardly supernatural. Heneghan said he had to shoot craps even if he had to come up against a bust-out man because the name Carmelita was related so actively to prophecy and she had seemed so very fond of him.

They were interrupted en route to Sans Merci by a suggestion from the driver that they might consider stimulating, or in any event a novelty, to witness a cockfight. They took his tip but it was very dull stuff because chickens are so stupid, born to be killed anyway, and their blood in no way a threat to man, although Heneghan did take the trouble to explain that at one time in India and Russia it was a desecration to put such fowls to death, although the Aztecs had believed in killing cocks for sacrifice and Hungarian bridegrooms had carried their chickens in marriage processions, not so much as an assurance for fertility as because they knew full well that if they left the birds at home the mayor would send someone in to steal them.

At Sans Merci Heneghan shot craps. Peggy and Dan watched the floor show, then they danced. They moved slowly to the designedly persuasive music in sublime content, supreme in their world, serene beyond sublimity. Heneghan looked up twice from his field research with the dice and although he was drunk and his mind was not exactly a fist of steel for reaching images and grasping them, he smiled like an elderly uncle at what they had to share, as the sun is shared.

Dan looked invincible: a big man with a face slashed by three furrows on each side, which were lines left from the grinning and grimacing when he had been ambitious and too poor, and a crook in his nose where he'd been hit by a drunken cop when he'd been twelve. His eyes were clear and light blue, ashine with love and awe and pride, edged with lust. Peggy's cheek rested on his shoulder. Her full, pink mouth was slightly open, her breathing was shallow and, as she clung to him, her ash-blond hair against his dark, filled suit, it seemed to Heneghan, far across the room, that Dan was carrying a chalice of lights against his bosom. They did not speak as they danced, yet, eyes closed, Peggy smiled at what she owned and what possessed her.

Heneghan had not only won thirty-six dollars by ten minutes to four but he had, miraculously, found Carmelita somewhere. They were joyous, even agitated, at the fortuitous reunion. Even Peggy got to marveling over it until Heneghan remembered he had, many hours before, made a date to meet Carmelita there at three-thirty. Heneghan began to share his joy in Spanish, but was corrected in time. He asked Carmelita's pardon for needing to speak English for just a moment, kissed her hand, and turned to the Tiamats.

"Isn't this beyond belief? Here I have been mourning her supposed loss—gambling to forget, if you will. Why, all the afternoon and into the evening Carmelita and I had been planning merriment together, such as the celebration of the true rhumba for this morning. Then I forget, somehow, that we had pledged to meet right here, just about now, and that I had not actually gotten out of the cab to buy those three cigars but had been thrown out by the two guitarists, who, as it turns out, are admirers of Carmelita."

"A true rhumba?" Peggy asked tentatively. "Is there a false rhumba?" Heneghan immediately translated this for Carmelita, who looked wide-eyed and said, "Hah!"

Beyond them a gigantic retina opened with astonishing, rolling speed, letting in the raw, yellow sound of a Cuban trumpet. The color moved faster than its internal light and it smote them. It could not be stopped. The maracas came in with the sound of sand and pebbles, chanting a plot to escape from the hollowness. A metal voice began to sing in Spanish, fixing its words in the air in front of them with bright, brass brads of sound. The music put wild teeth into the mind and dragged it to single concentration upon what was happening under the narrow circle of light.

A sweat-polished banana-colored boy and a glistening purple girl were dancing the rhumba, the boy ithyphallic under a straw hat, the girl with a red and green rag tied around her waist, their twenty toes at right angles to their legs, their feet stirring dust in the night under the brazen light. They danced as cock and hen, to help crops to multiply, to catch the substance of life at hot fullness at the center of a woman and a man, then to hurl it forward and upward in the rhythm that creates life while it reveals what is at the center of the sun. The light, striking like a war club from directly overhead, splintered all perspective.

The rum careened inside Dan. He left Peggy there, staring from the ring of sweat and flesh. He talked to the man at the bar. He shook hands with him and left paper money in the man's hand. All the eyes of all the watchers were black spots at the center of flat white. Peggy imagined she could hear their heavy breathing, despite the incitement of the music, but it was her own breathing. Dan took her soft, moist hand and drew her along behind him, walking away from the ecstasy in the music and the transforming sobs of enormous pleasure from the shining, purple girl. He followed the man who had taken his money through a beaded curtain at the end of the bar, then to a metal-buttressed wooden door. The man opened the door. They went in, then he closed the door behind them.

The sun watched them. The taxi stopped. The driver explained that, because of the flood, this was as far as he could take them. Dan opened the door of the cab and looked down at the yellow water coursing like a river through the street, almost up to the running board of the ancient car.

"Oh, what fun!" Peggy said. She pulled her stockings off.

"I'm glad it's fun," Dan said, "because it's the only way to get back to the hotel."

She laughed and climbed over him to get out and into the water first. "You don't know the first thing about wading. Go on, take off your shoes and socks. Ooo! It's cold!" She laughed.

Dan rolled his trousers above his knees. "Hey! Wait!" He took his shoes off and tied the laces together and slung the shoes around his neck. He put his socks in his pockets. "I don't know anything about wading."

"I'll race you," she yelled, well ahead of him. She began to stride forward through the knee-high water, her skirts caught up in front of her with one hand, her shoes in the other, her pinknesses making small turbulences as she cut through the moving stream.

"Hey, Peggy! Wait! Wait for me!" He felt so marvelous that he, too, began to laugh when the icy water gripped him about both legs. He was fully ten yards behind her when he started, but she moved so easily, yelling back over a shoulder as she moved along what must have been the center of the street, that she increased the distance. "Wait till we tell Carrie about this," she called. "She'll burn that school down for keeping her there."

Dan heard voices shouting from somewhere behind the taxi. He turned and saw two policemen racing forward, shouting, *"No, señorita! No! Las alcantarillas están abiertas! Las alcantarillas! Señorita!"* Somewhere a woman screamed.

Confused, Dan turned toward Peggy. She was moving ahead steadily, but she was looking back at him, smiling her blessed and beautiful smile, saying "Come with me, darling, come with me" when she fell into the open sewer and disappeared forever to sleep on and on, somewhere far, far out to sea.

Weave costly songs. Tell me things so majestic in their love of us, so pressed into time that they lose their wings for flight. I have tired of empty hours sitting, lamenting, nodding blindly, counterfeiting the coin of my memory. Weave lights with your voice, lights that now seep through the floor of heaven; lights of a price so high that even I, fat with hope, should not find reason with them but only plait, match, and blend want with pride, the balancing weights described by the heavy untrained bridesmaids of longing, who, as we wed tomorrow's shadow, wait there under a horizon we have never seen. Carve deep your graceful marks into the trunk of the tree of my life. Freeze leaves falling from it: a park around it. Invoke a carousel of hours: reprieves revolving and repeating, not ending till the music stops, until I am eased by love into garishness. Weave costly songs. Weave lights with your voice. Carve deep my tree of life. Weave, carve, make a strong roof for the kingdom.

At eleven o'clock that morning, as he talked by radio telephone to Joe Downey in New York, Dan was stricken by poliomyelitis.

X V

It was four months before Dan was well enough, physically and mentally, to leave the Carnaghi Sanitorium, on a Van Winkle hill above the Hudson River opposite West Point, and return to New York to try to start all over again. The tragedy of the loss of wife and legs changed many things for Dan, not alone his impress into inner, utter bleakness, but beyond himself as well. It caused his daughter Carrie to be transformed from child into woman in one swift year. It scourged out of Joe Downey the enmity and dislike he had pressed like a power torch against Dan. It ripped out Dan's surface arrogance as pipes and wires are torn by wreckers out of condemned buildings. It made him grateful for Downey's apologetic offer of a job, even such a job, to help him fill the jars of time until permission came through for him to die. Miss Friendship, the club Downey had once planned to use to bring Dan to his knees, became a sudden chance for salvation from a mission that would have been to stare from a wheel chair into nothing, waiting.

All these things the tragedy changed. It did something else. It created a balancing force, a residue of opposite power. The power sank into Dan Tiamat as a meteor might fall into the lava of a volcano. Its basis was the bitter resentment that he, of all the men walking on the earth, should have been singled out to be so cruelly and senselessly struck. This power was arrogance, of course. Dan's surface arrogance was gone; his inner arrogance he nurtured in darkness.

When he had returned to consciousness in the Havana hospital, he had not been able to forget his impression of Peggy's last steps on earth, along that flooded street, her lovely face turned to him, smiling. His memory of it was a loop of Technicolor movie film running endlessly through a projection machine that he could not reach to disconnect. He had to be drugged to shut off his yelling. Later, they used hypnosis, and the edge of his agony was thickened. They could not make him stop remembering but it ceased being eternally continuous. The images became somewhat blurred and did not threaten his sanity as before.

With the partial withdrawal of that torture, Dan was able to accommodate the agony of the shrinking tendons in his legs. Then, when Peggy's and his own disasters assaulted him as one force, they became, in his mind, fused into a single incontinent injustice on the part of a stern God whom he imagined looking rather like Bernard Baruch with a beard; sex, indubitably male; color, white; religion, Catholic. Thus, the bitter arrogance was forged. He showed it to no one. He took it with him, as it grew, wherever he went. He held it, brackish and poisonous, inside himself the first day he returned to the *Press* to take up his work as Miss Friendship.

He rolled out of the elevator on the editorial floor in his shining wheel chair. He was not sure where to go, but he was sure that the apartment of offices he had had in the far past was not his any more. The receptionist, an Italian girl, Brigida Natale, who had eyes like oiled hummingbirds, saw him but she did not look directly at him.

"Oh! Mr. Tiamat!" She had been alerted when she had come

on duty, and she had been sweating out his arrival for an hour and a half.

"Hi, honey. Where do I go?"

"Why—uh—right this way, Mr. Tiamat." She slid out of her chair and glided hurriedly ahead of him toward the corridor. Virginia Le Fanan Street, the Homemakers Editor, and Bob Landry, the movie critic, happened to appear. Seeing Dan in his wheel chair, they turned around as one soldier to rush back to wherever they had come from. As Dan rolled himself along the hall made by the glass cubicles everyone working in each of the tiny offices seemed to be looking the other way. The receptionist indicated the office that Dan was to occupy, then tried to flee. Dan caught her wrist.

"What's the matter with everybody, Bridge?"

"Oh, Mr. Tiamat! I—everybody—all of us, I mean—we feel so terrible about all your troubles!"

She stared down into his eyes, her own seen as a doe's eyes behind a mist, and they both knew that what nobody could really face was not that his wife had drowned, and not that he had lost the power of his legs, but that an affable murderer had been cut down to less than nothing, that one of the greatest names in the newspaper business was now to be used as a letter clerk for a lot of slobs and jerks. This was what Dan's mountainous bitterness allowed him to see in Brigida Natale's sulphurous eyes. He let go of her wrist and dismissed her by moving his wheel chair forward into the tiny room. The telephone rang. He rolled to it.

"Hi, kid. Joe."

"Yeah, Joe."

"They told me you had just checked in. Everything okay? Is that office all right?"

"Great, Joe. Everything's great."

"The Friendship ad broke yesterday. This morning's mail brought the first letters for you. Ten altogether."

"For me?"

"Yeah. Miss Friendship."

Dan looked across the desk. There was a thin stack of mail dead center on the big green blotter.

"Have you got them?" Downey asked.

"Yeah. They're here."

"All you do is pick three for the first column. Hang some three-line answers on them. That's for tomorrow. Then just route the stuff to Reyes like it was regular copy."

"Sure. Like regular copy."

"Then, if you can—I mean, if you feel like it—maybe you could send sort of a short, personal note to the others. Give them a little aid and comfort like we offered in the ad. You know, just mail them a little note. Okay?"

"Sure, Joe. Certainly. Okay."

"Good. Fine. I'll check you later." Downey disconnected and Dan hung up slowly, staring at the pile of letters on his desk, each one a token of his humiliation, each one a chain to the years of mediocrity to come. He pulled the heavy typewriter table toward him slowly, his seamed face expressionless. He squared up some gray copy paper and rolled it into the machine. He looked into three drawers of the desk until he found a new file folder. On its tab he wrote, with an old-fashioned black fountain pen covered with tarnished gold vines: MISS FRIEND-SHIP (TIAMAT), JULY 19, 1949. He took the rubber band off the packet of letters and marked the first one #1. He read it carefully.

> Dear Miss Friendship: I am going to kill myself. You are the only one in the world I have to tell this to. You don't know me but it will shock you to read this and maybe for one moment someone in the world will care something about me. Good-by,
>
>   Esther Carney

Dan typed his reply, his mouth clamped as tight shut as a purse. His fingers moved without hesitation.

> Dear Esther Carney: You should kill yourself but you won't. Your miserable, cold, sickening little vanity

which permits you to write such disgusting self-pity is
the slow way to kill yourself. You are a whiner and a
faker and the lowest kind of a blubbering nothing who
feeds off the minute charge of power you can get by
thinking you can frighten people by this symbolic suicide. It won't work for just the reason you set down.
Nobody in the world cares enough about you to be
frightened or to react in anyway except with this revulsion and disgust for you which I feel now. Sincerely,
                                        Miss Friendship

He addressed the envelope, stuck the letter into it, sealed it,
then placed the carbon copy of the letter face down in the new
file folder.

He marked the next letter #2 and began to read it, his eyes
as blank as the statue of Laocoön in the Cortile del Belvedere.
The handwriting was spidery, the paper splattered with ink.

Dear Miss Friendship: I am an old lady eighty one yr.
I got 4 suns. I dond have no place to go. I no my suns
wand me but they got hard jobs they to think about
and the families they go to also think. My husbin ded
21 yr. a good man. We marrit 65 yr. next month. For
everybody remember my husbin I want all suns to-
gedder dinner 1 night. How can I do that? Truly yours,
                                  (mrs.) Ernia Mae Phillicoe

Putting the letter face down on the file folder, Dan turned
to the typewriter. The sunlight came through the high panes
of the window like a yellow pipe from the sky to form a bright
nimbus around his head.

My dear Mrs. Phillicoe: You are a lucky old woman.
In most societies you would have been killed by your
family long before this. In some of the Arab cultures
they bury their old people alive or leave them out to
starve to death because, as you know better than I will

ever be able to tell you, the old are useless and you are very old. Instead of wasting the time and the money of your sons and disturbing their wives and children, why don't you tell each son you will take ten dollars a week from each one to stay out of their lives? With forty dollars a week you will be welcomed by most social agencies, as they are all big philanthropists, too. Go sit around with a lot of other useless old people and complain about what your children have done to you, with never a word or a question about what you did to them. Your job is finished. Let go gracefully and give your grandchildren a chance at some mental health by staying away from them. Sincerely,

Miss Friendship

Dan pulled the page briskly out of the machine, signed it, folded it, and slid it into an envelope. He addressed the envelope, sealed it, and tossed it into the OUT basket. He clipped the carbon of his letter to Mrs. Phillicoe's letter and placed it in the file folder.

He opened the next letter and wrote #3 neatly across the top of it. He answered it. He numbered and answered the fourth letter. Then he read and processed number five.

Dear Miss Friendship: I have to talk to someone or write to someone. It is tearing my heart out and I don't know what to do. My husband is a wonderful man in every way. He is a kind man, Miss Friendship, who would do anything in the world for me, but he has this one thing in him which he cannot always keep under control. He has set fire to our drapes and bedspreads twice in one month. He does it only when he is feeling happy. He never drinks. He wants only to be with me. He is a man who works very hard; perhaps too hard. I ask if you think if we went to the country and we burned things in the woods in the country, it would help him to get this thing out of his system. He doesn't know why he does it. He hates it. I mean when it is all over he hates himself for having done such a thing. He wants to stop it somehow and although I would swear forever that he would never do one thing to hurt a hair of my head, I am afraid if this should come over him again and he cannot fight it, he will set fire to the bedclothes when I am asleep. I take caffeine pills so that I can wake up at the slightest sound. Can you recommend a pill that will work even better? I am sorry to bother you with my troubles but I needed desperately to say this to someone.

Edna Kennan

Dear Edna Kennan: Your husband is insane. I will give you exactly three days to start the machinery to have him committed to an insane asylum or I am going to have this newspaper move in with all of its power to see that he is put away where he cannot endanger the lives of all those who live around him, in the building with him, and in the houses adjoining it. Because of your sodden, maudlin selfishness, people are being endangered. Your husband will be put behind bars with other crazy people where he belongs. Sincerely,

Miss Friendship

He read more letters and answered them, his face tight with disgust. He filed his carbon copies with the efficiency of a Nazi major of the *Sicherheits Dienst* issuing receipts for the dead. He struck at his supplicants, then struck again and again, bludgeoning them with the dripping stumps of the arms of their hopes upon the starved faces of their dreams.

When he put the last answer, sealed and addressed, in the OUT basket and called for a copy boy to pick up and mail, he leaned forward on the desk and buried his face in his folded arms.

Grandpa Downey had moved into the big apartment on Fifth Avenue while Dan had been away in the sanitorium, so that Carrie could comfort him after her mother's death. Very quickly he returned to the pattern of 1928, when Peggy had been twelve years old, and the great fountain of his interest had flowed and sparkled. Carrie looked very much like her mother and through that wonderful example had learned her mother's graceful, gentle movements and expressions. The deep, scalding grief Downey felt over the loss of his daughter vanished under Carrie's ministrations, and the four months he spent with his granddaughter were the second happiest set of days in Downey's life. He recreated all of the diversions and discussions he had had with Peggy when they had been very young. He spent less time at the paper than he had in thirty years and didn't care whether it could run itself or not. They went to theaters, to movies, to ball games, on boatrides, and to concerts in the park. The twelve-year-old Carrie realized her most affluent dream, a ride through the park in a horse-drawn carriage once a week with her grandfather. Because he got great pleasure out of her pleasure, he wanted them to take the carriage ride each evening, but she thanked him, declining, saying that she could not enjoy it as much once a week if she rode in a carriage every day.

Every Sunday they borrowed Charley O'Neil's limousine and drove sixty-two miles north to visit Dan in the sanitorium. He was very hard on all of them for the first three months. Carrie was so much like her mother that Dan could not look at her without feeling anguish, which screwed up his face like a chimpanzee's and left him limp with self-pity after she had gone. Downey, who had had the best of the Peggy-become-Carrie vision, understood mistily what he thought Dan must be feeling. After the first visit, when Dr. Youngstein had given Downey and Carrie his progress report on Dan, as they rode back to New York in the big car, Downey wondered how to explain her father's condition to Carrie.

"Daddy's legs must hurt him very much," Carrie said, looking out the window and trying to sound casual. "I never saw him cry before."

"I don't think the pain in his legs is why he cried," Downey said tentatively.

"Then *why?*" She swung around to face her grandfather. "Because of Mommy?"

"Yes. I think that is partly why."

"Did the doctor tell him he won't ever be able to walk again?"

"Yes. That makes him feel badly, but it wouldn't make him cry. What happened to your mother makes him feel very badly, but I don't think—it wouldn't make him cry so suddenly. I mean, I don't think so."

Carrie stared at the back of Charley O'Neil's chauffeur's head for some time. "Do you think I could be the one who is making him cry?"

"Why?"

"I could remind him of Mommy. And because he won't be able to walk, it might make him feel that I might be disappointed because he was different from other fathers. Both those things together could make him cry. Couldn't they?"

"Yes, they could."

The following Sunday when they got to the sanitorium Carrie asked her grandfather if he would like to visit with old Dr. Youngstein while she went in to see her father. Downey said that sounded like a good idea.

She kissed Dan, then sat down next to his bed, her head at a level with his head as he lay on his back. He lay with his eyes closed. She came directly to the point.

"Daddy, I've been thinking all week how badly you must feel because I look so much like Mommy. I looked at one of her pictures and all of a sudden I realized that I *do* look very much like her, and I can guess how terribly hard that must be for you."

"No!" He moved as though he would try to sit up in the bed, but then fell back. "Please, sweetheart. That's not true. It isn't.

It's a blessing. Don't say that. How wonderful it is that you look like Mommy and that I can see just a little bit of Mommy when I see you. But, I see *you*. Mostly *you*. You are your own person, yourself altogether and wonderful, not Mommy. Please don't say that, Carrie darling. I can see what you *mean,* of course. I can see how that might occur to you, but it just isn't correct or in any way accurate, darling girl. No, no. Not at all. It couldn't be. Don't you see that it could never be that way?"

"Yes. Daddy. I see. I'm glad."

"Don't cry, sweetheart."

"I'm not. Really I'm not. My eyes just got fogged up, that's all. Because I love you and I think that you are worrying so much about your legs and—and other things."

"I won't worry any more. You give me much more than the power of my legs. Much, much more."

"Oh, Daddy!" she cried. She stood up and threw herself into his arms. "You always make me so happy!"

The evening of the day Dan wrote his first ten Miss Friendship letters, as he and Carrie and Downey ate dinner at the apartment, Downey was full of Dan's first day back at work. Carrie was quieter, listening.

"How were those first letters I sent along, Dan?"

"Pretty awful."

"Sad, you mean?"

"Embarrassing. Even disgusting. I don't know how people can possibly get anything out of washing their dirty laundry in public like that."

"What kind of letters *were* they, Daddy?"

"Well, you have to know these kind of people, hon. I mean if I just told you about the letters you might think the end of their world had come. Complaints and whining? You never heard anything like it. All to get attention for themselves. That's all. Just to get a little attention for themselves."

"But—why would they want to get *that* kind of attention for themselves?"

"Like I said, you have to know these kind of people."

"People get lonely, Carrie," her grandfather said. "They don't have anybody to talk to so they might write this kind of letters just to sort of visit with somebody."

"But what *kind* of letters?"

"Just slops," Dan told her. "The first was from a woman who ranted on and on about how she was going to kill herself. Probably she's been writing that same silly letter every week for years to every newspaper and magazine in the city. And maybe there are some people who would go rushing over there to her when they get a letter like that. But not me. No, sir. Not me."

"How did you answer her, Daddy?"

"Oh, I sort of kidded her along. I told her she wasn't fooling anybody. You know, these kind of people can get pretty sloppy about getting a lot of attention, and all that foolishness is pretty darned disgusting when you have to read it in a letter from a stranger."

"What did the other letters say?"

"Well, one bordered on the criminal side. This woman who wrote it said her husband was always setting fire to things in their apartment and she was afraid he might burn her to death while she was sleeping. Burn *you* to death, I told her—he just might burn a lot of innocent people to death, I said, and I gave her exactly three days to report the situation to the police and have that man committed to an insane asylum. Or, I said, the *Press* would have him committed. Can you imagine such a thing?"

"I never thought we would get *that* kind of letters," Downey said slowly. "I thought they would just be letters from a lotta lovesick kids."

"Well, they aren't," Dan told him. "What you need in that spot is some psychiatrist or a social worker or something."

"But can't you help any of those people, Daddy?"

"Oh, sure. Some of them. Some are perfectly normal people, I suppose, but what I can't stand are fakers and goldbricks. The best thing you can do with people like that is to be tough. That takes the exhibitionism out of them. They catch on."

There were no letters for Miss Friendship in the next day's mail, but it was the first day the Miss Friendship department appeared in the paper, and the sight of the functioning entity was what would generate letters from readers. Dan figured that he would soon be able to settle down with the full, irritating routine of his job.

He ate his lunch in his wheel chair at his desk. At one-thirty the receptionist telephoned to say that a Mr. Hubert Phillicoe and his brother, Mr. Alexander Phillicoe, were outside to see him. Dan said to send them in. The name was familiar. He riffled through the correspondence file and found the letter from the old lady with the sons who begrudged her her life.

The door to his office crashed open. It hit the partition so hard that the glass in the door shattered. Dan wheeled around. Two tall, well-dressed young Negroes stood there. They were breathing heavily.

"Where is she?" the taller one demanded.

"Who?" Dan answered stupidly.

"Miss Friendship! Where the hell is this Miss Friendship?"

Drawn from their desks by the noise of the crashing glass and the shouting, *Press* employees began hovering behind the Negroes. Joe Downey, wearing a straw sailor hat, came elbowing through the knot of people like a giant, fleshy termite. "What the hell is going on here?" he snapped. "Who broke that door?"

"I did. Me," the tall Negro said. "Who the hell are you? Where is this Miss Friendship?"

"I run this newspaper," Downey barked. "And that's Miss Friendship right there. What the hell did you break the door for?"

The two young men rushed at Dan. One lifted his great

torso right out of the chair by the lapels of his jacket. "A goddam cripple," he said. "Wouldn't you know it would be a mean,
goddam, hate-thinking cripple would write a letter like that to
an old lady. You dirty, low, cowardly cripple." He dropped
Dan from a height into his chair. Dan was bewildered. He did
not understand what was happening. Downey, with the fierce
expression of a belligerent mother cow, rushed in and pulled
one of the men away from Dan while the other said threaten-
ingly, "A cripple, nothin' but a goddam sick, low cripple. Oh,
you lousy, low son of a bitch!"

"What's *happening?*" Downey yelled. "Why are you *behav-
ing* like this?"

The tall Negro handed him a sheet of paper. "Where's our
mama? That's all, little man. You just tell us where's our
mama."

Downey read the letter. Then he stared with a bloodless face
at the young Negro before he looked slowly over at Dan. "You
write this letter?" he demanded in a choked voice. He handed
the letter to Dan. "Just make sure. Read it and tell me. Did you
write this letter?"

Dan looked at it. "Yes," he said. "Yes, I wrote it." His face
had flushed deeply. As he looked at the words it was as if he
were seeing them for the first time. He could not lift his eyes
above the level of the knees of the people who were around
his chair and in the corridor.

"All right," Downey said to the young men. "He did it.
Later on I'll try to think of why he did it and how he could
have brought himself to do it. In the meantime, you two come
to my office. We're gonna get every cop in this town out to
find your mother, but let me tell you this: a lady who can keep
going and stay interested for eighty-one years of age, and get
two of her boys upset enough to take on the biggest newspaper
in this city, is not going to do anything that sounds like quit-
ting, because she don't know how. You gotta believe that. Now
come along with me." He held them both by the arm and
moved them out toward the corridor. "All right, everybody,"

he barked, "back to work. This isn't a sideshow." The knot of people broke up. Downey started the two young men toward the City Room and his office.

"One moment, please," the taller one said. He broke free from Downey, returned to the shattered door, looked coldly at Dan, and then spat at his feet.

"I made a mistake! I made a terrible mistake!" Dan yelled after him. He stared at the two Negroes moving off with Downey beyond the distorting glass walls. The telephone rang. Reflexively his hand went out for it. The receptionist told him that a Miss Esther Carney, who had an appointment, was on her way along to his office. As he put the phone down, a thin woman with mottled skin and watery blue eyes was coming in the door. "Are you—is this the right office?" she asked timidly. "I'm so sorry. I was looking for Miss Friendship."

"I'm Miss Friendship," he said hoarsely. "Are you the Miss Carney who wrote yesterday that you were going to—" As he spoke she continued daintily across the summer-warmed room to the open window, which was thirteen stories above the street. She climbed carefully up on a chair and stepped across the radiator to the sill.

"*No!*" Dan screamed.

She ducked under the half-open window and rolled her body over until it fell downward, out of sight. Her scream streamed behind her like a ribbon of colored paper.

XVI

In the early summer of 1959, when Dan was fifty years old, the buildings and pavements of New York reflected sheets of heat that wet everything with their heaviness. Thirteen million people were embedded in the heat. Their mass stretched for fifty-five miles in the horizontal directions. They existed in eighty-nine million steaming rectangular rooms where, every evening of every year, an average of sixty-four people hanged themselves because of loneliness. The inner millions, at the center point from which the fifty-five miles of mass was reckoned, lived upon a heated rock that was twelve miles long and, at one place, two miles wide. New York had become a city mutated beyond the original meaning of any city into the most ominous meaning of all cities. Within it, living had become a palindrome.

One thousand three hundred and forty tons of soot, stuffed with unlikely amounts of radiation distributed under the brand name of strontium 90, fell upon every square mile of New York every year. Six hundred and ninety-three thousand dogs soiled its avenues, which were scarred with the debris of seventy million death-inducing cigarettes each half-day and nine million two hundred forty-seven thousand wads of chewing gum. Tens of thousands of tall buildings were arranged in attitudes of rigid suspicion. They stared from five million sightless eyes at either side of the endless streets, incapable of forgetting what they could not see. To the north lay the city's shame, to the south its greed, to the east its pride, to the west its past, where cockroaches gummed yesterdays in thirty-nine thousand two hundred and six furnished rooms. The thirteen million prisoners of this delusion scurried across it with desperate haste, as though in panic or pain, like old people in a pogrom.

The Press building was on the east side of the city. From the south windows of the City Room there was a good view of lower Manhattan, part of Brooklyn, some of New Jersey, a confluence of rivers and an expanse of harbor through which millions of people could all have escaped any dark night.

In the City Room the old-fashioned flat-bladed fans turned slowly from the ceiling. Everyone seemed wet with sweat, dampening everything he touched. Two rewrite men typed in their undershirts. Copy boys wore handkerchiefs around their foreheads. Some men had trouble breathing. Some faces were pale and some were bright red.

Jolly Times O'Neil, the younger brother of Charles O'Neil and a full partner in the *Press's* ownership, had been Promotion Manager for nearly two years now. The paper was eighty-six years old. Jolly Times was twenty-four. He had tripped through life lightly, careening on the silver roller skates of youth, pursuing Hope, which was built close to the ground with a wet, black nose and a fine high tail, like a dachshund. Jolly Times was the first Promotion Manager the paper had ever had, and he had come to his job when the third generation took over the business department. His office, which was eight times the size of a regulation telephone booth, was always disorderly. Among the masses of printed matter on his desk, two telephones could just be seen. Into the small area he had managed to cram two of the claimed tools of his craft, a table-model radio and, separately, a twenty-one-inch television set.

Jolly Times's work was anomalous. He was a press agent for the paper. He supervised pistol-shooting competitions among city policemen so that the grateful Police Department would tell the *Press* first if anything really good happened. He managed amateur dance contests. He advised a rehabilitation center that attracted only a few juvenile delinquents because the psychiatric social worker gave them such a bad time. He was chairman of a panel of citizens who examined the election promises of the two major parties every year, with one-half supporting the Democrats and the other half supporting the Republicans so that the outcome was always predictable and not controversial. He was also a director of an outfit called the National Parent's Forum, whose influence extended as far as Teaneck, New Jersey. The fact that the *Press's* Promotion Department was new and excessively active had given it no more muscle than the same department on other papers. Joe Downey had said they weren't ready yet to give the paper away to any press agent, even if the very plotter who seemed to threaten integrity happened to be paid by the paper.

The younger O'Neil had received his enduring nickname, Jolly Times, from Downey. During his first week as Promotion Manager he had insisted that on his last job, wherein he had assisted in sending aloft a passenger balloon in Paris for an

American film company, he had had an expense account. Downey had told him that the *Press* didn't believe in old-fashioned nonsense like expense accounts for promotion managers.

Jolly Times's legal name was Francis Xavier. He was a tall, skinny, extremely attractive young man whose permanent expression was that of a farmer's youngest son wandering around a carnival grounds trying to figure out the shell game; which is to say he resembled most other young men of twenty-four. Jolly Times was ambitious, which was a good thing because he came from a family that had the habit of success, but he was not yet clear what his ambition would be when it revealed itself; it had life but no useful shape as it lay within his impatience waiting to be born. He had no way of disarming the gnawing suspicion that he would suddenly and disappointingly be seventy-seven years old. He was aware that he had been six years old only a reasonably short time ago, and running like hell, pursued by an older playmate who was trying to split open his small skull with a sailboat. He had the annoying conviction that time would continue to be just so quixotic, and that then, when a great deal of it had passed, there would be far too much time for looking back, for searching for the meaning he was afraid he was going to miss.

The working area of the *Press* was a desk-packed, paper-strewn conception of order through disorder, covering an area of approximately two acres. In a U-shaped fringe around it were transparent cubbyholes in which some of the feature people sat. Jolly Times's office was furthest away from everything. When he stood up at his desk in his glass box he stared through the two glass partitions to where Dan Tiamat wrote his Miss Friendship letters.

Dan did not yet know that he was Jolly Times's antagonist. No matter how ingeniously Jolly Times had designed promotions to utilize the Miss Friendship Department, Dan kept telling the management that he would not let the people be exploited by such idiocy. His people were stained and ex-

hausted, he had said flatly, and he would not let them be used
as promotion geishas by a half-baked kid.

Jolly Times had never spoken to Dan face to face, because
Dan had taken down a big reputation in his day and this made
Jolly Times feel shy. He made his representations through
Downey. Jolly Times's natural reactions to these continuing
failures were not against the quality of his promotion ideas.
Instead, he decided that Dan Tiamat was against him. He
came to resent Dan so deeply that he acquired a compulsion to
watch him work through the glass partitions. The conflict
sharpened him in his professional capacity. After much brood-
ing, he finally stumbled onto a dodge that Joe Downey agreed
to let him take in to Dan for approval.

The day it came to him he was staring at Dan's meaty, battered, committed face as it flinched under the whispered agony
coming from a young woman whose lips moved incessantly like
a pilgrim's over beads, whose extinguished eyes seemed to have
been sketched on her face with a soft pencil by a bathroom
artist. While Jolly Times watched them through the glass partitions the radio beside him gurgitated the lyrics and melodies
that would tell future anthropologists so much about his civilization. Jolly Times could see Dan's hand hanging down at his
side, out of sight of his visitor. It was clenching and unclench-
ing. His face was wet. His mouth was rigid. There were dark
stains on his thousand-mile blue shirt. His face was florid with
small purple veins. His permanent expression was that of a
mute forced to watch a spinal operation on a patient who has
been denied an anesthetic.

The promotion idea came to Jolly Times. Abruptly, he
dialed Joe Downey's intercom number.

"Mr. Downey? Frank O'Neil. Can I see you?"

"What about? I'm jammed."

"I have a terrific promotion idea for Miss Friendship."

"What are you, kid? Some kind of a masochist?"

"Mr. Downey, if you tell me you won't take this idea into
Mr. Tiamat after you hear it, I promise you I will never bring

you another Miss Friendship gimmick. Okay? Is that fair
enough?"

They flicked a small amount of silence at each other. "That
is not only fair enough, it is extremely tempting," Downey said
at last. "You have my permission to take your last idea to
Tiamat personally." He disconnected. Bemused, Jolly Times
stared at the telephone in his hand.

The young woman two offices away held Dan's eyes with
her own as though she might die if he so much as turned away.
Her lips moved steadily but with slight action. Her voice was
soft and monotonous. She had been over her story to herself
so many times, unable to find any meaning in it, that it had
come to have a mercifully hypnotic effect upon her. She rocked
almost imperceptibly as she spoke, her roughened hands held
in her lap. She was young, but her dark hair line was receding.
She wore too much rouge and she had missed her mouth's edges
on the left side with the lipstick. Her face was finely boned,
but more tubercular than aristocratic. Her vocal tones were as
aspirate as dry leaves in a down draft:

"And then I had the third baby. He hates the kids. His own
kids. We had three of them, the most beautiful kids you ever
saw, but he hates them. What am I gonna do? Nothing? What
can I do? Nothing. It's like a big joke on me. I thought marriage
was gonna change him. Everybody else can change their husband. I love him. He knows it. Even if only in some little ways
he would change. But not him. He can't change. I'm not complaining about that part and I'm not being sarcastic. If he can't
change, so he can't change. He comes home every night from
his job, that I got to say for him. He comes home and he sits.
He won't even look at TV. He won't read a newspaper. If I
talk to him or if one of the kids talks to him he wouldn't pay
any attention. Finally, when this happens, we are at my
mother's, which is on the island, fourteen months ago. I make
him take the little girl for walk because he hates my mother
and I figured it's better if they get out of the house for a while

and take a little walk. It's in the country, my mother's, but it's still nice. So they take a little walk but he don't touch her, the baby. She's two and a half years old, a little baby, so beautiful. He don't care where she's going or what she's doing and she falls in the water. In the little river there. My baby. She drowns in the little river there."

Standing beside his radio, Jolly Times watched this as a distant pantomime. After a long time, the young woman stood up, a welcome bit of action. Dan said something to her. Jolly Times moved out of his office. He waited until the young woman, whose grief made her a leper to the lucky, got a five-yard start toward the elevators, then he walked along the corridor to Dan's open door, took a deep breath, and knocked resolutely on the glass pane. Dan looked up from his wheel chair with dull eyes.

The Miss Friendship office was a little larger than Jolly Times's but it looked smaller because Dan Tiamat's working tools took up a lot of room. Prominent was a large carton of vitamin complex tablets. Next to that was a carton of men's black cotton socks with white feet; three pairs of the socks hung over the edge, held together with a white rubber band. In a corner of the office another cardboard carton held ten gross of packages of individual servings of dehydrated soup in four flavors, including dietetic salt-free minestrone. Disorderly stacks of the paper-back editions of Norman Vincent Peale, and Bishop Sheen, their covers commercially gay, were lined up against the wall opposite Dan's desk. On the floor and on the far side of the desk, almost out of sight, were two cases of half-pint bottles of rye and gin. (The reformed Dan never drank from these; the liquor was on hand to tonic some of his more distraught readers.) The office smelled like a general store, with something added: the effluvia of many different kinds of people who perspired grief and exhaled misfortune.

Rising above the piled paper debris on the desk was the framed picture of a pretty, young blond woman standing beside a great, grinning hulk of a man at a ship's rail. They were waving. They had movie-star teeth. The woman held the man with her entire left arm linked through his right arm, leaving no doubt as to who belonged to whom and as to the length of the lease.

"Yes, son?" Dan said tonelessly at the knock.

"Mr. Tiamat—uh—I'm Frank O'Neil. Promotion Department."

"Come in, Frank."

Jolly Times moved crab-fashion through the piles, stacks, and bundles and was gestured into the chair facing Dan. "I was watching through the partitions," he said. "That girl could certainly talk."

"Yeah," Dan answered laconically, "her husband is murdering their children. Two gone so far. One left. It was out in the reception room because she's afraid to leave it alone. What can I do for you?"

"I'm sorry. I didn't know."

"Forget it. What can I do for you?"

"I—um—well, something absolutely electric occurred to me a little while ago. I haven't really thought it through, but since I know I will never get another idea to top this idea, I called Mr. Downey and said if this idea wasn't accepted, I would never come back with another one for your department."

"I see."

"Anyway, he didn't even ask me what it was. He sent me right to you. I mean, after seven straight turn-downs."

"What's the idea you have?"

"Please try to keep an open mind, Mr. Tiamat."

"Shoot."

"The tenth anniversary of the Miss Friendship feature is just about due."

Dan blinked.

"My general idea," Jolly Times said, "would be to round up the first ten people who wrote in for help and give them a nice birthday party at some hotel."

Dan's face sagged out of an intelligent expression into no expression at all.

"We'll get some great human interest copy out of it," Jolly Times said, "and I know we'll get real TV coverage, and the way I figure, it answers any objections like you used to have because all these people will be ten years away from their troubles so nobody can get hurt."

Dan's face had turned as white as marble, then as white as milk.

"Whatsa matter?" Jolly Times asked.

"Get out!" The old-time snarl had come back into Dan's voice.

"But, Mr. Tiamat—"

"Out! Out!"

Jolly Times's hands lifted in silent supplication for an instant, then he dropped them. The young man stared at Dan for an instant, looking as though he were going to curse him, then he turned and shuffled out of the office. He walked slowly along the corridor to his cubicle. About ten minutes later he went to the elevators and punched the DOWN button savagely.

After the Promotion Manager left him, Dan slumped forward in his wheel chair facing the framed photograph on his desk. He licked his lips, staring dully, then he let his hands decide for him. The right hand dipped downward out of sight, then reappeared holding a half-pint bottle of gin. The left hand took the cap off it, solicitously and unobtrusively, then stripped the broken plastic seal neatly away from the neck of the bottle. It raised the bottle to his mouth and tipped it. His head went backward obligingly. He gulped the gin in rapid swallows until the glass flask was half empty. It had been seven years since he had drunk anything stronger than soda pop. He jerked the wheel chair around so that Peggy could not stare at him from the photograph. Within himself he shrank from the atonal singing that rose from deep inside the invisible casket of his fear. It was a casket without locks, containing nests of boxes built of the coldest stone. He belted at the gin again then tried to kid himself out of the coldness and the fear by saying aloud to the empty room, "Excuse me if I taste not thy muse, nor join thy carols with my usual glee."

He had come to the end of his journey because time had completed its great circle.

Jolly Times tunneled through the heat on the streets. It seemed like no other heat. It melted the city's lust for privacy. People slept on fire escapes in dirty underwear, or they slept like rows of disordered vegetables in the parks, and they conversed as vegetables might converse—about what Nature had brought them today and what tortures or relief she might send tomorrow. The summer city was like the hell people had long been promised by their clergy. The sealed trains moving under the streets compounded the body heat of the millions they carried. The heat reached into the minds of everyone trapped in that city, and part of each mind was lost forever, burned away. People were pressed into each other to stare blindly at each other's stinging, glistening faces. Some tried to screen out all images of themselves by holding up newspapers that told them of murder, violence, lust, greed, fall-out, and of children maiming their teachers in the public schools. Many relinquished hope for peace in the world as they lost it within their minds. *How can I love you, dearest Lydia, until I can love myself?* The enforced pitch of hatred for self and the hatred held by their images pressing from all around, grew and grew until the world no longer seemed quite so tragic in its daily pursuit of its own destruction. Each man within himself became the reason for the end of the world, never understanding, ever deploring from whence all this hatred and this gnawing need for killing could have come.

Jolly Times had not had any practice at losing. He thought about the 50 per cent of the stock he owned in the *Press* and he felt mean as he stared into a highball glass in the mahogany-lined saloon. He was a co-owner of the paper and he didn't

even have the muscle to put through a lousy lonelyhearts promotion. If he pressed his authority, people would begin calling
his brother and threatening to quit, then Charley would get
sore at him and that would be no good. Jolly Times didn't like
to drink but he didn't know what else to do when he felt
bitter. He had always tried to link his psyche with that of the
late Humphrey Bogart, and it figured naturally that Bogart,
thwarted beyond a chance of unthwarting himself, would head
for a bat and a jukebox. Jolly Times wondered briefly how
things would be changed in the world if every time the Good
Guy in movies got his elbow into the wringer he headed for
a public library instead of a saloon.

The manufactured coldness of the saloon wrapped its legs
around Jolly Times and stuck its tongue down his throat. The
whisky, the merciless heat waiting outside, and the unhealthy
cold all plaited themselves across his mind while the apple-
cheeked bartender polished glasses and whistled fake folk songs.

Jolly Times paid for the three drinks, left a quarter on the
bar, and decided to go back to work as if nothing had happened. If he didn't go back right away, he wouldn't feel like
going back tomorrow, and heaven only knew where a thing
like that could end and where it would leave him. He stepped
into the heat outside the saloon and moaned as he plowed
slowly through its viscosity. For a young man and a rich man,
Jolly Times was frugal. He ignored the cruising taxis and
moved toward a bus stop at the open stretch of sidewalk nearby.
A bus rolled to a stop before him. He moved toward its opening door. Seven maniacal women materialized magically, as
they do at all bus stops in New York, elbowing him back, away
from the bus and out of their course. Each woman fought
against the others to board that bus as though it were the last
transportation to safety before the arrival of an advance patrol
of enemy troops, or as if it were a mythical love-ferry that had
been fitted out by a sensual fantast and was known to set out
without warning only once every ten years, stocked with aphro-

disiacal viands and rare wines and staffed by insatiable Greek
youths who lived only for physical love under the roof of that
bus where anything could happen and everything did.

In the end there wasn't room for Jolly Times. Angered and
disgusted, he took a cab. The cab crept slowly across town.
He stared out at the mire of people stretching out in every direction around him, and he allowed himself to see that each
mote in that mire was grimly intent upon causing something to
empty the city of people and sound. Not until it lay as silent as
a vine-bearded Mayan capital, mourning its nine thousand
miles of empty streets, warted with waiting gadgets, tunneled
by its uncountable and incomprehensible mazes of pipes,
mains, and sewers, would the real meaning of this city be
found. Two centuries after the mire of people had succeeded
in willing destruction upon themselves, those left alive far out
toward the prairies, inbred with spoiled genes, could come east-
ward and sit with their legs dangling over the edge of the New
Jersey Palisades to contemplate the rock on which thirteen
million people had swarmed and struggled against each other
to survive in hate, becoming more and more murderously hys-
terical in their mass will to be destroyed; planting money, growing money, and harvesting money until at the end they had
only money to feed upon and the taste of it had killed them.
The prairie folk would direct the gaze of their children across
the crystal river to the twisted spears of steel planted in the
rock speaking, pointing them out as the marks of a way of
life that all who had survived must shun.

Jolly Times shuddered. He could not look into the mire
any longer. He closed his eyes and leaned back on the seat.

**Fifty million humans in a huge living room had been
sitting there for years, watching light and shade. When
they had to leave to die, more entered the gloom, all chewing brand names as the heroine got laid. 'Twas monstrous concubinage! Droit de voyeur extended now ten
million times. But who had who and who got paid was
known only to the Frères Warneur and the trade associa-**

tion folk who paid their dues. Does it not seem passing
strange? The mayhem there, the palmistry of lewdness
taught to tots at such low cost? A pod of wattage for a
chair, to enjoy in congress busts of stellar consequence.
But, wait! Keyholes to pain are not all it reaches. It
proves that the possession of money, that reason for paradise, is why we're here; that leeches may try to get it,
therefore the murder season is all year round. As is the
lying, cheating, arson, beating, duping, treason, dishonor,
rape; prayers by mockers, tears from bawds, jeers at
parsons. Don't sit there disaffected, please. We beg, don't
jape.

All these things it teaches. A few amperes a chair is
all we charge. What if that warhead falls bringing fish-
scale skin or iridescent hair? Why, blame the Communists! What if all greenery is charred until singing people
build cults around snake plants in flowerpots, or ferns in
window boxes? Why, blame the Communists! We have
TV! It is not true that if we keep what we've got that we
need to fear that such unlikely things can be.

It is not true that the whole nation will pack into living
rooms, hunched forward toward the brand names in the
dark, listening to lyrics that have set them far back; staring, spittling, at colored fleshy harks, waiting for the
bell to ring, amassing gaily, which would send them
marching to the screens, seeking new thrills, then into the
screens, urged by some hard-sell Barnum and Bailey,
finding their wills; as once those dancing children did
under the Koppelberg Hill.

Twenty minutes after Jolly Times had left the *Press* building and gone to the saloon his brother Charley strolled into
Downey's office and shut the door carefully behind him.

"Hi, Joe."

"Hi, kid."

Charley sat down, somewhat elaborately, self-conscious
over the role he had chosen to play. "I'm not complaining,
Joe," he said slowly and carefully, "and please keep that clear,
but I knew you'd like to know that Dan Tiamat is drinking in
his office."

Downey sat bolt upright, frozen like a tin soldier as the dawn appears. "Drinking? Tiamat?"

"Yeah."

"Drinking *what?*" Downey asked shrilly.

"It looks like gin. From one of those half-pint bottles he hands out to his shook-up readers."

"This is terrible. It's been years. I mean maybe seven or eight years. This could kill him."

"You want to talk to him? Would it help if I talked to him."

"No, thanks, Charley. Time has caught up with him, I guess. We can't black that out, either of us." Downey got up and looked out of the window. "I'll think of something. Let's give him a chance to get a few belts under his belt. Once he starts we might as well. We'll let him go till he passes out, then give him to the doctors."

"I'd be a drunk myself if I did his work," Charley said. "I've watched him in there. Frank talks about him a lot. He sits there and they talk to him. They plead with him but he never answers. He just sits there like a boozy god and stares at them."

Downey turned slowly. "Charley, you're a young fellow and Frank is younger, so I'm going to tell you something. We can talk about him now anyway, while we wait for the gin to work. No use trying to get anything done right now. He doesn't just run a lovelorn department." Downey sat down and looked over at the publisher sadly. "It's a three-way spread the way he has it organized. You probably think everybody he deals with is an idiot."

"Maybe I do. I never really thought about it."

Downey reached over, took up a fresh copy of the *Press,* and flipped it open expertly on the worktable between them. He read aloud. "Dear Miss Friendship: My boy friend hasn't called me for two weeks now and also my father had the telephone disconnected. What should I do? Signed, Perhaps Proud." He looked up at Charley. "That's pretty idiotic, but what the hell, Charley, that little broad is in the same spot as Juliet. We run it because a newspaper is supposed to entertain as well as inform. After that letter comes the tougher part of Tiamat's job. The so-called unorthodox problems. He writes them long letters. Personal. Unpublished. He doesn't have to. We pay him to fill that column, that's all."

Downey leaned back in his swiver chair and stared at the ceiling as he started to talk about the second stage of Dan's work. "Dear Miss Friendship (this kind of a letter goes): I had to write again. Two nights ago when I was fast asleep he came home and he beat me while I was on my back in the bed. I was asleep when he hit me and it broke my cheekbone. He broke my nose while I was laying on the bed with my arms under the covers. I couldn't protect myself. Then, in the morning when he wakes up and he is like sober he don't know what happened to me and he cries when I tell him and he says this can't be because he wouldn't do anything in the world to hurt me. And I believe him, Miss Friendship. That is the terrible part. I mean, he is so boxed in by everything and they have him so scared that maybe I am the only one he can hit, but he doesn't know it when he gets drunk. What do you think, Miss Friendship?"

"Jesus," the publisher said. "Stuff like that actually goes on?"

"It goes on. What the hell, Charley, why shouldn't it go on? And it's only middle-bracket stuff. Take the third part of Tiamat's work: the absolutely hopeless problems, the utterly impossible ones that sneak up from behind the kitchen door on a sunny morning and whack people over the head like an insane, red-nosed clown with an iron baseball bat. Tiamat is pretty expert at these. He's had a few himself. I can still remember one letter he got. I found it on his desk and I read it, and this is how I pay for that—I remember it. 'Dear Miss Friendship: I have twin daughters who are going to be married next Saturday. They are wonderful and beautiful girls. They have been very, very dear girls from the moment they were born. After a routine physical examination, which seemed like such a good idea, the doctor got in touch with me and asked me to come to the hospital to talk with him. He told me in technical terms that they have some form of flash cancer all along the right sides of their bodies. In his opinion they will be dead within two months. I write to ask you whether you think I should permit them to go through with this double wedding next Saturday. If not, how can I tell them? If not, how can I tell the boys who love them?"

O'Neil stared at Downey in horror. He did not speak.

"They are the ones Dan asks to come in to the office to talk to him. Yes, he sits there like a boozy god and doesn't answer them because there is nothing to say." Downey stood up suddenly. "I can't sit here any more," he said. He slammed out of the office and moved rapidly across the City Room. He almost ran along the glass-lined corridor to Dan's cubicle. He went in and shut the door behind him.

"What the hell is the matter with you?" he said.

Dan stared at him dully. "I had a shock. I'm working it out. Get out of here. I'll be all right."

"Not if you drink you won't be all right."

"I stopped. It's over."

"What was the shock?"

"You sent the O'Neil boy in here to tell me about that gimmick."

"The hell with that. What was the shock?"

"He wants to hold a tenth anniversary banquet for Miss Friendship. He wants me to be the host to the first ten people who wrote in for help."

"Jesus," Downey prayed. Turning, he left the office and walked slowly along the corridor and across the City Room. Locking his office door, he cut off his incoming calls. He gazed north over Manhattan Island and began to remember the days when they had thought they would never get Dan Tiamat off the booze. He looked old as he remembered how his son-in-law had blown his corks for sure in England. And now Jolly Times and his gimmick were probably going to ruin Dan all over again.

Not knowing what to do or even where to start, Downey telephoned his granddaughter.

Carrie was enjoying the bathtub part of the afternoon when he called. Before her, on a wide tray, she had letters and note paper, a pen, some magazines, and two chocolate bars. The telephone, which had been brought within reach by its long cord, offered a chance for electrocution in a handsome shade of blue.

Like all young people, like elderly bishops of the Anglican Church, visiting agronomists from the Soviet Union, department-store Santa Clauses, and labor-union leaders, Carrie wore a series of sharp sensations in a secret way. In her mind there were strange, exciting people upon exotic streets. Her vagaries concerning large amounts of money had authority. Her personal popularity in the eyes of every living thing expanded exquisitely like a perfectly sounded musical note. She wore these sensations cautiously because she was still young and not yet intolerant of reality. Like all other young women of her nation and time she pursued the possession of love with the constant, if abstract, preoccupation of any lyric in any popular song. Love was an unknown and faceless man whose suit was pressed and who was desirable to other women.

"Carrie?"

"Hi, Grandpa."

"How's everything?"

"Fine. I'm in the tub." She paused slightly to allow her intuition to catch up with her. "Is Daddy all right?"

"Well, you see—"

"Say it right out, Grandpa."

"Well, he's been drinking." Downey exhaled slowly.

"Grandpa!"

"It's my fault."

"What *happened?*"

"Well, the promotion manager—that O'Neil kid—I let him go directly to your father instead of screening him like I always do, although the last six or seven gimmicks he's come in with certainly have been innocuous enough. I let him go direct because he guaranteed me—"

"But what *happened,* Grandpa?"

"The boy told him he wanted to have a tenth birthday banquet for Miss Friendship and invite the first ten people who wrote letters to your father."

"Oh."

Neither of them spoke for a long moment. Carrie stood up in the tub, water running off her youth, the telephone pressed to her ear. She stepped out of the tub, staring straight ahead, pursuing something across her imagination. Then her eyes closed as if she could not bear to watch what she was thinking. "I'm glad," she said. "I'm glad, Grandpa."

"What?"

"We should have thought of this a long time ago and those psychiatrists should have thought of it, too." She inhaled with deliberate need. "Let's just drag Daddy's terror right out into the open." Tears filled her eyes and her voice trembled. "Oh, Grandpa! After all of the things that have happened to us, we can finally help him. It's out in the open at last where we can finally help him." She hung up absent-mindedly.

Jolly Times strode with self-conscious belligerence out of the elevator on the City Room floor of the *Press.* Riding up, he had begun to think of the day when he and Charley could announce that he was one-half owner of the building and the paper so he could nod pleasantly to the people in the car instead of pretending he wasn't there. He had convinced Charley that wasn't a very good idea while he was only the Promotion Manager and was only paying himself $92.50 a week.

After his three drinks, Jolly Times was flushed from the heat. His clothes were damp and rumpled. He walked slowly and silently along the glass-lined corridor. The City Room was darkened and quiet although a light seemed to be on in Downey's office. Without thinking, as he walked past Dan Tiamat's cubicle and saw him sitting there in the semidarkness, he bounced off his own resentment by stepping in the door and flipping the light switch. Dan wheeled his aluminum chair around silently, his great head sunk into his enormous shoulders.

"Ah. You."

Jolly Times wished he had gone home instead of doing a foolish thing like this.

"What do you want?"

"Wrong office. Mistake. Sorry." Jolly Times tried to back out.

"Sit down," Dan ordered, and Jolly Times surprised himself by doing as he was told. He was sitting where that crumpled young woman had been sitting and talking. He was sitting where all the silly, life-stained people had sat as he had watched them implore at Fate with mumbles.

"What is on your mind, Frank?"

It came out all of a piece, and there seemed to be no way that he could stop his own voice.

"I have never related very well to this business, Mr. Tiamat," he said. "I don't seem to fit into it anywhere, and I put a lot into my work. But, it is a family business so I had to give it the big try. I was an English major at college and the second half of the twentieth century turns out to be no time or place for an English major, although nobody goes to the trouble to explain that. It's about as useful as a degree in Druid recipes. It just happens that nobody is hiring Druid cooks at the moment, or ever will again. And nobody has any place to put English majors. Good heavens, Mr. Tiamat, can you imagine the plight of the guys who studied history or how to be a historian? Who can use them? I happen to like English literature, but if that goddam, little, dead-eyed Admiral Rickover has his way we'll all be ordered to dream in plastic and to hell with learning to read anything but a printed circuit. Good heavens, Mr. Tiamat, who wants to be a space dentist? Can a man who specializes in learning to take off right shoes ever find time to learn how to take off left shoes? I'm kind of mixed up, you might say. I've been watching you through these glass walls for so long that I probably see you as some tin god by now."

The young man rambled on but for a moment Dan stopped listening. Dan was dazzled by the sudden flash of light from a truth he had never been shown before. A tin god. That was it, that was right. He had seen himself as a tin god whose power of arrogance had broken those ten mere mortals who had once turned to him for help. That was how tin gods thought. That was the conscious attitude of a tin god who was as arrogant as ever he had been, the attitude of a tin god who believed in the destructive power of his own curses and tin thunderbolts.

Jolly Times was saying, "What I ought to be doing is something like teaching. A kindly, donnish sort of man, they could say, as I bumbled past under the elms or whatever those trees are that the botanists developed for university towns. Learn to smoke a pipe. Business of dottle and cleaners and never having matches. Become an authority on arctic mosses and lichens or something else abstruse and unassailable. Or, it may turn out that I belong in a monastery. Top man in the human vegetable racket and have all my living done for me. Write endless best sellers under a vow of silence. But I'm not being sarcastic, Mr. Tiamat. I mean it. I want to thank you for letting me see myself by turning me down for the last time on such a useless, fruitless, childish idea as holding a tenth birthday party for a couple of sticks of type."

"I didn't turn you down," Dan told him, slowly and hoarsely. "I turned away from you because I had to think." Dan felt a chill enter his body and his mind. "I accept your suggestion, Frank. We will go ahead with the tenth anniversary dinner."

Downey stood in the doorway. He could not get the picture. He could not understand how these two men could be sitting and chatting so amicably. He stared blankly at Dan because he seemed to be almost sober. "What the hell's going on here?" he asked. Although Jolly Times had not been able to absorb the meaning of what Tiamat had said, he looked up and said, "Mr. Tiamat has okayed the tenth anniversary dinner, I think."

"Dan, is that right?"

Dan nodded his answer, his eyes looking frightened. Downey

pulled up a chair. He popped a huge cigar into his small mouth and put a match to the end of it, turning the cigar and making small puffs that looked like the sounds of a motorcycle. "Well, then," he snapped, "let's get this thing organized."

Jolly Times began to talk rapidly, spilling out his plans. Downey's answers tried to keep up with him, but he addressed everything he said directly to Dan, sure that each remark would be canceled before he could finish it. But when Dan spoke, he spoke slowly, generally affirming, which had the effect of turning Jolly Times into a ball of fire.

"I have to have a Contest Page all my own for not less than ten days," Jolly Times crackled.

"You've got it," Downey answered, watching Dan's eyes. "But no full page. You can have whatever space is left on the Miss Friendship page."

"Left after what? After the Friendship column or after advertising?"

"Of course after advertising. What the hell is the matter with you?"

"Listen, Mr. Downey. I need a lot of space for this dinner. You'll get sensational results with this. I'm going to do an interview with every guest as he accepts."

Dan's voice was hard as he declared, "I invite the guests."

"Yeah, yeah," Jolly Times said impatiently. "This dinner is gonna get this paper big hunks of free, prime television time and maybe I'll even get a sixty per cent discount at the hotel where we'll hold it."

"Sixty per cent?" Downey gaped at him.

"Well, maybe eighty per cent."

"Eighty per cent?"

"After all, Mr. Downey, I can't get it for nothing."

"You can get it for the cost of the whisky! They'll be getting fifty thousand dollars' wortha free advertising."

Dan stopped them, speaking hoarsely. "Do you know that we can find those first ten people. I happen to know that the very first one is dead."

"I'll find the rest. Just let me get started."

"How?" Dan's voice was urgent.

"Don't worry about that part. I'll take care of that part."

"Come on! Come on!"

"Aaah, for heaven's sake, Mr. Tiamat! Telephone books and voter's registrations. Merchants. The post office and social security records. Credit bureaus. Labor unions. The marriage license bureau and the reverse book of the telephone company. Utility companies. Police and parole records. How can anybody escape in the twentieth century? Anyway, why would any of these people *try* to disappear except maybe a couple who might have died?" The words had come tumbling out of him.

Dan nodded solemnly.

"I also happen to control the Contest Page, don't I? I can run provocative stories telling them 'Come in, come in, wherever you are,' and telling other people to look for them, can't I?"

Dan looked at Downey sourly. "And he was just telling me how he doesn't think he relates to this business."

"Yeah. Him and his grandfather, too."

"You free for dinner, kid?"

"Why—uh—yes, sir."

"Come on, then. We'll work on this at my house. Joe?"

"Not tonight, Dan. Thanks."

Downey watched them go, Dan wobbling intensely on his crutches. He waited for the elevator door to clang, then he waltzed around the little office, bellowing a chorus concerning a man named Casey and a strawberry blonde, with his right hand spread out over his heart and his left arm extended stiffly. After that he sat down at Dan's desk in the wheel chair and pretended to knock out one more chorus on imaginary piano keys in the manner of the late de Pachmann. Then he picked up the phone and dialed.

"Carrie?"

"What happened? Where is he?"

"You'll never believe me. He approved the tenth anniversary dinner."

"He—*what?*"

"That boy did it."

"What boy?"

"Jolly Times. The O'Neil boy. I can't tell you *how,* but he did it. Wouldn't take no for an answer. Your father just left with him. He's bringing him home to dinner."

"Bringing him home?" Carrie wailed. "But, Grandpa, I look like the wreck of the Hesperus!"

"What a pity," her grandfather said and hung up softly, grinning from ear to ear. He walked and skipped across the City Room back to his own office. He snatched off his brown working beret, pigeonholed it in his desk, and from a drawer took his straw sailor and put it on at a jaunty angle. He removed the polka-dot bow tie that clipped to his collar and took a dark blue four-in-hand from another pigeonhole, where it had lain wrapped in crumpled white tissue paper, used too many times. He threw the tie around his neck and knotted it while whistling "Sweet Marie." He polished his shoes with a soft cloth, drew on a seersucker jacket, and sang out his good nights to the City Room crew as he left the building.

He stopped at a saloon on Third Avenue for two rye whiskies with a few sips of water and some conversations with the bartender about sciatica, jockeys, the civil-service retirement system, the geology of the Arkansas bauxite region, the Middle East, the Newcastle disease in poultry, sinus infections, and several of the products of the Burpee Seed Company. Although Downey had been patronizing the saloon regularly every evening for twelve years, the bartender had always thought he was a minor leader in the municipal government, employed in the Department of Licenses, although Downey never knew that.

He took the Third Avenue bus north after the second double rye had been put away. When he got off the bus he went into a supermarket and bought a little bit of this and a little bit of that, careful to avoid specials and bargains. As he walked toward Second Avenue on the way to his apartment house, paper bags in his arms, he stopped to pick up all the late opposition papers. He started up alone in the automatic elevator. A woman got on at the third floor to ride to her daughter-in-law's apartment on the ninth. She instructed him to understand that the building was certainly getting run down. He wanted to say "Aaah, shuddup!" but instead gave the impression of agreeing with her. He got off at the fourteenth floor and let himself into his four-room apartment. It was neat because a housekeeper came in every day and made it that way. They rarely met, which was a good thing because they usually had violent arguments over his insistence on shopping for his food. What the hell was he, she would demand, some frowsy little old bachelor, or a big newspaper executive? He would explain the difference between a bachelor and a widower. Did he actually think she would cheat him if she bought the food? Did he? And would he please stop staring at her so meanly with those little blue eyes?

Downey wouldn't trust his housekeeper to buy a soda cracker for him because she was a diet nut. She had made a blooper of a mistake by going to the *Press* one time to get some bail-bond money from him for her nephew, and she had found him wearing that brown beret, and things had never been the same between them since then, because with that head covering and his insistence on doing his own shopping and cooking she had been possessed with the conviction that he had turned effeminate. She had been cleaning his apartment for twenty-three years, and she'd been a favorite third cousin of his wife, but he'd be damned if he'd let any blowsy biddy go out and buy a lot of stuff he couldn't chew or swallow, and then stuff him with a lot of gab about how she was keeping him alive and healthy with a lot of molasses and grass.

Downey lived almost exclusively on ground round steak or frozen imperial crab, canned spinach or string beans, and apple pie with ice cream. He drank a quart or two of skim milk while he read the newspapers or watched television. It was a baffling regime for the woman to observe. The last time he had stared her down about it, she had clamped on her horrendous hat and rushed out of the apartment crying, "What the hell your poor system does for iodine, I'll never know, you little weasel."

By ritual, after he had cooked dinner, eaten standing up, and washed the plate, Downey read the papers, smoked a big cigar, and kept his feet up. He looked at his watch at ten-fifteen, as always. He got up and dressed for the street, just as he had at his office. He met no other tenants as he descended in the elevator. He left the building and walked a block and a half east to First Avenue and into a large granite church on the northwest corner. He was alone in the chapel. He knelt in the gloom in the last pew. It was the half-hour of every day in which he permitted himself to think of his daughter. He knelt in the dark and thought of his beautiful Peggy through all the moments in all those other years when they had both been young and she had all of the life and the warmth and the love that one sweet, sweet child could ever have had.

There is no true present except at the moment of birth and at the moment of death, Downey told himself. He assured himself each night that this was how it had to be because of all of the kinds of time. He was sure the present was the only true mirror for men, but men's faces had grown too ugly for him to allow himself to see himself. Man is allowed to tell himself that he has had beauty in the past. He is permitted to promise himself that he will make beauty in the future. He walks on the treadmill into the future and it rolls behind him, becoming the past. Birth is now, the pure present for a frozen, held instant when the mirror can be used because the face has not grown ugly yet. Death is then, the future forever until it suddenly becomes the threshold of the present that men must cross. Could he bear to look into the mirror then? The present is recurring beads upon a string clasped in a circle, repeating itself again and again. Man looks upon himself at birth, at death, and at birth again; the only moment of the present.

The present was being held out ahead of him now; he would hold it outstretched in his hand before him to illuminate his way from birth to death and birth again. That which he held and which lighted his way was his vanity, called by him his immortal soul.

XVII

Dan Tiamat drove his specially equipped car with the abruptness of flight with which he drove his wheel chair. He wove the car in and out of the ultimate traffic in the ultimate city as though the other cars were fixed warts on the back of a concrete porcupine.

Miles and miles of neon tubing, the veins of the city, had begun to bulge and throb with horrid varicosity, their colors conveying despair. The car inched or zoomed past many faces as Dan cursed it forward and Jolly Times passed the time by wondering just when it could have been that men had thrown up their hands and abandoned any thought of relaxing. The faces were mostly handsome faces, in that well-fed tightness and good health counted for beauty. They refused to look at the other faces as they moved along, but threw fast glances out the sides of their eyes as dust is cast under a rug, as though they were fearful of being charged a large sum of money for looking. Most of the faces looked baffled. Almost all the faces looked suspicious, as though each had had a partner in business and each day more and more money had been unaccountably missing from the till. These were the people who had all been subtly promised a million dollars each by the schoolbooks, newspapers, comic books, television sets, and movies, but who had not received it yet. Their faces seemed to understand clearly, the way very poor children know there will be no Christmas, that somebody must be getting what was promised on every page of the big, slick magazines, but it wasn't them.

It started to rain lightly. Dan felt that he needed a drink as badly as he had ever needed one. He turned the car into the garage under his apartment building at four minutes after eight. They reached the apartment four minutes later and Dan's bawling out by his daughter started two seconds after that. He was pushed off his crutches gently into a wheel chair and rolled into the large, square kitchen. Jolly Times followed, bemused. Carrie dropped to her knees in front of the wheel chair to remove her father's braces. She chided him steadily through it all, but she was so happy to have him home after all her imagination had delivered to her that the lecture was pure banter, mainly concerned with his being a half-hour late for dinner. When she had spent her reproaches, Jolly Times was introduced. With Jolly Times it was a case of *whoooosh!* like a stoker being sucked into a furnace, or like an off-course space ship falling into the sun, soundlesssly and inevitably. Either way, after seeing Carrie Tiamat for the first time, there was no Jolly Times O'Neil left the way he used to be.

Carrie was her hauntingly lovely mother in miniature. She had the right kind of contrasts to demonstrate. She had big eyes and small feet. She had fragile wrists but tenderly swelling thighs under a printed cotton skirt. The top of her head reached a point midway between Jolly Time's elbow and shoulder. The surfaces of her eyes seemed to him to be three-dimensional, and he kept imagining that they conveyed the sound of incessant finger-snapping like a tribe of drunken gypsies working to break a lease. The atmosphere all around him shimmered through new sets of prisms.

"What's the matter with you?" she asked him abruptly, as though he should have had the sense to insist that her father telephone before he brought a stranger home for dinner.

"Me?" he answered dreamily as she moved across the room to the stove. For the moment that was all. Dan guided him along through the pantry so they could wash.

They were seated, at Carrie's orders, at the large, round kitchen table covered with a brightly patterned linen cloth under a brass captain's light. Before they broke bread, as senior male present, Dan undertook to recite the city man's evening ritual. "Today was the second hottest day in thirty-two years," he intoned.

Jolly Times, as junior male present, made the first ceremonial response. "It was not the heat—" Then he paused appropriately.

"It was the humidity," Carrie chanted. The ancient city rite had been completed, permitting them to eat.

Jolly Times accumulated recklessness like a miser snatching at new dimes. He felt the rising sense of power that set the upper rungs of time solidly under his feet, something new for him, a mystery having to do with the recognition of the need to reproduce oneself. His face was pale and his eyes were slitted, as though, unbeknown to its owner, he was in the act of borrowing something he did not intend to return. Carrie could feel his advancing maleness and understood the buttoned recklessness. She was moved by his thin face under the black hair, by the lost nose that defied convention. She pondered the position of his head. It was cocked at a slight angle as though one of the large ears didn't work very well. Or was the floor slanting? She was absorbed as he piled physical movements on top of one another like a skilled croupier working a wheel, raking in chips, then squirting them out again; moves with hands, shoulders, hips, chair, and with his shuffling feet as he sat. She listened intently to his chemical clamor, astonished by feelings of need for him, and she began to think of them both as a flooding mountain stream, rising higher in a stone gorge, ready to roar to get free, to tumble out toward the world and into an unknown sea.

While Carrie and Jolly Times feinted each other cautiously, Dan tried to play the serene host, thinking simultaneously about the threat of the tenth anniversary dinner and his need for whisky. He could almost convince himself that he felt the accusing presence of the first ten supplicants, as though they were in the room, standing behind him, staring. He pretended to eat. He could feel retribution accumulating speed, as though it had donned skiis to escape the huge, threatening glacier of his gelid past. Tenth Anniversary Dinner: he could not stop the words running through his mind like ticker tape stripped from human skin and printed with bile and blood. The integration and disintegration of the past with the present, the fear of the past and the fear of the future, exchanged places again and again like swains at a barn dance, producing patterns and figures that were glazed with the tragic perspiration of Miss Friendship's first unrequited loves. He had to have a drink. He had to get them out of here.

"Mr. O'Neil is Promotion Manager of the paper," he said.

"Really?"

"Call me Frank. Please."

"Everybody at the paper calls him Jolly Times."

"Why?"

"You know the kind, Carrie." Dan shrugged elaborately. "Up all night. Showgirls. Jolly Times."

"That is not true! Mr. Downey happened to name me Jolly Times because I used to be in show business."

"You were?" Carrie seemed happier.

"Yes. In Paris. I helped to launch that balloon from the Place des Invalides for the opening of that *Around the World in Eighty Days* movie."

"You did? Oh, what a wonderful movie!"

"Actually, we launched from the Esplanade des Invalides."

"Well, Daddy is very lucky to have a man of your experience to be running his tenth anniversary dinner."

"Who told you?" her father asked.

"Grandad did, actually."

Dan excused himself from the table quite formally. He turned the wheel chair and glided silently out of the kitchen to the pantry. He closed the door behind him and Carrie watched it close out of the corner of her eye. He found the bottle where he had hidden it years before, inside an old three-quart picnic thermos in a low cupboard. He held it tightly before him and stared at it. Then he began to pull at the cork, slowly at first, then faster. He returned to the kitchen as soon as he could.

"Frank has been telling me about the wonderful plans for the dinner," Carrie said. "What a wonderful idea it is. I've been thinking about it a lot ever since this afternoon and I really think it is a truly wonderful idea."

"Why, thank you, Carrie," Jolly Times murmured.

"It is a very good idea, I think," Dan replied. He was suddenly grateful for his paralysis because he could not get up and run. Carrie felt prayers gather behind her eyes.

"May I see that list again, please?" Dan asked. Jolly Times searched in his pockets and gave his host the list of the first ten letter writers. "Why don't you two go to a movie?" Dan suggested.

"That's all right, Daddy."

"If it's all right with you, sir, I—uh—would very much like to go into the background of these people so we can get sort of a head start on the planning."

"Very well," Dan said in a strained voice. "I'll get the file." He wheeled out of the room almost before he had finished the sentence. Carrie stared at the pantry door as it closed. Then she turned nervously to her guest. "We are certainly grateful to you for thinking of this wonderful idea, Frank," she said softly.

"I've been after your father for a long time to okay a promotion," Jolly Times answered diffidently.

In the pantry, Dan took a deep slug of the whisky. He stoppered the bottle clumsily and returned it to the vacuum bottle shell. He held an office file folder in his lap. He wheeled himself back into the kitchen.

"All right," he said harshly as the chair came to a halt. "Here we go with Number One. Esther Carney." He read aloud in a toneless voice, somewhat rapidly and absent-mindedly. "Dear Miss Friendship: I am going to kill myself. You are the only one in the world I have to tell this to. You don't know me but

it will shock you to read this and maybe for one moment someone in the world will care something about me. Good-by."
He put the letter back into the file. "Esther Carney signed it,"
he said.

"You get *that* kind of letters?" Jolly Times asked in alarm.
"That's awfully emotional stuff. I mean, well, I sort of thought
the letters you got came from lovelorn people."

"I suppose Esther was lovelorn," Dan replied.

"Well, what happened? Did you send the cops to her place
in time to stop her?"

"No."

"What did you do?"

"I sent her a letter. It was the first letter Miss Friendship
ever warmed a lonely heart with. I told her she was a whiner
and a faker."

"What happened?"

"She came to my office so I could watch her do it. She went
out the window. I couldn't stop her."

"My God!" Jolly Times whispered. "And did you answer all
the first ten in the same way?"

Dan put his hand over his eyes. "I didn't know any better
then."

"But you couldn't possibly have helped her, Daddy," Carrie
said. "Please read Frank the fourth letter. Then he'll understand."

Dan shuffled through the letters in the file. "I still get letters
from Number Four about twice a year. She's my stand-by. As
far as I'm concerned she's the only one of the ten that I would
have the guts to meet at your dinner."

"Why is that, Mr. Tiamat?"

"Because I spat on them all and worse than that when they
wrote to me."

"Read the Number Four, Daddy, please."

Dan found the letter and read it to them. "Dear Miss Friendship: I am glad your people decided to give us readers some
place to go for advice. When somebody has been hurt it helps

them to have someone to say what he thinks they should do, whether the advice happens to fit exactly or not. It makes you mean something to yourself when somebody tells you that you have the right to have trouble, that it is all too normal to have trouble, just like everybody else. God sends the trouble to make the good things seem better. My husband is unhappy in his work. This makes him so miserable that it is hard for him to live with himself. He is a fine man."

Dan looked up at Jolly Times. "Number Four always signs herself just 'Loving.' "

"How did you answer a letter like that, Mr. Tiamat?"

Dan grunted like a man taking a punch. "I told her not to bother me. I asked her how many people she thought there were in the world who liked their jobs." Carrie got up abruptly and went to the sink. She ran the cold water faucet for want of something else to do, her back to her father.

"She kept writing to me," Dan continued. "She thinks I'm a dame. Her husband was a drunk. Her husband got sick. We have a lot of things in common, Loving and I."

"Oh, yes?" Jolly Times answered politely. "How's that, Mr. Tiamat?"

"I'm a drunk."

Carrie wheeled around tensely but she spoke smoothly. "That is not precisely true, Frank. Daddy means he *was* a drunk. Once. A long time ago."

"Oh."

Dan spun the chair on its spot, facing the pantry. "I think that's enough of these letters for tonight," he said. "We'll pick up again tomorrow. Good night, children." He rolled rapidly out of the room.

Carrie began to clear the plates from the table. Jolly Times leaped up to help her.

"I noticed that my father has a bad cold coming on," she said.

"There are a lot of summer colds around," Jolly Times said.

Carrie stacked the dishes in the washing machine. He watched her as though she were assembling a language-translation computer. "There *are* a lot of summer colds this year and they are the worst kind to get rid of," she said.

"Would you like to go for a walk? Or maybe hear some music?"

"Well, yes. I think that's a wonderful idea." She steered him out of the kitchen, through the darkened living room, toward the front door. Behind them, the sound of a cork leaving a bottle resounded like a heartbeat in a sepulcher.

While they walked, Carrie was able, without much difficulty, to get Jolly Times talking about himself. In this way she seemed to be an accomplished listener while her mind stayed in the apartment with her father and it pored over ways and means to banish the settling dread.

After a few blocks, walking along the edge of the park on Fifth, Jolly Times thought of a small club she might like because the singer didn't seem to know a single jump tune. Carrie nodded in agreement, not because she had heard his suggestion, but because his face looked as though it expected a nod.

In the café the little man sang in a circle of light. His face was folded in creases of dissipation and he sang to help his audience remember what had never happened, promising a wet, vague unhappiness for everyone in the world, excepting the favored, blessed few who happened to be then assembled in that dark room.

Jolly Times had now found the pace and he talked steadily on about his past, present, and future because this beautiful, attentive girl seemed to be determined to have him tell every reasonable and discreet detail about himself. "My brother Charley says I'm unbalanced by innocence, but that is far from correct. What I do need is to pick up a sense of evil along the way, the way people can learn to eat oysters if they have their heart set on being a gourmet or of finding a reliable aphrodisiac. Sophistication is a perfectly good, if misused, word. All it means is 'deprived of original simplicity.' My brother

Charley gives a great deal of thought to obvious things, which he says are the truly unexplored areas. My own suspicion is that so much of our character is formed by the statistics of our experience. I mean true statistics, as cold as a baseball player's batting average. Just as asparagus grows above the ground and potatoes grow under the ground, everybody finds what his or her character is fairly early. Miserable people have almost always been miserable. Their own statistical repetition of a miserable point of view keeps them that way. Really poor or improvident people, you know, never seem to win the Irish Sweepstakes. There are women who keep marrying men who give them black eyes, and it's all quite unplanned. It's all something like saving up and buying a new hat, then having somebody drop a paper bag full of water on it from the fourteenth floor of some building one has never entered."

Carrie was open to hear him. Like a summerhouse far back in the years, swollen with his memory, she faced him from wherever he approached and welcomed him, and her offer of shelter gave him strength. Her openness softened all the jaggedness of his uncertainty. As he talked to her he marveled over her. She was loaded with peace. Her secret was there to take, he knew, but he was aware, as a part of himself, that if her peace could have been put in a big package with a bright red label that stated exactly what the package contained, and the package was placed beside next year's model of any kind of merchandise, and he and everyone passing were given the choice of taking either one or the other for only ten cents, the red-labeled package would never move an inch and the hucksters would run out of the new merchandise.

After an hour in the café they walked slowly up Third Avenue. A red bus rolled downtown to pick up the franchise to take it back to the carbarns to keep the relay going until the warheads fell. A hackie stared at a punched fender outside an all-night restaurant.

The city scattered itself through the night heat far ahead of them. It was late and the streets seemed like the dirty cellars of the palace of a potentate. The sounds from everywhere around them, far and near, were muted chants of unknown, octagonal words. Hysteria had been calmed by illusion.

They turned west on Fifty-eighth Street and walked toward Central Park and the center of the deceptive silence. They rode through the park in an open carriage. The walls of the city shone from trays of dull gold upon the many ledges of the night. Her head rested on his shoulder. His arm was around her. They rode toward a different dawn, like a fairy prince and princess with convictions about happy endings, behind a weary horse, behind a rheumy old man who had lost the power to remember lost summer nights and fancies.

He kissed her good night. They had been walking toward the entrance to her building. Arriving, they had turned and fallen into one another's arms, jostled by their joy in each other as actors in silent western pictures had to be jostled into bussing by their horses. They kissed. Then, to Carrie's surprise, Jolly Times shook her hand as though he were a life-insurance salesman, mumbled something about telephoning her, and turned to stalk off down the street and out of sight.

Carrie found her father unconscious on the kitchen floor, holding an empty whisky bottle. She turned him on his back, stood over him, gripped him under his shoulders, and dragged him slowly along the corridor to the bathroom. She stretched him out on the white-tiled floor, then knelt beside him. She stripped off his shirt and undershirt, handling him like frozen beef, the undershirt requiring the help of a pair of nail scissors. His torso was massive and heavily muscled. The hair on his chest was white. Carrie dropped the shirts in the laundry hamper, then returned to the kitchen. She emptied all the ice trays into a large bowl. She made six cups of hot coffee. She walked with the ice bowl and a large pitcher of ice water to the bathroom. Her father hadn't moved. She put a layer of ice cubes into the wash basin, then a layer of washcloths, then another layer of ice. She went back to the kitchen and poured a large cup of black coffee, pouring the remainder into a silver thermos jug her father had stolen from a Pittsburgh hotel while living it up on a movie junket a dozen years or so before. She walked deliberately back to the bathroom and set the coffee out of the way, upon a shelf, then she brought her father's chair from the kitchen. The flat electric light, bounding from so many white surfaces, dropped emphatically upon every line of her father's ravaged face as he lay upon the floor. She would not allow herself to think of anything but the job at hand. She worked slowly and well, recognizing only one thought at a time.

She stood directly over him, the ice-water pitcher four feet above his stomach. She emptied the pitcher upon him. He groaned and moved. She took two ice cubes in each hand and began to rub all the exposed skin from the top of his head to his belt line; roughly, heavily, and hurtingly. Her large eyes were wide. Her face was expressionless. Her hot tears fell upon his chest around the skating, burning ice cubes. He struggled under the frozen friction but he had no legs for leverage. He began to talk brokenly, trying to complain. Carrie wrapped the cold, coarse washcloths around more ice cubes and began to scrounge them heavily into her father's armpits. She wedged one cloth-wrapped ball of ice under the belt of his trousers, upon his lower abdomen. She slid a cold, rough cloth behind his neck and pulled roughly and alternately at each end of it to make friction. Groaning, he managed to prop himself up on one elbow. She forced his back against the wall. She unscrewed a vial of benzedrine tablets and held one pill in two fingers while she reached for the cup of black coffee. She pulled on his chin to open his mouth. She popped the pill into it. She made him sip the coffee while she spoke to him in a low, soft, earnest voice.

"It's okay, Papa. It's okay. Just drink the coffee. I know. It's hot. That's good. It's good and hot." He opened his blood-red eyes for an instant but slammed them shut as the brilliant light struck at them.

"Here. More. Another cup, then another cup after that. Then

we'll get you up in your chair and put on a warm bathrobe and we'll sit in front of an open window in the living room and watch the dawn come up. Keep drinking this coffee until the pill works because I have to talk to you, Papa. You have to understand something if I have to say it over and over again, a hundred times. Everything is different this time. We have a chance this time. We'll shake free from the past, at last, this time. Good. Now let's try getting up. Brace yourself on the tub and lift. Brace and lift. Sit on the edge of the tub. That's it. Good. Now hold on. I'll bring your chair over. Stay there. All right. Slide in. That's it. That's fine, Papa. Here's the robe. Fine. Now the scarf. Remember, I want you awake with a clear head."

She got behind the chair and pushed it out of the bathroom and along the corridor to the living room, which was beginning to lighten with the promise from the eastern sky. She opened the window as far as it would go. She pulled a straight-backed chair near his wheel chair, and sat where she could look into his haunted eyes. He was fully conscious, able to listen and to understand. She made him sip another cup of black coffee, but she skipped the benzedrine.

"Papa, this tenth anniversary dinner will be one of the most important things that ever happened to us. To both of us. You are going to have a chance to face those people once and for all and learn once and for all that God isn't angry with you. I'll bet you anything you say that meeting those first ten people won't be one-tenth as terrible as you have imagined it. You are lucky because you know where all of your fear is hidden and now you are just about to wipe all those fears away. Do you see what I mean? Do you understand why this tenth anniversary dinner is so important to us?"

"Yes," he said thickly, "yes, darling girl."

"You'll have to keep remembering that every instant of every day and night from now until that dinner is over. We'll have to keep talking about it morning and night, every time we're together, because this is something you have to remember. You'll have to stay sober, stone sober, until you've talked to every one of those people, so you can look right at them and hear what they have to say and become a free man. Free forever."

They sat side by side and waited for the morning. The dying summer night foamed with silence.

XVIII

Jolly Times worked hard to get the dinner organized. He stayed with it an average of fourteen hours a day. The investigations took him into three boroughs outside Manhattan. He started out with the names and the original addresses of Miss Friendship's first petitioners, excluding Esther Carney, of course, and soon found himself standing in nine blind alleys. He started on a Monday morning. The following Saturday he reported to Dan Tiamat and Joe Downey. Everything had worked out with far more difficulty than any of them had foreseen, and Dan had been on his neck every day, snarling and demanding. Jolly Times had not been able to spend much time at the office but when he was able to get there, no matter what the hour, Dan would be waiting. The fourth such bitter check-up had involved some shouting, and Dan had knocked the radio off the desk in Jolly Times's office because its sounds seemed to be drowning out what they were yelling. Joe Downey had had to intervene. Both Dan and the boy were operating on each others' nerves. The future pecked at the past and the past shook its fist at the future.

At the Saturday meeting in Downey's office Jolly Times gave his discouraging report. Number One was already known to be dead. Numbers two and three—old Mrs. Phillicoe and Mrs. Kennan, she of the pyromaniac husband—were also dead. Jolly Times had learned that Numbers Eight and Ten had left the country. "Out of the original bunch, that leaves us five possibles," the young man said, "and Number Six is definitely on tap. Her name is Eva Meyer. It was Bader ten years ago.

She lives away up in Woodlawn." He tore a piece of paper from a small pad and handed it to Dan.

"You'd better call her before you go all the way up there, Dan," Downey said.

Dan stared at his father-in-law, and Jolly Times thought Dan looked frightened.

The car moved along the eastern rim of Manhattan Island. Driving with his hands, Dan watched the heat dance ahead of him. The city lay as limp as a Dali watch on an Eliot wasteland. The river had been painted in with tempera. The parks were burned. The sun moved meanly.

It was a trim white two-story house with green shutters at the windows and four pairs of roller skates on the front porch. He slid out of the car and onto his crutches without a slip. He had the deep shakes. He knew they would grow worse if he didn't get a drink. He swayed on the crutches for an instant as though he were being pulled back into the car by the sight of a saloon at the corner, sixty yards away. He inhaled deeply. He decided he wanted to listen to Eva Meyer more than he wanted a drink, so he made his way up the short steps. The ringing door bell set up a shrill excitement of children's voices inside the house.

A girl about four years old opened the door. She had black curly hair and eyes like the buttons on dancing shoes. A smaller boy stood behind her. He wore a large pistol and held the hand of a fat pink parcel who was another little girl about two years old. Dan's anxiety pounded within him. He felt nausea. His voice rasped when he spoke. "Some service," he did his best to say. "Three door men."

"I'm not a man," their leader said. "I'm a girl."

"Is your mother home?"

The question turned the three children as one and sent them running into the house yelling, "Mama, Mama, a man is here. He's a cripple. He's a cripple." He could hear a woman's voice chiding them gently for saying such a thing.

Dan faced a hallway, a staircase, a blue and white ceramic umbrella stand, and an old-fashioned coat tree. Beyond the stairs, at the end of the hall, which was covered with a Lincoln green carpet that would have matched Robin Hood's business suits, a door opened and a darkly handsome woman came through, taller than most, wiping her hands on a flowered print apron in the manner of a reliable character woman in a television soap opera. The bright light from the street behind Dan made him a black, hulking shape from her viewpoint as he stood in the open doorway leaning on his crutches.

"Come in and close the door, mister," the woman said with a Germanic accent. "I can't hardly see you on account of the light."

"Thank you," he answered and moved into the hallway to close the door with the tip of his left crutch. The woman pulled open sliding doors to a living room and motioned him inside. "The kids don't mean anything fresh when they said that about you being a cripple," she said easily, "but I bet you if you ever come back here, they don't say it again."

"They are beautiful kids."

"Thank you. Have a seat." He lurched to a straight-backed chair. "What can I do for you, mister?"

"I—I'm from *The Daily Press*."

"I'm Mrs. Meyer. You're in the right place?"

She sat across from him in the pleasant, musty parlor, on an overstuffed sofa. She was serene. A cop could come to her front door, Dan thought, and if all her children were accounted for she would remain serene. He wondered what she had been like ten years before. As he wondered, she decided it was essential that he have some coffee. She left him alone in the room.

It was mid-August but a sprig of mistletoe was hanging from the center chandelier. He tried to begin to think of what he was going to say to her. It made him close his eyes tightly as though the past lay there bleeding on the rug in front of him.

When Mrs. Meyer returned with the coffee the three children were following her closely. When she had served him she sat

down on the sofa with a child on either side and the youngest
in her lap, waiting calmly for him to explain why the *Press*
had sent a man to call on her in Woodlawn. His words came
out of him in a rush, then slowed to a stammer. "Mrs. Meyer,
what I have to say—uh—is unusual but—uh—I can assure
you—uh—please understand that there is nothing wrong
about it."

"I am sure."

"Mrs. Meyer, before you were married, was your name Eva
Bader?"

"Yes. And what is your name?"

"Dan Tiamat."

"How do you do?"

"Mrs. Meyer, you see, I—"

"Peter! Don't hug the baby like that! It could smother her.
Come, sweetheart," she said, recapturing the baby from the
little boy and kissing a pink cheek absent-mindedly while she
looked at Dan with polite interest. "Please," she said.

"Mrs. Meyer, at the beginning of the department, my department, on the *Press,* and for many years since then, I have
held a job called—well, I am Miss Friendship, Mrs. Meyer."

"Miss Friendship?"

"Yes." He gripped the arms of the chair.

"A man is Miss Friendship?"

"Yes, Mrs. Meyer." His voice choked.

"Well, I—I don't know what to say to you."

"I know."

"At last we meet."

Dan closed his eyes and spoke slowly. "My newspaper is
about to celebrate the tenth anniversary of the Miss Friendship department. We—the management of the paper, that is,
would like to give an anniversary dinner party for the first
ten people who wrote to Miss Friendship for advice."

"And for comfort."

"Yes."

"That is what the advertisement said, I think."

"Yes, Mrs. Meyer. The files show that you wrote me my sixth letter."

"You have my letter?"

"Yes."

"Would you read it to me, please?" She spoke the words in a softened voice.

"I—I find I've left it in my car."

"The children will get it."

"It is the brief case on the front seat of the car right outside."

Mrs. Meyer smiled at the little girl and nodded. The girl and her brother scampered out. "When you read what I wrote to you, Mr. Tiamat," Mrs. Meyer said, "I will read to you your answer. Were you crippled when you wrote to me?"

"No, Mrs. Meyer."

"I did not think so. However, whatever happened to you, I am sincerely sorry."

"Thank you."

The children ran back into the room with the brief case. "My uncle has a new Buick," the little girl told Dan as she gave him his case.

"Time for naps," Mrs. Meyer said suddenly. "Excuse us, please, Mr. Tiamat."

Dan listened to the children complaining ritualistically while they climbed the stairs with their mother. He opened the brief case but he was unable to take out the letter. He felt sicker. He pushed his crutches over suddenly, causing them to fall far enough away from him so that he could not reach them unless he crawled. He was afraid he might try to run away.

He stared at his feet. He concentrated upon making out the expression he imagined he saw on the faces of his shoes. It helped him to blank out his shame. The black shoes had the smug look of a man who can sign a check for more than he could have signed it the day before. It must be shoes that are smug, he insisted upon telling himself, because feet were never smug. He remembered paintings of crucifixions in books that he had turned upside down in order to judge the art of the painter by the expression of the feet. If the feet held the expression of a forgotten face he knew he saw art, but if the feet were merely handles for the toes and the painter had a reputation, he would consider that one a fraud. Feet must always look quizzical, he had decided. Feet must look unconvinced of what the mind has embraced. Dan broke his gaze away from his feet and stared helplessly at the threatening staircase. He needed a drink. He needed a drink. He had to leave and get a drink. Then Mrs. Meyer was standing in the doorway with a letter in her hand.

"You look ill, Mr. Tiamat."

"I have a cold."

"You must have a schnapps. You are deadly pale." She walked toward a cabinet.

"No!" She turned to stare at him. "I mean, no thank you, Mrs. Meyer. I do not drink." He clasped his arms tightly around the brief case at his chest and tried to smile at her. She sat down again on the overstuffed sofa.

"Please read the letter to me, Mr. Tiamat."

He took the folder out of the brief case and found her letter with numb fingers. He placed it on top of the folder and the folder on top of the brief case so he could hold the whole kit tightly in his fists, which would then not shake if he propped his arms on the arms of the chair. He began to read the letter aloud but there was nothing to support his voice against shock. Through the reading he had to stop frequently.

> Dear Miss Friendship: I am an Austrian girl who is here only four months. I live with people who are kind, but the husband is not always. He comes to my door at the nighttime. He stops me on the stairs. I am afraid his wife will see him and feel shame. There is a baker who makes me to marry. He is sick in his lungs. What could I do? I cannot go back to Austria. Signed Sick-in-Heart

When Dan finished, he could not look up.

"The letter brings back many things," Mrs. Meyer said.

"Yes."

"I was young and I felt fear."

"I know."

"When I got the letter which you sent to me in answer, Mr. Tiamat, I didn't know what to do, at first. It was such an angry answer. Much, much later, of course, I realized that you—I believed you were a young woman then—had been placed in this work because you were a master psychologist. When I understood everything, how I admired you! You produced within me exactly the effect which you desired. You fired my blood and my brain. I got so angry that you could write to me such things because I was a human being who had asked for help. Later, of course, when I understood God's way, I saw that you had been the single architect of my happiness."

Dan, listening to the incredible words, fought to control the muscles in his face. Mrs. Meyer put on a pair of black-shelled glasses, took up the yellowing sheet of paper, and began to read aloud.

> Dear Eva Bader: You signed your letter Sick-in-Heart but maybe you are a tramp in your heart and if you are, don't write to me. If you enjoy his hands all over you when he stops you on the stairs what are you waiting for when he moans outside your bedroom door at night? Do you expect me to give you an alibi? One thing you can be sure of is that you cannot have any pride or you could not possibly write such a letter to a complete stranger. If you had either pride or honor you would leave that house and fight for your place in this country, if there is any place here for you, which I doubt.
>
> Neither you nor I care about the baker. His lungs are his problem and you would only use the baker's offer as an excuse to get away from those hands on the stairs, if you really do want to get away from them.

With all your faked anxieties you did not once mention the words love or respect. You should have stayed in Austria. You were born ten years too late. Just a few years earlier and Hitler would have seen that your troubles were over.

Very truly yours,
Miss Friendship

Mrs. Meyer stared steadily across the room at Dan.

"God forgive me," Dan mumbled.

"He always forgives."

"I must be allowed to tell you about that letter and how it could have been written, Mrs. Meyer. You see, it was—"

"Psychologically, it was a masterpiece! It was a profound letter! It built a great and strong bridge for me, Mr. Tiamat. It gave me every beautiful piece of my beautiful life, almost beginning with the moment I got the letter."

"You have to let me tell you that—"

"When it arrived, I will be frank with you, Mr. Tiamat, I cried. I cried a whole night. You made me feel cheap and rotten. The next day, all day, I rode on the subway. I went and I went. I made myself think. I made myself face what you had said to me. Today, ten years later, and only to you could I ever tell this—I know I did not altogether reject that woman's husband. I searched through all of me, right into where the lust lives, for your meaning. I searched and I found that maybe I had pretended not to want that man with his hands, but that secretly, I mean it could be that actually, I wanted him. I rode on that subway and I began to understand what you were telling me in your wisdom and your kindness. Kindness is not always a gentle thing. I could see that. I understand that now. That night I went to the sick baker and I told him I hoped I could become worthy to accept his kindness and his love, and that if he still wanted me I would try to be the best wife I could learn to be."

Dan's bloodshot eyes were knobs of agony. His thick hair

hung down on either side of his pale face. He stared at the
crutches out of reach on the floor and tried to will them to
come to him.

"I told the baker everything, Mr. Tiamat. I showed him your
letter. At first he didn't understand. He wanted to get into a
taxi and rush to your paper and beat you." She smiled at the
memory of the day. "He was a little man and not strong. After
he had beaten you he was going to find your boss and show him
your letter and tell him you must be fired for striking with such
unpardonable cruelty at a helpless girl." Mrs. Meyer's eyes
pulled Dan's gaze into them and held it.

"He was a brave man, the baker. His body was small but his
spirit was very big. He taught me kindness. He taught me how
to forgive, Mr. Tiamat." Her back was straight. Her hands
were in repose in her lap. "That day, he took me to the place
where I lived. He closed his store in the middle of the day and
took me there and made me pack and leave with him. I married the baker, Mr. Tiamat. For that, I will always be grateful
to you."

"Mrs. Meyer," Dan croaked, "please bring your husband to
the dinner. I promise you he will not be embarrassed. No one
will be embarrassed."

"No, Mr. Tiamat."

"Please invite him. I will be honored and grateful if he
would come."

"He cannot come. He is dead." She smiled. "But we had
much life together. It is not a sad thing. He told me when we
were married that I must not expect him to live long. He accepted that. He had a way to ignore the inconvenient part of
his body. But he did not die until last year, Mr. Tiamat. We
had together nine wonderful years. When he was very sick, at
the end, he told me I had kept him living longer than he had a
right to live, and this was a man who had the right to live for
a thousand years."

Tears filled Dan's eyes. His shoulders shook convulsively.

He had been released from torment. At that moment he felt that if he could stand before her, he could walk.

"I envy you your three beautiful children, Mrs. Meyer," he said, "and what you remember."

"I have eight beautiful children, Mr. Tiamat. And you are right to envy me. I am the happiest woman in the world."

XIX

A week after he had located Mrs. Meyer, Jolly Times discovered the whereabouts of Number Seven, Olga Jorgenson, now Mrs. Steve Szabo. She lived on Seventy-third Street between Second and Third Avenues.

It was three o'clock on a Friday afternoon when Dan reached her door. He gripped his brief case firmly in his teeth and slung himself on his crutches across the lobby of the apartment building to the elevator. The cab driver had told him that his mother-in-law had bad arthritis and how he was always amazed to see what a person like her could do on crutches. He told Dan that plenty of times he had danced with his mother-in-law on crutches. Dan told him to drop dead. He paid exactly what was shown on the clock, no more. "What are you trying to do?" he snarled. "Work me for a big tip?"

"Whatsa matta wit' chew?" the cab driver said in astonishment. "So I happen to have a clever mother-in-law!"

When Dan rang the Szabo door bell, he could hear a woman's voice shout inside, "What the hell is the matter now, Pop?" It was a big voice. From the back an old man's voice crackled as indistinctly as crumpling cellophane. Dan rang the bell again. "Coming! Coming!" The woman's voice boomed with good nature. The door was flung open with exuberant force. Dan faced a tall, bony woman with slightly protruding, impeccably white teeth. She surveyed him neutrally. She had an enormous bosom that was made to seem even more heroic by a brightly

flowered wrapper that could have been advertised on Fourteenth Street as a genuine sari. Electric blue, it was splattered
with giant white daisies. The woman's hair was straw blond
and was arranged on either side of her head in matching buns
as large as Air Force earphones. She was a fine figure of a
thirty-five-year-old woman.

"Yeah, friend?"

"I'm Dan Tiamat from *The Daily Press*. Mrs. Szabo?"

She reached out and grabbed him by the lapels and pulled
him in, crutches or not, almost bringing him down, holding
his huge body erect with her own strength. "What happened,
friend?" she demanded. "Is Stevie okay? Is anything wrong
with Stevie?"

The old man's voice squeaked like a prop mouse somewhere down the corridor. "What, Olga? What is it? Who?"

"Take it easy, Mrs. Szabo!" Dan yelled. "Take it easy, fuh
gossake!" He felt like a giant Raggedy Ann doll in her
hands.

"Nothing happened to my Steve?"

"Not that I know of, dammit. Now let me go and give me
my crutches." She let him go slowly, and balanced him solicitously until he was able to gain purchase again, reaching down
and handing up his crutches while she held him.

"So how come you know my name?"

"That's what I'm here to tell you."

"Listen, if you're selling subscriptions, don't waste time. My
husband brings your paper home."

"Mrs. Szabo, do I look like I'm working my way through
college?"

"So whatta we standing here for? Come on in." She backed
along the corridor. "You have aroused my woman's curiosity
arreddy." She led the way into a spic and span living room.
"Siddown, friend. Those crutches ain't no rest, I bet."

Dan lowered himself into a wing chair covered with green
material on which had been printed yellow eagles with terrible

hang-overs. The old man's voice shrilled with impatient excitement from the other room. "Olga! Tell who is it!"

"A newspaper guy!" she yelled. "I don' even know nuttin' myself what he wants so shuddup a minute."

"So ask him what he wants," the old man screeched.

"So wait a minute so he can tell something, fuh gossakes. So when I know, you'll know." She looked down pleasantly at Dan, who was buffeted by the sounds. "You wanna glassa beer?"

"No, thank you."

"Okay. What can I do for you?"

"Well, I—I write a feature for the *Press* called Miss Friendship."

"Ho, ho, and ho." Not laughter; just four words.

"You remember the feature?"

"Remember? Boy, oh, boy. Now ask me if my husband remembers. Then ask me if my father—he's in there—remembers."

"Well, that's what I came here to talk to you about, Mrs. Szabo."

"A fella could get a lotta lumps talking about a thing like that."

"Please sit down, Mrs. Szabo. It's very hard to talk with you standing over me like that."

"Afraid I might sock you?" She stared at him grimly then walked across the room and sat down.

"Let me explain," he said tentatively. "Next week the Miss Friendship feature will be ten years old. The paper would like to give a little birthday party for the first ten people who wrote in for advice. Like you, for instance."

"What a memory you got!" She clapped her hand to her forehead. "And you must get about fifty letters a day."

"Olga, dammit," the old man yelled from the back, "tell! What does he want, the newspaperman?"

"Papa! Remember a certain letter which was sent to a certain newspaper about ten years ago which said Steve was a bum and should I marry St. Francis across the hall?"

"What letter?"

"The *letter,* Papa. *The* letter!" Her voice filled all the rooms, all the closets, and all the drawers of every table and bureau. "The time you were yelling at me all day I should marry St. Francis and I was crazy for Steve, which I still am, crazy for Steve."

"Steve is a bum."

"You can't remember the letter? You have forgotten Miss Friendship?"

The old man's high-pitched shout filled the apartment like the racket of a drunken parakeet. "Miss Friendship, I remember! Believe me! Yeah yeah yeah, what a friendship, that Miss Friendship. My worst enemy shouldn't have such a friendship!"

"So, that's who is this newspaper guy is."

"Who?"

"Miss Friendship."

"Miss Friendship is a fella?"

"A fella on crutches. Also the newspaper wants to give a dinner after what happened."

"Yeah?"

"Listen, it's free." She looked over at Dan abruptly and questioningly. "It's free, the dinner?" she asked in a much lowered voice. He nodded. These people were so relaxed when they shouted that he wondered if they ever met face to face.

"Don't take it, the free dinner!" the old man yelled merrily. "Poison you'll get at a free dinner from Miss Friendship."

Mrs. Szabo shrieked with laughter at that sally. When she recovered she said to Tiamat proudly, "My pop is some character. Believe me, he's a million laughs a day."

"I want a drink," the old man yelled. "You got me all stimulated up laughing like that."

"The doctor says no."

"The doctor said no fifteen years ago," the old man yelled

as though behind an electrically powered megaphone. "The first doctor is dead. Every day I have a couple little drinks. The second doctor who said it is dead. The third doctor don't look so healthy and *he* says no drinks. So bring me a drink."

"Excuse me, please, Mr. Tiamat," Mrs. Szabo said demurely. "I'll be right back. Say, how about a liddul belt yasself?"

"No, thank you. We'll have a belt together at that dinner, I hope."

"Listen, any time." She left the room. Dan could hear the old man grumbling, then silence. Mrs. Szabo returned to the living room. "Papa is eighty-nine years old," she said. "He's been in bed for twenty-two years. He's like a liddul baby. Some baby." They heard a key scraping into the lock of the front door.

"It's my liddul doll!" Mrs. Szabo cried, springing to her feet. A short man with a happy Slavic face, wearing the coveralls and cap of a railroad engineer, and carrying a lunch pail, came through the archway into the room. Mrs. Szabo rushed him. He scooped her up as one would a small girl, held her high, and kissed her warmly. "Who's the company?" he asked cheerfully.

"Is that the bum home?" the old man cried. Steve Szabo grinned, faced down the corridor, and said loudly, "You know what, Olga? I sneak back in here while you was on jury duty last week. So I count inna ice box. Then I get back fomm work that afternoon and I count again. Plenty of food is gone. When nobody is here the old man gets up an' walks alla roun'. He's a big faker, your pop."

"Listen," Mrs. Szabo shouted, with great delight in their daily game, "if Poppa's a faker, he some faker."

"So who's the company," Steve asked again.

"Sit down first. I'm afraid you'll start laughing and fall down and hurt yasself."

Grinning, Steve sat on the edge of a chair facing Dan, ready for something marvelously comical to happen. "So go ahead," he told his wife. "I'm sittin'."

"First, I'll interduce evveybody by their right names. This here is Mr. Tiamat of the *Press*—"

"We won something?" her husband cried joyously.

"Not yet," his wife said. "And *this*—this is my husband, Mr. Steve Szabo."

"How do you do?" Dan asked gravely.

"I have a little cold," Steve said, "but otherwise okay. How about you?"

"Now comes the part. The beauty part," Mrs. Szabo exclaimed. "Mr. Tiamat happens to be a certain party from the *Press* and the certain party's plume name happens to be Miss Friendship."

Steve's face went utterly blank. His right arm lifted slowly. His right forefinger pointed directly at Dan's nose. "Him?"

"That's the one," his wife cried proudly.

Steve began to laugh. He beat on the arm of the chair with glee. He doubled over laughing, making as much noise as his wife's laugh and her father's combined. He stood up laughing. He staggered. He reeled. He clung to the spinet piano for support, laughing. He caromed off the piano and bumped into his wife. They hugged each other and laughed together. He tottered to Dan's side and whacked him repeatedly on the back until, at last, he was able to gasp out, "Now I know what it means—as funny as a crutch."

He began to laugh again and it was like the belling of a hound. Olga's laugh was laid under it with the depth and rhythm of a slap bass. Dan started to laugh in the middle register. The old man's high-pitched cackling joined in. It sounded like the quartet from *Rigoletto* as rendered by a mixed troop of animals.

Steve pumped Dan's hand and said, "Boy—I mean girl— have I wanted to meet you all these years!"

The old man yelled, "So he's with Miss Friendship talking, the bum?"

Dan was not only baffled, he was speechless. He heard the knob of the front door rattled impatiently.

"He's early today," Steve said.

Mrs. Szabo shrugged and walked to the door. Without bothering to see who had been entreating for entrance, Mrs. Szabo opened the door and returned to the living room.

An enormously fat man with skin like white paper rubbed with bacon rind closed the door, then floated past her back without speaking or glancing into the living room, and disappeared down the corridor.

"Francis? That's Francis?" the old man shrilled in the distance.

"That's Francis," Mrs. Szabo said over her shoulder, "and I just might vomit."

Dan heard a door close at the rear of the apartment. Then he became aware that Mrs. Szabo was staring down at him.

"I don't know what kinda guy you are, Mr. Tiamat," she said slowly. "You are probably a louse like most of them, but I wanna tell you you taught us a coupla very important things. Me and Steve have talked about you plenty over the years."

Dan could feel the coldness overtaking him.

"The most important thing you taught us," Mrs. Szabo said, "is never to take advice. Also, never ask for advice. Maybe you wanna have a tooth pulled or something, that's different, but where conversation is concerned, believe me, evveybody is too busy or too knocked around to do anything but listen to the sound of their own voice. Believe me. Better people should figure something out for themselves. If I hadda taken your advice, my life woulda been miserable. In evvey way. Worse, Papa woulda had to go to a home or something."

"Listen," Steve said, "that ain't all."

"I'll say," his wife replied.

"Mrs. Szabo, and Mr. Szabo, if I may, I would like to say that—"

"You remember you told me not to marry Steve? Boy!"

"Mrs. Szabo, Mr. Szabo, I brought the letters. I would like to read them to you. To both of you."

"Hah?" Steve said incredulously. "You kept a dopey letter like that?"

Dan drew the two letters from his brief case. He glanced at the Szabos. They were watching him soberly. He began to read:

> Dear Miss Friendship: My father wants me to marry a nice boy but I love a man who is a no-good bum. He drinks. He is a mean man. My father is old and he is very sick. All he wants is for me to marry and settle down and be happy with some good man before he dies. What shall I do?

As he read, Dan had to keep raising his voice; for some reason the letter had set them off again. The laughter reached hurricane proportions after he finished reading. Steve was staggering in tight circles like a poodle with worms, and Mrs. Szabo was knocking her head against the wall as she brayed. It was as though some mad scientist had given life to a pair of broken bagpipes.

"What the hell is so funny?" Dan demanded.

"Wow!" Steve said.

"Now let me read the answer!" Mrs. Szabo yelled. She hurried to the mantel and drew a folded piece of paper from behind a clock.

"You kept that thing?" Steve asked.

"Wait till you hear, Tiamat!" she said. Holding the yellowed paper at arm's length and stifling her laughter, she read the words Dan knew too well.

> Dear Olga Jorgenson: You sound like a bird-brained, wasp-hearted creep to me. If your father is sick, stay with him and get all those men out of your alleged mind. Take four or five cold baths a day. Later on take the good man and throw out the bum. You sound so dumb it is probably impossible to insult you. Let your father do your thinking for you. Sincerely,
>
> Miss Friendship

Steve Szabo flopped into a chair. "I swear I can't laugh any more," he said weakly.

"You know what I did a half-hour after your fine advice arrived here?" Mrs. Szabo asked Dan. "I went right out and married the bum, Steve."

"Then why did you write for advice in the first place?" Dan broke out. He had had about all of this perverted mirth he could stand.

"Who wrote?" Mrs. Szabo replied. "Who asked for advice?"

"Yuh big dummy," Steve said. "Olga din't write you no letter. Pop wrote the letter."

"That's why you are the best joke we ever had," Mrs. Szabo cried happily. "The letter says Pop wants me to marry a nice boy. That's Francis. You saw him. A slob. But with Pop he's a real catch because he plays lousy pinochle. He's across the hall with his mother for twenny-three years and evvey night, to get a little relief, he comes in here and he plays pinochle with Pop."

Dan gaped at her, cruelly cheated out of his tragedy.

"And you know why my Stevie is a bum? Because he hates to play cards and because he keeps proving Papa is a faker who likes to rest twenny, thirty years onna bed."

XX

Jolly Times began to break his ten-years-of-Friendship promotion in the *Press* three Mondays before the day of the dinner. It was, of course, only a silly promotional gambit, not to be taken seriously, because it would have seemed very odd indeed if a great newspaper had suddenly begun to think of itself in the terms of friendship for its readers. The single commodity a newspaper sold was violence, which is antipodal to friendship. The *Press,* along with every other paper but one in its community, survived on violence, crime, hopelessness, lies, indignity, anarchy, and fear because that was what sold papers.

That and sports news. "Give 'em what they want" was the
modus operandi of the *Press*. The newspaper industry worked
hard to manufacture the attitudes and rationales of indecency
and violence, which they then claimed to report objectively,
as news. The industry invented and sustained the common
fodder of the idiot forms like television, motion pictures, and
comic books, then had the overweening dishonesty to deplore
that these three rogue media could have so reflected "life" as
to subvert the moral intentions of youth. The industry had
begun its incitements to murder and shame from a dark, foul
cellar of the edifice marked by it for all to see, as though it
were an Orwellian ministry, as Freedom of the Press, and in
lieu of patriotism it "cooperated" with world governments in
reporting the true consequences that had been projected from
the peacetime fall-out of atomic radiation. But, as a great institution, the industry worked only for itself. It made money,
but only for itself. By various usages it persuaded the public
to view it as one of the professions, and so, indeed, did under-
takers and the producers of musical shows. Journalism was
taught in the colleges to the growing generations of the savage,
simple-minded people, and the profession was so grafted to
the body of the nation that it did not take one backward step,
amok or berserk in its zeal to self-service, that it did not claim
that majesty in the rolling *R*'s of freedom of the press, and in
the name of the Republic for which it stands. All that was accepted. No one cared that newspapers bred death, ate filth, and
survived on chaos, but it was odd to think that a newspaper
like the *Press* could seek to show that it had been doing all
these things in the name of friendship for its readers.

On the first Monday of the build-up for the dinner, Downey
let Jolly Times have four columns, held down with a three-
column picture of Dan Tiamat with Mrs. Eva Meyer. Jolly
Times had gotten the picture the previous Saturday by inviting
Mrs. Meyer to bring her own children and any neighbors' for
a tour of the inside workings of the *Press*. He had sent his
brother's limousine to transport them.

On the big Contest Page, Jolly Times boxed the rules for something he called The Miss Friendship Big Ten Contest. Considering the extent and value of the prizes, the contest was painfully simple. The entrants were called upon to guess how many of The Big Ten would have survived; of those, how many would accept; and of whatever number accepted, how many would be men, how many women.

The first prize was an all-expense round-trip ticket to visit the tomb of Miss Juliet Capulet in Verona, Italy, with a side trip to nearby Venice and free gondola rides on two consecutive nights chosen in advance for their coincidence with a full moon. Jolly Times hadn't promoted the hotels in either city yet, but he planned to be ready with a case of fine Bardolino wine when the winner got home, if he or she should have to pay personally for hotel space. The lesser prizes included quantities of transistor radios and two hundred appropriately shaped one-pound boxes of candy, each to be delivered to any person of the winner's choice the following St. Valentine's Day. In reserve, should any of the promoted prizes fall through, Jolly Times had a year's supply of Idaho potatoes and a hundred and twenty-nine nine-pound, eviscerated, full-frozen turkeys.

Jolly Times finally cleared a network TV show to telecast the key ceremonies at the dinner by telling the station people to drop dead and going directly to the sponsor controlling the time slot he wanted. The agency for the sponsor demanded to be allowed to assign two of its writers, but Jolly Times refused. It was his show. He would write the script. They compromised. If he didn't have a script in the network's hands for approval three days before the dinner, their writers would take over. Five days before the big event the *Press* had generated so much excitement across the country that the network split the time with the first sponsor and sold it again to a co-sponsor. The co-sponsors picked up the tab for time and production, all paper hats, and a large quantity of Rodie's Rosé, a waif wine of exceptionally low cost, from Bundaberg, Australia.

By the second Thursday of the promotion, the paper had

received six hundred and forty letters from readers demanding, or requesting, or pleading that they be allowed to attend the dinner. A third of these stated that they would pay their own way if the *Press* would make the arrangements, and over 80 per cent went into exhaustive detail in describing what Miss Friendship had done for them. By the following Monday, at the beginning of the week immediately preceding the dinner, the number of requests had reached nine hundred and twenty-four. Neither sponsor wanted to pay for that kind of an unexpected cost. Jolly Times didn't have any budget for it. He was tired out and discouraged because he had not been able to find more than two people out of the original ten, while six had definitely been eliminated by death or plain twentieth-century disappearance. He had begun by doing all of the leg work himself. Then the pressure of time and Dan's relentless goading had caused him to engage a private detective agency. Three expensive men had gone on the job on a full-time basis. Jolly Times had paid for them out of his own pocket. He would pore over the agency's daily reports until late at night, trying to think of one more method they might use, one more lead they might uncover, one more unanticipated path they might follow, but the detective agency was the best in the business; its operatives shuffled forward through the inexorable routines of detective work, eliminating and discarding. There seemed to be nothing overlooked. Soon there would be nothing left to eliminate.

Despairing, Jolly Times worked through the heat under double anxiety. As far as he could see he had too many guests and not enough guests of honor, and he dreaded the time when Dan would find this out. Dan believed that there would be at most three or four guests of honor and no other guests. Four days before the dinner, Jolly Times decided he had to discuss a lot of matters with his brother and Joe Downey.

Hungarian Charley's, across the street from the *Press*, was a restaurant with a simple credo: noise for the sake of noise. Charley O'Neil and Joe Downey were at a table far in the back when Jolly Times found them. Years before, Joe Downey had explained to the fat proprietor that if he bothered them in any way, such as by greeting them or coming within eight feet of their table, he, Joseph Downey of *The New York Daily Press,* would see to it that his license was taken away. In a sentence that was the kind of a self-effacing, lovable guy Hungarian Charley was, sort of a legend in his own time.

Both the newspapermen had been crumpled and used by the summer day. Their faces, which had been pink that morning, were now fish-belly white, and smudgy shadows seemed to be drawn into the texture of their skin, showing them up rather like Daumier sketches or Walpurgis spectator sports by Doré. Charley O'Neil drank his whisky straight and made wet, interlocking rings on the bare table with the sweating bottom of his glass in the manner of all people held captive too long in a saloon, staring down at his work moodily like a careful artisan. Joe Downey had a large glass of beer in front of him, placed between his propped elbows. He sipped at the beer by ducking his head and mouth into the froth of it, like a small boy at a soda fountain. The fatigue the heat had given them kept both men silent. Charley O'Neil, facing the front, could see the early-evening stalkers going past the joint in the bright sunshine. Jolly Times came in the front door. He looked around hopelessly for a moment, then saw them and waved. He joined them at the table, weighing the social dangers of going to sleep in a saloon while cold sober.

"Hi, Frank," Charley said.

"How's Dan?" Downey asked.

"He's crazy, that's how he is. Furthermore, I have a slight suspicion that every idiot who ever got himself given a testimonial dinner acts crazy just like this. I say good morning. He grabs me. 'What about the dinner?' he says."

"How is the dinner building up?" Downey asked.

"Listen, Mr. Downey, there is a little problem. A *little* problem!" Jolly Times clapped his hand weakly to his forehead. "Nine hundred and fifty-odd people want to come, and

I made arrangements for twenty-six. By Saturday there'll be about twelve hundred demands for invitations, and don't forget the impulsive ones who don't believe in calling ahead. They'll just drop in."

"Drop in? How many?" Charley asked.

"Well, maybe two thousand altogether."

"Two thousand?" Charley looked dumbfounded.

"Can I help it that this has turned out to be one of the most sensational newspaper promotions of all time?"

"But, Frank, you said twenty-six people!"

"So I underestimated."

"By nineteen hundred and seventy-four people? Let me tell you, that's the kind of underestimating that sent Lenin to Russia in a sealed train."

Jolly Times nodded gloomily. "Out of the first ten people who wrote in, I can only find two. Count them as three. One has a husband."

"That's not so bad," Downey said. "After all, Dan is the star. He's the one they'll all be coming to see."

"They know that," Jolly Times said hotly, "but does Mr. Tiamat know that? He still thinks we're all going to sit down to a cozy family-type type dinner in a private dining room. Just him and four or five of the survivors and a few buddies from the paper."

"So we'll surprise him," Downey said. "We'll get better human-interest pictures that way anyway. We'll put him into the hotel a whole day ahead of time—I'll say it's because it's air-conditioned and I want him to be fresh for the affair. Then if there's a lot of action downstairs he won't know anything about it till the last minute and it will be a wonderful surprise for him."

"Very good, Joe," Charley O'Neil said.

"I hate surprises myself," Jolly Times agreed reluctantly, "but in this case it sounds like a very good idea. Now what about the nineteen hundred-odd extra guests?"

"What about them?" Charley asked.

"Well, who's going to pay for their dinners?"

"Don't look at me."

"Then who? The hotel? The State Department?"

"Let the TV sponsors pay."

"I tried that. No soap."

"How much are the dinners?"

"Three-fifty. That's absolute cost."

"Then it's out of the question."

"We could give them hot dogs and potato salad and beer," Downey suggested. "To hell with that wine. We might make a deal at a buck a plate."

Jolly Times gaped at him with admiration. "That's it! Hot dogs. A buck a plate. But we keep the wine. Beer costs a lot more than Rodie's Rosé, and the wine has that delicate flavor that actually was meant for hot dogs."

"Kid, that's still two thousand dollars, which is about seventeen hundred more than any promotion this paper ever handled," Charley said.

"I'll pay for it," Jolly Times said.

"No."

"Please, Charley."

"Would you say that no matter what happens, this can't cost more than five thousand dollars?"

"Five thousand! It won't even cost two."

"Let's figure five. The paper pays. It's worth every penny, too, Frank, but I wanted to have a top figure because that's the only way to run your life. Always try to know in advance what every sheer folly is going to cost."

XXI

The following afternoon the detective agency uncovered the last survivor of The First Ten, a Mrs. Calvin Tunert. She lived at the Hotel Getty, facing Central Park from Fifth Avenue.

Dan telephoned her immediately, gave his name to her maid, and endured a long wait. Finally, Mrs. Tunert came to the phone. "Yes?" she said carefully.

"Mrs. Tunert, this is Dan Tiamat of *The Daily Press*. I would appreciate it very much if you could see me."

"May I know what your visit would be about?"

"It *is* rather complicated, Mrs. Tunert. I run a department called Miss Friendship, and we're about to celebrate the tenth anniversary of the department, and as I understand it you were one of the first ten people who wrote into the department for advice and comfort. Is that right, Mrs. Tunert?"

"Quite right."

"Well, I wanted the chance to meet you, Mrs. Tunert, to explain the things that happened and how they happened, and to—"

"I have the feeling that we have already met, Mr. Tiamat."

"No. I don't think so. I mean, I'm sure we haven't, Mrs. Tunert."

"Could you come by this afternoon? Say at six o'clock, for cocktails."

"Thank you, Mrs. Tunert. I'll be there."

A uniformed maid opened the door on the thirty-seventh floor of the Getty. She took Dan's name and hat away with her and left him waiting in the wide, square foyer on his crutches. The foyer was lined with large, carved pieces of jade within illuminated cases lined with ivory silk damask. The walls were covered with ivory paper of a high gloss. The carpet was a soft ivory in color. In the center of the room, upon a pedestal four feet high was a twenty-inch jade carving of some Hindu deity, lighted by pencil spots from the ceiling. The god rode a parrot of jade and was attended by nymphs of jade, one of whom bore his banner. He was armed with a bow, the string of which was a line of bees. He carried five arrows, each tipped with a different flower, to conquer each of the five senses.

Pulled to this exquisitely sensual work of art, Dan read the golden plaque attached to the pedestal:

KAMA, GOD OF LOVE
Who Connects Entity with Nonentity

Hearing a door open, Dan turned and watched a woman with a broad scar running from the base of her jaw to the corner of her mouth come into the room. He swayed dizzily on his crutches as Pilar Castaños smiled into his eyes. Despite the scar, she was as incredibly beautiful as she had ever been. It was twenty years earlier for an instant. She was barefoot. She wore Chinese red: house coat, fingernails, and lips against ivory skin, black eyes, and black, black hair. He could imagine the snow spilling up Riverside Drive far behind her head and he could see the faces on the people in the street near Washington Square as he had fled from her.

"How kind of you to come on such short notice, Mr. Tiamat," she said in a low, deliberate voice. "I cried when I read that you had lost your wife—and your legs—ten years ago."

"You cried?"

"Please come with me," she said. "You must meet my husband." She walked slowly through the open door behind her, mindful of the pace of crutches. He followed, staring dazedly at the back of her gleaming head. They went into a large salon at the southwest corner of the building. The room was high over Central Park. He could see the Hudson and he imagined that he saw the feet of the purple Dutch mountains away to the north by northwest. Two men stood waiting for him but they had the light of the sky at their backs and, from the doorway, he could not clearly see their faces.

"Mr. Tiamat, may I present my husband, Calvin Tunert? Darling, this is Mr. Tiamat of the *Press,* who has come here on a mission it would have been impossible for you or me to anticipate." Pilar, Dan perceived, had thrown her fire away, her self-indulgent, melting passionateness. She had now become as a duchess might seem beside a *gamine*. She was as smooth as an incoming tide, but underneath that Dan could feel the excitement she made, that movement she had which was like a noise fused from a scream, a gasp, and a sigh.

Calvin Tunert shook Dan's hand so vigorously that he was almost pulled off his crutches. Mistakenly, Mr. Tunert expected great strength from the hand of a man whose legs were useless. As Dan recovered himself, it crossed his mind that Pilar had married herself an intelligent conservative.

"And," she said, moving Dan with her eyes and the attenuation of the conjunction, "my twin brother, José Castaños— Mr. Tiamat of *The Daily Press*."

Dan almost cried out. He gripped his crutches as though they were each a halberd and looked fearfully, while Pilar smiled into Pepé's mad face. Twenty years afterward, that face was still as empty and caddish as the face of the Jack of Clubs.

Pepé had traveled too many planets within the tilts and ascensions of his mind to recognize Dan after two decades. He remembered only the Dan of long ago. In a hopelessly twisted context, "age had not wearied him, nor the years condemned; at the going down of the sun and in the morning he did not remember him." From his perch on the ledge, through his binoculars, Pepé had seen Dan writhing and supple, quick, bold, and thirty; he had never before seen this broken, gray, seamed, veined, smashed, and crippled time-server of fifty.

"You are a newspaperman, Mr. Tiamat, so I suspect you are thinking of my notoriety of the past. Am I right? Of course I am right." Pepé smirked and handled his tiny mustache. He seemed like a stock cocktail guest, government issue; relatively normal, entirely pleasant, hardly insane.

"What will you drink, Mr. Tiamat?" Mrs. Tunert asked.

Dan knew enough to feel afraid. Even across the measureless chasm of time that separated them, he was one of the men living who knew the validity of the terror that infected him at certain sounds within her voice, at her seeming control, and at the way she allowed him to see behind her eyes, for a punishing instant, each time she looked at him. "I would like some ginger ale, thank you," he answered gravely.

"I'll wager you are surprised to find me here, Mr. Tiamat," Pepé said. He was a short, muscular man, with white hair over dark skin. He could have been forty, but he was Pilar's twin so he was forty-four. He wore a white planter's shirt, sewn as a jacket for the tropics, with four pockets and needle adornments. His dark skin had florid underpainting. He smiled in grimace then dropped it instantly to a normal somberness. His eyes were mad. The blackness in them had massed tensely at the centers of the flat whiteness, so white his eyeballs seemed painted. His eyes had no expression other than madness and were as feeling as a jewel on the finger of a disinterred pharaoh. His shoulders were compact and powerful. His fingers, as he held the lapels of his jacket in the manner of a country squire, were as stubby as a badger's and almost as hairy. Dan could imagine that machete gripped in them.

"We hope you can stay for dinner, Mr. Tiamat," Calvin Tunert said.

"I would be happy to," Dan heard himself lie.

A houseman appeared with the ginger ale. Pepé cleared all hedges by seeming to forget entirely his remark to Dan. "Pilar and Calvin! How wonderful to see you again! I have thought about you every day and every night of every month in that confounded hospital, but no matter how much I yearned to see you I decided that I would do so only on the one strict condition."

"My brother has been institutionalized for some time, Mr. Tiamat," Mrs. Tunert explained primly.

Dan shuddered. He had never been able to defeat her except by running from her. After a life, after stepping across the bodies of beloved dead, he had traced his way back to her. With wet apprehension he began to understand that she was going to exact an enormous payment from him for having run from her.

Pepé extended his index finger and held it high over his head with an emphasizing gesture. "I told myself sternly that I absolutely would not see you again until I had been pronounced absolutely cured, three times. On my honor! Not once. Not twice. Three times."

He turned pleasantly to Dan and, with the musty courtliness of a golfer who must brief a new member on the hole-in-one he scored in 1927, said, "I had been mentally ill for a while because I had been under severe strain." His accent was barely more perceptible than his sister's. "I had become unnecessarily worried about sin. We should have the greatest attention for sin at all times, of course, but I had overextended that obligation. Heaven knows these things happen frequently and to many, many people in this ragged twentieth century, but just the same I must thank heaven that it is all over." He took his left hand into his right hand and spread it, preparatory to counting. "I absolutely insisted upon them giving me three complete and separate examinations in each one of the mental institutions where I had received treatment in the past— in this country, that is. In Florida." He ticked off his fingers. "In California—no, no, I mean in New Mexico. And in the state of New York. It was entirely voluntary, you understand, and they kept telling me, over and over again, that it was not necessary."

Pilar languidly watched Dan as he watched Pepé. Calvin Tunert watched his wife, nothing else. Pepé watched the distant past, not where it joined the present but where it was invisibly, inseparably seamed into the future.

"The private man I always use when I feel myself under strain," Pepé continued, "said flatly that I would be wasting the valuable time of pressed psychiatric staffs, but I couldn't be half-safe. You understand? *I had to be sure so that my loved ones could be sure,* I insisted. I made the journeys, over six thousand miles, at my own expense, of course, and mind you I will not travel in any other manner than first class. Eleven hundred dollars. Oh, yes. I convinced the top men at every one of those hospitals that I would not leave their premises until I had received their complete, written bills of good health. They cooperated. It is indeed a commentary upon this ragged twentieth century that one is required to obtain absolution from medical men concerning an overextension of what is wholly a theological problem, the consequences of the examination of sin, but I was given complete bills of health. Not one bill. Not two. Three complete bills of health."

"We are all very happy to hear that news, naturally," Mr. Tunert told Pepé and Dan while eying his wife.

Dan dined beside his crutches at Mrs. Tunert's left hand, at Mr. Tunert's right, and facing Pepé. Mrs. Tunert was intent upon hospitable joviality. Her lovely hands and long fingers moved as she talked, lending the illusion that she was engaged in typing her own conversation in the air. She strove with dedication to make all of her pressing senses of physical excitement increase, to have their presence confirmed again and again through signals that could be most clearly read. Only her husband lent a note of sober reality to the dinner. His eyes were always at ready.

The dining room was circular. It had high pink walls and an oyster-white ceiling. The carpet was French blue. The upholstered chairs, were pink and blue and had come to the room by an indirect route from the fourteenth Louis, king of the sun.

"And you may well believe me when I say that I could spend the rest of the evening telling you wonderful stories about this luscious, beautiful, exciting woman," Pepé said, gesturing intimately toward his sister, who laughed lasciviously, "but most of them would be set in a time which probably never happened and in a place which undoubtedly never existed, but which I would call Cuba."

"*La perla,*" Mrs. Tunert said to no one at all.

Pepé beamed at her fatuously. "It is said that when God made the world, the last thing he created was the island of Cuba. When it was finished, all the people and the animals and the birds elsewhere set up a frightful cry that He was unfair to give one place on earth more beauty than any other place. 'Ah,' the Lord replied, smiling and nodding, 'what you say is perfectly true. However, I can assure you that everything is going to come out much more than even, for I haven't put the Cubans in there yet.' " Pepé exploded with harsh laughter. His teeth emerged, glistening and threatening, in a snarl. It stopped as suddenly as it had started. The feral teeth were withdrawn into his head.

"Now, Pepé," Pilar said, "Mr. Tiamat is a very busy newspaperman and we must no longer keep him from speaking to us of his mission."

"Ah, yes. Forgive me."

"Mr. Tiamat is the famous Miss Friendship, the friend of the lovelorn." Pilar told her brother. Her husband stared at her implacably, willing her to speak of other things.

Drawing his hands from the table to his lap, Dan had to grip his left wrist with his right hand to keep them both from shaking. He did not yet know what she had decreed must happen to him. He could not grasp how he must defend himself because he had never been able to see how to defend himself whenever she had decided to punish him.

"What does that mean, the friend of the lovelorn?" Pepé asked politely.

Pilar patted the back of Pepé's stubby, hairy hand as it rested upon the blue damask cloth near her. "When young ladies are troubled by naughty sweethearts and have no one else to turn to for help, if they have a desperate need for objective, dispassionate advice, they write to Mr. Tiamat." She turned to look into Dan's eyes. "I did once, a long, long time ago," she said. "Although I did not know it was Mr. Tiamat I had written to." She passed her hand lightly across her eyes. "And had I known, of course I would not have sent it, and we would not have had the pleasure of seeing Mr. Tiamat tonight."

"Why would you have not sent it?" Pepé asked quickly.

"When one reads Miss Friendship one thinks of a kindly

older woman, not a man. However, Mr. Tiamat's affliction must have brought him much understanding. And please don't be so tense, Pepé. It displeases me."

"You have come here on business relative to your work, Mr. Tiamat?" Pepé asked.

"Yes."

"Relative to my sister's letter?"

Dan cleared his parched throat and his memory tasted whisky. "I have come to explain that in a few days, on the evening of August second, that is, my newspaper will hold a dinner commemorating the tenth anniversary of the department called Miss Friendship, and the dinner is to honor the first ten people who wrote to the department for advice."

"Formidable!" Pepé exclaimed.

"Ten years ago, when I was still quite childish," Mrs. Tunert said with smooth ingenuousness, the blinds drawn over her emotions, "and when I could not quite make up my mind whether I should marry Calvin or whether I should—"

"Pilar!" Mr. Tunert's electric voice slapped at her. She broke off and lowered her eyes becomingly. At once Mr. Tunert began to stuff velvet into the open sound he had made. "Why go backward, darling?" he said soothingly. "Yesterday is misplaced somewhere, and it is all so boring for the others. Come along. We will have coffee in the salon and watch the lovely lights move through the park."

"My dear brother Calvin," Pepé protested with uncontainable delight. "How can you stop little sister at such a delicious moment. But this is charming! I must hear it! Calvin, please relent. I beg of you, please relent. I can actually taste sin here."

Pilar shut him off momentarily by turning away to Dan and saying firmly, "I must tell you this and only this, Mr. Tiamat. I vowed at that time that someday, somehow, I would find some way to repay you for your prompt answer to my letter."

"But what did he do for you? What did he say?" Pepé asked impatiently.

"I wrote him a letter and he answered it, my darling," she said with a bland, perfect smile, "and someday soon I shall show you both my letter and his answer. I promise you that."

Mr. Tunert stood up abruptly. "That will be all," he said. "We will have coffee in the salon."

Mrs. Tunert stood up. Pepé hastened to pull her chair aside. He took her arm. They led the way. Dan got his crutches together and swung after them. Mr. Tunert brought up the rear. His face was haggard.

As soon as he had drunk his coffee, Dan announced that he would have to leave. The Tunerts and Mrs. Tunert's brother all agreed that they would be delighted to attend the tenth anniversary dinner. Mrs. Tunert said she would see the guest out. She led the way to the jade and ivory foyer and waited for him in front of the statue of Kama.

"Pilar! Mr. Tiamat!" Pepé called after them. "Would it be possible to hitch a ride with Mr. Tiamat?"

Pilar raised her eyebrows in question. Dan nodded. "Yes, Pepé," she called out, "if you hurry."

Dan stood two feet away from her. "Do you remember what I had tattooed on my back twenty years ago, Dan?" she asked.

"Yes."

"Do you remember the words?"

"St. Joseph bless and keep Daniel Tiamat who is my life."

She unbuttoned the red house coat and pulled it down over her shoulders. She stood staring at him, her padded mouth slightly open, her ripened breasts lifting themselves. She turned after a moment and he stared. "Pepé burned it off for me," she said. A purple and carmine scar defaced the golden skin of her back. She turned again. They could hear the noisy Pepé coming along the corridor as he called good night to Mr. Tunert. She slipped the house coat across her shoulders again and buttoned it unhurriedly.

"He would kill you if I told him who you are," she said slowly and matter-of-factly.

"As he might kill you," Dan said with a rasp.

"As he would kill you if he ever saw your answer to the letter I wrote in all trust to Miss Friendship," she murmured. Pepé burst into the foyer. "All set? I hope I didn't keep you. Well, good night, little sister!" He kissed her on the cheek. "Awfully good of you and Calvin to have me over."

Dan shook hands with his hostess and tottered off toward the elevator on his crutches.

Pepé prattled on about rain forests, men's tailors, and grades of cigars until Dan dropped him off at a hotel on Park Avenue in the Fifties. Dan then drove back up Fifth Avenue to his apartment building. Parking on the street instead of taking his car into the subterranean garage, he brooded. After a long time he reached across the seat and pulled the brief case into his lap. He took the file folder out of it. Snapping on the overhead light, he studied Pilar's letter in his shaking hands.

> Dear Miss Friendship: I am a young Cuban woman of good family whose heart is torn and whose pride and sense of justice have been twisted and broken long before this.
>
> I am very, very close to a countryman whom I had thought I had loved in a more sisterly way at one time and to whom I had given all that he had asked to prove that I loved him differently. I came to see, in a terrible punishment, that what I did was wrong.
>
> Now I love an American man. He is older than I by twelve years. He is calm and sure and safe and dear, where my Cuban admirer was cruel and wild. What we did in the name of love has made that man sick with guilt and fear, and I am afraid he will do terrible things if I marry the American. What shall I do?
>
> Mrs. C. Tunert Questionmark

To make his agony complete, Dan read the carbon of the letter he had unknowingly written Pilar.

> Dear Cuba: If one of you Cuban women moves in with an old American there won't be much left of him.

Something will snap, but since the unstated factor you are probably *actually* in love with is money, my advice is to marry the old chump and keep your Cuban on the side for those cold North American nights. Did you write that letter to have an alibi ready in your hope chest? Did you plan to use it to show how sincere you were if you ever got caught by Old Moneybags when you were being more than sisterly to the lad from the island? I know you Cubans. You are nothing but rutting animals.

Tiamat sat motionless in his car, clutching the letters.

"Carrie!" She wasn't home. He slammed the door behind him with a crutch tip. He flicked on the light switch with his elbow and moved as fast as the crutches would take him across the foyer and into the pantry. He flipped on the pantry light. He opened a cupboard and dragged out a tool chest. He opened it and took out the top tray. A bottle of bourbon lay exposed. Without hesitation he snatched it up and threw it into the pantry sink. It smashed. The whisky ran through the broken glass down the drain. He moved on, into the kitchen, worked the light switch, then propelled himself to the side of the refrigerator. He fumbled behind it. His hand came away with a string that had been taped to the back of the white machine. A bottle of whisky was tied to the end of it. He tossed the bottle into the air, then swung backward, out of the way, on his crutches. The bottle fell like a hanged man. It shattered against the side of the refrigerator. The smell of whisky moved around him like a talking snake.

Dan swung himself to the other side of the kitchen facing the long corridor from the front door. Bracing his back against the wall, he let himself sink to the floor in exhaustion, his useless legs sprawling helplessly. He picked up each leg with his strong hands and set them out ahead of him as props. Holding one crutch at a time over his head like a spear, he flung them as far up the corridor as he could make them go, where he could not get them without agony or help from Carrie. Panting, he leaned his head back. He sat there sweating, fighting his need for whisky, waiting for Carrie to come home, and thinking how many times he had met death in his life.

Carrie came home almost two hours later. By the time she reached the kitchen she was running. When she found lights on, the crutches yards apart on the floor, and the smell of whisky it sent her running, yelling for him.

She knelt beside him. She held his lined, anguished face between her hands and stared into it. "Are you all right, Papa?"

"I'm better now, sweetheart."

"What happened? No—I can see what happened. You have had a terrible, terrible night and you've stamped it out under you." She kissed his cheek. She held his huge right hand in both of hers and she kissed the back of it. "Oh, Papa, we're winning. We're winning!"

"We have to find Number Four. Of all of them, I have to find Number Four."

She stared at him. "Frank O'Neil found her tonight."

He surged upward. He held her tightly by the upper arms as they sat beside each other on the kitchen floor. "He found her? Who is she?" he beseeched.

"She was Mama," Carrie said quietly, "then she was me. Mama wrote the first letter and showed it to me and talked to me all about it when I was a little girl. Then we lost Mama, and I became Number Four." Tears filled her eyes but she smiled at him as she continued. "Mama was Number Four, Daddy, and if afterward I wrote the letters, Number Four was still always Mama."

Dan stared at her, blessed and transformed with the wonder of his life. He began to laugh. He laughed and while he laughed he wept, and while he laughed and wept he took his child in his arms and pulled her close to him.

XXII

On the afternoon preceding the dinner for Miss Friendship, some seven hours before it was scheduled to begin, Jolly Times sprawled and listened to his brother Charley play the piano, as was their Sunday custom, in the penthouse apartment they shared overlooking the Metropolitan Museum of Art. The apartment reflected the tastes of two vigorous bachelors who had a combined income of four hundred and ten thousand dollars a year after the sharpest tax axes in the business had chopped away both Federal and state returns.

Charley was playing the Brahms First Concerto. He believed it expressed his personality. In succession that day he had played Señor Albeniz's *Iberia* and some of the work of Mr. Charles Ives, a temperate insurance man who had more than evened the score with his climate by composing his Sonata Number Two, a musical assault that had the power to make even a virtuoso of the level of, say, Artur Rubinstein sound as though he were continually hitting the wrong keys. Charley had played these pieces, too, because he believed they expressed his personality, which indicated the extent of his estimate of his own spiritual terrain.

The Sunday concert was a practice of long standing. Charley always got to the piano as early as possible on Sunday and remained there, eating rosettes of rare roast beef and sipping a brave Burgundy, Romanée Conti, from a bottle marked 1947. Today he had agreed to be best man at a wedding, so, upon arising at eleven, he had dressed in striped trousers and a swallowtail coat because he did not like to think of leaving the piano once he had settled down to it. With his wing collar and a silk hat on his head as he played, he resembled a portrait of Boss Tweed as a young man. Jolly Times was stretched out in a low, modern chair, covered with Sunday tweeds. The Brahms shimmered as silk does before a fire, and the halls of the two brothers shimmered with the spirit of gold. As he listened, Jolly Times gazed out across the gardens of the penthouse grounds on the twenty-eighth floor over Fifth Avenue, where two full-sized shade trees were growing and just the tailored corner of a plot of tall corn could be seen growing. Two large, live sheep dogs, looking like fugitives from an expensive toy store, drifted across Jolly Times's field of vision, following one live sheep. This working rural tableau was Charley O'Neil's idea of a joke.

"Cholly?"

"Yes, Brother?"

"I just decided to get married."

Charley stopped in mid-arpeggio. He swung around, full face, and waited attentively, as alert as an alarm clock. He did not speak.

"Dan Tiamat's daughter. Mr. Downey's granddaughter."

"My God, you won't have children, you'll have Nieman Fellows!"

Jolly Times grinned.

"It's great. That's all I can say. Is she ugly? I mean warts on the face. Anything like that? Does she wear a little beret like Joe?"

Jolly Times could not seem to stop grinning. "You'll see. She'll be here any minute. We're going to the museum. Spanish painters."

"Oh, one of those."

"You'll see."

Charley swiveled into position at the piano and began to play a Catalonian sardana. "What's her name?" he asked.

"Carrie."

"Have you proposed yet?"

"Not yet."

The front door bell rang. Far off in the distance a Japanese houseman crossed the large foyer and disappeared. A moment later, Carrie appeared. She was wearing white and pink and, counting her eyes, a lot of blue. She made her way down the several living-room steps, perilously on flagpole heels, into an appreciative, not to say awed, silence. She stood there for a moment gazing happily and silently at the brothers. Whatever Jolly Times had told her had lit bonfires behind her eyes and their glow had rubbed itself into all of her; the sheen had softened every part of her. The mechanism that made her a woman had begun to whir quietly and surely across the fantastic distances of its universe, subtly changing the color of her hair, the tilt of her breasts, the balance of her purpose.

"I have never seen such a magnificent apartment in my life!" she gasped.

The brothers came to life. They leaped to their feet. "May I present my brother Cholly," Jolly Times said. "Charles, this is Miss Carrie Tiamat, who is my best chum and a positive peach."

"How do you do, Miss Tiamat? And he has never called me Charles before."

"How do you do, Charles?" She strolled in small circles, gaping at the dimensions and the decor, then ventured out across the tundra toward the far terrace, trying to see everything at once: the carved crystal; the wall-to-wall marine-garden fish tank underfoot (swaying green fronds in blue water, shot with canary-colored fish); the walls, on which she saw a Moïse Kisling, two Eduardo Rosales, a Dali, two Banne Hellers, three Picassos; the French blue glass drapes; the furniture, which seemed to be upholstered with English money; the chromium pipe organ. She reached the doorway to the terrace and looked out at the shade trees and the miniature corn field, which was scaled as high as a pygmy elephant's eye, the two dogs trailing the sheep, the patch of lawn, which had been barbered by a blue-haired man who had formerly been with Helena Rubenstein, and the sylvan pool so high above the city. Then she turned to the two brothers who were gazing after her rapturously and asked, "When will this apartment apply for statehood?"

Charley rushed across the room and gave her an enormous hug and several warm kisses. Jolly Times beamed like a drunken clergyman.

They toasted Sunday morning everywhere with a cold pint of champagne while Jolly Times sweated out his anxiety that his brother might burble on about the marriage state before he, Jolly Times, could have the chance to ask her how she felt about such things. But all was still safe when Charley departed to act as best man, crying out from the doorway that he would see them both at the Miss Friendship dinner at eight o'clock.

Jolly Times led Carrie to a terrace overlooking several states of the Union. He noticed that her manner had begun to seem somewhat strained. He offered her iced tea, iced coffee, ice cream, brunch, lunch, tomato juice, wine, beer, spirits, stewed fruits, chocolates, and finally jazz records. She declined each offering. This convinced him that a coldness had entered his paradise. Neither was he able to draw her into conversation. She may have been listening to him but he felt he couldn't be sure.

"What's wrong?" he asked.

She studied the sturdy construction of some magnesium window boxes.

"I said, what the dickens is the matter with you, Carrie?"

"Nothing."

He gritted his teeth. He ground them. It made a disturbing sound. "Have you gained the impression that you have contracted some strange malaise and that you must give me up forever?"

"That *I* have contracted a disease?"

"Well, have I?"

"You never told me you were wealthy."

"What?"

"You heard me."

"Well, what the hell, Carrie! Do other people go around taking girls in their arms and whispering, 'I am very, very rich, darling, so stop worrying'?"

"I didn't mean that and you know it."

"Well, I certainly don't know what you mean. I don't even think my brother would know what you mean."

"What does he have to do with it?"

"He understands women."

"How can the promotion manager of a newspaper live in a place like this? *That's* what I mean!"

"Well, gosh, Carrie, I—"

"Ever since I've known you," she wailed, "you've been talking and talking about how the future confuses you and how you are just fumbling your way and how you're not sure of where you're going or how you'll get there."

"What does my having money have to do with that?"

"What does money have to do with—?"

"It has nothing to do with me! I'm underweight and my brother happens to be overweight. Our parents left us certain genes and we had nothing to do with it, and because my grandfather left them money and a newspaper, do you really think that has any bearing on what I'm going to do with my life?"

"A newspaper? What newspaper?"

"What newspaper? The *Press.* Where I work. You don't think Charley and I would be working for an opposition newspaper?"

"Charley?"

"He's the publisher."

"That—that little round man who was just here is Charles Thomas O'Neil, publisher of *The Daily Press?*"

"Little?"

"You *own* the paper?"

"Don't make such a disgusted face!"

"This is shocking! Does my father know this? Does my grandfather know this?"

"Why the dickens shouldn't they? You make it sound like some horrible crime."

"Answer me!"

"Of course they know it!"

"It isn't fair!" She began to weep. "They never told me! I thought you were such a nice boy who was trying to pull himself up and become somebody, and all the time you were a rich man." She sobbed inconsolably.

He crouched beside her as she sat and held her in his arms.

He kissed her again and again on the temple and cheek, talking to her brokenly. "Don't be so goddam middle-class, Carrie," he said. "It's only money. I climbed down out of the crib and there it was. At the rate I'm going now it would take me four hundred and six years to earn the money Charley and I are handed every year. But I have to build something myself, on my own. And I couldn't do that without you, Carrie. Please, honey. Just say you'll marry me and let's get started. Don't cry. Please don't cry."

She shook him off gently and sat up as straight as a rod on the chaise longue, then swung her lovely legs over the top of it to the far side, to turn her back on him.

"I am humiliated," she said.

"You want me to move out of here? This isn't actually a home anyway. It's Charley's idea of something funny. I'll move out."

"I didn't mean that. I meant I've humiliated both of us by being silly. I just couldn't help it."

"Please don't feel that way, darling."

"It was such a shock! I can't explain it. I never saw anything like that silly sheep grazing in carbon monoxide fumes. Then to have you own the paper where my father has worked for much longer than I've been alive. I still can't get it through my head that you own the paper."

"Only half of it, honey."

"I imagined you in a life that was very easy for me to imagine and then, when I found you here—" She twisted her handkerchief as though it were salt-water taffy. "I—I had the terrible feeling that you had never existed at all, like the Frog Prince, and that if you *had* existed at all, I had lost you."

He threw himself across the chaise to land in a scatter at her feet. He stared at her gravely, kneeling in front of her, then he held her lovely face in his hands and kissed her. "Are we going to get married, Carrie?" he asked slowly.

"Oh, yes. Just as soon as we possibly can."

In that way was a summer afternoon drawn away from the moment of their beginning on a dazzling carriage of young love, at the speed of beauty and as soundless as the pressure of time.

At five-twenty, Carrie returned to the hotel where her father had a suite. Although she was too busy remembering other things to notice, there were already evidences of the huge crowd assembling in the lobby for the dinner. Her father was napping when she let herself into the suite. She was able to bathe and dress before he awoke at twenty minutes to seven. He was dressed and ready at seven-fifteen, at which time, until the phone call came from Jolly Times, she read aloud to him from *Tom Jones*. She did not tell him about what had happened to her that afternoon or that she was going to be married. It was uncharacteristic, but she needed to get used to the massive idea of actual marriage for herself before she could announce it to anyone, even her father.

The summoning call came. They went down to the Grand Ballroom in the freight elevator. The operator wore a horrendous sports shirt of lemon-yellow silk figured with what seemed to be purple fried eggs. Her father stared at the floor of the car all the way down as though he were going over mental notes for his welcoming speech, and Carrie slipped easily into her reverie about Jolly Times again.

They waited in the wings as Charley O'Neil wound up his introduction. She felt her father's physical recoil from the shock of the exultant, uncontained shouting and applause that struck at them so unexpectedly from the darkness out to their left, from the area in front of the speaker, but she moved the chair forward instantly before he could collect himself enough to turn around to face her accusingly. The brilliant lights came on. The chair rolled slowly forward and her father stared out across the hundreds and hundreds of eager faces turned up to him. She halted the chair at the center of the dais behind the microphone, under a barrage of utter bedlam.

"The crutches," she heard her father say hoarsely. "Give me my goddam crutches." She slipped the sticks out of their holster on the chair quickly and expertly. He took them from her and

pulled himself to his feet. Because she had not been told where
else to go she walked directly across the stage to the far wings
where Jolly Times was standing. He drew her into the shelter
of the wings and kissed her swiftly on the cheek. She heard her
father's voice roar out its will and the noise of it re-echoed from
wall to wall all over the enormous room.

"Those who have legs will stand," he cried out. She stared
at her father's tortured profile as it was embedded in the hosed
brilliance of the spotlight.

"Those who have not been blinded will look about us, then
above us," he voice commanded.

Pepé Castaños was impelled to rise up from his seat at the
center of the dais. Carrie felt Jolly Time's arm go about her
shoulders, softly and lovingly.

"All of us, in one voice and with one mind and wish, if the
brutality of our living and the shock of it have not snatched
our voices and sanity—all of us, with that one voice—let us
curse God together."

Pepé shook the long, slender machete out of his left sleeve.
He moved forward rapidly and struck Daniel Tiamat heavily
with the machete on either side of the base of the neck, as unmoved by the performance of his duty as would have been the
angel of death.

> *Some angry angel,*
> *Bleared by Bach and too inbred,*
> *Climbed out of bed,*
> *Pulled on a sock,*
> *And, glancing downward,*
> *Threw a rock*
> *Which struck an earthbound peacock's head.*
> *The peacock fell.*
> *The peacock's yell,*
> *Outraged by such treason,*
> *Cried out to know why it,*
> *Out of billions,*
> *Should be hit,*
> *And instantly invented a reason.*

ABOUT THE AUTHOR

Richard Condon is a playwright and successful novelist. When his first novel, *The Oldest Confession,* was published two years ago, reviewers greeted it with a chorus of praise as loud as it was harmonious. His second novel, *The Manchurian Candidate,* was also widely acclaimed. Mr. Condon shows every sign of establishing a literary tradition all his own, and of finding a large and willing audience to share it with him.

155